EMPEROR

Andrew Frediani

About *Emperor*

Octavian has defeated and killed Caesar's assassins, but the road to absolute power is still long and treacherous. Threat now comes from Sextus Pompeius – a cunning pirate active along the Italian coasts, who terrorises Perugia's citizens with his constant attacks.

Octavian and his associates don't have time to celebrate their victory in the final battle in the civil war before another even more bloody threat arises: the one presented by Sextus Pompeius at sea.

The long campaign against the pirates proves frustrating, and often sees Octavian close to defeat and even death. Everything seems to conspire against him: his enemy appears to be receiving divine assistance, public opinion is against him, the soldiers lack confidence in their commander, and rebellion is just around the corner…

I

It was better not to get too close to the two severed heads that hung from the rostrum in the middle of the Forum.

By now, they were no more than lumps of decomposed, rotten flesh peeling from skulls, the orbs of the eyes empty, the remaining tufts of matted hair plastered to the cranium and the lips stretched out in a grim rictus of death.

A shiver of disgust went through Gaius Cilnius Maecenas as he contemplated the awful things.

He was surprised by the small crowd that had gathered around what was left of Brutus and Cassius, two assassins of Julius Caesar who had been killed at Philippi just over a month ago. It was extraordinary that people continued to go to the forum to watch them rot after they had already been there for a week.

He turned to Octavian. "Why do you think they are attracted to these two disgusting trophies?" he asked. As he spoke, he felt a throb of pain in his side: it happened every time he spoke since he had been injured in Macedonia – and by a friend, not by the enemy.

"I was just wondering myself whether they come here on a pilgrimage out of some kind of veneration for the murderers of Caesar or whether they do it to express their contempt…" replied Octavian, who was also unwell and still weakened by the disease that had prevented him fighting in the first battle of Philippi. Yet, he had more than made up for that in the second, fighting on the front line despite not yet having fully recovered, but the effort of it had cost him dearly over the following weeks, and he had been taken ill while they were aboard the ship returning to Italy.

"Probably both, I would imagine," remarked Agrippa, pointing to the heap of rubbish at the base of the Rostra beneath the two heads. "This stench isn't the smell of decomposition. They come here to throw stuff at them…"

"Especially when they see that there are members of the triumvirate present," added Salvidienus Quintus Rufus, the fourth member of the brotherhood that the young heir of Caesar had been assembling for the last two years with the aim of avenging his adoptive father and succeeding him in power. Rufus indicated a plebeian who threw a stone at the two heads, then looked round at them for approval. Soon afterwards a woman with a basket of vegetables hanging from her arm copied him, then smiled at the four men who, surrounded by their bodyguards, stood off to one side observing the scene. Not content, she then began to insult what remained of Brutus and Cassius and those nearby hastened to imitate her.

"It's no coincidence that there are no senators about, then..." commented Maecenas. "These two are martyrs to freedom, as far as many of *them* are concerned and they would rather not compromise themselves by coming here. Quite apart from the fact that it would be beneath their dignity to shout insults or throw fruit – if there are actually any of them who hated Brutus and Cassius enough to do so, which I doubt."

"Yes. If any of them have been here, then they've done so in disguise – perhaps dressed as commoners," mused Agrippa. "And certainly not to insult them – to honour them, perhaps..."

"It remains to be seen just how strong this opposition in the Senate actually is. And what measures we will have to take in that regard," said Rufus, who, as always, went straight to the point. Maecenas was beginning to find it hard to tolerate the man. Just before the Battle of Philippi, the sect of Mars Ultor, which Octavian led with their assistance, had been on the verge of falling apart: rivalries, suspicions, failures and murders had compromised the mission that was the reason for the group's very existence. And then at Philippi things had gone well, mainly, it had to be admitted – in private, at least – thanks to Mark Antony, the unwitting ally of the sect who had led Caesar's armies to victory. It was thanks to that success that Octavian had been able to consolidate the group and resume his role as triumvir. There was still much to do, both in order to build the society that he and the other members of the sect desired and to finish avenging Julius Caesar and the other fallen members of his family.

"We will find that out soon enough," answered Octavian. "I won't be able to completely ignore the wishes of the senators, particularly now that I've started to requisition land to assign to the military veterans. And many of them have clientele where we will be requisitioning that land. I expect protests, but none will dare to react now that we have so clearly defeated the murderers of Caesar, though Sextus Pompey's blockade of supplies to Italy might cause some unrest. Anyway, we'll have to wait and see what Lepidus does when he discovers that the triumvirate is now only nominal and that he will have to settle for Africa. By the way, Rufus – I want you to leave right away for Spain and to install yourself there as the new proconsul before Lepidus thinks of some way of keeping it for himself."

"Spain? *Now?*" said Rufus resentfully. "That's hardly somewhere where I can hope to conquer anything – apart from some rebellious tribe up in the north, perhaps. I want to stay here and fight Sextus Pompey or go to some eastern province to expand our borders… We've always said that we wanted to push forward Rome's frontiers!"

Maecenas grew angry. Rufus had had his chance against Sextus Pompey and he had thrown it away, allowing his fleet to be defeated by the son of Pompey the Great and he was certain that Octavian would not give him another chance. He decided to intervene before Caesar's heir did.

"You're an imbecile, Rufus! The expansion of our borders *must* be preceded by the consolidation of our power!" he snapped. "Does it *really* look to you as though we are firmly in control of things? There's Lepidus to deal with and several of Caesar's murderers still need to be eliminated, Sextus Pompey to stop, and Mark Antony, who thanks to the victory at Philippi is currently the most powerful man in the world. And even if he has gone off to the East, he still enjoys undisputed prestige and he is watching us closely. And you are already thinking about new conquests?"

Octavian put a hand on Maecenas's arm to restrain him.

"All in good time, Rufus," he said in a more conciliatory tone. "Spain is a land where Sextus Pompey has many supporters and I need a man I trust there to prevent him from obtaining recruits for his fleets. We have to isolate him until we are ready to tackle him again face to face. *Have you forgotten what happened the last time we tried?*" he concluded, a subtle reminder of Rufus's failure which provoked a shiver of gratification in Maecenas.

But Rufus showed no embarrassment. He never did, in fact. "Yes, except that now I know how to face him and to defeat him. But you want to give that opportunity to Agrippa, don't you? You always hoped that I would fail just so that you could give the job to him," he complained. "It's no coincidence that you're keeping him by your side while you're sending me away, is it?"

The Etruscan looked at Agrippa, wondering if he would intervene but the embarrassed expression on the face of Octavian's young friend confirmed what he already knew: the man was too noble of mind to rub in Rufus's defeat in the battle that Octavian had initially assigned to him. All Agrippa said in a quiet voice was,"Don't be stupid, Rufus. You are the one who has the task of greatest responsibility of all of us now."

Octavian, however, was much less delicate. "Stop constantly challenging my decisions, Rufus!" he declared loudly, attracting the attention of the nearest plebeians. "You are going to Spain and that's an end to the matter as far as you're concerned."

Rufus was about to react when a slave who was attempting to push his way through the cordon of bodyguards around three other members of the sect

– the centurion Popilius Laenas, the latest addition to the Mars Ultor cult, and the two Germans Ortwin and Veleda, old lieutenants of Julius Caesar – asked loudly if he could speak to the triumvir. Octavian seemed to recognise him and waved him over.

"Caesar!" said the man, reaching out to him, "The domina Octavia asks that you go to her house! Senator Marcellus has tried to kill himself!"

The young man looked at his friends and then raised his eyes to the sky in annoyance.

"And now here is another problem which we must remedy immediately!" he said, before heading off briskly towards the home of his sister.

*

Octavian barged into the home of Octavia and Marcellus without even giving the caretaker time to announce him. He didn't know whether he should be angry or frightened. Marcellus mustn't dare die: it would be too easy an end for that traitor. No, he couldn't just die and leave them all up to their necks in problems, not after two members of Octavian's family – his fifth cousin Pedius, a member of the sect, and his mother Atia – had already met untimely ends within a few months of one another. If yet another one died, people might start suspecting that he was vulnerable and abandon him. Or they might wonder if he was particularly unfavoured and unloved by the gods, with the same result.

Marcellus had to live so he could atone for his guilt by making himself useful to Octavian and to the sect.

The guilt of having caused the death of Atia, the mother of Octavian.

He was told that his sister was in her husband's chamber, so Octavian hurried in and saw them, she beside the bed, he laying upon it, with a doctor applying a bandage to his naked abdomen.

"Will he live?" Octavian asked the doctor brusquely, neither deigning to look at Marcellus nor to speak to Octavia.

"Yes, triumvir, he will," was the reply. "It's nothing serious. The tip of the dagger has only scratched the flesh, but he has lost quite a lot of blood. All he needs is a bit of rest."

"He started screaming as soon as the knife cut his skin," said Octavia, getting to her feet, "and when I heard him I rushed in and stopped him, with the help of the slaves."

"Get out!" snapped Octavian to the doctor.

The man gave him a hesitant look and then obeyed: these days, it wasn't a good idea to ignore the orders of a triumvir.

"Why did you do it?" Octavian asked Marcellus as soon as the doctor had left.

The senator kept his eyes lowered, just as he had done since his wife's brother had entered the room.

"To avoid you doing it for me," he said eventually.

"And what makes you think that I was going to?" replied Octavian, leaning closer to him.

"It's obvious that you can't wait to get your revenge and punish me for having caused the death of your mother. I expected you to act as soon as I got back to Rome, but then I realised you wanted me to cook in my own juice for a bit, and… and I couldn't take it any longer."

"I can vouch for what he is saying," said a glacial Octavia. "He's been living in fear even of his own shadow. The slightest noise makes him jump. He is expecting you to send an assassin any moment."

Octavian looked at them both. Yes, he would like to have Marcellus killed, or perhaps even kill him with his own hands, but he had not thought about it much since returning to Rome: as head of the triumvirate and the sect of Mars Ultor he had other priorities.

"Do *you* want him dead?" he asked his sister.

Octavia did not answer, but her expression remained emotionless. There was no pity in her face, no trace of the fearful, naive woman she had been before joining the sect. Her expression was eloquent: she deferred to her brother's will.

"You will live, then, Marcellus," he said finally.

Both the senator and Octavia peered at him uncomprehendingly.

"Yes, I need you alive," the young man explained, "so don't you *dare* die. And not simply because I don't wish to be thought of as the triumvir chosen by fate to watch all his relatives die. The harmony between you and my sister must serve as an example and an incentive so that peace may reign between the factions in Rome. Everyone knows, Marcellus, that you were not in favour of Caesar and that since his death you have been a covert supporter of his murderers. Well, if they see that you continue to be a contented part of our family, people will say that I favour peace between the various factions. And that it is possible for those who loved Caesar and those who hated him to get along. "

"So you're... you're *not* going to kill me?" asked Marcellus incredulously.

"Quite the contrary. I am relying on you to provide me with nephews. I cannot touch my own wife. If I were to have a child with her that would make it more difficult for me to take on Antony when our interests eventually clash once more, and I have no intention of putting up with the man forever, so when his stepdaughter is no longer of any use to me, I will rid myself of her. But I have to make sure that the family line continues and so I want you to have a child. In fact, I want you to have at least two. And I will tell you again – you *must* show that the most absolute harmony reigns between you."

This time it was Octavia's turn to look at him in shock.

"Are… Are you joking? Have you forgotten that this man had our mother murdered?"

"The needs of the state require that we put the past behind us," said Octavian. "We are not ordinary people and each of us has a role to play. Yours is that of continuing our family's line."

"No. I could *never* do that," said Octavia, standing up and making to leave the room.

Her brother seized her by the arm.

"I said that you *have* to do it," he ordered with a fierce glare, enjoying the shocked, terrified expression on his sister's face. "And I want to make sure that you actually try. Do it. Now. In front of me."

*

Agrippa throbbed with the desire to make love to Fulvia. What with the war against Sextus Pompey – where he had been kept busy in Apulia while Rufus had been in Sicily – and the subsequent battle of Philippi against the murderers of Julius Caesar, it had been many months since he had indulged in those wonderful sessions of lovemaking with her. And he had missed them immensely. He had once been in love with Octavia's handmaid Etain, but Etain had left him when she had learned of his frolics with Fulvia. It had been no use trying to explain that he had only done it on Octavian's orders because she was the wife of Mark Antony and a valuable source of information. Etain hadn't fallen for that – she had understood that what he had been doing went far beyond the simple call of duty.

And now the girl was dead, killed by Quintus Labienus, who he was still hunting, and in the end Agrippa had invested all the passion that he had hitherto divided between the two women into Fulvia alone. Was it love? That was a question Agrippa often asked himself, without knowing the answer. He was aware that she was a dissolute, fierce, dangerous woman, and that his feelings were influenced by the overwhelming desire he had for her and her skills in the art of love. But since he had got used to being with the woman in private, he could no longer take pleasure with anyone else, and he had actually been bored when he had tried to give vent to his impulses during the campaign in Greece. If it was not love, then, it was certainly something much like it. He knew that she was the wife of the most powerful man in the world and that she was a woman fourteen years older than himself, but he couldn't help thinking about himself with her. Even out of bed, at this point.

Octavian had encouraged him to pursue the relationship in the past. Indeed, he had commanded him to do so, in order to be able to extract information from her – information which had, in fact, proved useful on more than one occasion. But now his friend didn't want him to see her again. He was finally on good terms with Antony and didn't want to do anything that might annoy him, therefore Agrippa had been forced to ignore her since his return and he hadn't even written to her before that.

But he couldn't take it any longer. He had to see her, touch her, smell her heady scent: Octavian would understand. Or maybe he wouldn't: his friend never seemed to feel those cravings and had even managed not to actually touch Clodia Pulchra – Fulvia's daughter, the beautiful young wife who loved him – because he needed to keep her pure.

But at the end of the day, Agrippa didn't really care. He arrived outside Pompey's Gardens, the home of Antony and Fulvia, and had himself announced by the doorkeeper. The slaves bade him enter and took him directly along the route to the matron's bedroom that he knew all too well, even if he hadn't taken it for a while. Good, he said to himself: Fulvia was already waiting for him in the bedroom. Would he find her naked and arrayed in some provocative position, ready to make love, as she used to in the past? Agrippa had no intention of wasting time on pleasantries. He knew that she had no time for them and that she preferred rough ways.

But when the servant opened the door for him, the scene he saw was not the one he had been expecting.

Fulvia was being taken by a young man of about his age and sitting on a chair next to the bed was the consul designate Lucius Antonius, younger brother of Mark Antony, who was fondling himself under his tunic.

*

Octavia could not believe that her brother was serious. She looked at Marcellus, whose expression increasingly resembled that of a whipped dog, and then at Octavian, who was staring at her grimly. No, he was not joking at all: in that moment, he was not her brother at all but a perverse triumvir – Caesar's ruthless heir, and above all, the leader of the sect of the pitiless Mars Ultor, the avenging god.

But he couldn't ask that of her. She walked over to him.

"I won't do it," she whispered. "I'd sooner kill him, even if he *is* the father of my daughter," she added, referring to little five year old Marcella.

Octavian pulled her aside. "You swore. You swore to Mars Ultor that you would do everything in your power for the sect. And now Mars Ultor requires peace and an heir to guarantee it."

Octavia stared into her brother's eyes and saw the ice that formed in them when he wanted to scare someone. And it worked perfectly, as always. She felt a shiver run down her spine and wondered if Octavian would actually be capable of hurting her if she disobeyed. She decided not to find out, especially because she had no intention of prompting him to investigate the reasons that had led Marcellus to kill their mother in more depth. Only Octavia knew that she had been her husband's real target: he had discovered her affair with another member of the sect, Gaius Chaerea, and had always known that they had a child together that had been born before their marriage. Octavia had made her husband swear not to say anything to Octavian because she knew that he would take brutal retribution against the centurion who had dared to violate his sister when she was a little girl, and that any attempt to explain that Chaerea had continually fought off her attempts to get them back together, loyal as he was to his duty and his family, would have fallen on deaf ears.

She felt tears well up in her eyes and streak down her face. Octavian softened and embraced her. "Can we do it… later?" she ventured.

"No. Now."

Octavia bowed her head and walked over to the bed. She pulled back the sheet, raised Marcellus's tunic, slipped off his thong and began to massage his flaccid member, and when she saw that he was ready, she took off her own thong and mounted him, her tears falling into his chest. Overcome with disgust, she began to move her pelvis, her eyes closed.

For a moment, she opened them and turned her head to look at Octavian, seeing that, if nothing else, her brother had had the decency to look away. But the thought didn't console her: she had never felt so humiliated in her entire life.

She kept moving, feeling her husband's hands squeezing her hips, and Marcellus's moans only made the scene even more grotesque. Octavia tried to imagine she was elsewhere, with her beloved Gaius Chaerea.

She felt fortunate that her husband's pleasure soon reached its peak.

"I'll come back tomorrow at the same time," said Octavian, standing up and leaving the room.

II

At last, he was finally free to do what he had been wanting to since returning to Rome, Maecenas said to himself after he bade Octavian farewell. The last few days had been hectic ones for all of Octavian's general staff. They had wasted a great deal of time on all the people who had rushed to congratulate them on their victory without being at all sure whether they were sincere or not. Several senators had insisted on inviting them to dinner parties at their homes where no expense had been spared. In some respects, Octavian had also accepted the compliments intended for Antony, who would not be returning to Italy in the near future, judging by how much work there was to do in the East to re-establish the rule of Rome and loyalty to the triumvirate.

But the two triumvirs had also been busy assigning new magistrates for the years to come and annulling out all that they had once decided upon with Lepidus. And Maecenas had been working to hide how minimal Octavian's contribution to the victory on the fields of Philippi had actually been. He distributed propaganda and put up posters throughout Rome and the various regions of Italy to convince people that the youngest of the triumvirate had been at the head of his troops despite the illness that plagued him, and had killed three of the murderers of Julius Caesar with his own hands in the middle of the battle and at huge personal risk. In reality, he had only killed one, but the rumours would remain etched in the memories of the citizens far longer than any subsequent corrections. And Antony's absence from Rome allowed the sect to portray events to their advantage, without there being anyone sufficiently authoritative around to contradict them.

And above all, they had begun to study the delicate question of allocating land to veterans and the appropriation of property this would necessitate. Between upsetting the army and upsetting the civilians, he was in no doubt as to which took priority: the soldiers had become the power base of the triumvirate and there was still much work to do to reorganise those units which had been decimated and redistribute the soldiers to other units that had fought for Caesar's avengers. On the civilian front they needed to find ways to limit the discontent of those who possessed the resources to oppose them. He and Octavian were having to juggle several issues: finding ways to exclude those cities which had shown strong support for the triumvirate from land confiscation, avoiding further antagonising those in favour of Sextus Pompey or who had provided patronage to the murderers of Julius Caesar and satisfying the senators' urgent requests in favour of those they wished to protect.

In practice, it was an impossible task. Octavian was right, it was like a snake biting its own tail: protests were inevitable, and revolts avoidable only by paying off the soldiers – a gesture that, of course, would only exasperate those affected by the confiscations of land.

But it wasn't that which was worrying him now.

The principal cause of the anxiety which he was no longer able to contain was Horace.

The man had bewitched from the first time he had set eyes upon him. They had told him he was a brilliant poet and he had always sought him out under the pretext of wanting to sponsor his art as part of the project which he had been cultivating for some time. When the civil wars were over, he wanted to create a literary circle which would nurture talent and bring renewed vigour to the culture of Rome, which had been practically annihilated by the decades of internecine conflict that had crushed the city's intellect. He'd always enjoyed helping others, as he had with Octavian, with whom he had created a deep bond: he saw more potential in him than in other politicians and had decided to make his ingenuity and his wealth available to the young man.

He wanted to do the same for others, in the belief that helping them realise their ambitions was not simply rewarding and a source of pride when they were eventually successful, but that it was also in his own interest: life was so much easier in a world full of debtors.

In truth, he had never actually read one line of Horace's verse. He sought him out because he was attracted to him in a way he had never been to any man previously, and the fact that Horace had sided with the assassins of Julius Caesar and had moreover behaved hatefully towards him had in no way cooled his ardour.

However, at Philippi he had finally glimpsed a glimmer of hope.

Maecenas had managed to find out when Horace's unit had returned to the homeland and where the survivors were stationed, and had asked if his name was on the list of survivors: with the carnage that had taken place at Philippi, he could quite easily have been amongst the fallen. His heart had suffered a violent jolt when he had learnt from the freedman he had charged with the investigation that Horace was alive, headquartered a few miles from Rome on the Via Appia and waiting – with all his fellow soldiers – to be assigned to another unit and posting.

As on the previous occasions they had met, once he entered the camp, Maecenas waited with pounding heart for Horace to be brought to him. As tribune of the triumvirate's general staff, officers hastened to fulfil his every wish, despite his anything but martial appearance. Every officer, that is, except Horace, who he had left in Bologna with the rank of *optio* and encountered again in Philippi as a tribune.

Maecenas couldn't help rushing forward to meet him when he finally appeared, and after hastily dismissing the soldier he had sent to summon him and ordering that they be left alone in the praetorium, he looked at Horace. The defeat, the campaign and prison had taken their toll, but you could tell that his spirit was still indomitable. It was that which attracted him most, of course, but it was also that which had prevented them from ever having any more than fleeting contact with one another: Horace saw him as Octavian's errand boy, a despicable symbol of the stifling of political and civil liberties.

Well he would make him change his mind about that.

"Where has your obstinacy in supporting those murderers brought you, Horace? You are no longer even a tribune from what I can I see," he began, on noticing that Horace had been demoted to legionary.

"Have you come to humiliate me, Maecenas? I was no tribune when I fought for Antony either. At least they let me feel the thrill of command, though, for what it's worth..." replied Horace with his usual sarcasm as he stared into his eyes.

Mesmerised by his gaze, the Etruscan remembered the power those eyes had to lower his defences.

"No. I came to thank you for saving my life at Philippi," he said, thinking back to when the poet had allowed him to escape from Brutus's camp, where he had ended up along with hundreds of other prisoners after the first battle. "And to find out why you did it. When I asked you then, you didn't answer me."

Horace smiled. "Must there necessarily be a reason?"

"Yes, because you risked your life to do it. You knew that Brutus was keeping an eye on me."

"And what if I told you that I had anticipated the defeat of Brutus and the Republicans and I did it to ingratiate myself with Caesar's avengers?"

"I wouldn't believe you. You do not seem the calculating type. And in any case, you're a staunch republican yourself. I'd more easily imagine you sacrificing yourself for the cause..."

"Let's say that there is no cause for which I would actually sacrifice myself," specified Horace. "Life is too precious to waste it upon goals whose realisation depends exclusively upon men, and men's motives are never fully clear. I wouldn't die for anyone, not even if they claimed to fight for a cause in which I believed, because nobody – not even Brutus – sacrifices themselves for something or for an idea which would bring them no personal advantage. But there are things worth fighting against – the tyranny, for example, which chokes free thought and which your master pursues with such determination, should be fought against."

"And what if I tell you that you are wrong?" replied Maecenas with conviction. "That Octavian wants to build a new order that puts the people and the Senate on the same level. No more eminent families deciding the fate of Rome, its citizens and the whole world amongst themselves from within their comfortable villas. Under Octavian, all will be able to make their voices heard and anyone with talent will be able to rise in society."

"... of course, as long as they don't say anything that he doesn't like..."

"If there is harmony and all are devoted to the common good, there is no disagreement. If everything functions and all are represented, why would anyone *want* to go against it, unless it was to take power for themselves and to crush the others?"

"We are always at the same point: anyone who wants to put his good ideas into practice plays his part in killing them. Your Octavian is ambitious and above all he wants absolute power."

"And what's wrong with a bit of healthy ambition, if it is accompanied by the will to work for the common good? Or do you perhaps know of someone better than him?"

For the first time Horace had no answer and Maecenas felt optimistic. Yes, he would manage to get the man onto their side.

And then, everything else would follow by itself…

*

Agrippa flinched in disgust. He knew that Fulvia's debauchery was limitless and he had himself participated in it many times in the past, but he had expected a welcome worthy of their past. He had prepared himself to tell her how much he missed her and realised how important she was to him. For the first time, he had felt… well, sentimental. And now here she was enjoying herself with a handsome young man while an ageing onanist drooled over her.

"Well look who it is! Agrippa! I'd gladly invite you to join in but as you can see the room is already full. I don't think there's room for you…" said Fulvia when she became aware of his presence, her voice choked by the pleasure the youth was giving her with obvious expertise.

Other times he'd found her rolling around in bed with the slaves and once even with a servant, but this time Agrippa sensed immediately that the situation was different: the young man taking her wore no slave *bulla* round his neck and his presence was incompatible of that of the consul designate had he been a servant. And Fulvia wasn't staring at him seductively with eyes full of desire as she always had previously when she welcomed him.

The thing was that he had begun to think of her – of the two of them – differently, and those orgies now made him shudder.

He wanted her to himself.

Antonius was deeply engaged with his business and only noticed Agrippa's presence after some seconds. He jumped up, visibly embarrassed, then shot Fulvia a withering look. When he spoke his voice seemed almost choked. "Why did you let him enter without telling me?" he spluttered indignantly. "Have you no decency…?"

"Oh, don't worry – he has seen worse in here," replied the woman casually, gesturing to the young man to continue. For a moment the youth looked somewhat confused, then he shrugged and began to move over her again.

Agrippa felt ridiculous and hated himself for having wanted to confess his feelings to a woman like her. But it took him but a moment to realise that he desired her more than ever – and he hated himself the more for it. He pounced on the man taking her, took hold of his shoulders with his massive hands and hurled him from the bed. Ignoring the shocked consul, he lay on top of her, seized her wrists in his hands and put his face up to hers. He could smell her fragrant breath which had so often mesmerised him. He pressed his erection against her pelvis so that she would feel it.

"And I thought about you so much, even in battle..." he whispered, his voice sounding more desperate than he would have liked.

She gave him a wicked smile. "Well, I stopped thinking about *you* months ago. I have no use for men who prefer playing with toy soldiers. Manius is young and vigorous too, but *he* is always here – and available. He's smart too, so he lets imbeciles like you go and fight wars..."

Agrippa looked back at the youth Fulvia had so effortlessly replaced him with. Manius glared at him but did not dare approach: as muscular as he was, he was no match for Agrippa, nor did he have the controlled aggression of an experienced soldier. Meanwhile, Lucius Antonius had vanished.

"I remember you told me that you felt something for me that you had never felt for anyone before..."

"Did *I* say that? Really? I think you must be getting confused," said Fulvia immediately, with no trace of emotion in her voice.

"The fire that burns so bright is swiftly spent, I see," said Agrippa, barely able to hold back his anger and pain. He had lost Etain for her. For a woman who had forgotten him overnight.

"But perhaps an ember remains beneath the ashes, if you only know how to rekindle it..." said Fulvia, looking increasingly amused. She was in control of the situation and she was well aware of the fact. Agrippa knew that she was playing with him, but he couldn't help heeding her words and decided he would take her there, in front of everyone, to prove that he was the strongest, the only one able to master her. He had only just begun, however, when Fulvia summoned Manius closer. The boy obeyed meekly and she reached out, took his member and placed it in her mouth just as Agrippa, his face but a few inches from hers, was about to kiss her.

He couldn't do it.

He pulled away from her, got to his feet and left the room in silence. From behind him he heard the echo of a laugh.

*

Rufus remained in the Forum thinking for a long time after Octavian bade him farewell. As hard as he tried to make the leader of the sect appreciate him, it was clear that Caesar's heir would always prefer Agrippa or even Maecenas. And the Etruscan hadn't even been there at the beginning – the three of them formed the original brotherhood two years earlier when, on learning of the death of Caesar, they decided to avenge him. But in supporting Octavian to become one of the greatest leaders that Rome had ever known, Rufus saw a career opportunity. He had reckoned on being second only to the young heir of the dictator – at least for a few years – but not on having to compete with those other two, who were both younger and less experienced than he in military matters.

He was dissatisfied and decided to go and speak to the only other member of the Mars Ultor sect that he felt might be equally unhappy with the turn events had taken: Pinarius. Since two members of the triumvir's family had been killed, the cousin of Octavian had been progressively marginalised, left behind the lines at Philippi and – at least at first – deprived of any public office. Later, Octavian gave him the consulate to quieten his protests, but he hadn't involved him in meetings of the sect for some time and everyone had noticed. During the trip back from Greece the triumvir revealed to the other members that he had been tricked into becoming suspicious of them all until he learnt that it had been Marcellus who had caused the death of his mother. Pinarius, who had been the person most under suspicion, had shown himself to be offended by the lack of trust, especially after all he had done for the sect and for his cousin.

An idea was forming in his mind. Pinarius had always seemed pretty spineless to him, but who knew that he wouldn't back him up.

The consul received him as he wished a senator farewell. One of those known for not supporting Octavian.

"I could tell our leader that you have relations with people you're not supposed to have relations with," began Rufus as soon as the guest had taken his leave.

"I am the consul. I am required to have relations with everyone. Even with those who are not well-disposed towards us," replied an annoyed Pinarius. "Even more so with them, actually, in order to make them more… malleable."

"Oh, really? I'm not so sure you were the one making him more malleable. It looked more as if he was making *you* more malleable…" Rufus continued to goad him.

"I don't care for your tone. Let me remind you that you are talking to the chief magistrate of the Republic."

Rufus burst out laughing.

"Oh, do me a favour! With the triumvirate around, the only supreme magistrates are the triumvirate and the others are nobodies! You know very well that you are nothing more than a lackey. As, unfortunately, am I…"

"I've heard that you're now proconsul of Spain. Over there you will have more autonomy than if you stay here. You shouldn't complain."

"Maybe. But that's not what I want."

"And what *do* you want?"

"I want to be the one who decides for himself what orders to give his men. I have earned the right."

Pinarius thought for a moment. It was obvious that he was trying to measure his words carefully.

"You have sworn allegiance to Octavian and to Mars Ultor," he said. "If you are not afraid of our leader, you should at least be afraid of the god: he is the god of vengeance and his wrath may befall you if you betray him."

Rufus made a dismissive gesture with his hand. "Don't tell me you still believe in that nonsense! The gods are for children and for the credulous. He who has ambition cannot afford to believe in them, nor to choose his actions on the basis of their purported judgment."

"Very well, but Octavian is powerful. Especially now that he is taking the credit for Antony's victory at Philippi."

"And those who oppose him and the triumvirate are very powerful too. Especially now that Octavian is about to make plenty of enemies thanks to the land seizures. If we lead the opposition we could create a powerful party – an alternative both to him and to Antony. And maybe we could even bring Lepidus along with us. He must be anxious to get his old influence back."

Pinarius looked around him as though terrified that the walls had ears.

"Are you insane? Aren't the civil wars already underway enough for you? You want more? What do you think would happen if there were a third party involved in the fight? No, if anything..."

"If anything?"

"If anything, if – and I emphasise *if* – I chose to leave the sect, I would do so to join Antony."

"He and Octavian are big friends nowadays!" snapped Rufus.

"Ah, and you think that will last for long, do you? They both want supreme power and agreements are nothing but truces for those like them. There isn't enough room in the empire for both of them."

‘Well I’m not giving up being Octavian’s lackey to become the Antony’s lackey.”

“Then in that case we have nothing to talk about. And remember, this conversation never took place,” said Pinarius decisively, whilst indicating the door.

Rufus made a gesture of irritation, turned and walked away without saying goodbye. That coward was no use. He needed to think of something else.

*

Octavia’s eyes were still wet with tears when she stopped her litter in front of the house of Gaius Chaerea. Immediately after concluding the forced sexual act with her husband, she had washed and rushed out of the house toward the Suburra. When the other members of the sect had returned from Greece a week ago, she had forced herself to leave the centurion time to be alone with his family despite being desperate to see him. Now, after what had happened in her house, she could wait no longer.

And this time she did not want to see him simply to be with him and because she loved him more than ever.

This time she needed to apologise to him.

It did not matter if his woman was there. She had to make him understand how guilty she felt. There would be time for her to win him back: now more than ever she wanted to be with him, take care of him, make him feel like a king in a way his partner would never be able to do. What Octavian had forced her to do had sickened her and she could see no more reason to sacrifice herself for the sect, even if it meant a total renunciation of her affections. And then there was Marcus, their eleven year old son. She wanted to be with the boy, she'd had enough of a stranger bringing him up in her place. She no longer cared about causing a scandal, nor about hurting a woman who, after all, had raised Octavia's son as if he were her own.

She was willing to fight for the only man she had ever loved. She was willing to commit whatever madness was necessary to have him all to herself.

The presence of a matron of high rank in the Suburra was always news. A crowd of children and adults had gathered in front of the insula, and someone must have already gone to warn Chaerea because little Marcus had descended the stairs to come and meet her, anxious to see what gift that rich lady who came to visit him from time to time had brought. Gaius and Fabia had agreed to tell him that she was simply a noblewoman of the triumvirate's family that Gaius was escorting. Fabia had begged her never to let him know the truth, but now Octavia was no longer certain she would respect her will: he was her son, and she finally wanted to be his mother.

Even at the cost of kidnapping him and bringing Gaius with her, far away, perhaps to the East, under the protection of Antony and far from the clutches of her brother and the obligations of the sect.

She had never regretted what she had done with Gaius when she had been a young girl, nor had she blamed the soldier for having taken advantage of her all those years ago. In a moment of weakness when he was acting as her escort, they had made love, and later Marcus had been born. Her parents had avoided a scandal by making her give birth in secret and forcing her to get rid of the child and never see him again. And she had complied with this for years, letting Gaius look after the boy by himself. She had never encountered Gaius again until the events surrounding the death of Julius Caesar and the birth of the Mars Ultor sect had brought them together.

Gaius had actually left the sect in order not to be tempted by her any longer, but Octavia had asked him to join the other recruits in Greece to inform her brother that it had been her husband Marcellus who had caused the death of their mother, and not one of the Mars Ultor sect. Gaius had readily consented, though whether out of love for her or devotion to the sect she could not tell.

But it had cost him dearly and now she wished that she had never asked him.

"I'm sorry, Marcus. This time I left home in a hurry and I didn't bring you anything," she said to the little boy who had greeted her so hopefully. "But I'll make it up to you soon, you'll see."

Marcus was a little disappointed but he bowed his head in deference and went off to play with some of his friends. Octavia immediately went up the flight of stairs that led to the first floor where she found Fabia in the doorway, her arms folded across her chest and a hostile expression on her face. In the past she had at most looked scared, but never hostile.

"What do you want?"

"To honour a hero of Rome, what else?" Octavia said, more resentfully than she would have liked. In any case, though, she needed to prepare for a fight: Fabia would not give up her family so easily.

"Haven't you done him enough harm? Leave him in peace."

"I want to hear it from him, if you don't mind. Let me pass," she insisted.

"It's thanks to you that he's in this state. He was fine and happy before you sent him off to the East. Because I know for certain that it was you who sent him, even if he hasn't said so. He'd stopped having anything to do with you lot. What more do you want from him now?"

Fabia wasn't giving in either. Octavia, however, had no intention of letting a plebeian walk all over her. "Out of my way," she said curtly, advancing toward her with decision, "I want to talk to the father of my child."

The other woman did not budge. The matron pushed her out of the way, but the plebeian tried to block her entry.

"Fabia, come here a minute!"

The voice of Gaius from the bedroom stopped them just before a fight could break out. The woman glared at Octavia, then turned and went inside. The noblewoman stood there, not knowing whether to follow her. She decided to wait and, if anything, to insist on entering if Gaius had told his woman to send her away. She had reckoned on him feeling resentment for what had happened, but she had no intention of giving up. The alternative was a life at the side of the man who had killed her mother and who had tried to kill her too.

But there was no need. Fabia emerged from the bedroom and then walked out of the front door, walking past her without a word and giving her a scornful look. As soon as she was alone, Octavia approached the bedroom. She felt her stomach tense as she crossed the threshold, and even more when he saw the man she loved sitting in a chair. His face was pale and unshaven, his muscles less pronounced than in the past, and his eyes looked tired.

And he was missing a leg.

Octavia threw herself at his feet.

"I'm sorry, I'm sorry, I'm sorry," she repeated, while clutching his hands.

"Don't blame yourself. I had to go. I couldn't have left them there alone. Not at such a difficult time. And I will never be able to thank you enough for allowing me to do that," Gaius reassured her, with that warm voice of his that made her always feel safe.

"I would go back in time if I could…" she murmured, comforted by his reaction.

"No. It is all right," he said. "We actually saved the sect, that's what Octavian himself told me. You were right: warning him made all the difference."

Octavia summoned up all her courage. It was time to tell him what she intended to do. She raised her head and looked him in the face and then stood up and, still clasping his hands to hers, said, "Now we have done our duty, and you, above all, have paid dearly for it. But I am paying too. If you only knew what I must suffer to fulfil my vows to the sect… But I will tell you later. Now, though, it is time for us to do what we must. We must get away from here and from our obligations. We will escape to the East, away from all this, along with our son and my daughter, and live the life that has been denied us these last twelve years."

He looked at her quizzically.

"I cannot. You know that," was all he answered.

"Why not? I love you and you love me too – I'm sure of it, though you attempt to hide it. Let's go together."

"Octavian would find us wherever we were and would make us pay."

"We will flee to the other side, then, and go where his hand cannot reach us."

"And you would give up your position in Rome to spend your life somewhere with a cripple?"

"With the man I have always loved."

He was silent.

"And what about Fabia?" he said finally.

"Fabia? You kept her with you because you could not have me."

"Maybe it was that way at the beginning. But then I learned to love her, and I am happy with her. I will be able to make her happy even like this, I'm sure of it. Indeed, perhaps even more than before, because now I'm no longer able to be a soldier she will have me all to herself."

Octavia was appalled. She had not expected this. Not this obstacle.

"It cannot be… You love me."

"What I feel for you means nothing in the face of everything else, as I have told you once already. My place is here, with them. Yours is at the side of your husband and your brother."

"I don't believe it! I don't believe it!"

She flew over to him, wrapped her arms around his neck and tried to kiss him. "Let me atone for my sins! I have made you an invalid, but I know how to make you forget. Don't hate me, don't send me away!"

She couldn't hold back her tears and Gaius gave in to her lips and let himself become entangled in a kiss. But only for a moment. He drew back saying, "Don't let your guilt control you. I don't want to punish you nor be pitied. And you only want to do it out of pity..."

"No," she protested vehemently, "it isn't true! It's not true! I truly love you! You know I have always loved you. Nothing has changed, I have been pursuing you for two years!"

He looked at her with a poignant expression on his face.

"Fabia only left because I reassured her that she has nothing to fear. And it is true. I'm staying with her, whatever I feel about you."

"But I'm not giving you up," she said defiantly.

Gaius seemed to reflect a moment. Then he reached out and took a knife from among the objects on the table beside his chair. She shivered, suddenly frightened and fearing that he wanted to attack her.

Finally he spoke. "Do you feel guilty because I lost a leg in the war? You have no reason to. But if you insist on putting my determination to the test..."

He paused, and before she could stop him he put his palm on the table and with a sudden gesture dropped the knife onto the little finger of his left hand, severing it completely and flooding the surface of the table with blood.

"... I will cut off a finger each time you come to tempt me," he added, his voice choked with grief. "And then you *will* need to feel guilty..."

III

War was in the air. Ortwin could feel it. He was warrior with a long military career behind him – first in the service of Ariovistus, then in the service of Caesar and finally in the service of Octavian – and he could immediately sense an impending conflict. And he couldn't say that he was sorry: without a war, Octavian used him simply as an assassin and with so many of the murderers of Julius Caesar still at large he could be kept busy for a long time. When an official rival to fight appeared on the horizon, however, his commander did not hesitate to send him to the front, aware as he was of Ortwin's value as a warrior.

He had been fighting civil wars for a long time now, however, and they seemed more and more senseless. In the last three years, he had fought Julius Caesar's enemies, then returned to his native Germany to reclaim a throne for his woman, Veleda. But he had failed and became a mercenary in Rome, putting himself at the service of his old commander's heir and entering the sect of Mars Ultor to avenge the most worthy man he had ever served. He had killed with his own hands at least two of Caesar's assassins – Trebonius and Decimus Brutus Albinus – and been present at the deaths of the Casca brothers, Cassius Longinus and Marcus Brutus. And he had already fought in civil wars at Modena and Philippi.

Amongst the troops there had been rumours that the defeat of Brutus and Cassius would put an end to the infighting, but they had turned out to be about as far from the truth as it was possible to be. Sextus Pompey was stronger than ever and had no intention at all of bowing down before the triumvirate. Lepidus had been confined to Africa but was certainly contemplating his revenge and still possessed a vast clientele. Mark Antony was in the East and, yes, for the moment he and Octavian seemed to be getting along, but Ortwin had been around ambitious men for too long not to know that sooner or later they would come into conflict.

And now he foresaw the arrival of a civil war in Italy against Lucius Antonius.

The rebellion was already taking place – it had been dormant for months and over the past few weeks had begun to manifest itself. Ever since he had assumed the consulate, Mark Antony's brother had been voicing virulent support for the rights of those whose land was being confiscated; instead of promoting and facilitating the provisions of the triumvir regarding the allocation of plots of land to veterans as chief magistrate of the Republic, he was fanning the fire of discontent and defending the alleged rights of all those whose land had been seized for the soldiers. For months now he had been blaming Octavian for applying the law with excessive zeal, accusing him of all sorts of crimes: of insufficiently compensating the dispossessed, not consulting Antony, confiscating land in cities not covered by the legislation so as to curry more favour with the soldiers, honouring not only the veterans of Philippi, as had been agreed, but also other units which had had nothing to do with the war; continuing to enlist recruits in Italy and increasing the size of his army despite the agreement he had made with his counterpart, which involved the two triumvirs dividing the empire with an equal number of legions.

"You know very well that everything Lucius Antonius accuses Octavian of is true," said Veleda, interrupting his thoughts. "So what are we doing here?"

The woman rode by his side, as always. And as always, she liked to provoke him with rhetorical questions, never failing to remind him of her contempt for the Romans. She had never managed to grow fond of the memory of Caesar, who was responsible for the ruin of her father Ariovistus, let alone feel any kind of bond with Octavian – although she too was part of the cult of Mars Ultor and despite having saved the man's sister.

"We will carry out our orders," he said quietly, urging his horse on again and gesturing to the squad following him to do likewise. It was time to scout farther afield from the place chosen for the meeting where Octavian and Lucius Antonius would attempt to resolve their differences and avoid war. The consul did not appear to have prepared an ambush, but there might be troops hidden further away. Octavian, on the other hand, had positioned his reserves well beyond the reach of his rival's cavalry. "Even when the orders are wrong?" said Veleda, wiping the perspiration from her face with the stump of her right arm and urging on her own horse.

"I see nothing wrong in patrolling to determine whether Lucius Antonius has laid a trap there," he protested. Their bickering had been a constant throughout their life together, but neither of them questioned the love each felt for the other. "You know as well as I do that, given the way things are at the moment, this meeting would be a good opportunity to capture Octavian."

The meeting had been arranged under bad auspices. The antagonists had met at Teanum and Octavian had been accommodating towards the requests the consul advanced on behalf of people suffering because of the confiscations. Lucius Antonius, however, had immediately exploited the situation to increase his own popularity and with his new prestige, he began to challenge virtually everything the triumvir now tried to do. According to him it was not true that there was no money to pay the dispossessed and he protested when Octavian used money taken from the temples. He complained that the famine afflicting Rome because of Sextus Pompey's blockade was due to Octavian's inaction and urged him to arm a fleet as soon as possible to deal with the pirate. He had even suggested that they abandon power since the period allotted to the triumvirate was due to end, and he challenged the renewal of it which had been agreed upon in Philippi.

His attitude had irritated Octavian, who felt the man was breathing down his neck, watching his every move: just what he wanted to avoid when he created the triumvirate and allowed Antony to go East. He had expected to finally be able to dominate the West unchallenged, crushing any opposition with the support of the army gained through indiscriminate bonuses. But he had discovered that the discontented had found a champion, with whom he now had to contend, in his rival. The two then organised a new meeting in Gabii, near Rome, on a plain where two grandstands were assembled from which each would argue his case as in a court. But Ortwin had the distinct feeling that this meeting would get them no further forward. The two antagonists faced one another in a climate of mutual suspicion.

"Octavian has placed armies near the grandstand too," objected Veleda.

"Of course, but he is only doing it to protect himself. He's not going to attack Lucius, as far as I am aware," answered Ortwin, always loyal to his master, whoever he was.

"You can't know that. No one knows what goes on in the mind of that man... Not even his lieutenants, in my opinion. He is much more unscrupulous and ruthless than Caesar."

"Ruthless, yes, but not cruel. And these days, some ruthlessness is inevitable, if you have a bit of ambition..."

He paused. A group of horsemen suddenly emerged from the woods they were riding alongside and began galloping towards them.

The German made a gesture of irritation. Realising that they were about to be discovered, the enemy riders had decided to take the initiative and attack so as to leave no witnesses. He reflected for a moment upon whether there was any way to avoid them but saw that they were cutting off any route for retreat. He would have to fight his way through them.

Even though they were clearly outnumbered.

*

She had sent for him. Agrippa could hardly contain his excitement. Fulvia had denied herself to him for six months and now, suddenly, she had sent for him. The young man knew he should have been paying attention to what was happening in Rome, but he couldn't think of anything except that invitation. Her previous refusal now seemed just another of that fierce woman's punishments for having left her behind. She had done the same in the past, subjecting him to perverse games, mental and physical tortures, just for the fun of seeing him willingly suffer for her, especially when she believed she had something for which to reproach him. He remembered when, during the negotiations for the triumvirate at Bologna, she had savagely bitten his member, causing deep cuts, and then forced him to make love to her until he was exhausted.

That Manius was just a disposable trinket, Agrippa was sure of it. He could barely wait to run to her, but her invitation had arrived just as he was going out to suppress a sedition in the Forum and he could not fail in his duties: in the absence of Octavian, who was busy meeting Lucius Antonius, he was responsible for public order in the city. And at that time it was no easy task: Sextus Pompey was starving the city and the citizens were taking out their frustration on those who administered it.

Agrippa had brought Popilius Laenas, the most recent and least able addition to the sect, along with him; the centurion commanded a handful of legionaries, who drew their swords as they reached the Forum and saw the crowd that thronged the space between the basilicas. Agrippa was tempted to leave the job to Laenas, but he was sure that, given the ferocity which the centurion had shown in the past, it would mean the situation rapidly degenerating. And it wouldn't take much for these riots to turn into an open rebellion.

"Bread! Bread!" shouted the people at the sight of the soldiers.

"You spend all the money on your wars, and nobody cares for the common people!"

"At least the proscriptions only affected those who were condemned! With these confiscations you punish entire communities!"

"I don't know what to give my children! They are dying of hunger because of you!"

"Everything to the soldiers and nothing for the rest of us who slave away from morning to night! It's not fair!"

Agrippa observed the protestors: poor people for the most part, even women and old men, asking for no more than survival. Some were so frail that he was amazed they were actually able to stand, and to judge by the cries, Lucius Antonius must have planted some agitators amongst the crowd to get them worked up: it made no sense for Romans, who were unaffected by the confiscations and the privileges granted to soldiers, to be protesting about the expropriations.

"If we kill a couple, the others will certainly go running home with their tails between their legs," commented Laenas.

Agrippa was not surprised by the suggestion: during the proscriptions, the centurion had revealed himself to be the cruelest and most sadistic executor of sentences, killing personally and with great pleasure many of the proscribed. It had been he who had cut off the head of Cicero. Octavian had wanted him in the sect because he felt they needed a man who could ruthlessly carry out the most unpleasant tasks – the ones which for the rest of them might cause pangs of conscience.

But now was not the time for violence. At least, not yet. "Haven't you noticed those troublemakers there in the middle of the crowd?" he said to the centurion. "If we kill anyone they'll use the crowd's resentment against us and exploit the deaths to get the whole population up in arms."

Laenas did not hide his disappointment, but Agrippa was a minister of the sect, and the centurion had no wish to appear insubordinate. "So, what do you think we should do?" was all he said.

Agrippa thought for a moment, and looked at the people gathered before him. He should have climbed onto the rostrum and attempted to speak to them, but he was neither Octavian nor Maecenas, and he was no good with words. Hoping to make the right choice, he studied their faces, excluding the most determined, who were probably in the pay of the consul, as well as the most agitated, until his eye fell on a stout woman, getting on in age, in whose face he read despair but no madness or malice. She was in the front row, but seemed to have been pushed there by others, rather than having arrived of her own will.

Then he drew his sword and waved it in the air, gesturing to those nearest to be silent. Some stopped shouting immediately while others took a few more moments. Agrippa raised his voice and shouted, "Citizens, do you not understand that we are all in this together? Pompey is an enemy of the state and he controls the sea, especially now, after admirals who took part in the murder of Caesar like Staius Murcus and Domitius Ahenobarbus have joined him with their fleets since the defeat at Philippi. But if the situation in Rome and Italy is calm, and if the soldiers are satisfied, we will have the opportunity to get rid of him once and for all. These rebellions work in his favour! Do you want to kill the triumvirate and their representatives? And then what? Do you think Pompey will feed you? He doesn't care about you, he's a pirate, a criminal! But if you want to kill us, help yourselves! Maybe there are some among you who think they know how to resolve the situation better than we do!"

When he had finished, he took his sword by the tip and handed it to the woman he had identified.

Just as he had expected, he watched as she stared at him and started to tremble. Laenas stepped forward aggressively, and Agrippa, fearing that he might ruin everything with his stupidity, reached out to stop him. "Are you crazy?" he heard him say, while he watched the reactions of the woman and the crowd.

Many of those around her were disorientated. They looked at each other in cofusion, while the woman stared at the sword she had suddenly found in her hands. Agrippa heard someone in the crowd shout to her to use it, and for a moment feared that she actually might. He was afraid, but for his tactic to work he must remain fearless in front of her, with his chest out and his gaze steady.

"By the gods, you crazy bastard…" murmured Laenas, who made to take another step forward. The other soldiers were just as nervous. A stone struck a legionary on the helmet, but Agrippa gestured to them to hold their positions. Right now, the spark that could ignite the situation was just as likely to appear among the soldiers as it was among the civilians.

"I will kill the first man who dares react to a provocation myself – if the crowd doesn't kill him first!" he hissed at Laenas and the soldiers.

A civilian shoved aside some of his neighbours and approached the woman with the sword and, realising his intentions, Agrippa felt his chest tighten. But he did not move. The man tried to take the weapon but the woman held it behind her back.

"No!" she said. "He's right – us poor people can't do anything. We have to rely on them – and if they disappoint us then, yes, we'll kill them!" And so saying, she offered the sword back to Agrippa, who did not hesitate to take it: now the weapon had served its purpose and if his plan didn't work, he was going to need it.

The people around them remained immobile. Even the man who had tried to take the sword appeared disorientated. Some shouted insults and recriminations, but they were isolated voices without conviction and they found no support. The woman turned and pushed her way through the crowd to leave. Agrippa would have liked to embrace her and thank her, but he continued to watch for a reaction until he saw that the others around them had started to move away, some with their heads bowed in shame, others still shouting insults and threats, but all keeping well out of the reach of the legionaries' swords. Before long, the space in front of the cordon of soldiers was empty and the people were flowing back to their homes.

Agrippa breathed a sigh of relief. Now he could go to Fulvia.

"I'll be damned…" Laenas murmured in disbelief. "You did it!"

No, before he went to her there was one more thing to do, Agrippa said to himself. He walked over to the centurion and punched him in the stomach, making Laenas double over in pain.

"Dare to insult your superior again and I will use my sword on you. After the things I saw you do during the proscriptions, it is you who is the crazy bastard…" he said, before turning on his heel and walking away.

*

Veleda exchanged a glance with Ortwin. Her man's only eye gave her the usual warning that preceded any battle: she was to remain in the second row behind the other horsemen. But Ortwin knew very well that she wouldn't obey him: she never had, and after the battle he always berated her for making him use his one eye to watch both his opponent and her.

"One day you'll get me killed," he used to say, and she would laugh about it. She was the daughter of a king, who had lived first among Germanic warriors and then among the soldiers of Rome, and she could not help but be a warrior. And there was a good chance that if she was on the front line it would one day be her who saved him, she replied defiantly.

They felt no need to say any more before the battle. Veleda knew what tactics Ortwin intended to use. "Wedge formation!" the German shouted to his men. "We have to break through and move on!" He put himself at the head of the unit, which had immediately assumed a triangular shape, and she placed herself right behind him, earning a new look of disapproval but no protest: Ortwin knew that it was pointless to insist.

The charge began. Their group was going to have to break through the line forming in front of them as horsemen flowed in from the woods to their side. Veleda knew what worried Ortwin: it was not just that their opponents outnumbered them – it was that the two of them had brought with them only light reconnaissance cavalry, while the enemy had several men with heavy weaponry.

Then she heard the sound of hooves behind them. She turned and saw that yet more men were emerging from the woods.

They had been trapped in a pincer movement.

The situation couldn't have been worse. Ortwin didn't panic, though: he was born to command and was able to instil confidence in his soldiers. He was also consistent and faithful, the ideal lieutenant for ambitious men like Caesar and Octavian. Antony had been a fool to reject him when he and Veleda had returned defeated from Germany and had offered their services first to him and then to the young heir of the dictator who had only just appeared on the scene. At the time they had considered it but a stopgap: Octavian hadn't given the impression of being an effective leader. But now, two years later, he was starting to actually look like he might be victorious.

Ortwin urged on his steed and let out a war cry to boost his men's morale. He held his spear in front of him and selected one of the horsemen lined up ahead: that was where he intended to break through. Veleda cried out too and waved her spear while with her the other arm, the one lacking a hand, she protected herself with the small circular shield she always used in battle.

Veleda smashed into the line an instant after Ortwin. In no time at all, there was a crowd of horsemen from both sides in the confined space, whilst those on the sides hastened to converge. Meanwhile, the soldiers behind them advanced: a few moments more and Veleda and Ortwin risked being encircled. The woman stretched out her spear toward her nearest opponent and simultaneously parried another's attempt to stab her in the side with her shield. The violence of the blow unbalanced her and she was knocked over to the opposite side, bumping into one of her comrades. She bounced back off his massive body and ended up once again on the other side of the saddle, tossed from one side of the horse's back to the other.

She found herself face to face with the opponent who had struck her and, still balanced precariously, she had to hold on to him to keep from falling to the ground. An idea struck her: she dropped her spear and grabbed him with both arms, preventing him from moving while in the meantime using him to lever herself directly onto his horse and seat herself behind him. Before the man could get free, she released her grip with one arm, pulled her dagger from her belt and cut the man's throat.

She was about to throw him to the ground when she saw that another opponent was aiming his spear at her. She used the dead man's body to block the attack, holding it out in front of her and the point of the weapon pierced it, emerging a foot from the man's back and brushing her stomach. Only then did she push the corpse away with enough force to knock her new assailant from his mount. He fell under the hooves of the other horses. Veleda saw a large gap open up before her, but she couldn't leave without the others. She turned toward Ortwin and saw him engaged with two opponents, but so tightly wedged between his own men and the enemy soldiers that he was unable to defend himself with his usual vigour.

Suddenly the German was unbalanced by a violent blow from a shield to his side. He was forced to lower his guard, and one of his opponents was quick to take advantage, charging against his undefended chest. Realising that Ortwin would not have time to react, Veleda urged on her commandeered horse, approached the enemy from behind and, with her shield, struck the man a blow on the temple. He swayed in the saddle, and Ortwin, who by then was back in position, quickly shoved his spear into the man's throat, immediately afterwards passing the butt of the weapon in front of his head and, without pulling the spearhead from his victim's body, used it to block the other opponent's lunge. As the man came towards him, Ortwin freed his spear and, with deadly precision, struck him with in the eye with it.

He smiled over at Veleda and then looked in front of him. The way was clear. He helped the men closest to him fight off their opponents and only then did he urge his horse forwards. Veleda followed him, as did the others, who all took advantage of the open breach. They set off at a gallop and soon had a reassuring advantage over their pursuers who were hindered by their heavier armament. When they could no longer feel the enemy breathing down their neck, Ortwin and Veleda took a headcount: they had lost four – a fifth of the men who had set out with them. Given the circumstances, that was acceptable.

"Well it looks as though you were right: this time it was you watching over me," admitted the German, giving her a tender look full of gratitude.

"I am always right!" she said, well aware that it was by no means the case. If anything, the opposite was true: if she hadn't persuaded Ortwin to abandon Caesar and join her futile attempt to regain her kingdom in Germany, Ortwin would now be an important figure in the empire instead of an obscure soldier and assassin. He had tried to talk her out of it, explained that they didn't have the resources to stand a chance against the other pretenders to the throne of the Suebi. But she had not listened. And as her man had expected, things had ended badly and they'd been forced to return to Rome to start again after having thrown away all that Ortwin had built with Caesar. If he had not abandoned the dictator in Munda, he would probably have become at least the decurion of some important Gallic city.

Ortwin did not answer, nor give any sign of scepticism. He knew that she needed to maintain the attitude of the haughty queen she should have been, and he never reacted with irritation. Another of the many of his ways that his love for her dictated. Veleda often wondered how she could have managed not to choose between him and Quintus Labienus for so long…

They arrived at Octavian's camp, a short distance from the place established for the meeting with Lucius Antonius, and Ortwin hastened to confer with the triumvir. He burst into his pavilion even before the sentinels could announce him: as a member of the sect, he and Veleda could afford to take such liberties. They found the young commander with Maecenas and surrounded by scrolls and wax tablets, as was more and more often the case. However, Octavian looked more comfortable with the work of intellect and reasoning than on a battlefield, and it was in this above all that he differed from Caesar, Ortwin often thought.

"Triumvir, Lucius's horsemen were stationed about three miles from the meeting place," said the German after receiving a nod from the young man. "They clearly wanted to ambush you. I doubt very much that Lucius Antonius had any intention of coming to the meeting. When they realised we had spotted them, they attacked. We made it, but it was a close call, and we lost several men."

Octavian nodded gravely. With a grimace, Maecenas shook his head.

“I knew I couldn’t trust him. He wants war,”said the commander. “Well then, in that case, let there be war!”

“Let’s not rush into it, Octavian,” said Maecenas. “Right now, we are pretty well outnumbered: Lucius Antonius has the six legions he has assembled since he became consul, plus the eleven assigned to his brother. He also has the resources of the eastern provinces, which have been pacified. We only have four legions – the ones allocated to Capua – in addition to the praetorian cohorts in Rome. We cannot rely on the resources of the provinces assigned to you: there’s fighting everywhere, with the exception of Sardinia and we can assume that the people and the cities would side with Lucius in the case of conflict, which would force us to use troops to quell rebellions. Not to mention Sextus Pompey, who would certainly support the consul in order to make like difficult for the triumvirate. Either that or he would take the opportunity to land in Italy and go about his own business in the midst of all the chaos. And finally, we do not know how Antony will react when he finds out about this business: will he respect the terms of the triumvirate or will he support his brother’s attempt to get rid of you? At the moment, they say he is busy enjoying himself with the queen of Egypt, but for how long?”

Octavian seemed even more worried. "But I cannot simply do nothing," he said. "That would be tantamount to a surrender. The West is mine, and I must show that I know how to govern it. For now I think it suits Antony more to respect the agreements than to follow his brother in this lunacy: he too has his veterans to keep happy, if he doesn't want to lose the support of the army. And there's no proof that his legions would be enthusiastic about joining Lucius Antonius's party: remember, we are the ones who serve the interests of the army, and the soldiers know it. I'll get Rufus back from Spain: his six legions will be useful, but he must come immediately. We cannot know which side the other provincial governors like Fufius Calenus and Ventidius Bassus might choose, and they could prevent him from entering Italy. "

"Good idea," admitted Maecenas. "And we need to act quickly: Lucius has numerical superiority, it is true, but only in theory. And then, he is the champion of the civilians and so much of the army is with us that it will not be easy to convince the soldiers to fight for him. But we must pray to Mars Ultor that Mark Antony and Sextus Pompey don't lift a finger to help him..."

Octavian swallowed. "Yes. I will offer a bull as a sacrifice tonight, as soon as I get back to Rome," he said, adding in a softer, more disheartened voice,

"After Philippi and with Antony away in the East, I though that we had made good progress towards achieving all our goals, and instead we are hanging on by an even thinner thread than ever..."

Veleda felt a chill run down her spine. She looked at Ortwin and wondered if they had really chosen the best side: no matter how hard they tried, how many victories they won, it seemed there was always a new battle to fight.

Would it never end?

*

When Agrippa reached Fulvia's home, he was greeted with much more enthusiasm than he had been six months earlier. Despite the disappointment he had felt then, he had tried repeatedly and in every way possible to meet her again, aware of the fact that she enjoyed challenging him, putting him to the test to see how much he cared for her. But despite all his efforts, the terrible woman had never granted him a hearing. Maybe now, though, Fulvia had decided that was enough: she understood how much she meant to Agrippa and was satisfied.

His feelings were confirmed when he saw her walking towards him across the hallway of her home as soon as the slave announced him. She had a radiant smile that made her look younger than thirty-six, though in any case she carried her age exceptionally well. She threw her arms around him and kissed him in front of the servants, without any shame.

"What a dear you are to come so soon! Another man would have felt compelled to behave proudly after all the times I rejected you!" she chirped.

Agrippa was disorientated, not knowing how to take her words, which seemed slightly sarcastic, but he didn't resist and abandoned himself to her lips, letting himself become intoxicated by her perfume and experiencing again all those wonderful feelings that had bewitched him in the past and which he had been craving for so long. And he knew instantly that it would always be worth it. He would have subjected himself to further indignities just to have her in his arms again, and for a moment he even regretted having walked out that day just so as not to have to share her with Manius. After these six months of abstinence, if she proposed an amorous triangle anew, he would not hesitate to accept.

But there seemed to be no other guests. Fulvia took his hand and led him to her bed chamber, where Agrippa saw only the bed that had already been the scene of their embraces in what seemed a distant past. He wanted to pounce on her, but did not intend to humiliate himself more than he already had, so he tried to keep a cool head. "You were really perverse this time," he said, taking a firm hold of her waist. "You've never been so ruthless before – and you've treated me pretty badly in the past..."

She stroked him almost tenderly, without the sensuousness she had always displayed in the past. She no longer seemed the proud woman who craved powerful emotions, who was always seeking the boundary between pleasure and pain. Her behaviour was almost maternal – and she was, in fact, easily old enough to be his mother.

"I needed to know if you really cared for me. You had already abandoned me in the past, and for another woman. I didn't see or hear from you for months after the Battle of Philippi: how could I know if you still had the same feelings for me? Maybe there was another Etain..."

He squeezed her hands reassuringly. "My feelings have changed. They are more intense than before. I realised that I cannot live without you, and I left you only because the war made it unavoidable, I assure you. I no longer have any interest in other women: only you exist."

At one time, he thought, he would never have said anything like that, and certainly not in such a heartfelt way. Not only because he hadn't felt that way then, but because he knew that she would have laughed in his face. Now, though, he needed to make her understand that he really loved her. It was not just physical attraction or passion – it was a genuine addiction.

She didn't laugh in his face. Indeed, she only smiled condescendingly, and added, "I'm glad. That's exactly what I was hoping to hear. You're still the man I desire most, and now that events are precipitating, I need to know you are near." She moved a step back from him, undid the belt of her robe and then took off the garment, displaying herself for his admiration as she liked to do, well aware that the years had no effect at all on her magnificent body. Agrippa threw himself to his knees at her feet, grabbed her buttocks and pressed his cheek against her sex.

"I know. There may even be a new war in Italy. Your brother-in-law doesn't want to listen to reason, it seems," he said, kissing her repeatedly. "But this time I will not leave you. I promise I'll be back to see you whenever I can. I would do anything for you."

"That is not enough. I want you always by my side, Agrippa."

"You know I cannot," he said, standing up and kissing her neck now. "Octavian wants to give me the command of the operation, if war does break out. But let's not despair: Octavian and Lucius are at this moment in Gabii, discussing ways to find an agreement that satisfies everyone."

"It will be a truce at best, just like in Teanum. War will break out sooner or later, everybody knows that."

Agrippa made a gesture of impatience, picked her up and laid her on the bed. Then he began to undress.

"Why do we have to talk about politics now that we are finally together?" he protested.

"I told you. Because I need to know you are at my side. I need you, now that my husband has abandoned me."

"Abandoned?" asked Agrippa with a surprised expression.

"Yes, abandoned. I don't expect him to return to me in the near future: he is in the arms of Cleopatra, so they say. I have lost him, Agrippa. That harpy already had her claws into Caesar, who was much more level headed. Antony is easily influenced and Cleopatra will do what she will with him. I cannot *stand* it!"

"I didn't think that you loved him so much. After all, you're forever cuckolding him…"

"It's not that. Being the wife of Antony meant that I had a lot of power and I cannot abide the idea of losing it. I want to continue to be the *prima donna* of Rome. Once you have got used to them, it is not easy to give up certain positions."

Agrippa began to sense something disturbing about her reasoning. What was she getting at?

"And so?" he asked suspiciously.

"So I seduced my brother-in-law and I encouraged him to promote the cause of the dispossessed, inducing him to break off negotiations with Octavian and press for war."

"By the gods!" cried Agrippa, appalled by the perfidy of the woman, which never ceased to amaze him. "But what do you hope to achieve?"

"That should be obvious. In the event of war, Antony will be forced to return to Italy to rectify the situation and I will be able to reclaim him: apparently he has forgotten that I am no less a mistress of the arts of the bedroom than that whore! And if he doesn't return, Lucius will win the war and I will convince him to marry me. At that point, he will be the most powerful man in Italy..."

Dismayed, Agrippa remained silent for a long time. "Your lack of scruples leaves me dumbfounded..." he muttered finally. "And where do I fit into all this?"

"I am counting greatly on you, Agrippa. If you love me, you will support me and you will be my lover when I marry Lucius just as you were when I was with Mark Antony. Lucius has no idea how to be a general, but you do. And Octavian isn't much of a strategist either. So, if we have you on our side, victory is certain."

Agrippa's eyes widened." Is that why you summoned me? To make me betray my friend? What makes you think I would ever do it?"

"The fact that you love me. You just said that you would do anything for me. Otherwise, it must means that you weren't telling the truth, and I will never again give myself to a man who takes me for a fool."

Agrippa could not believe it. She had tricked him. Furiously, he jumped on the bed and lay down on top of her, grabbing her wrists and preparing to take her with the violence that she had always demanded from him. But Fulvia held her legs together.

"I take it you are with me, then?" she asked.

Agrippa would have liked to scream his refusal in her face. Shout his contempt for her ruthlessness. But he collapsed on top of her then fell to the bed beside her and whispered, "You can't ask me that..."

"But I *am* asking you," she replied. "So? Are you with me?"

"I... I don't know. I will have to think about it," he muttered, before getting up, dressing and leaving the house.

IV

"Attack! Aim for the rearguard, come on!"

Octavian attempted to shout loudly enough that even the men at the rear of the three cohorts entrusted to Agrippa would hear him. His friend might be the one leading them, but the men must always be aware that he was the supreme commander. As soon as the legionaries began to go forward, heading quickly back down the slope towards the enemy column crossing the valley, he moved alongside them, keeping a safe distance from the flank: as Maecenas always said, it made no sense for a commander to risk his hide in battle, especially when he had lieutenants as skilled as Agrippa to rely upon.

The army of Furnius had been warned of the assault thanks to the light cavalry that Lucius Antonius had dutifully posted at its sides. They rushed over to their fellow soldiers and urged them to form an *agmen quadratum*. Rapidly halting their march, the legionaries attempted to get into a series of square groups, but Agrippa and Octavian's men were now almost upon them and when the clash between the two armies took place, the geometrical formations were still only half-finished. Many of the enemy soldiers were surprised with their backs still turned towards them, while others got in their comrades' way, allowing Agrippa and Octavian's men to penetrate their ranks.

The triumvir drew his sword and continued to urge on his men from the saddle of his horse, moving closer to the line of combat behind the protection offered by his bodyguard, in which Ortwin and Veleda acted as his forward shield. His men had blocked the enemy's rearguard where it was, but the rest of the column, contrary to his expectations, was already heading off before it could be surrounded. That was no good at all: the plan was that Furnius would rush to the aid of his rearguard only to find his escape route had been cut off, but instead the coward was abandoning the rear portion of his army to save the rest.

He had to change tactic. He couldn't allow the *legatus* to take all those men to Lucius Antonius, further strengthening the consul's army: the legionaries had to become his. At *least* those legionaries. He motioned to Ortwin to stay with him and rode towards the position occupied by Agrippa, who was fighting in the front line. The German understood the danger and moved close to his commander, creating a barrier of shields with the other soldiers. Octavian watched his lifelong friend engaged in battle, his massive frame towering above the other soldiers, both comrades and enemies, while with every swing his sword became more and more crimson. And he envied him: the lad had strength and courage to spare in a way that he never would. It occurred to him that it would not be a good idea for him to fight beside his friend – they should always fight separately whenever it was possible, otherwise sooner or later the soldiers would inevitably start making comparisons and begin thinking Agrippa was a better commander than he was. And perhaps even force Agrippa to take his place. It mattered little that his friend was a commoner and he was the son of Caesar. For all the blind trust he felt in the friend he had grown up with, Octavian knew about human weakness and preferred to keep him out of temptation's way, for Agrippa's sake, above all: he would never want to have to get rid of him, and not simply because he was the most valuable lieutenant he had. He was also the person Octavian felt the greatest affection for – that is, if you could define the mixture of feelings Agrippa provoked in him as affection: a blend of the usefulness, familiarity, friendship, pleasure and comfort with which Agrippa provided him.

He sent Veleda to get Agrippa's attention. The woman urged her horse forward and sliced through the combatants, forcing them to clear the way for her. She reached him without showing a trace of hesitation or fear and motioned for him to follow her. Agrippa did not alter in any way what he was doing: he continued slashing away, but instead of advancing deeper into the enemy formation, he headed toward Octavian, clearing his path with blows from his sword. His brow beaded with a film of sweat, he appeared before the triumvir, who was still in the saddle and with his armour as immaculate as for a parade.

"I can't see the rest of the column from here," Agrippa said. "What is Furnius doing?"

Octavian grimaced. It was just as Maecenas had said: a commander who took part in the fray lost sight of the overall progress of the battle and had no way of making the necessary adjustments. In addition, of course, to risking death and leaving his army in disarray. He was wise to keep out of it.

"He's making a run for it. Sacrificing his rearguard to save the rest of the troops. There is a hill further up ahead, and if he manages to reach it before dark, we'll never be able to flush him out," he said. "And right by it there is Sentinum. The city has sided with Lucius, so it will give him support. And it's not the only one here in Piceno: we're also running the risk of someone attacking us from behind."

"Wonderful. We'll have to detach at least one cohort to cut off their communications with the city," said Agrippa. "We'll surround him, and eventually he will have to surrender."

"Triumvir! Horsemen approaching!" shouted a despatch rider who was racing towards them.

"How many?" asked Octavian.

"Several squadrons. At least five, I think."

Octavian glanced at Agrippa in dismay. "Is it possible that Lucius is already attacking us? Or are they troops from one of the cities of Coppice hoping to trap us between two fires, as I feared?"

"In either case, we're in a bad position," replied Agrippa. "We need to send this cohort off to defend ourselves from this new attack. Furnius will get away, damn it"

Octavian nodded with a gesture of annoyance, and ordered the tribune in command to take the unit up to the ridge and prepare for an attack from behind. As soon as the cohort distanced itself from the line of fighting, the pressure on the enemy column eased and a part of Furnius's rearguard began escaping the battle. Octavian waved to Agrippa to follow the tribune.

When they reached the top of the ridge, they saw with their own eyes the column of horsemen approaching. Two of them, including a despatch rider, came towards them.

"My lord, he is one of Lepidus's horsemen, come to announce the arrival of the triumvir!"

Octavian looked at the despatch rider.

"You mean that Lepidus is with them?" he asked incredulously.

"Yes, sir."

The ousted triumvir was the last person that Caesar's heir would have expected to encounter. He was responsible for guarding Rome, where Octavian had left him with two legions to keep watch so that Lucius, busy trying to procure support in Italy, didn't manage to seize it, and the fact that he was no longer in the city was not a good sign.

And in the meantime, thanks to him they had lost their opportunity to surround Furnius.

As soon as Lepidus eventually reached him – sweaty and dusty, more flabby than ever, and with the hang-dog expression he had assumed since the victors at Philippi had relegated him to a secondary role in the triumvirate – Octavian could already sense the bad news, but he waited for Lepidus to speak.

The man stood with his head bowed for a while, after greeting him with a wave of his hand. However, Octavian said nothing. Finally, when the other spoke, it was in an unsteady voice.

"Rome is lost, Caesar. By now Lucius will have seized it."

"What do you mean? You don't even know if he is inside the walls or not?" snapped Octavian. "Why did I leave you two legions?"

Lepidus spread his hands in resignation. "There was nothing I could do. Three cohorts, the vanguard of Lucius's army, appeared outside the city. The Senate began to protest and to call for the arrival of the consul and the end of the triumvirate. So I took the troops and I went to the Curia to scare those old windbags, entrusting the custody of the walls to my tribune Nonius. But as soon as night fell, the traitor let the enemy in and handed over the legions to him. The only thing left for me to do was get out of there before they blocked off all the escape routes and..."

He didn't have time to finish. Octavian slapped him across the face. "This is what I deserve for having allowed you to remain as part of the triumvirate, you idiot! Any centurion would have done better in your place!"

Lepidus rubbed his reddened cheek and glared at him with eyes full of hate while his men gripped the handles of the swords in their scabbards. All those present could sense the tension in the air, but Octavian didn't care: he had just lost two legions and the city, the Senate was against him, Lucius was somewhere in Italy with an army that was growing by the day, and Furnius was escaping before his very eyes.

The war couldn't have got off to a worse start.

*

Maecenas awoke at dawn and realised that the streets of Rome were full of soldiers and gladiators.

Lucius Antonius's men.

When the slaves came to tell him what was happening on the streets, where groups of armed men were marching from one neighbourhood to the next, apparently carrying out round-ups, his first thought was for Octavia. She was about to give birth, and with Lucius's entry into the city, she became the most obvious hostage. He had to find a way to get her out of Rome.

He dressed hurriedly and had himself taken to the woman's house, in agonies of anxiety all the way from his home on the Esquiline to the Palatine hill. He noticed that Lucius's squadrons were converging on the Forum, and he ordered his litter bearers to take side streets so as to stay out of sight: someone might recognise him as one of Octavian's men and capture him.

He saw a gang of gladiators and suddenly was afraid. They were not soldiers, and tended not to be controlled by any form of military discipline. Nevertheless, he ordered the bearers to stop and waited for them to pass. But they paused in front of a tavern and then went inside, and by the cries the Etruscan heard emerge from within, they were looting the place. He took advantage of the distraction and urged the bearers to run on quickly before they emerged again. They rapidly reached the Palatine and began to ascend the slopes, encountering only common people hurrying to take refuge in their homes. When he reached the house of Marcellus and Octavia, he saw an empty litter surrounded by a group of bearers, and after a moment, he realised that they were those of Lucius Pinarius. Evidently, he had had the same idea. He approached the door hurriedly and Octavian's cousin appeared in the doorway.

His gown was smeared with blood.

Maecenas winced. "What happened? Are they already here?"

"No, but they soon will be, I'm certain of it," replied Pinarius. "That's why we have to stop him."

"And… what about *that*?" asked Maecenas, pointing to the blood.

Pinarius spread his hands. "I had come to get her out of the way, but that's no longer possible. When I told her what was going on, she panicked and went into premature labour. I had to help with the delivery. Fortunately everything went well. It's a boy. Even Marcellus was pleased. But now Octavia is in no condition to travel."

"And how are you planning on stopping them from coming? From what people are saying, all the soldiers have been handed over to Lucius and

Lepidus has escaped," objected Maecenas. "We can't defend the house."

"No, we can't, so I'm going to talk to Lucius," said Pinarius. "I will offer him something in exchange for him guaranteeing the safety of Octavia, and of yourself. He is a man of honour, and if we make an agreement he will keep his word."

Maecenas looked at him suspiciously.

"What will you offer him?"

"You will have to trust me."

"No way – I've noticed the way you've been distancing yourself from the sect lately, and it hasn't been particularly reassuring."

"I would rather say that it has been the sect which has been distancing itself from me, don't you think? In any case, I have no intention of doing any of you any harm, so I ask you again to trust me. Anyway, what choice do you have? Lucius holds the city, and so he holds us too. Our only hope is that he doesn't take advantage of the situation and that he decides to make use of a go-between. Which cannot be you: you're not a senator, and right now it is the Senate he needs more than anything else."

He was right, Maecenas could not deny it. All he could do was put all his hopes, as well of those of the sect, in a man who now seemed to be one of the least committed to the cause he had sworn to uphold before Mars Ultor. And this was further proof of how troubled the cult was for at that moment Octavian had all of Italy against him.

"Go home and wait there. I'll send for you when Lucius delivers a speech to the people and the Senate. Because he will do soon, you can be sure of it," Pinarius said to the Etruscan.

Maecenas departed uneasily. Pinarius seemed overly sure of himself.

He spent the next few hours brooding and expecting the worst. He read dispatches from the other members of the sect and learned that Octavian was stuck in Coppice outside the walls of Sentinum, and that Rufus was having trouble entering Italy: Antony's generals, Ventidius Bassus and Fufius Calenus, commanded armies along the border and were threatening to block him. If they hadn't yet challenged him openly, it was only because Mark Antony hadn't yet informed them of which side he would be supporting. And that was the real problem: no one knew whether Antony approved of his brother's rebellion – which also looked like a rebellion against the triumvirate – or whether he was piloting the whole thing from afar. The triumvir hadn't made an official statement and may not even have been aware of the recent, dramatic developments.

He spent the whole morning the same way until he heard solders at the door asking for him.

Maecenas winced, fearing they had come to take him away, but his doorkeeper told him that he was to go to the Forum and handed him a waxed tablet that turned out to be a pass. If it was a trap, it was a well organised one, he said to himself, resigning himself to going along with it. When he arrived at the square between the two basilicas it was already packed, but the pass reserved him a place in the front row amongst the senators and knights.

Lucius was already on the platform of the Rostra and began to speak. The stage was surrounded by his gladiators, who were far more menacing than common legionaries and it was clear that his intention was to intimidate.

Just behind the consul was, amongst others, Pinarius.

Maecenas still didn't really understand what was going on. Meanwhile, Lucius was becoming increasingly passionate. He lacked the rhetorical skills of his brother but he was still capable of expressing himself effectively.

"The triumvirate is illegal! We were forced to accept it as the judiciary of the Republic, but no one asked us what we thought!" he shouted. "We would have said that we did not want a king or a Caesar, and that we certainly didn't want three!"

Pinarius nodded with conviction, indicating his agreement.

"We must punish Octavian and Lepidus for the abuses they have been responsible for and for the continuing violations of the law they have perpetrated. They refuse to submit to our judgement so we will have to defeat them on the battlefield. We did not ask for this civil war: it was they who abused their prerogatives by harassing the population with these unjustifiable seizures and contravening the provisions agreed upon with my brother. I am sure that when Mark Antony finds out what is happening, he will renounce his position as triumvir and assume the consulate, a far more legitimate judiciary!"

Cries of approval rang in Maecenas' ears, many of them from the rows of senators and equestrians. It didn't look good: the Senate was taking advantage of the opportunity to ride the wave of indignation caused by the confiscations and seizures and deprive Octavian of authority, which had always been their goal.

Then he noticed that Pinarius was chatting amicably with the man alleged to have allowed Lucius into the city despite Octavian's provisions. Nonius, he was called, and it was clear that the two knew each other well. They actually seemed to be congratulating one another. And suddenly, everything was clear.

He rose and walked around the stands, trying to attract Pinarius's attention. Pinarius tried to ignore him but when he could no longer pretend not to have see him he climbed down from the stage. "What do you want?" he asked. "If you're worried about yourself and Octavia, you can relax: I have made an agreement with Lucius that you will not be harmed."

"You had already agreed on that before all this, hadn't you?" Maecenas snapped at him.

"What?"

"All of this. You made an agreement with the consul to let him into Rome, with assurances that he wouldn't harm the family and associates of Octavian. Nonius is your man."

Pinarius reacted with exaggerated indignation. "How dare you? I have risked my life for the sect," he protested. "And in return I offered to go to Antony in the East to inform him of the situation and to discover his intentions."

"Oh really? Well the way I see it is that you are going to the East to escape the revenge of Octavian," he answered. "Wait till he finds out you are a traitor. He did well to be suspicious of you!"

Pinarius became even more indignant. "It would seem that there is no point being a faithful member of the sect if I am in any case suspected of such ignoble crimes. If I now no longer wish to be involved with you, it is precisely because I was treated unfairly! I'm no traitor: I am simply going my own way, and I mean no harm in any way to

Octavian. And it is true that I obtained a promise that no harm would be done to you, and I intend to work for peace: that is why I am going to Antony now. Mars Ultor will forgive me, knowing as he does what I have been forced to suffer!"

Without another word, he turned and climbed back onto the grandstand.

Well, he had at least admitted his betrayal, albeit indirectly, said Maecenas to himself. The sect was about to lose another member, after Etain and Gaius Chaerea. But the thing that worried him most for the immediate future were the words he heard emerge from the mouth of Lucius Antonius, who had begun to speak again once the ovations had ceased.

"… we have more legions than them, and we will be victorious. Especially if we prevent Salvidienus Rufus from entering Italy with his army. We leave immediately for the border with Gaul and we will take those units too, and then Octavian and Lepidus will have to surrender and undergo a fair trial. Do not worry about these soldiers you see around the city: unlike them, I respect the laws, and will not force you to live under the shadow of swords and shields like a conquered people… the way they did! You are the citizens of the most important city in the world and you have the right to be free. I will be sending troops to Sutri soon, leaving only a few soldiers inside the walls of Rome to maintain public order and guarantee your peace of mind."

Maecenas did not wait for him to finish. He walked briskly away from the Forum in the direction of home. It was time to act.

*

The enemy soldiers had finally turned their backs to the ramparts of the camp and began to flow through the breach, chased off by spear and sword. It was dawn now and it was easier to identify targets thanks to the fires caused by their attack. Popilius Laenas threw the second of the spears he had at his disposal and struck a fleeing legionary in the shoulder. He let out a shout of triumph, motioned to his men to follow him and leapt through the breach, risking the flames to give Furnius's men a lesson for once and for all. He soon reached the slower ones and began slicing away, literally chopping the less cautious ones in two. His men followed suit and soon the ground in front of the fortifications was strewn with corpses. Only then did the centurion pause, aware that he was almost within range of the archers posted on the ramparts of Furnius's camp. He told his men to fall back and hurried off to report to Octavian.

It had been a good fight, but pointless, just like all the others. Popilius Laenas had had enough of inaction. For some time now he had been asking himself when the triumvir and Agrippa would give the order to raise the siege, and he was increasingly afraid they would be overtaken by events. What were they waiting for? For Lucius Antonius to attack them, perhaps with the help of the legions he had taken from Rufus? Rome was back in the hands of the consul and it seemed that Rufus was unable to get to them to offer them assistance. Sextus Pompey was ready to support Lucius, and they were wasting time in front of that secondary goal. If he had been one of the leaders of the sect, he would have given completely different orders.

But he was not a leader. Or rather, he wasn't yet. He was determined to earn himself a higher rank through his successes on the field. And there were no glorious victories to be won up there in those mountains., The city was too difficult to conquer with its granite walls and the meagre forces available to the triumvir, and even starving them out was not an option: sooner or later, someone would surprise them from behind, exactly as had happened to Caesar in Alesia. But this time it wouldn't be ill-equipped barbarians that were easily defeated but experienced Roman soldiers, intent on ending the rise of the dictator's young heir.

They had no siege engines, and Octavian didn't fancy risking his men in an assault with ladders. He wanted to let hunger conquer the city defence and Furnius's troops camped on a nearby hill. Meanwhile he was losing men in the frequent sorties that the besieged soldiers undertook at night. They repelled them but after each battle, despair spread deeper among the triumvir's troops: they could see no way out, and heard only disastrous news from all over Italy.

Laenas approached the commanders having firmly decided to urge them to action. But he paused a few feet from them when he saw them saluting someone he struggled to recognise. The ridiculously dusty and sweaty little man hurrying towards the triumvir with his awkward, effeminate walk was Maecenas.

He was supposed to be in Rome.

Laenas put aside current events and tried to hear what he had to say. Octavian invited Maecenas to enter the praetorium with them and the centurion followed, certain that as a member of the sect he had every right to attend the meeting. And no one stopped him although no one invited him to enter either. Once all four were inside, Agrippa closed the curtain flap and Octavian invited the Etruscan to speak.

The poor man was decidedly out of breath, "I have terrible news for you," he finally managed to say.

"If you are about to inform us that Rome is in the hands of Lucius, we already know," said Octavian.

"No, that's just *bad* news. I said terrible. It is that Pinarius handed it over to him."

"Pinarius?" Octavian and Agrippa exclaimed almost in unison. "*Our* Pinarius?" Octavian added.

"He is no longer ours, it would seem. He must be one of Mark Antony's men now, because he informed me of his intention to join him in the East."

Octavian quivered with indignation. "I knew I couldn't trust him!" he shouted angrily, slapping his fist into the palm of the other hand.

"He says he did it because he was offended at the way you had treated him. But at least he did not let Lucius enter until he had agreed to guarantee the safety of your sister, who has just given birth," explained Maecenas, who seemed to have recovered his eloquence. "To a boy."

Octavian did not appear interested in his new nephew.

"What else did you hear about Lucius Antonius?" he urged.

"Ah, that brings me to the most interesting part," said the Etruscan. "The consul is preparing to leave the city to confront Salvidienus Rufus and prevent him from bringing reinforcements. But, so as to avoid upsetting the Romans, he has left some of his troops in Sutri, and that has given me an idea…"

*

She was there, beyond those walls. Agrippa felt a chill run down his spine as he began to make out the lines of Sutri's defences behind which Lucius Antonius's men were quartered.

And where Fulvia was.

He'd had a start when Octavian had ordered him to take a cohort and march from Sentinum in Piceno, where they were besieging Furnius, all the way to Sutri. Maecenas insisted that the consul would be forced to retrace his steps to defend his soldiers and abandon the idea of keeping Rufus and his six legions out of Italy: that should give Octavian some breathing space.

He told the unit to distribute themselves at regular intervals and begin digging a ditch to encircle the city. Meanwhile, he began to think about what he should do about Fulvia. He had not yet given her an answer because in reality he had not given one to himself. He was too fond of Octavian to betray him, but he was also obsessed with the woman and didn't want to risk losing her so soon after finding her again. If only there was some way to maintain his relationship with both… but there wasn't, Fulvia had been clear about that. She instigated Lucius Antonius's revolt: the consul would never have had the courage to do anything that might provoke the anger of his more powerful brother by himself. The woman was able to make any man she had decided to use completely lose his head.

He must keep in mind that when he thought about Fulvia, he was not entirely objective himself, and only this awareness had prevented him from immediately joining her cause in the hope of finally having her all to himself. He knew it was wrong. Nevertheless, he was desperately seeking some pretext, some excuse, which would allow him to join her.

Towards evening he inspected the fortifications. The men had done well as had the peasants recruited for the occasion. A rampart and a moat ran all around Sutri and no one could leave without a battle. If the blockade was attacked with sufficient numbers it would probably break, but thanks to his expedient of dressing the peasants up as soldiers, they would think carefully before deciding to take the risk.

He went to bed thinking about the strangeness of that siege. He had no real army with him and wasn't supposed to storm the walls but only act as bait. And inside the city walls was the woman he loved: Fulvia was a few feet away from him on the other side of that wall and he could neither touch her nor see her.

He had only a few soldiers with him and a bunch of peasants who, if there was a battle, would only be a hindrance. He had done some strange things for the sect and for Octavian, but this beat them all.

He rose at dawn to the prospect of doing nothing all day unless the besieged tried to break out. It was frustrating for a man of action like him. The inaction forced him to wallow in his dilemma: Octavian or Fulvia? His mind and even his heart compelled him towards his friend and his loins and perhaps something else towards Fulvia, but it was a terribly hard compulsion to control. He told himself that he had shared many dreams with Octavian since childhood that were just now beginning to be realised – that they had done it together, and that together they would change the world. But then the image of the woman burst into his fantasies and crushed all his reason. When he saw her appear, flesh and blood, before his eyes in the middle of the afternoon, he could scarcely believe he wasn't hallucinating.

He had the presence of mind to keep her party a reasonable distance from the fortifications so that her keen eye didn't notice how undermanned his army actually was. He stared at her, riding astride and accompanied by a squad of armed horsemen, on the plain that separated the city walls from the trenches and felt his heart jump. One of his soldiers told him she wished to speak to him. How she had known of his presence was a mystery, but in any case, Agrippa felt a sense of euphoria mixed with anxiety begin to come over him, and ordered ten soldiers to saddle up and accompany him across the trenches. When the two squads came into contact, Agrippa beckoned Fulvia to him so that the others could not hear them talking. He moved away, trotting over to a nearby chestnut tree, where he dismounted and stood by the trunk under its wide branches. She dismounted slowly and approached him with a mischievous smile.

"So, you've decided that you don't want me any more, have you?" she said, breaking the silence.

She was more enchanting than ever, thought Agrippa, swallowing hard. "Actually, I haven't decided anything," he said in an unsteady voice.

"Well, that's not the way it looks to me. It looks as if you've chosen, all right: you are here to besiege me on behalf of your little friend. The war has begun and you already know which side you're on."

"That's not true," he protested. "Much can still happen. War has not yet broken out!"

"So I do still have some hope with you, then?" she said in a soft voice, taking a step closer and holding out her arm to stroke his cheek.

But Agrippa flinched. "Are you crazy?" he shouted. "They're all watching us!"

Fulvia smiled contemptuously. She was about to speak when a courier arrived on horseback, stopping a few feet from them and gesturing for Agrippa's attention.

"Legatus! I bring urgent news from the triumvir!"

"Off you go," Fulvia urged him sarcastically, "go and wag your tail for your little friend!" He gave her an almost apologetic look and then walked over to the messenger.

"Legatus, the message is verbal to avoid running the risk of it ending up in the hands of the rebels," said the soldier. "When he learned of your march on Sutri, the consul was afraid of being caught between two fires and he decided not to go and face down Rufus!"

"So he's coming here, I imagine. What orders did Octavian give?"

"No, Legatus. Apparently, to avoid being caught in a pincer movement between you, Rufus, and the triumvir, Lucius Antonius has gone to Perugia and barricaded himself inside. Therefore you are to abandon the siege and to head to Umbria. When Rufus arrives, you will lay siege to the city together."

Agrippa nodded thoughtfully, then turned and walked slowly back to Fulvia. "As we knew, Lucius is a coward: if it weren't for you, he would never have dared do any of this," he said. "Instead of fighting he has gone to hole up in Perugia, and that will be the end of him, because we will put him under siege. You have lost, my dear."

"No, I have not lost. Not if you stand down your fellow soldiers besieging Perugia when I send reinforcements," she said, without hesitation. "Which I am sure that you will – if you want me."

V

When Salvidienus Rufus saw the outline of the city of Perugia perched along the top and down the slopes of a series of hills, he thought, not for the first time, that it would be a good idea to turn back. The only thing that stopped him from actually doing so was that he feared a mutiny amongst his legions: many of his soldiers were blindly loyal to Caesar's memory, and so to his heir Octavian too.

He had struggled to accept the idea of leaving for Spain, where he had feared he would be cut off from the centre stage of the struggle for power, interpreting the proconsulate as a kind of exile the leader of the sect had sentenced him to. But on the way to the Iberian Peninsula he had begun to see the benefits of the marginal position he was preparing to take up. As things stood, bands of legionaries led by a variety of generals travelled around Italy – some were loyal to Octavian, others to Lucius Antonius, others still to Mark Antony – and the country was surrounded by fleets commanded by the admirals of Sextus Pompey, from his freedmen to the assassins of Caesar, Domitius Ahenobarbus and Staius Murcus. He himself had almost run into columns led by Asinius Pollio, Ventidius Bassus and Fufius Calenus, who were gravitating towards northern Italy without a clear idea of what they were doing: they wanted to support Lucius Antonius, but lacked the conviction that would only derive from very specific orders given by their actual leader, his brother Mark Antony. Without those orders, by explicitly hindering Octavian they feared contravening the seemingly iron pact of the triumvirate's agreement.

In short, Italy was in chaos, and Rufus had concluded that he could only benefit by keeping out of the way. He would leave the protagonists of the political and military action behind to slay one another and would return when they were too exhausted to stop him, and the population was completely exasperated, and would seize power for himself. Perhaps in conjunction with Mark Antony who, he was sure, knew very well what was happening in the west. The protests against the confiscations and the threats of rebellion had been going on for nearly a year now, and it was unthinkable that in all that time nobody had informed him or asked him for instructions on how to behave – not even his own brother Lucius. But Antony, of course, was pretending not to know so as to be able to obtain the maximum advantage from the situation: in fact, if his brother won, he would be given control of the west, and if he lost, all he would need to do would be to distance himself and decry his foolish brother's actions.

If it had been up to Rufus, he would have made an agreement immediately: he was sure that if he helped Lucius, the man's brother would reward him sooner or later. By now, he had realised that he was not destined to rise high in the sect and was condemned to forever occupy fourth place in the hierarchy, after Octavian, Agrippa and Maecenas. With Antony, at least he would be the second in command, and perhaps one day even the first, considering how much older than he the triumvir was.

But his soldiers wouldn't have understood. Not yet. Even less so now that Octavian was in trouble: they would have thought he was stabbing him in the back by siding with Lucius. And anyway, he didn't have enough money to buy their loyalty at the moment. The proconsulate in Spain would make him rich – as it did Caesar in his first job as provincial governor in that very same province – and then he could really turn those six legions into a personal army. For now, though, he had to make the best of a bad job and wait for more favourable times.

Nearing the city, he noticed large scale fortification work by both the city's besiegers and its defenders, and saw movement along the slopes of the hill. He had no time to work out what was going on before Ortwin came galloping towards him.

"Proconsul!" shouted the German. "You've arrived in the middle of a sortie by the consul's men who are trying to prevent us from completing the trenches! When the men on the city battlements saw you coming they recalled them, and the triumvir wants you to send a cohort to Perugia and cut off the raider's retreat before they can get to the gates."

"A day will come when you no longer give me orders, you little shit," said Rufus mentally to Octavian, but he replied, "Certainly, Ortwin. I will lead the attack in person. Centurion, have the first cohort blow its horns!" His men admired his courage, as well as his money, and would follow him more willingly if they saw that he exposed himself to as many risks as they did, so he was determined to never miss an opportunity for a bit of visibility.

He led his soldiers off at a rapid march, heading directly for the foot of the hill, towards which was flowing a column of defenders pursued by Octavian's troops. Approaching the head of the enemy column, he passed an unfinished *vallum*, only partly excavated with embankments of varying height and paling erected only for a few yards. From the besiegers fortifications cries of joy arose at the sight of his cohort bursting onto the battlefield and he began to shout encouragement to his men as they clashed with the enemy.

Some of the enemy forces were making their way through the city's external boundary wall, which Lucius must have had built in a hurry to re-inforce Perugia's defences, but it was still incomplete and Rufus was able to take advantage of a breach and rapidly break through. His men immediately set about massacring Lucius Antonius's men, who also had to contend with the Octavian's legions in pursuit and their own comrades fighting their way through the *vallum*.

On realising he had advanced too far inside the walls, Rufus gave the order to fall back, fortunately for him, Antonius's men were too confused to set up a coherent defence. He realised that had been reckless, but how many times had Caesar been reckless too, obtaining his most spectacular victories in precisely that way? Only at Gergovia had his gamble not paid off – but he had soon made up for that with Alesia. And an even bigger gamble.

Many of the enemy were now manning the gates of the fortifications at the foot of the hill and he was trapped between them and those near the walls. His men and those of Octavian who had remained outside pressed forward along the rampart, forcing Antonius's men to watch their backs, but getting out would be difficult. He urged the men with him to attack along the rampart, but he also had some facing the wall to defend the main line from attacks from the rear. Breathing heavily now, he took advantage of the momentum and charged downhill, his sword swinging. It worked, after a few moments of resistance the enemy forces fanned out to let him and his men pass.

He reached Octavian's soldiers, who were scattered across the plain, and revelled in their cheers. Glowing with satisfaction, he headed towards the triumvir's fortifications, which appeared to go all the way down to the Tiber – Caesar's heir was obviously planning to cut the city off completely. But what would protect him from the generals who supported Antonius and who were currently roaming central Italy?

His friend met him whilst the legions Rufus had brought with him began to flow past the fortifications, with some centurions already laying out the plan of a camp.

"What were you thinking? Who gave you the order to penetrate their defences?" said Octavian, visibly annoyed.

Rufus stiffened. "You did. You told me to cut of the enemy's route, didn't you? And I think I made a pretty good job of it," he said with undisguised irritation.

Agrippa appeared from amongst the crowd of milling soldiers. So he was already there. And then Maecenas appeared too. The whole gang of his alleged 'superiors'.

"Octavian just means that you exposed yourself to an unnecessary risk, Rufus – you could have been killed in there," said Agrippa in a conciliatory tone.

"Yes. And I bet you'd have been happy if I had," Rufus replied angrily.

Agrippa did not see fit to answer. He never did, the hypocrite, because he always wanted to look accommodating and reasonable in front of Octavian, who now tried to change the subject. "Anyway, now that you're here, we have three armies with which to besiege the city. Mine, yours, and the one that Agrippa brought back from Sutri. It is thanks to him that Lucius didn't attack you from the rear."

Rufus thought that if Lucius had attacked him the two of them might have made an agreement, but said only, "We will also need the three armies to defend us if the other generals attack: Asinius, Atinius, Ventidius and Calenus might well appear at any moment. I hope you're all aware of that."

"Of course we are, and that is why someone will have to go and stop them," cut in Maecenas. "Now that we have a dozen legions, some of us will go to the Umbrian border and prevent them from approaching the city. We know that Fulvia has also mobilised Munatius Plancus in Spoleto, as well as Ventidius Bassus."

"But if we disperse our forces, Lucius will be able to retaliate..." objected Rufus.

"No – Lucius has an army made up mainly of recruits, and he won't dare do any more than a few sorties," pointed out Octavian. "And the sooner we finish the fortifications around the city, the sooner we prevent the risk of that too. Now you're here, Agrippa and I will go to take on the other generals: Your men are tired from the forced march so let them rest and finish building the fortifications. I am sure you will not disappoint me and will refrain from taking any inopportune initiatives, Rufus," he added in a vaguely provocative tone.

Rufus clenched his fists and nodded at what he considered yet another humiliation. They had brought him back from Spain to play caretaker to a bunch of recruits while Octavian was taking his chosen one to seek glory against experienced generals like Ventidius and Plancus... But the day would come when he would make them pay for all of their arrogance...

*

It would have been easy. He had him right there, within arm's reach, the man who was his lifelong friend and, at the same time, the greatest obstacle to the fulfilment of his desires. Agrippa stared at Octavian, who was intent on deploying his troops against those of Ventidius already in formation at the foot of the Spoleto hill. They hoped to dissuade the general from attacking – to scare him so much that he would hole up in the city and then leave enough troops there to ensure that he did not set off to assist Lucius Antonius.

But Agrippa hoped that the battle would take place. He had decided that in spite of the affection he felt for his friend he was going to give Fulvia what she wanted. He knew that the woman was evil: he had watched as she stuck a hairpin through the Cicero's tongue after she had demanded his decapitated head, he had heard her spit venom about all and sundry, he had seen her threaten Etain and betray him… But he needed her in a way he would never have imagined possible. And if the only way to get her, to make sure that she didn't take up with Manius or marry Lucius Antonius, was to eliminate his closest friend… well, he would do it. That was why he was hoping for a battle: in the fray he could find a way to get a spear into Octavian's back, then he would take command of the troops, join Ventidius Bassus and together they would liberate the consul from the siege. And it was likely that there would be a battle, because he and Octavian only had four cohorts, a number that could easily entice Ventidius, who was in possession of a legion, though not at full strength.

But what if there wasn't one? He wouldn't have had the opportunity to kill Octavian without being considered a murderer. He had to make sure that the battle took place. He approached the triumvir and said, "Caesar, it seems strange to me that Ventidius has so few men. We cannot rule out him having more lurking in the woods over to the side there and ambushing us when you declare battle. I would like to patrol the area with a platoon of scouts. If I find something, we can extend the line to avoid being surrounded."

"Well send someone else," Octavian objected. "Why should you have to go? Claudius Marcellus, the ancestor of my brother-in-law, was killed during a perfectly normal patrol during the Punic Wars after being victorious in many renowned battles and having stood up to Hannibal. Generals shouldn't…"

"Generals shouldn't put themselves at risk, I know," Agrippa replied promptly. "It's that theory of Maecenas's. He's explained it to me as well. But I don't think that it's risky. I'll be very careful. I'd rather check the situation first hand, if you don't mind. I'll be back soon, safe and sound, you'll see."

Octavian made a gesture of resignation and returned to what he had been doing while Agrippa called over a decurion and told him to mount up his squadron. They set out at a brisk trot while he was still pondering exactly how to go about it. He wasn't convinced he would find any hidden soldiers – there was no evidence that Ventidius had actually planted any – but he was determined to cause an incident which would unleash a confrontation. They trotted through a dense thicket, Agrippa almost hoping to be attacked, but nothing happened. He strained his ears, but all he could hear was the sound of their passage through the undergrowth.

He saw a little villa beyond the forest, almost at the foot of the city, and decided that it was his opportunity. There would certainly be civilians inside. He would attack it and set it on fire, thus attracting the attention of enemy troops: Ventidius, who had assumed responsibility for these people, would come to their rescue and that would be enough to trigger a battle of greater proportions. And afterwards… afterwards he would complete the job by ensuring that Octavian – Octavian, who was so careful to avoid taking risks in combat – was amongst the fallen.

He trotted over to the fence that bordered the edge of the property and jumped neatly over it. There were, he saw, peasants at work in the part of the property where they lived, but he paid them no attention – he was only interested in the palatial building which Agrippa took to be the main residence and chose as his target. He wasn't planning to kill anyone, merely to create chaos. "Someone get some torches! Throw them onto the house!" he cried, while the terrified farmers and slaves fled in confusion.

His men obeyed him promptly and zealously, and almost instantly appeared bearing torches while others carried pieces of wood which, thanks to their more enterprising companions, were soon turned into kindling. Agrippa didn't care that Octavian might criticise his initiative: he would justify it by saying that he had wanted to eliminate a potential stronghold for enemies. Anyway, the point was irrelevant, given that afterwards he was intending to do away with the triumvir altogether. He hesitated for a moment before giving the order. He was about to start something he would not be able to stop even if he wanted to, and he considered the enormity of the situation: he was betraying his best friend and was actually going to kill him. For a woman who could never be any more than his mistress. He wondered which would cause him the most pain – losing Octavian or losing her – and he had no doubt: Fulvia had bewitched him, and he felt he would lose his mind without her.

His thoughts were interrupted by shouting and a group of soldiers appeared. His trained eye counted at least a hundred swarming out of the main house and heading for his squadron.

There must have been a unit in the rear: the possibility should have occurred to him when he decided to go behind enemy lines. It wasn't an ambush but trouble that he had gone looking for under his own steam. A centuria: all he could hope to do was escape, but he was trapped deep within the property and couldn't just disengage: they were too close to avoid combat. And with a ratio of almost ten to one, he had little chance.

He'd been an idiot: blinded by his lust for Fulvia, he had long since ceased to use his head, and now he found himself isolated behind enemy lines facing a contingent that could quite easily wipe out his men. It was the end. He gave no order to retreat, knowing that he must die honourably and without a pilum in his back, so he drew his sword and gave the signal to attack.

He heard the sound of arrows flying past him and thudding into the shields and bodies of his opponents. Astonished, he turned and saw a team of Cretan archers – the ones stationed in Octavian's Pretorian court – positioned just outside the fence firing off arrow after arrow with unerring aim.

Seemingly Ventidius's men hadn't expected this turn of events either and they immediately broke ranks and ran to take refuge inside the house, leaving their fallen comrades on the ground. Incredulously, Agrippa glanced at his men, who let out a huge sigh of relief, then back at the archers, who did not stop firing until the last enemy legionary had disappeared through the door of the building. Only then did the young man retreat. The archers led them to the field occupied by the triumvir, and one of them went off to report to the commander in chief before Agrippa had a chance to speak to him.

Apprehensively, he approached his friend, who was waiting impatiently on his horse. Fortunately, he had prepared a credible excuse, but it wouldn't save him from looking like a fool.

"Would you mind telling me what you got into your head?" asked Octavian, more agitated than angry, in greeting. "Why did you set fire to that villa, damn it? And why did you go so far away from camp?"

Agrippa snorted. "I saw it and I thought it might be a valuable defensive position for them in the case of battle or siege. So I wanted to destroy it... How was I to imagine that it was full of soldiers?" He paused, then couldn't help adding, "Why did you send the Cretans after me? Don't you trust me?"

Octavian looked at him in amazement, a vague expression of despair appearing on his face. "Of course I trust you! You are the only man in the world to whom I would blindly trust my life. I just wanted to protect you. I told you that missions like that can be risky – and I was right."

"... You wanted to protect me?" murmured Agrippa, feeling himself overcome by a wave of unspeakable shame.

"Of course. What else? I could lose anyone else, but not you," said Octavian, who, for once, seemed inclined to speak from his heart. "I only took up the mantle Caesar bequeathed me because I knew that you would always be by my side. The gods have rewarded me not only with a powerful and generous great-uncle but also with a true friend – the kind that only a lucky few meet in a lifetime. Friendship as you and I understand it is even rarer than the perfect love the poets write of, is it not? It's the most precious thing I have, and I will always do everything possible not to lose it. Everything. So of course I worry about you running unnecessary risks!"

Agrippa struggled to hold back tears of emotion. It was as though his friend's words had awakened him from an enchantment, and he suddenly realised that the spell Fulvia had cast over him was no match for the relationship that bound him to Octavian. His fate was tied to that of the heir of Caesar, not to a woman much older than him who probably didn't even care for him at all and to whom he could only ever be a slave. What he had thought he could find with Fulvia after losing Etain was not love, and what

Octavian offered seemed infinitely more genuine and profound. He would never question it again.

*

The son of Caesar ordered Ortwin and Veleda to close ranks in front of him: fighting at night made him even more nervous than usual. He had the constant feeling that danger was everywhere, and that at any moment the enemy might emerge from the darkness but feet away and attack before he could defend himself. At first, on seeing the besieged forces attacking his fortifications, he had panicked and had ordered his men to light as many fires as possible to illuminate the barricades as bright as day. Agrippa had advised against it, though: for if they did, it would be easier for the enemy to locate them. To avoid revealing his fear, he revoked the order, but he faced the battle with more caution than usual, his stomach churning and his heart pounding wildly. He was shivering from the bitter cold which assailed him that night in early January despite wearing three woollen tunics under his armour.

He started and almost fell from the fort's internal battlements when he saw the head of an enemy soldier appear just beyond Ortwin's Germans. They dealt with him easily with a horizontal sword swing and forced back those who were climbing the ladder behind him. He wanted to see how their opponents were crossing the ditch in front of the rampart but was afraid of being hit by one of the arrows or spears flying through the darkness. He realised angrily that he couldn't just stand there at the back shouting orders while his men were dying though: he had to show himself on the battlements to reinforce their faith in him, and so he had Ortwin compose a tortoise, under and behind which he placed himself, thus arriving at the edge of the battlements.

In the dim light, he peered down at the ditch, which he had taken steps to broaden and deepen only a few days before, and which was now full of debris. Just beyond it were the abandoned mobile shelters Lucius's soldiers had used to approach the trench and fill it in without being detected. And now the enemy soldiers flocked in droves over the embankment and then helped each other over the palisades. Many had been held at bay by spears, but Octavian only had to look around to see that Lucius's surprise attack had been partially successful in that the besieged had managed to break through in places.

Reinforcing the defences after he returned to Perugia from Spoleto with Agrippa hadn't helped much. He had not only had the ditches widened, he had also had the palisades raised and doubled the number of the towers to increase surveillance. He had also built an outer ring of fortifications to defend against increasingly likely assaults from Lucius Antonius's allies. The size of the resulting construction was almost equal to that built by Caesar at Alesia. There were embankments, one facing the besieged city and one facing open fields and the vibrant Umbrian landscape where, from behind one of the many surrounding hills, an army could appear at any moment.

But they hadn't expected Lucius to attack by night, particularly not on the eve of a day of celebration like the first of the year. Until then, he had been carrying out repeated sorties, but always during the day, and had been repeatedly repelled. Caesar's young heir blamed himself, though, for failing to predict that a desperate man would be capable of anything. And Lucius was now nothing if not desperate, for his only hope was the arrival of external assistance. No supplies had been delivered to the town for some time, and the consul had not prepared a long stay in Perugia. Deserters reported growing famine and increasing tension within the walls, and for a few days Octavian had nursed hope of a citizen's rebellion obliging the consul to surrender. But nothing had happened, and it was clear that Lucius had made an agreement with the local notables: once he had conquered Perugia, Octavian said to himself, he would make the elders pay dearly for having chosen the consul's side instead of his.

Now he had never been further away from defeating him. The few enemy soldiers who managed to open a breach had overcome the small number trying to garrison it, and rapidly, what had seemed no more than an annoyance had become an unstoppable flood of soldiers swarming over the fence, palisade and ditch, slaying those climbing down from the stands to take positions in the area between the two walls in an attempt to repel them. In the feeble torchlight, darting figures cast long shadows along the ground between the two lines of fortifications.

"Triumvir! There are too few of us here to attack their flank! We need Maecenas, his is the closest legion to hand!" shouted Popilius Laenas.

"Send someone! Perhaps hasn't realised what's happening!" replied Octavian. The centurion beckoned to a soldier who immediately climbed down from the fortifications, but his journey ended only a few steps away. As he cut across the courtyard he encountered two enemy legionaries, who, almost simultaneously, ran him through with their swords. Octavian grimaced. He was about to urge Laenas to send at least two more when shouts at his side caught his attention: he turned and saw that it had only needed three of his men to fall for a gate to be opened and now the enemy had penetrated his sector too.

He was appalled: they had ceded even more ground now, and he couldn't stay there without risking his life, but more importantly, he couldn't leave without looking like a coward.

He thought quickly. "Laenas!" he cried. "Stay there with your centuria and hold the fort. Me and Ortwin will go for Maecenas. We'll be back soon!"

He motioned to the German and the rest of his bodyguard to cover him, descended from the battlements and set off in the direction of the Etruscan, to whom he had entrusted the legion under his direct command. After only a few yards, three enemy soldiers appeared before them, but Ortwin and his men formed a wall of shields to protect him and began to retaliate without delay. Flailing their swords, the barbarians drove back the enemy and soon won the skirmish. They killed one, another escaped after suffering an injury in the shoulder and the remaining man disappeared as soon as he realised he was alone.

But then another appeared from behind them.

Octavian saw him at the last moment: just as he had been dreading right from the beginning of the battle, he found the man practically on top of him as he emerged from the shadows. The enemy soldier swung at Octavian's side with his sword, but just as the young man felt he was done for, another blade intervened to parry the swing.

It was Veleda. She pushed her opponent's weapon aside, opened up his guard and took the opportunity to stab him in the groin. As he slumped to the ground, the German woman threw Octavian a quick look and moved behind him before he had the chance to give her a nod of thanks. Now he was protected from all sides and he and his entourage found a clear path to their goal. They found Maecenas already struggling: the legionaries were in formation, but few were on the battlements where there seemed to be enemy activity.

Octavian went over to the Etruscan, who was getting a column of soldiers into formation.

"You're ready?" he asked him in surprise. "Had you heard about the enemy penetrating my sector?"

"What?" cried Maecenas in amazement. "No, actually I have just learnt that Plancus, Ventidius and Asinius have freed themselves of our contingents in front of their bases and are converging on the city. I was preparing to reinforce the outer wall in anticipation of their assault on our rear…" was the dismaying answer he gave his friend.

VI

Maecenas was grateful to Octavian for having allowed him to play courier rather than warrior. Both of them knew very well that his contribution as a soldier was infinitely less valuable than that he could provide as an adviser and politician. While the triumvir was returning to the fortifications in front of the city with reinforcements, he rushed to the sector held by Agrippa and Rufus to share the plan he had devised with his friend. The area between the two rings of fortification was empty and dark: all the soldiers had now been positioned along the embankments and on the towers. Occasionally, though, some fiery bolt would hiss through the darkness, missing him by a few feet and impaling itself into the ground. Each time Maecenas started, hysterically demanding more protection from his accompanying escort.

He hated being in the midst of a battle and could barely wait for the day to arrive when Octavian no longer needed all of them by his side and could leave him to consolidate their goals among the civilians. Agrippa and Rufus were men of action, he and Octavian men of strategy, and even if his friend was forced to march at the head of his men to earn the esteem of soldiers loyal to the memory of Julius Caesar, he could quite happily do without such dangerous obligations. If Lucius hadn't forced him to flee Rome, he could have remained in the city, working on his schemes and being undoubtedly more useful to the sect than he was here, on the battlefield. His experiences at Modena and the Philippi had been enough for him, and he wanted nothing more to do with blood and death. The chill of the Umbrian winter night caused his bones to ache intensely and made his muscles stiff and painful. He would have given anything to be in the comfort of his home, surrounded by his perfumed and accommodating slaves and kept warm by the expensive new heating system invented by Murenus that heated the domus through its floor. He had been among the first to have it installed – and one of the few who could afford it.

He found Agrippa and Rufus talking animatedly. He called for their attention and started to speak, but Agrippa cut him off. "Where have you come from? We were trying to decide who should provide support in the inner circle and how many men to send."

"But first we wanted to know how much trouble they are in," said Rufus. "The imminent arrival of Antony's generals means we need to keep a lot of men on the outer circle."

"Neither of you must go to the slope in front of the city!" panted Maecenas. "We can't risk two simultaneous attacks on the fortifications. Octavian has decided that both of you will advance with a legion to head off the arrival of Munatius Plancus, Asinius Pollio and Ventidius Bassus and keep them away from our fields until we have forced Lucius to cease his assaults."

Agrippa nodded in agreement, but Rufus, just as Maecenas had predicted, began to argue. He was a troublemaker, there was no doubt about it.

"Both of us? What's the point of that? And who will take command if there's a pitched battle? I want to be free to move as I judge best!"

Maecenas snorted. "You both have to go because if the enemy armies split rather than join up, or if they choose to attack us in several places rather than trying to break through in one, you have to be able to separate and face them. And you must not engage in battle unless it is absolutely necessary, but only block their passage until we have dealt with those from Perugia!" he snapped impatiently.

In silence, Agrippa took Rufus's arm, but he wrested himself free. "Let go of me! I'm not your subordinate!" he snapped. "This whole thing seems absurd to me. We'll see who makes the decisions once we're out of here!"

Agrippa looked at Maecenas, shaking his head in resignation. The Etruscan felt compelled to tell him what he had learned. “By the way: Fulvia is with Plancus…” he added, seeing his friend swallow hard and go white.

*

Gladiators. Lucius Antonius had sent gladiators to attack them, and in the melee there was no way to slow down their momentum. Popilius Laenas couldn’t remember the last time he had been afraid in battle. Probably when he was still a green recruit. Even when he’d gone up against those truculent barbarians with Caesar in Gaul he hadn’t hesitated or trembled. Never, in the many campaigns he’d been in.

But now he was afraid. Those thugs fought in a way he’d never seen anyone else fight. As one by one they appeared over the fortifications and climbed down to the battlements, it became increasingly difficult to stop them or force them back down the embankment. They somehow managed to unite barbarian fury with legionary combat techniques and were practically unbeatable in the fray. Only with superior numbers would he be able to defeat them, but there was still no sign of Octavian and the reinforcements, and he wouldn’t last long against warriors like this, who were able to overcome any regular soldier.

He saw a young legionary pierced through the chin by the sword of a giant who roared like a beast whilst blood spurting from the wound sprayed his face and chest. The gladiator then lifted the corpse with his sword and, with another roar, hurled it against two approaching legionaries. The body struck one of them, who lost his balance and fell from the battlements, breaking his back. The other stared in terror at the brute approaching him, for his face was now a vermilion mask with bloodshot eyes, deformed by a demented expression,and, seized by panic, he abandoned the idea of tackling him and jumped down to the ground below.

"Coward!" cried Laenas, but he couldn't really blame the man. He knew he should take on the assailant himself, but deliberated just a moment too long, giving the gladiator time to bring his sword down on the back of another soldier attempting to hold off an adversary who had just scaled the fortifications. The centurion cursed himself for his hesitation: if Octavian arrived and saw the defences had been overcome, he would blame him for the defeat and he would no longer have any chance of climbing the ranks of the sect.

The only thing preventing – for the moment – the complete collapse of their defences was their greater numbers, but it was only a matter of time. And not much time, at that. His mind finally made up, he set off towards the giant while other gladiators continued to flow over the battlements. His opponent did not seem to have noticed him, and Laenas prepared to sink his sword into him. But then he turned round and saw him about to attack: demonstrating surprising speed for his size he parried the blow with his sword, then stepped forward and rammed the centurion with his body, crashing into him so that he lost his balance. Laenas staggered backwards, his guard down, and when he managed to regain his balance, his opponent was already on him, those long, powerful arms ready to crush him. The gladiator hugged him and tightened his grip until Laenas could barely breathe. The centurion seemed to feel his bones creak, and yet somehow he managed to headbutt his opponent, the visor of his helmet smashing into the man's nose.

The giant momentarily released his grip and put his hands to his face with a scream of pain, but immediately regained lucidity and advanced on him again with a look of hatred. Laenas, meanwhile, took a step back, and then another, until his back was against two soldiers attempting to hold off a second gladiator. His opponent, however, had decided to settle his account and continued to advance on him, his sword at the ready. Laenas looked at his two fellow soldiers and had an idea. He waited until the last moment for his opponent to attack, let the man's sword approach him and then suddenly moved behind the soldier closest to him, who had no idea what was going on. He pretended to stumble and bumped into him, pushing him into the trajectory of the blade, and a moment later, the legionary fell to the ground pierced by the sword of Laenas's opponent, while Laenas took advantage of the instant it took his opponent to free his sword to attack. His own was in the man's side before the gladiator had a chance to lunge again, and he twisted the blade frantically, ripping open the man's organs.

When he thought he had caused enough damage to the man to put him out of action, he pulled his sword free but to his amazement the gladiator didn't collapse to the ground, but lumbered unsteadily toward him with his sword held out and roaring like a lunatic. He moved heavily, as if dragged by many ropes, but still looked dangerous. He swung his sword at an incredulous Laenas, who felt the flesh on his arm burn.

The glancing blow snapped the centurion out of a fog of confusion and he swung a backhand blow that the giant, no longer as sharp as earlier, could not avoid. His sword sank deep into the man's thigh, causing him to fall to his knees, but the gladiator still had the strength to react: he parried another blow the centurion swung at his head, and Laenas it felt as if his arm had hit a stone wall. He moved sideways and aimed a blow at the gladiator's forearm – and this time it hit its mark. The giant screamed and waved the stump, from which sprayed an unquenchable flow of blood through the air.

Laenas now felt safe enough to advance on what was left of his opponent, preparing to strike the final blow, down between his neck and shoulder, but the gladiator somehow found the strength to reach for Laenas's ankle with his remaining arm. The centurion's blade penetrated his body just as he began to squeeze. Laenas pushed down with both hands and all the strength he had left until the blade sank in almost to the hilt. Only then did the giant fall to the ground, and the centurion emitted a shout of triumph. Then the outline of another gladiator with his sword in his hand, ready to attack, appeared.

In that precise moment, though, he heard his men cheering the arrival of the triumvir and the legion of reinforcements.

*

Dawn was breaking, although the dense mist made the surroundings as indistinct as they were the night before. The cold, damp air of the winter dawn seemed to be warmed by the tension from the two armies facing one another on the gentle slopes of the Umbrian countryside.

Here was the pitched battle he had sought. If Agrippa didn't get in his way, he would win a prestigious victory, said Rufus to himself, as he observed the formation of the enemy troops. The scouts had told him that they were all there: perhaps fifteen cohorts in total, including the three armies of Plancus, Pollio and Ventidius. They must have decided to try and force their way through, but they had not expected that the besiegers – now the besieged – would emerge in force from the double ring of fortifications to take them on.

No, not to take them on – only to hold them back, Octavian insisted, and Agrippa had reiterated as soon as the scouts had described the situation.

But it would be stupid not to take advantage of it: if he had been there, there was no doubt that Octavian would have opted for an attack, given the favourable situation in which they found themselves.

"Forget it," said Agrippa, sensing his thoughts as he rode alongside him, he too, intent on observing the opposing armies.

Rufus snorted. "What is it you think I want to do?"

"Attack, of course. I know you too well to imagine otherwise," said his friend. "But Octavian's orders are clear. We don't go looking for trouble."

"Looking for trouble? It's an obvious victory!" exclained Rufus. "Look at them: they were in a column formation before to try and break through along the fortifications, but now that they've seen us they are starting to get into line: if we attack them now, we'll surprise them with their units still broken up and their ranks disrupted, and we will annihilate them! We even outnumber them!"

"You can't be sure of that," objected Agrippa. "It's barely dawn and there's a lot of mist and there are high plains around here where they might have other units stationed. We could be drawn into a trap. And in any case, there's an ongoing attack on our base and it would be madness now to throw ourselves into other operations that are not purely for containment. Remember that we are here to protect the camp, not to seek personal glory!"

"The best way to protect Octavian is by wiping out his opponents, you fool!" snapped back Rufus. He had no intention of giving up. "I have no intention of missing an opportunity like this, that's for sure. I'm going to take my legion and attack – if you want, you can follow me and avoid a disaster or you can stand here watching and take the responsibility for a defeat." He had decided to put Agrippa up against the wall.

"You're mad." The usual patience Agrippa showed towards Rufus disappeared. "What I will do is stop you myself with my legion, you damned idiot!"

Rufus gave a wry smile. Agrippa had never reacted to his provocations and had always maintained an affectionate, conciliatory attitude which he had known couldn't be sincere. "Finally! Finally you've stopped playing the hypocrite and expressed what you actually think, now that Octavian isn't here to see how patient and tolerant you are! And perhaps the reason you're doing it because you're afraid that you'll look bad in comparison with me, now that there are only the two of us!"

"Don't be ridiculous," replied Agrippa glacially. "If it weren't for Octavian, I'd challenge you to a duel to settle you once and for all!"

He had lost all control. Rufus decided to continue his provocation. "Or is it that you are afraid I'll attack your woman? Because you're still fucking her, even if she is our enemy. In that case, I could call you a traitor..."

Agrippa's features changed radically in the space of an instant. He leapt from the saddle and pulled Rufus from his horse, both fell to the ground, one on top of the other.

"I've had enough of you: I've put up with you for too long!" shouted Agrippa, blindly throwing punches which Rufus returned with greater accuracy and effectiveness, it having been he who had provoked the fight. They rolled about on the muddy ground beating at each other. When Rufus hit his the target, he felt a thrill of satisfaction at giving vent to the frustration he had repressed every time Agrippa had outshone him, for all the victories that he had snatched from him, for the women he had stolen from him, for the mistakes he had forced him to make, as well as for the admiration and affection that Octavian had for him and for all the underserved praise that he had been given.

Suddenly, Agrippa broke off and rolled away before climbing to his feet and raising his arms. He looked shaken.

"We are giving our men a pitiful spectacle. Two commanders, two of the triumvir's right-hand men, two of the lieutenants of the heir to Julius Caesar, in a fist fight in front of an enemy army that could attack us at any moment. Let us stop now," he said, struggling to resume a moderate tone of voice.

That was something that Rufus hadn't considered. He cast withering glances at the astonished faces of the men who surrounded them and quickly tried to assume a dignified demeanour before turning back to Agrippa.

"So be it. But I haven't changed my mind. I'm going to attack, you can do what you like," he said with a tone of finality, and then leapt back into the saddle and ordered the *primus pilus* to close ranks and prepare to march forward.

He paid no more attention to Agrippa. He was sure that he would follow them. But this time it would be him, Rufus, giving the orders.

*

Octavian realised that he had arrived just in time. With the reinforcements he had brought with him, he didn't see how they could be overwhelmed, but if he had arrived even a few moments later it would have been too late to hold the breach. He ordered the head of the column to concentrate on the two areas of the fortifications where the stakes had been pulled out, the embankment flattened out and the ditch filled in, and the soldiers split into two groups, each of which pounced on the assailants, who were suddenly forced to halt their influx into the fort.

Now the balance of power had been reversed. The disciplined legions, moving rapidly with closed ranks, smashed into Lucius Antonius's men, who were already disorganised and lacking cohesion. They were mixed groups of legionaries, gladiators and auxiliaries who together were unable to summon up even a semblance of a formation. As long as they had been fighting in the darkness below the battlements with every man for himself, they had managed to create a serious problem for the defenders, but now that they were on the flat ground between the two walls of the fortifications and exposed to heavy infantry, they had no idea how to behave. And thus each man acted for himself, allowing Octavian, who had climbed up to the battlements to observe by the light of the coming dawn, their progressive retreat, which soon began to resemble a rout.

The massive gladiators could do nothing against the solid line of legionaries, who first targetted them with their spears, decimating their ranks, and then swept through to finish off those who hadn't fled back up onto the embankment in time to escape the onrushing tide of the legion. Octavian watched with pleasure as the enemy thugs were literally crushed under the boots of soldiers who then finished them off with the bottoms of their shields. Now the assailants thronged the breaches they had created, rushing to retreat through them, and many even leapt into the ditch just to escape the swords of their enemies, while others raised their hands in surrender and were immediately surrounded and immobilised.

The young leader raised his eyes to look beyond the battlements onto the plain between the ring of fortifications and the hills of Perugia. The landscape was dotted with fugitives, some running swiftly, having liberated themselves of their shields and sometimes even their armour, while others, the wounded, dragged themselves along wearily, alone or supported by helpful comrades.

It was a clear victory, thought Octavian with satisfaction – the first following numerous sorties that could not be classed as any more than skirmishes. But to be absolutely certain of it, he would have to wait for the outcome of Agrippa and Rufus's battle. It had been a risk, sending them outside the double ring of fortifications like that – for they could easily have been trapped if things went wrong. There was no guarantee that Rufus would behave wisely, but he trusted Agrippa to keep control of the situation and use his head: if they managed to keep Lucius's allies away from the fortifications then he could be considered the undisputed victor of the day that – he had the distinct feeling – would be decisive. Lean times were approaching for the consul and his men, and that rabble of recruits, civilians and gladiators he had fighting for him would never be able to break through their blockade without outside assistance.

Always provided that Rufus and Agrippa had succeeded in their mission.

He felt a sudden lump in his throat. If Antony's generals defeated the two members of the cult of Mars Ultor, he would soon be watching the same situation he was now observing but with the roles reversed. It would be difficult to prevent the enemy breaking into the courtyard between the two rings of fortification.

No, the battle was not yet won. Everything depended on Agrippa and Rufus.

*

Agrippa found himself facing one of the hardest decisions of his brief military career. After what had happened in Spoleto, he no longer had any doubt about his unconditional and eternal support for Octavian, which his foolish passion for Fulvia had for a time threatened, but now he had to understand whether that support also presupposed a war against another member of the cult – and under the very eyes of Fulvia.

There was no doubt that a battle between Rufus and himself was exactly what she had been expecting since she had given him her ultimatum. If that happened, it would give the wife of Mark Antony the impression that he was doing as she had commanded and would in any case be exactly what she wanted, favouring her intrigues and turning him into precisely the tool she desired.

Agrippa's decision to remain with Octavian had not completely eliminated the feelings he had for Fulvia. They were still in him, corroding and consuming him like malignant weights that he must always drag with him, weighing down his every move. And it was a struggle to keep them at bay and to prevent them from overwhelming him like some inner demon that continually tempted him. He must always remind himself that Fulvia was an evil and perverse woman who cared for no one, not even him, and that following her would be his downfall. Continually convincing himself of this cost him a huge effort and drained the energy he needed to face the dramatic situations in which he often found himself.

Situations like the one he was facing now.

Rufus seemed quite determined to attack and was apparently convinced that he would support him to avoid a defeat. But that was not what Octavian wanted: being well aware of Rufus's recklessness, he had sent Agrippa with him precisely for the purpose of restraining him from committing such folly. Agrippa too, thought it was unwise to risk a pitched battle with an evenly matched army. And in the end, although he had to struggle to admit it to himself, he could barely stand the idea of attacking an army with Fulvia in its ranks.

He had to find a way to stop this madman. But Rufus had already arranged his legion in battle formation and given the order to attack. The centurion asked Agrippa what he should do, and the words seemed to flow from the mouth of the young commander of their own accord.

"We must stop them," he murmured, and then repeated it louder, as though to convince himself.

The centurion looked at him blankly, waiting for clarification.

"Stop them? But how, without attacking them in a battle between fellow soldiers in which many of the men will probably refuse to engage?"

He decided that he would bluff. Rufus was probably doing the same – preparing to fight and taking it for granted that he would give in and come to his aid in order to avoid a disaster.

"Turn the cohorts around and tell them to get into formation by the proconsul Rufus's flank!" he shouted to the centurion. "And as soon as they start moving, attack them!" Then he mounted his horse and rode over to the other member of the cult.

When he reached him, he shouted, "If you proceed, I will attack your flank."

Rufus looked at him wordlessly, then turned and continued to observe the formations of his men without saying another word to his subordinates.

Agrippa looked at the faces of the soldiers: there was bewilderment in their expressions and many no doubt did not understand why it was necessary to attack without the support of the other legion. This was no way to launch an offensive: with uncertainty like that, they were destined for defeat in any case. He returned to his men and saw them just as baffled as they stood at right angles to the other units. He queried his own intentions. Did he really want to set brother against brother right under the nose of the enemy? But he had no intention of giving in to Rufus either. He waited for what seemed like an eternity as he watched his men complete their deployment, with the right flank stretched out until it almost touched the left flank of the armies of Antony's generals, observing the disorientated expressions of his men. He hoped that Rufus would not give the order to attack. He hoped that his ranks wouldn't break. He hoped that the enemy generals were already on the move. He clenched his fists and almost ceased to breathe from the tension.

But then, with the haze now reduced to thin banks of mist hanging here and there, he saw Rufus raise his arm and give the signal, and realised that he had to act in one way or another. Even if he did order the attack, he thought, the disagreements between the commanders and the bizarre arrangement of the men would prevent the legionaries from fighting at their best, and the chances of failure would be high. How would he ever dare face Octavian when he came back... if he did actually come back?

Yet he could not put thousands of men in jeopardy, not allow them to be slaughtered by attacking their flank, and Rufus knew it. He raised his arm in turn, and said to the centurion, "Order the soldiers to turn round. We will attack in column formation with the aim of penetrating the enemy flank – at this point, Ventidius Bassus and his companions must believe that we are advancing obliquely, as the Thebans did at Epaminondas, while Rufus keeps the whole front busy. And let's just hope they fall for it..."

The centurion did as he commanded and the trumpeter sounded the order to rotate to the right. At another signal from Agrippa, the men began to march towards the enemy ranks, only a few moments after Rufus's army had set off. Both legions advanced with measured, unhurried steps, so as to preserve their energy for the running that awaited them when they came within range of the enemy spears.

Agrippa looked at his opponents, arranged in a long line dotted with the emblems on the shields and on the standards which towered above each unit. The moment when he should give the new order to advance at a faster pace and to close ranks was approaching, which would be followed soon afterwards by ordering them to halt and throw spears. But it seemed that the enemy formations were getting further away instead of nearer. Suddenly, he realised that he could not see their shields.

They had broken ranks. In a few moments, the scattered units were climbing the slopes of the hills behind them.

Antony's generals did not intend to engage in battle and were removing themselves to safety. He immediately gave the order to halt, and soon afterwards, Rufus was forced to follow suit.

They had won without even having fought. They had forced Lucius Antonius's reinforcements to stay away from Perugia.

*

The message, wrapped around an acorn and fired from a sling, fell right at Octavian's feet when he had gone to inspect the fortifications at first light. He picked it up and before reading the litany of insults which it bore – it was only the latest of many – he sighed at the thought of the bleak sight that awaited him on the other side of the battlements: dozens and dozens of slaves who traipsed around the area between slopes of the hill and the fortifications in search of edible weeds. Three days ago, in fact, Lucius had begun expelling from the city, which was now on its last legs, all the mouths it no longer intended to feed, starting with the slaves. Some of the soldiers along the battlements had softened at the sight of them, especially when they saw the women and children, and threw them bits of food as one might to a dog, only to then sit and mock them along with their fellow soldiers as the poor souls fought over the scraps.

And Octavian ensured that he carried a vial of perfume around with him, which he would smell as soon as he was exposed to the breeze in the stands, which brought with them the stench of those who had died from starvation. There were hundreds, some piled up just below the city walls and some hastily buried in mass graves to prevent outbreaks of disease. And it was from those makeshift graves that the slingshooters fired their shots, sometimes advancing a few steps and, as a demonstration of courage in the face of their disheartened comrades, trying to provoke those who held them under siege with their insulting messages.

There was not much point in them trying to provoke anyone at this point, he thought to himself. Lucius was done for, and even if the increasingly frequent deserters who left the city by night to join the triumvir's army, principally in the hope of getting a good hot meal, hadn't told him, he would have noticed how slow the activity on the walls and in the sorties had become.

Expecting to find the usual insults, he looked at the message, but instead read, "You're in for it today."

At first he was surprised that they still had the energy to be making foolish threats, but then he smiled and handed it to Agrippa and the other members of the general staff so that they could read it too. His friend smiled back and said, “It’s much more likely that they’ll be surrendering,” he said with a smirk. “For weeks now they haven’t even had a chance of being rescued by the other generals.”

But just as they began climbing the stairs of a turret, the guard stationed up above them began calling for their attention. They raced up the rungs of the ladder and once on the covered platform Octavian realised what had shaken the soldier so.

A full army, complete with siege machines, was pouring out of the city gates as if they were aiming to lay siege to a city themselves with all means available.

The alarm spread throughout the battlements before he had a chance to raise it himself, and as the enemy rushed down the slopes of the hill and began to approach, Octavian was able to see them in detail. He told Agrippa to handle the defence as he thought appropriate and began assessing Lucius’s forces. His eye fell on a series of four mobile towers, then on some ballistae… no, wait, they weren’t ballistae, they were harpoons. And as well as that there were the covered vehicles called testudos, no doubt full of waste material to fill in the ditch and allow them to cross.

He stood there in dismay. He would never have expected Lucius to pull off something like this – the man must have rallied all his remaining resources. But with men reduced to ghosts by hunger, few legionaries available, and those recruits taken by force from among the civilians in the city, the gladiators and the auxiliaries, Lucius had no chance against his men, who were hardened by years of battles. He observed the enemy advance as he watched Agrippa deploy units along the fortifications, assigning each responsibility for a sector. He heard him call to the archers to move scorpios and ballistae to the areas in front of the advancing four towers.

The first testudos reached the ditch. Pushing them from behind were groups of soldiers who, once they had arrived at their destination, began to empty them and throw their contents into the ditch. Agrippa gave the order to fire projectiles at any who exposed themselves, and immediately a hail of arrows, spears, rocks and stones began to rain down on them. The ones carrying ladders arrived, ready to move as soon as the ditch was bridged. They faced a storm of projectiles, and only a few made it to the bottom of the rampart. As they positioned their ladders, the defence, as yet not under any real pressure, converged on them and pulled up the ladder, or impaled those who had managed to climb a rung or two on spears.

Then Octavian heard a sudden thump from beneath his feet. The tower vibrated for a few seconds and then began to move outwards. The triumvir peered tentatively over the railing, whilst two watchmen rushed over to hold their shields in front of his face. In the slit between them he saw a large grapnel, to which was attached a thick rope, projecting from the surface of the fortifications. They had been harpooned! He followed the rope with his eye and saw that far beyond the moat and out of his spear-throwers reach there were catapults, and that some men were now dragging them backwards. He felt violent jerks, and the beams of the platform creaked.

"Triumvir, let's get down from here before the whole thing collapses!" one of the guards shouted.

Octavian had no choice but to do as the man said. He raced down the ladder whilst the tower vibrated alarmingly, and was thrown to the ground before he managed to climb down the final rungs. A moment later the tower disintegrated and only the quick thinking of two soldiers who protected him with their shields prevented him from being hit by debris. Octavian stood up and patted them both on the back in gratitude. But he couldn't leave the battlements now for it would give the men the impression that he was afraid. He saw Ortwin and Veleda arriving, alerted by the attack and immediately ready to act as his bodyguards, and with a nod he urged them to follow him along the battlements. Once up there, he noticed that the number of attackers under the rampart had increased tenfold but that none of them seemed able to reach the top of the fence. The defence kept them at bay with a steady hail of projectiles.

But a siege tower was approaching. It crossed the ditch and halted only a short distance from where Octavian was standing. The young commander took it for granted that his troops could cope with this new threat easily: as soon as the enemy let down the gantry onto the battlement, any of them who emerged into the open would be rapidly greeted by an arrow to the chest and have no hope of escape.

But then something happened which left him and the other occupants of the sector so stunned they were actually paralysed for an instant.

The tower split into two, and the top half fell over the fence, anchoring itself to the sharp tips of its poles. Octavian's soldiers found themselves faced not with the expected ramp – too narrow and light to allow the passage of more than two men at a time – but with a platform substantial enough for many men to cross together, and protected by the sides of the tower.

And a tidal wave of armed men suddenly poured onto the battlements.

VII

Things looked bad, said Agrippa to himself when he saw the two towers catapult their hordes of soldiers onto the battlements. He could only see two in action – one to his right and another to his left – but like everyone else, he had noticed that four had left the besieged city. And the other two had gone in a different direction to attack another portion of the ring of fortifications.

Instinctively, he wanted to throw himself into supporting the nearest defenders who were being submerged by the river of Lucius Antonius's men flowing onto the battlements, but Octavian had entrusted him with responsibility for overall defence, not just one sector, and first he had to work out how to tackle all four towers. Although there were only a few of them, they could facilitate deeper penetration if the men that they contained were able to occupy the resistance for long enough to get down into the area between the two fences and open up the gates.

He thought quickly. It seemed that the only possible solution was to set up a reserve in the middle. He called to his centurion, shouting, "Gather the legion and position it one hundred paces from the fence, between the open space and the centre of the area under attack." Fortunately, Lucius did not have a sufficient number of men to put pressure on the entire ring of defence but only on a portion of it. "Then find out where the towers have attacked and send a cohort against each one with axes and picks, leaving the other six in reserve. If after about half an hour the threat hasn't been put down, send more men to relieve those on the front line!" That way he would always have fresh troops to face the onslaught of men emerging from the tower who, for their part, wouldn't be able to keep up the pressure for long, especially given how exhausted and weakened by hunger they were. It was clear now that the key to the battle was the towers: if he could bring them down, their opponents would have no way of getting over the fortifications.

As he waited for the arrival of the reinforcements, he rushed with his squadron towards the sector under attack from the nearest tower, and immediately realised that the situation was critical. Many of the defenders were in a melee with the assailants who had been first onto the battlements. Behind them, a column of soldiers were pushing their way across the ramp to get onto the battlements in turn, and their movement assisted the action of their comrades at the front in the same way as in a phalanx, with the front line using the momentum of those behind them to drive them forward and increase their impact on the enemy.

Octavian's legionaries would not last much longer. Agrippa saw one fall backwards, dropping down to the ground from the battlements. His fellow soldiers retreated, and soon would fall too, unable to prevent the enemy from swarming into the space between the two rings of fortifications. He had to support them until the reinforcements arrived. The young commander shouted encouragement to his men and joined the defenders, swinging his sword and pushing back the enemy soldiers with his shield.

It felt as though he was standing in the path of an avalanche of boulders. Agrippa knew he was more robust than most legionaries, but ahead of him there were gladiators larger than him, and he realised that holding them back would be difficult. He engaged them in a brutal shoving match, trying to plant his feet firmly so as to avoid being thrown below. His opponents, though, had the weight of dozens of their comrades behind them, while behind him there were only a few subordinates. He felt the fetid breath of a gladiator whose face almost touched his own, and could distinctly hear the man's insults over the deafening din of screams, blades clanging, shields crashing into one another, scrambling feet, cries of encouragement and pain, gasping breaths and intermittent gasps that surrounded him, and saw the man's demented grin over the edge of his shield.

There was no room now to lift his arm and lunge or slash. The crush was such that the bodies almost seemed to merge into one another, and the only way to harm his opponents was to blindly stab at their thighs with his sword, hoping to hit the groin of whoever was nearest. But Agrippa also realised that in the crush there was a risk of injuring his fellow soldiers, it being impossible to distinguish the limbs of enemies from those of friends in the jungle of intertwined figures crammed into the restricted space on the rampart. Each time he heard a scream of pain, he saw one of the combatants nearby collapse, but – supported by the bodies of the soldiers who continued to press against one another – remain upright, perhaps with a wound in his leg or groin, only to lose consciousness due to blood loss while the soldier nearest him used his body as a shield against his opponents' swords.

This happened to one of the legionaries of his guard fighting at his side. Agrippa heard his desperate cry and then he moaned in agony for a moment while the gladiator in front of him tried to push past him to get to the man behind him. But the wounded man neither fell nor moved, and was now no use at all – in fact, he seemed unconscious, if not actually dead. The gladiator managed to move him just enough to take a stab at the man behind him, who, however, seeing the gladiator, grabbed his moribund comrade and used him as a shield. In an attempt to reach his him, the gladiator stabbed blindly several times, always, however, striking the dying man, who Agrippa saw convulse repeatedly while his comrade stayed carefully behind him. Suddenly, however, the gladiator flinched. Evidently, the legionary had managed to wound him.

The gladiator lurched away from Agrippa, freeing up a bit of space, and the young commander's adversary slashed at him with a relatively wide swing. Agrippa just managed to lower his shield enough to block his opponent's blade with the edge, but it banged into his legs, scraping the skin from his shins. He was about to retaliate but felt himself shoved violently from behind, and the dynamic of the battle suddenly and radically changed. The gladiator in front of him started to look worried, even frightened, and Agrippa managed to stab him under his shield. The man became a dead weight but began to shuffle backwards towards the siege tower, which could no longer contain the number of men who were swarming over it from the outside as well as those who were pushing their way back to it from the inside, driven there by renewed pressure from the defenders.

Agrippa saw the enemy falling over the fence and trying to escape along the battlements, and he did not need to turn around to see that the cohort of reinforcements had arrived.

*

Veleda brightened instantly when she saw the reinforcements. Things had been looking grim for the defence until then, but now they stood every chance of repelling the attack. The main problem was to take out those damn siege towers, and she wanted to do it herself. Being part of Octavian's bodyguard meant that she had never really fought during the siege, because he tended to stay out of the fray. Along with Ortwin and the other Germans, she had always been just a step away from the front line but had not engaged in combat. And she'd had enough. Over the years, she had become a warrior in every respect, and standing by while others were slaughtered was not for her. She was sure that this lack of involvement upset her man too, although Ortwin always did as he was supposed to, without complaint or query.

"I want to participate in the battle before it's over," she protested. Octavian was just behind her and could not hear her.

"You know that our role is to protect the triumvir," Ortwin said firmly.

"But he doesn't need any protection, not now! We are winning, and he is keeping out of the way!" she insisted. "Let me go over to the fence!"

Ortwin shook his head. "Absolutely not. And anyway, Octavian hasn't authorised it: he would never needlessly risk the life of one of the members of the cult."

Veleda made a dismissive gesture and moved toward the triumvir, who was intently observing the reaction of the defenders repelling the enemy back onto the ramp of the tower others were busily trying to cut it down using axes.

"Caesar, I ask you to let me participate in the battle, at least now. I want to prove to myself that I still know how to fight: it's been too long since I last did," she said, completely unintimidated. Since she had saved the life of his sister Octavia, she knew that Octavian, who initially had allowed her into the sect simply to satisfy Ortwin, respected her more than before, and she now felt able to ask him a favour. After all, the triumvir owed her something.

Octavian smiled. "Ortwin is in charge of my bodyguards. You must ask him," he said curtly, turning his eyes away and obviously considering the matter closed.

Veleda was puzzled for a moment, then she turned to her man, realising he had taken a step toward them to listen. "So?" she urged.

Ortwin snorted. “Even if I wanted to, I don’t know what you could do. Our men are pushing them back and they need strength above all. I can’t really see you helping much with that, frankly.”

Veleda could not argue. Apart from anything else, she knew she would loathe feeling the hands of the Romans upon her body, for they would surely take the fullest advantage of the opportunity to touch her. Then, however, she noticed the many still unused axes, lying on the platform. “I’ll use one of those to cut at the gantry like the others are doing.”

Ortwin gave her a look of pity, then, with a nod of his chin, indicated her stump. Veleda felt a blaze of anger surge through her. Did he think she couldn’t use an axe with one hand? Well she would show him just how wrong he was. She turned round and stalked away without another word, throwing down the small shield that she always carried in battle on the arm that lacked a hand and, sword in sheath, picked up an axe from the pile. She was furious. It had been years since she had thought of the time during the Gallic wars when she had accidentally ended up among the defenders of Uxelludunum, the town besieged by Julius Caesar, and Ortwin, following the orders of the proconsul and unaware of her identity, had cut off one of her hands, as he had done to all the survivors who surrendered. By now having only one hand had become part of her nature, she had almost forgotten ever having had two and she didn't blame her man for the fact. And in any case, years later she had taken out one of his eyes by accidentally striking him during his duel against Quintus Labienus. But now she felt her grudge against him resurfacing, and felt sure that it would be appeased if she could only prove to him, and to herself, that she knew how to handle the axe with one hand.

She pushed aside two soldiers who were obstructing her way and positioned herself near the battlements. The top half of the tower was still in place, resting on the wooden tips of the fence, and dozens of armed men were huddled inside attempting to resist the attacks of the defenders while a few legionaries were swinging axes against the sides of the war machine, cutting into its beams and taking chunks out of the ramp. Veleda took her place next to one of them and lifted the large axe, using her crippled arm to help raise it and then putting her stump on top of the shaft of the axe to bring it smashing down onto the wood.

She had to admit that the effect was not particularly impressive, and even the soldier beside her was looking at her in puzzlement, but she decided not to give up, and she prepared another swing, this time trying to refine her technique. This meant changing the position of the stump from below the shaft to above it in the shortest possible time. She looked over at Ortwin for a moment and, seeing that he was shaking his head with a grimace of pity, felt even more determined not to fail. She prepared a new blow, and this time it seemed to actually have an effect on the wood, but to be as effective as her fellow soldiers she realised that she needed to be faster. She raised and lowered the axe again, and again, and again, and with each blow seemed to gain greater expertise.

Before long she saw a fissure beginning to appear at the intersection between the side of the ramp and the platform. She persisted, ignoring the fatigue and the blisters forming on her hand and forearm. Meanwhile, around her some soldiers threw spears at the axemen while the legionaries in the stands used their swords and shields in an almost static melee, with neither side apparently prevailing over the other.

Suddenly, the platform gave a creak and began to tilt over to one side. Evidently, deduced Veleda, who was standing on the other side, it had begun to give way under the blows of axes, but thanks to the protection provided by its high sides, none of the enemy soldiers actually fell to the ground below: they were going to need to sever it entirely. She redoubled her efforts but in the meantime the men inside, frightened by the possibility of falling, seemed suddenly animated with new energy and began to prevail in the shoving match – in fact, a few moments later, some of them managed to claw back positions near the battlements. The legionaries engaged in the melee shouted to those who were hacking away at the tower to hurry. By now, Veleda was handling her axe almost skilfully, but she was getting weary. Then they managed to break the beams on their side, and the platform gave way again, forcing the soldiers to gather in the centre where it was still attached to the fence.

The damn thing still didn't completely detach, though, in spite of the weight of the occupants inside who, motivated by blind fury, seemed to be forcing their way onto the battlements with frightening speed. Veleda decided they needed to change tactics, and shouted to her companions, "The fence! Knock down the fence!" before immediately starting to swing her axe not against the siege tower but against the parapet itself. After a moment of bewilderment, the others followed suit, whether they understood the implications or not. Their axes fell dozens of times in a matter of moments and the beams of the fence began to break and crack, the debris falling onto the combatants below. The attackers were increasingly massing in the centre of the platform and suddenly it gave way, dropping a couple of feet but this time more evenly. Now it was below the top of the fence. Veleda urged her comrades to keep going and, at last, there was a sudden emptiness beside her.

Dozens of men disappeared suddenly in a terrifying crash of broken beams and bones, screams of panic and pain and the impact of bodies and armour colliding in the cloud of dust raised by the tower collapsing onto the embankment and into the ditch. Veleda looked down and saw the chaos below her. Men half buried in the structure's remains, their bodies broken and their limbs splayed out in unnatural positions, blood everywhere, soldiers moaning, struggling in a wilderness of death and destruction while their companions who had remained on the plain attempted to retrieve those from the wreckage who seemed to have a chance of survival. But the spear throwers in the stands targeted them mercilessly, and soon none dared approach to save their fellow soldiers.

There remained only a few isolated attackers in the stands, some of whom immediately raised their hands in surrender while others instinctively threw themselves from the battlements to escape the enemy swords. Veleda saw Popilius Laenas grabbing a prisoner by the collar of his tunic and throwing him over the side. His soldiers followed suit, looking down to watch them hit the ground and laughing out loud at what they seemed to find an enjoyable spectacle.

The German shook her head in disgust and turned her gaze to Ortwin, who was looking at her with a proud smile: you could never say that her man, so upright and noble, didn't know how to admit it when he was wrong. Meanwhile, there were still some soldiers enjoying themselves by pushing their surviving opponents off the battlements. Veleda would have expected Octavian to interrupt their fun, but the triumvir seemed content to leave them be.

She peered at him more closely.

And thought she could actually make out a twinkle in those cold eyes of his.

*

"I can't believe it! It's him!" said Maecenas, observing the solitary figure now advancing towards the ring of fortifications. "He's coming to us alone – without even his escort!"

Octavian shook his head in disbelief. It had been less than forty-eight hours since Lucius Antonius had launched the desperate attack and hundreds of his own casualties still dotted the land in front of the fortifications. And now, the former consul had emerged from the gates of Perugia and appeared alone in front of his enemy: a clear admission of defeat sanctioning the end of hostilities.

"Good!" said Octavian finally. "We will take him prisoner and send troops to plunder the city. That seems to me the least they deserve. The only thing I regret is that I cannot kill him without risking breaking up the alliance with his brother. I'd have every right to – he's a rebel, after all – but there is always the possibility that Mark Antony, at least formally, didn't approve of his actions… maybe if I act with some restraint towards Lucius, he'll continue to support this diarchy…"

"Your reasoning is good," said Maecenas. "But in this case, I think that it would be inappropriate to take him prisoner. If you really want to show Mark Antony that your behaviour has been impeccable, you must prove that you have not taken advantage of the circumstances in any way and that Lucius was able to decide the conditions of surrender freely, without the constraint of imprisonment."

"And what am I supposed to do if I find him here in the fort?" protested Octavian. "Everyone will think that I made a bargain for his surrender…"

"Simple. You go out and meet him. Alone. The soldiers will target him from the battlements in case he decides to play some trick on you. But I doubt that he will: we have flattened the area in front of the rampart, and if anyone is at risk, it is him. If you meet him and let him go, everyone will see that you're a reasonable man. Especially Mark Antony."

Octavian thought for a moment. Maecenas's proposal, like all of Maecenas's proposals, could be an important propaganda coup, and in any case, he was right: there was no risk. He nodded and gave orders to open the gates then went back downstairs and walked out of the fortifications to meet his opponent. With each step, he could better observe Lucius's emaciated face, his undernourished body and the armour that was now too large for his narrow, hunched shoulders. He was the shadow of the man that Octavian had met only a few months earlier at the meeting in Teanum where they hadn't managed to avert civil war.

No. Not civil war – rebellion. He would reproach him for it. But now, as Maecenas had said, he must act to avoid a civil war between himself and Mark Antony. Because a war between triumvirs would be an actual civil war, while a consul setting himself against a triumvir, who was superior to him in rank, was no more than a rebellion.

"I'm glad to meet you, Lucius," began Octavian as soon as the two stopped in front of one another. "I hope things go better than the last time we met and that we will find a way to agree."

"That's precisely what I'm here for," said Lucius, wearily. "I aim to put an end to this madness."

"I fully agree," replied Octavian. "It was madness. But it was not I who started it – I was only acting in accordance with the agreements we had made with your brother."

"When everyone except for the soldiers is complaining it means that either there is something wrong with the agreements or that you are applying them incorrectly. As a consul, I told you that many times, but you never listened. You have made the triumvirate into a tyranny."

"It is not a tyranny," objected Octavian. "It is an emergency judiciary, created to deal with a civil war against the murderers of Julius Caesar."

"Then you should have dissolved it after your victory in Philippi. Instead, you have not only continued, but have turned it into a diarchy by pushing aside poor Lepidus."

"I was not aware that you had been deprived of anything by this situation. You were a consul, one of the supreme magistrates of the State, and you were also growing richer than you would have been if the Republic had resumed its normal course..."

"That's not the point. I was a consul, yes, but a consul deprived of power. A consul should also have command of the army, but by giving the soldiers exactly what they wanted you set them against me and all that was left for me to do was assume the role of protector of the civilians. And when I saw that all I had left were new recruits and gladiators and that my brother's generals had no idea what to do, I realised that I didn't have a chance. If the veterans were all on the side of those who gave them more land than they had been promised and the generals were undecided, I had no hope. And unfortunately, my brother did not offer me his support."

"Your brother is politically astute. He pretended not to know what was happening and he took no position so as to avoid reprisals in case I emerged triumphant. You can be sure that he would have accepted the spoils of your victory if you had prevailed, though, even though you could never have succeeded… Who made you do it?"

Lucius hesitated a moment, an embarrassed look on his face.

"You know very well who…"

Octavian attempted to look Lucius in the eye, but the former consul lowered his gaze.

"Fulvia?"

Lucius nodded gravely. "That woman craves power and she knows how to make men do exactly what she wants. She seduced me, made me drink… She did a lot of things."

"I can imagine," said Octavian understandingly. He was certain that Lucius would have never initiated the conflict without Fulvia's encouragment.

"And then she abandoned me when she saw that I couldn't win. None of my brother's generals she was supposed to bring to my rescue ever came to Perugia. Your fortifications and soldiers were enough to keep them away. And that means she now considers me a lost cause and the others were unwilling to compromise themselves."

"So now do you offer me your unconditional surrender?"

"No, not unconditional. Many people believed in me and in my words, and I cannot simply throw away my honour. Beside the personal benefits that can be gained from the existence of the triumvirate and from giving the soldiers what they want, we both know that what I say is true: the triumvirate is unlawful and the soldiers are committing abuses. So I am here to propose a deal."

"Let's hear what you have to say then…"

"I know that by the right of conquest you would let the soldiers sack the city, but I cannot let the citizens suffer more than they have already done. So I ask you to preserve me and them from further hardships and violence and I in exchange I will surrender myself to you without further demands. Not only that: I have with me one of Caesar's killers, and I will serve him to you on a silver platter."

Octavian's heart jumped. This was something he had not expected. "Who is it?" he asked dryly.

"He has people here call him Cestius, but I know that he is really Marcus Spurius. I will point him out to you, and then… I have another gift for you," he added, pulling a wax tablet in a bag from the folds of his toga.

"What is it?" asked Octavian, greedily. That meeting was proving more valuable than he would ever have imagined. Just getting the head of one of Caesar's murderers was the best reward he could have expected after all that unfortunate and unwanted infighting.

Lucius's arm stopped in mid-air.

"Do I have your word that you will save the population from looting and leave me with my life?"

"You have my word… in exchange for the heads of the city elders. They must die so that the land confiscations may resume without opposition. All the decurions of the Italian municipalities must know what will happen if they do not respect the triumvirate. Sextus Pompey is still a serious threat and I cannot afford to appear weak. Magnanimous, yes, but not weak."

Lucius hesitated for a long time. Octavian gestured to him to hand over the tablet but the former consul held back once more before eventually giving in and handing it to him. Octavian removed it from the bag and read the short text:

I have had enough of Fulvia. See to it that she disturbs me no more.

While he read, he heard Lucius saying, "That's all Mark sent to me when I wrote to him at the beginning of all this to ask for his opinion. As you said, he didn't take sides but simply waited for events to unfurl to see if they were to his advantage or not. On the other hand, he made it quite clear that he has now chosen the Queen of Egypt. It was for that reason that I felt authorised to go along with my sister-in-law, who made me believe that she was interested in me when all she is actually interested in is power and a young man, Manius, with whom she has been making merry for months. As far as I am concerned, she is dead, and I think her husband feels the same. Do with her what you will, even though I assume that she is now fleeing Italy..."

A total victory, Octavian said to himself as he choked back a grin. All he had to do now was find a way not to upset the soldiers who felt that they deserved a bit of looting...

*

The courtyard between the two rings of fortifications that had surrounded Perugia for six months was full of people. The whole town was there, as were the soldiers of both armies, deployed in line and by unit around the grandstand erected for the occasion. Octavian sat on the podium with his bodyguards, his closest collaborators – Maecenas, Agrippa, Rufus and Laenas – and his adversary, Lucius Antonius, who was wearing a suit of shining armour, a fiery-red paludamentum cape and an immaculate crested helmet.

On the stage and in the ranks the atmosphere was festive, with the two adversaries exchanging broad smiles and the soldiers of the opposing armies fraternising and relieved by no longer having to attempt to kill one another. In the quiet of the parade, many recognised soldiers in the enemy army that they had fought alongside in the past, and greeted them with pleasure, declaring that they hoped to fight together again in the future, whilst the few surviving gladiators were kept apart, chained up outside the camps. They were slaves and they would go back to being slaves, reflected Octavian as he meditated upon how to play for time when he addressed his considerable audience. On the faces of the ordinary people, the people who had been forced to suffer the miseries of the siege, were expressions of relief, because they had heard that there would be no looting. Even the elders and decurions, gathered together near the grandstand, seemed content:

Lucius Antonius had not told them that he had sacrificed them.

The victorious soldiers, however, were excited and eager to break formation and get to work looting the city of anything of value.

Octavian, in fact, had been careful not to tell his legionaries that there would be no looting.

Meanwhile, he gave orders that they should light the pyre on which they would sacrifice the bull in honour of his father, the divine Julius Caesar, who had once again watched over him and allowed him to prevail in yet another challenge. And secretly, as only his closest lieutenants knew, the *taurobolium* was also in honour of Mars Ultor, to whom a new victim was about to be consecrated.

Indeed, by then the god had perhaps already received the new blood sacrifice.

As Pontifex Maximus, it was Lepidus who officiated at the ceremony. The triumvir, who was such in name only, covered his head with his toga, uttered the ritual prayers, gestured to his aides for the knife and then slew the animal, which had already been stunned and which fell heavily to the ground, spraying his white robe with its blood.

While the bull was being butchered by his assistants and cooked on the fire, Octavian stood up, raised his arms in front of him to attract the attention of the soldiers and began to speak.

"Soldiers!" he began. "You have fought another war that we would have wished to avoid, and once again the sins of the few have fallen upon the shoulders of the many! For their own personal ends, a gang of rebels attempted to prevent the soldiers from receiving their just rewards for the efforts they had made at the side of my father and of Antony, as well as at my own side, for the greater glory of Rome, in years and years of hard campaigns against formidable enemies, and sometimes even against their own brothers..."

*

Making sure that there was no one around, Ortwin and Veleda, accompanied by four other Germans, brought the man who called himself Cestius to the Basilica of the forum of Perugia. The population had been summoned down to the plain to witness the triumvir's speech and the city was now deserted. There might be the odd person about, but certainly nobody important enough to be able to refute the official version of what was about to happen, said Ortwin to himself as he yanked the murderer of Caesar along with him.

They entered the building and the German motioned to his men to give him the two torches they had brought with them, and then told Veleda to put a rope around the man's waist. She did so, then held one end of it.

"What are you doing? Why are you doing this to me?" babbled the increasingly agitated man. "Why me?"

"Because you dared to betray and to raise your hand against the divine Julius Caesar, Marcus Spurius."

The man blanched. Until then, they had not told why they had arrested him or what they were going to do to him.

"What? There's been some mistake! My name's Cestius and I come from Macedonia…"

"Of course, of course you do!" said Ortwin, paying no attention to his cries, which were becoming louder. Too loud: there was a chance he might attract someone's attention. With one of the two firebrands, he gave the man a blow to the head and watched as he slumped unconscious at his feet.

"Let's get a move on," he said to Veleda, advancing into the building.

*

"We must ensure that this never happens again and that everyone knows that the Republic must work as one, without argument, to make it the empire it deserves to be!" continued Octavian. "All the representatives of the state – from the supreme magistrates, to myself, to the most obscure town administrators – should be aware of their duty, which is to obey the laws of the State and not to flout them! Since returning from the campaign in Greece, I have committed myself in the name of the triumvirate to enforcing laws and to rewarding men who have sacrificed years of their life for the Republic, but some who were supposed to help us make the process straightforward and painless have fomented discontent and have ended up devastating Italy once again. Sextus Pompey's attacks that we are forced to endure through his acts of piracy were not enough for them! We were forced to spill yet more Roman blood and to impose upon ordinary people trials yet worse than that which they had been led to believe they would suffer from the land confiscations. You, the citizens, are as much victims of this deception as I! You should be angry with your city senate for having opposed the laws for their own personal advantage! The decurions and the senators deliberately provoked riots by refusing to give up even a part of their disproportionate possessions! Should not we punish them?"

From the massed populace of Perugia there came a murmur of assent. Many glared angrily and shouted insults at the nobles who, in the meantime, had begun to realise that they were in trouble. They huddled closer together, feeling threatened from every side.

"We all know that an administrator, much more than an ordinary citizen, has the responsibility for enforcing the laws, even when it is to his personal disadvantage! We triumvirs wanted to give the people like you a reward – because the soldiers are the same as you, they are your sons and brothers – by depriving these rich men of a small part of their immense wealth. So small that they would barely have even noticed it. But they are not in the habit of giving away anything. Well, now they will lose everything! And my divine father, whose memory and will they have violated with their behaviour, will witness their punishment!"

The crowd burst into an ovation while Octavian beckoned to the nearest soldiers to lead the senators over to the pyre set up in honour of Julius Caesar.

*

Ortwin set fire to all the corners of the building and left the torches inside when he went outside, and took the end of the rope Veleda had been holding. He uncoiled it until he was outside the entrance while the building was quickly engulfed in flames. Ortwin checked the wind and was satisfied: up there on the hill it blew strongly, and the fire would quickly spread to the rest of the city.

He stood by the entrance until he heard the screams of the murderer inside. They didn't bother him: the man who had killed Caesar in cold blood deserved to die amidst the most atrocious torments. With Trebonius and Decimus Brutus he was only sorry that he'd had to put a quick end to their lives. Veleda did not seem upset either, but then, as far as she was concerned, the death of a Roman was of little import – whichever Roman it happened to be.

He waited until the screams turned into gasps and only then did he begin to pull at the rope and drag out of the building what was left of the man's body. He looked dispassionately at the flesh eaten away by fire, the clothing fused to his blackened skin and his shuddering and finally took pity. He drew his sword from its sheath and sank it into what had once been the man's stomach. Meanwhile, the flames began to lick at the buildings nearest to the basilica. Very well, he said to himself. There was only one thing left to do.

"Fire! Fire! Help!" A woman holding up an old man emerged from an alley where flames had begun to spread. Ortwin motioned to one of his warriors to go and help her and the man took the two refugees with him, while more appeared from other streets.

"Come with us! Don't be afraid," cried the German. "We are here to help you. Caesar Octavian sent us here as soon as he saw the smoke. It was this man who started the fire! One of your townspeople! But he got the lesson he deserved!"

He set off back down the city streets towards the plain and the ring of fortifications, leading a procession of refugees which swelled with every step.

*

The cries of the senators burning on the pyre erected in honour of Caesar were suddenly drowned out by those of the citizens around the grandstand. Just as Octavian had expected: Ortwin's timing was, as always, perfect. He turned toward the hill upon which Perugia sat and pretended to be surprised and shocked to see tongues of orange fire rising over the wall into the clear March sky.

Moments later, he heard murmurs from among the ranks of soldiers, who saw their loot literally going up in smoke.

But not because of him, of course.

Now, however, he had to hurry to get to the point before the situation degenerated. Even Lucius was giving him a troubled look, and Octavian leaned over to him. "You wanted my men not to plunder the city, didn't you?" he whispered mockingly in his ear. "Well, they're not going to be able to..."

The ex-consul gave him an angry look, but the triumvir felt calm: Lucius could not reveal much of their agreement without losing that honour he was so concerned with maintaining.

The soldiers executing the senators by pushing them one after the other onto the fire stopped and looked in horror at the fire spreading across the hillside above them. Octavian commanded them to continue with the executions, and they were quick to drag forward another notable by his arms and throw him unceremoniously into the flames, but by now the audience was growing extremely agitated. What was Ortwin waiting for?

At last he saw the German coming towards them on horseback, followed by a column of citizens he had brought with him when the fire had started.

Octavian the victor, Octavian ruthless against his enemies, and now Octavian the saviour too.

He waited for the German to dismount from his horse and ascend the rostrum to tell him what happened – though only for the benefit of the audience. He already knew perfectly well what had happened and could have told the crowd had he so wished, but he needed it to look as though he had only just learned of the events. All Ortwin had to whisper in his ear was, "Everything went just as planned," and he raised his arms to ask for silence.

It took a long time for the people to stop shouting, and then it only happened when the soldiers intervened, and not always gently. At last he could give the speech he had been preparing since his encounter with Lucius and which he had perfected with Maecenas.

"Citizens of Perugia! I was just talking about the misfortunes that the rebellion of your elders has caused you, and now there is more: this fire and the destruction of your homes. This fills me with pain, because I have learned that it was one of your compatriots who started the fire: my men, who were inside the walls to prevent unrest, have led to safety those who remained there, but they also discovered the arsonist. They tell me his name was Cestius, and that he was from Macedonia. He must have thought I intended to vent my anger upon you and upon your assets and preferred to deprive you of everything before I did it myself! But he has already had his just reward," he said, regretting not having been able to throw Marcus Spurius onto the pyre in honour of Julius Caesar. But later, along with the other members of the cult, he would make a sacrifice to Mars Ultor for having taken another step along the road of vengeance, whose end was still distant even after the battle of Philippi and the deaths of Brutus and Cassius. There were too many of Caesar's killers still at large.

"But you promised us plunder!" protested an isolated soldier, and with a quick nod Octavian told Laenas to take note of who he was. Other cries of protest began, drowning out the civilians protests.

"I never spoke of plunder," he said. And it was true, he never had explicitly, though he had never denied the rumour that he would allow it once the city had fallen, as was usual in victorious sieges. And it was upon this ambiguity that he intended to play. "Firstly I wanted to see how the population behaved, because now I have an alternative. We have eliminated a greedy and corrupt ruling class, and thus all their property will be confiscated by the state, including their land, which will increase that available for the veterans. For *all* the veterans! Even those who fought in the service of Lucius Antonius but who once served under his brother, my esteemed fellow triumvir. Rest assured, soldiers: this way, things may perhaps go even better for you! And for you too, Perugia: do not weep over what you have lost, but rejoice for what you will gain: the state will provide funds to build an even more beautiful and prosperous city than before!"

And now he was *Octavian the Beneficent* too. He waited a few moments in silence, letting the crowd mull over what he had said and reach the expected conclusion, then let himself bask in the cheers and enjoy the look of undisguised admiration mixed with envy that Lucius Antonius was giving him.

VIII

Despite everything, Octavia was glad to see her brother. True, he might well have physically threatened her to coerce her into laying with her husband to produce more children, and then virtually excluded her from the cult of Mars Ultor, relegating her to being a mere instrument for perpetuating the family line and demonstrating to the world that harmony reigned in his inner circle. She should be angry with him for having deprived her of any chance of happiness now that Gaius Chaerea did not want her any more, but instead she tried not to be influenced by her personal experiences and to support Octavian's grand design. After all, her brother had shown that of all of them, he was the most far sighted, and each of his new initiatives was rewarded by further success. If he managed to bring all his projects to fruition, the *gens Julia* family would benefit, and she had no intention of doing anything to prevent that happening.

And perhaps, at the end of the day, he was also right about Marcellus. The man was her husband, and a prominent senator, and bringing him over to the family's side might be a wise political move: their thirst for revenge had consistently paved the way to power and to the succession to Caesar, and there was no need to add more blood. She would never be able to forgive Marcellus for what he had done but if Octavian had managed to overlook his crimes for the greater good then so could she, also proving herself a worthy member of the sect. For this reason, she and her husband hurried to meet her brother as soon as the doorkeeper had announced his presence at their entrance.

She had never seen Marcellus behave so obsequiously. It was clear that Octavian's treatment of him was paying off: the senator's opinion was rapidly changing and from being a Republican and against Caesar and the triumvirate he was turning into a staunch supporter of her brother. Octavia couldn't tell if that was because he had actually embraced the cause or whether he was simply scared: she hadn't asked him, nor – for the moment – could she manage to trust him in the slightest, and probably never would again. Unlike Octavian, she could not completely ignore what had happened, and for the moment her contact with her husband was limited to fleeting sexual encounters carried out to perpetuate the line, as her brother had ordered.

"... at your young age, you can already boast victories in numerous wars, my dear triumvir," Marcellus was already babbling to Octavian, without giving her time to greet him as was fitting. "Modena,

Philippi, and now Perugia. Not even Caesar dreamed of achievements like that at twenty-three."

Octavian had left the lictors outside the door and had brought inside only Popilius Laenas, that detestable individual from whom he seemed inseparable. What was that foul man doing at a family reunion? Octavia tried not to appear annoyed, however, while her brother nodded politely at her husband's words.

Eventually, he turned to focus all his attention on her.

"But look at you, my sweet sister!" he said, embracing her repeatedly. "So it is true, then: you're with child again. And how is the pregnancy going?"

"Very well, thank you," she replied, while Marcellus invited Octavian to sit in the triclinium. "Of the three that I've had, this is perhaps the easiest."

Octavian sat down on one of the couches, while Laenas remained obediently behind him. His presence continued to bother Octavia, but she knew that an important man like her brother must always have someone to guard his back, even when visiting his closest relatives. Marcellus was so effusive towards his guest that he scarcely seemed to have noticed the centurion. He clapped his hands, and soon slaves appeared bearing drinks, fruit and other snacks which were arranged on a table between three sofas in a moment.

"And what of young Marcellus, how is he?" asked the leader of the sect.

"He grows strong and healthy," said the boy's father, glowing with pride. "I cannot show him to you now because he is sleeping, but he will undoubtedly be a high ranking officer in your legions when you are the undisputed leader of the Republic!"

Octavian looked at him coldly. "I am already the undisputed leader of this Republic, at least in the West: Sextus Pompey will soon cease to be a threat."

Fidgeting nervously, Marcellus swallowed. "Of course… I wasn't referring to Pompey or to Antony… but…."

Octavian waved his hand to cut him off and his face relaxed once more. "But you are right, dear Marcellus, I still have a long way to go, and there are still many obstacles that prevent me from implementing my program. But now, with the defeat of Lucius Antonius, we have removed one of them, and soon we will remove the others too. As soon as we have allocated the land to the veterans I will devote myself to the conflict with Pompey. With Lepidus's help, I will make him regret deciding to become a pirate."

"Very good. And how are the confiscations going, by the way?" asked Marcellus, desperately seeking topics for conversation.

"Maecenas is handling it all. Now that those whose land is being confiscated have lost their champion and Antony's generals no longer want to risk getting involved, I predict there will be no further problems: within a few weeks we should have finished."

"But I heard there were new rebellions in Campania after the siege of Perugia had ended. Of course a man in your position doesn't have a moment's rest: once you have filled in one hole, another opens..." said Marcellus in an unctuous voice. Octavia found his behaviour extremely annoying, but Octavian seemed to tolerate it gracefully.

"Yes," nodded her brother bitterly. "And now, enemies who at the time of Caesar and the Philippi were suppressed by stronger personalities are beginning to raise their heads. Now they have space to manoeuvre, and seek their own moment of glory. But if they haven't managed it before, that means they can't be up to much: we have defeated those who were far stronger, and so will have no difficulty dealing with them."

"And in any case, they are slaves, after all..."

"Exactly. I do not know what this Tiberius Claudius Nero can have been thinking to get involved in starting a slave rebellion like that: a member of one of the most illustrious families in the city, a descendant of Claudius and the victor at Metaurus against Hasdrubal playing at being the new Spartacus… But all that it means is that he has no real army to lead. I've sent Agrippa to Campania, and you will see that he will settle the issue in no time at all."

"I am sure," nodded Marcellus, adding, "You will be victorious, as always," before raising a cup of wine to which the nearest servant had just added water. "I drink to a young man who is proving himself to be more prodigious than Scipio, more brilliant than Julius Caesar, more far sighted than Furius Camillus and more powerful than Romulus!"

Octavia was beginning to find him repulsive. Until a year ago, Marcellus had never hidden his distaste for Caesar nor for any of those who supported him. The only reason he had not explicitly supported the murderers of Julius Caesar was cowardice but he had secretly hoped that they would win at Philippi. And now, he gave himself over to ridiculous praise of her brother after having killed his mother and trying to murder his sister…

"I'm glad you have finally realised who genuinely cares about the good of the state. For a long time, you supported those who wanted to dissolve it and hand it over to external parties for purely personal benefit, and this led you to commit serious errors…" commented the triumvir.

Marcellus lowered his head, mortified. Octavian immediately began again. "But you have recognised your mistakes, and you too are working for the good of the family. Now I will have two new children of noble blood, and I thank you both for managing to put aside your differences and for having brought back the cohesion which is essential for our family in tackling the challenges that lie ahead. I am very satisfied with you, my dear brother, and I would like to thank you, as is proper, for having shown yourself to be so reasonable and helpful."

Octavia immediately thought her brother might be referring to a consulate. She looked at her husband, and knew he was thinking the same thing: his face was expanding into a radiant smile that made his features almost unrecognisable, so used was she to seeing him angry or depressed.

"Caesar, I don't know how to thank you for the opportunity you have so kindly offered me…" he began, but suddenly the imposing figure of Laenas materialised behind his couch and his dagger flashed rapidly across Marcellus's throat, opening a large gash like the red jaws of some wild animal. Blood sprayed everywhere, flooding the table, the couch and even Octavia's clothes. She screamed and shrank back in terror, staring incredulously at Octavian. Her brother glanced at her and then returned his gaze to contemplate his brother-in-law's corpse slumped on the couch in a vermillion lake, his face still contracted in an expression of amazement. He shrugged and said in a voice completely devoid of anger or hatred, "You didn't really think I would have let the murderer of our mother live, did you?"

*

There was always tension when one of Octavian's generals met one of Mark Antony's, and this time was no exception, said Rufus to himself as he headed to the praetorium of Fufius Calenus, proconsul of Gaul. The man who possessed more legions than anyone else apart from Octavian in Italy and the surrounding regions.

Eleven. Eleven legions the triumvir coveted, especially in the light of the impending war against Sextus Pompey. That they were just standing about idly in pacified Gaul instead of overseeing the Italian coasts threatened by that pirate was something Octavian simply could not tolerate. And, unfortunately for him, Calenus was under Antony who would never – absolutely never – deprive himself of them and hand them over to his ally and rival, even if Octavian did need them to defeat their common enemy on the seas.

Unless Rufus managed to bribe him.

That was his task en route to Spain. Once past the Alps Rufus had made a detour to Calenus's headquarters in Toulouse, camping his six legions – the ones which had been used in the siege of Perugia – near the town. And since Calenus had his units stationed in the four corners of Gaul and only three legions to hand, for the moment, Rufus possessed a stark numerical advantage. He could have simply relieved him and taken command of the provincial troops without a fight, but that was not what Octavian wanted. In the conflict at Perugia, in fact, he had been careful not to place himself in direct conflict with Mark Antony, saving the life of his brother and pretending to believe in the good faith of his fellow triumvir, who was theoretically oblivious to what was happening in the West. Octavian used to say that it was necessary to take one step at a time: he didn't yet feel ready to take on Antony openly – not with Sextus Pompey and several of the murderers of Julius Caesar still around.

It was a strategy with which Rufus did not agree, but then, for some time he had not agreed with the leader of the sect. Had he been Octavian, he would have requested a meeting with Antony, killed him and become the undisputed master of the empire. It was no good having too many scruples when you craved power, and any compromise was only destined to delay the inevitable, with the risk that, over time, your opponent would turn out to be more unscrupulous than yourself.

It was for this reason that he had decided to do things his own way and play the two against each other for his own ends… Octavian had proposed a consulate for him for the following year. It was just a way of keeping him quiet and nothing more, though, he was sure, and in any case, it would take more than a consulate to satisfy him: at the moment, consuls counted for very little.

He walked into Calenus's praetorium, leaving the bodyguards who had accompanied him into the city outside the door. When he entered the room, the proconsul rose from the table and approached him with outstretched hands.

"I am happy to receive a colleague traveling to Spain," he greeted him warmly. "You will have much to tell me of what has been happening in Italy… I know that you were right there at the centre of the action!"

Rufus remained aloof. "Yes. And you, on the other hand, sat here watching, like many other provincial governors, waiting to take advantage of the situation and declare yourself for the winning side…" he said, avoiding Calenus's proffered hand and going to sit in the chair in front of his.

The proconsul stiffened, and his brow furrowed in a frown. He took his seat too.

"You should reflect, Rufus, before making such accusations," he hissed. "But on the other hand, they warned me that you were impulsive. A very different beast to Agrippa. Since you don't mince your words, I'll tell you explicitly that I would have much preferred to receive him. And as regards your allusions, as well as having the responsibility for guarding this vast province, I take my orders from Antony. I had no reason to mobilise and Antony gave me no orders. Do not fool yourself that these tribes are under our control: Caesar's conquest was too rapid for it to be thorough as well. I must be cautious, and woe to he who neglects to keep the garrisons fully manned – at the moment, they are the only thing keeping these people in Rome's power."

"All excuses. The truth is that you, like all the others, are only interested in your own business and your own personal benefit."

"You accuse me of this because that is evidently how you think, and you cannot conceive of someone devoting themselves to what is necessary and not simply to their own lusts."

"A man without personal ambition is not a man at all."

"Ah, is that so? It is precisely those who think like you who have brought this empire almost to dissolution, with one civil war after another," snapped Calenus. "Do you think your six legions give you the right to aspire to absolute power?"

"No, not with my legions, they wouldn't be enough. But with seventeen I would…"

Calenus narrowed his eyes to a slit and peered at Rufus. "What would you want? For us to replace Lepidus and create a third pole of power?"

"Or perhaps a fourth: you are forgetting that Sextus Pompey still carries a certain weight…"

Calenus seemed to reflect for a moment.

"Yes, but I have no doubt that you would stab me in the back as soon as you had the chance. You are that kind of person."

Rufus looked at him with a grin. There was no sense dragging his feet any more. Calenus was right: he had no intention of sharing anything with him. With the speed of lightning, Rufus rushed to the other side of the table, grabbed the dagger his host kept on his desk and slashed the man's throat. It burst open, flooding everything with bright red blood. Rufus let Calenus slump gurgling in his chair, then pulled from the bag he had brought with him a wax tablet, which he deposited on the table, covering it in blood.

Finally, he put the knife in the right hand of his victim, went over to the door and opened it, saying to his bodyguards, "I have proof of Calenus's betrayal and his agreement with the pirate and outlaw Sextus Pompey. When the proconsul realised he had been discovered and when I offered him the chance to escape public trial with suicide, he took the opportunity, saving his dignity and his family's possessions. However, since his son is too young to take command of an army as massive as the Gallic garrisons, I will take command of his legions while I await new orders from the triumvir."

And at that point, if everything went as he hoped, his legions would have already surrounded the city and taken possession of the gates. Gaul was his, along with Spain. At least a third of the Roman world and almost twenty legions were now in his possession, and Antony and Octavian would have to reckon with him. In practical terms, he was as powerful as they.

But he knew how to be patient too, and now it was time to play both ends against the middle in his bid to become the supreme master of the empire.

*

There was nothing new about any of it. Tiberius Claudius Nero was certainly aware of Spartacus's feats but he was no match for them himself, and above all, he showed his limitations as a commander by attempting to replicate only the grandest, said Agrippa to himself as he watched his soldiers climb Vesuvius.

He had posted only half of them along the slope, expressly forbidding them to attack Nero's positions. He was waiting for his opponent's counter move, which – if he had guessed correctly – would not be long in coming. The exploits of Spartacus – the only leader apart from Hannibal and Mithridates who had been able to defeat the Romans repeatedly – were imprinted upon his mind, and he had a good idea what the man's less gifted imitator would do next.

An aristocrat at the head of a band of slaves. It would actually have been funny if the situation had not been so dramatic. But anyone in Italy wanting to rebel against the triumvirate had no choice but to resort to slaves and gladiators: the soldiers had all enthusiastically taken up Octavian's cause, for he had offered them real benefits. Nero, however, could promise nothing more than to free the slaves who adhered to his cause. But given how things were going, the only thing he would be freeing in the near future was his soul from his body.

He wondered what he would do when he found himself face to face with Nero. Agrippa knew that the man had embarked on this demented adventure with his wife, the young Livia Drusilla, who was also from a noble family, and with his little son Tiberius. He had dragged them through hardship and deprivation, hoping perhaps to provoke the intervention of Sextus Pompey, but the pirate was not the type to act unless there was something in it for him, and certainly not to merely assist others. Of course, Nero had been badly affected by the expropriations, but Octavian had been careful to leave him with considerable wealth, in spite of everything, so as not to alienate the powerful *gens Claudi*, which he might need in the future. But the man, who was as stubborn as many of the other senators, had not been able to tolerate them appropriating even a tiny part of his immense wealth, and now risked losing everything as a consequence.

Octavian had told Agrippa in no uncertain terms to kill him, preferably in battle because that way it would hide the fact that he had been summarily executed. Otherwise, they would have to have a trial, which might turn out to be embarrassing. The question was a delicate one, and Agrippa hoped that Nero would fight at the head of his troops, just like Spartacus, and offer him a chance to kill him. Otherwise, if he surrendered with his family, he would have no choice but to take them prisoner.

He looked up: stones and other makeshift projectiles began to fly over the heads of legionaries on the slope, and many of them crouched behind rocks and bushes. From the top, faces and arms were occasionally visible. Satisfied by the stalemate, Agrippa moved to the other side where the flanks of the volcano were steeper and climbed down, quickly arriving in the area where he had stationed a cohort amidst sparse scrub and sickly trees which offered some cover.

And he waited.

He didn't have to wait long. Soon, just as he had expected, he saw dozens of gladiators descending from the rock face on ropes, once on the ground they formed into columns and began to march towards the men Agrippa had sent to attack their positions. It was actually a good plan and would have been effective: it was only a pity that it was the same plan Spartacus had used to win his first victory, and in the same place, too. From his hiding place in the vegetation, the young commander tried to establish how many of their opponents there were and whether Nero was among them. He estimated their number to be at least three hundred, but couldn't see the nobleman among them. He knew Nero by sight, having seen him leave the Senate. He was probably up there at the top with the rest of the rebels.

He motioned to his men to wait and let the slaves enter the scrub thinking they were going to surprise the soldiers positioned on the ridge from behind, and only when he saw that the gladiators were arranged in a long, ragged column did he raise his arms, let out a war cry and leap out of the bushes, pouncing upon his nearest opponent. Unaware of his presence until the last, the warrior didn't even have time to turn round before Agrippa's blade sank into his side.

The same scene took place next to him and all the way along the column. The slaves were mostly devoid of armour and the legionaries' swords met with no resistance while they sank into the flesh with the ease as they did into the straw men they used in training. Moreover, to judge by their size, muscles and scars, only a few were gladiators – most were mere slaves who had fled villas in the surrounding area and who, puny and clumsy, lacked any military training at all. As he killed his umpteenth opponent without even breaking a sweat, Agrippa cursed Nero for having led all those poor people to their deaths, deceiving them with promises he could not keep: he decided he would do for the man willingly if he was given the chance.

But that meant attacking the position at the top of the mountain and thus losing some of his legionaries, and the life of that imbecile wasn't worth the life of even one of his men. Once there were only slaves who had raised their hands in surrender, and who knew that now they would be executed as rebels, left standing in the woods, Agrippa called the centurion over and said to him, "Get the men to cut off some heads, stick them on spears and go up the slope.

Make sure the defenders can see them and demand that they surrender, threatening that otherwise they'll end up the same way. Without external support, I doubt it'll take them long to surrender. They know they will be executed, so promise that you will spare their wives and children, if they have brought them with them."

In the meantime, he took the opportunity to wash, but longed to be back in action: every time he stopped, Fulvia crept back into his mind. He heard that she had reached Brindisi and embarked for Greece with her Manius. He wanted to talk to her – certainly not to win her back, aware that was now impossible and that Octavian would not tolerate it in any case – but simply to finally have the courage to face her without begging for her attention. In short, to humiliate her as she had humiliated him.

Since he had chosen to remain with Octavian, he had lain with a different woman every night in a vain attempt to find one that would give him at least the intense physical sensations that Fulvia had been able to. He was determined to forget her by all means available, but when he closed his eyes while making love, he couldn't help thinking that it was her skin that he was touching, her scent he was breathing, and when he opened them his excitement disappeared when he realised of how far from Fulvia the woman he was with actually was.

He was still absorbed in his thoughts when they called him. He climbed the slopes just as the slaves, unarmed and with their wives and children in tow, were beginning to leave their positions. He peered at the forlorn looking horde in search of Nero and his family, looking them over one by one and seeing their desperate and pleading expressions, occasionally punctuated by a fierce face with eyes still blazing with hatred. Not seeing the nobleman, he asked for their commander and after some hesitation, one of those who had been staring at him defiantly stepped forward proudly. Agrippa stood in front of the man who had the air of a gladiator. "I thought I would find Claudius Nero among you," he said. "Where is he?"

The other gave him a contemptuous smile. "From what he told me, he should be right behind you with another army of gladiators…" he whispered.

Agrippa looked at him with an interrogative expression. "There is no one around here for miles. I assure you that we have reconnoitred the entire area carefully."

The other spat. "Just as I imagined… That coward assigned me the task of leading my people to the mountain top to keep you busy with Spartacus's manoeuvre and told me he would sneak up on you from behind when you were convinced you had won," he groaned. "Instead, I bet he couldn't find anyone to come with him and ran off to join Sextus Pompey. Or never intended to continue the war in the first place and sent us to the slaughter when he realised he had no hope…"

Agrippa nodded. Yes, by that time Nero might well already be with Sextus Pompey. The number of men the pirate possessed grew day by day, he thought with concern. It looked as if it was going to be a hard war – as hard as the war in Philippi, perhaps – and they still didn't know what side Antony, always ambiguous, and even more so during the conflict in Perugia, would take. He shook his head, and brought his thoughts back to his own battlefield: every victory they gained led them to another, even more difficult challenge.

*

If it hadn't been for Plotius Tucca and Horace, said Maecenas to himself, he would have found the task he had so rashly agreed to undertake absolutely intolerable. The petitions, appeals, complaints, desperate supplications and solicitations were accompanied by a vast amount of documents which needed to be examined in order to proceed with the expropriations so as to avoid as much as possible any unfairness, injustice and oppression. Overwhelmed by paperwork, surrounded by shelves upon which were piled wax tablets and papyrus rolls, the Etruscan ceaselessly examined the maps of estates in senatorial, equestrian and municipal ownership so as to re-distribute them in a way which was relatively painless for the owners but without giving the veterans wasteland or land that was impossible to cultivate. He received the notables from cities subject to expropriation, who were sent by landowners, and patiently discussed solutions with them.

Eventually throwing them out when it emerged that they were unwilling to give up anything at all, which was the case most of the time.

He had established his office for the re-distribution of land in the antechamber of the Basilica Julia. It was crowded with people waiting their turn to present their claims, and soldiers were kept busy holding back people demanding appointments or complaining of unfair treatment. Many were demobilised legionaries who had come to Rome to ask their patron to intercede on their behalf or to ask the laticlavus tribunes under whom they had fought to put in a good word for them and get them a plot as close as possible to Rome, near somewhere they had been stationed, or just where they came from. Meanwhile they crowded into the forum awaiting news and making it difficult to even enter the basilica early in the morning when Maecenas was on his way to work. Fortunately,

Octavian had given him a strong escort who worked hard at keeping away the petitioners who, on recognising him, tried to attract his attention, or shouted out to him, asking for news of their case.

But it was still better than being on a battlefield. He continually repeated to himself that he was done with military life, and when he was sick of the paperwork and complaints and people hassling him, he forced himself to remember how awful the Modena, Philippi and Perugia campaigns had been, and how he had risked his life every day and found himself embarrassed by his inadequacy as a warrior compared with the skill and expertise, but above all the courage, of his subordinates. There in the basilica, at least no one could accuse him of not being up to the job: when it came to accounts and assessments he was without rival and feared comparison with no one.

"Here in Corfinium," said Plotius Tucca looking at a map of the city of Bruzio, "it's all rather complicated. Do you want me to show you how many petitions we have received? There's a pile of them over there. You cannot imagine how many senators support them. So far we have only managed to assign a few square miles far from the city, and not even good quality land at that: the veterans will not be happy..."

"I'm not surprised," chipped in Horace, who was busy sorting out some equestrian properties around Lucera in Apulia, as Maecenas had asked him to. "As the capital of the Italic League at the time of the Social War, Corfinium claims the right to be considered untouchable, just like Rome…"

"Yes," admitted Plotius. "And because many senators come from those parts, it also enjoys broad protections."

"The point is that it was not included in the list of cities to be subjected to expropriation when the triumvirate drew it up, as far as I am aware," Horace pointed out. "But then your Octavian decided to cosy up to all the soldiers of the empire and is now transferring practically all of Italy's land from civilians to the military… Even those who fought for only a few years now appear to be entitled to a pension…"

Maecenas lifted his head and smiled. "Those like you, you mean, Horace? I don't remember you having had a particularly long career. But you are a civilian now, and your father's properties have been returned to you."

Horace never got offended, and it was for this reason that Maecenas teased him. He knew that Horace took everything with a pinch of irony, and that was partly why he liked him. Instead, he replied in mock indignation, "I? But I have connections. I was talking of the ordinary people, of those poor people who have no one to protect them. Where is the advantage of this new order of Augustus if it forces them to give up their possessions?"

"You know that we only take from those who have too much. And among the senators, the prosperous cities and the richest equestrians, there are many who have far, far too much," pointed out Maecenas. "By satisfying the soldiers, Octavian will create a new, more willing and active middle class, and slowly supplant the parasites who led Rome to this point by shamelessly hoarding and putting their mark on everything and everyone."

"… a class ready to follow him where ever he goes…" replied Horace inevitably. Maecenas was about to retort, but his friend hadn't finished. "When you spoke of disproportionately rich equestrians, you *were* referring to yourself, Maecenas, weren't you?" he added with a mischievous smile.

The Etruscan gave up. "You have me at a disadvantage," he admitted, as a slave came in to hand him a wax tablet.

Maecenas glanced at it and snorted. "My friends, this is one that we have to receive. Plotius, get out the maps of Mantua, we're going to have to argue here. There is a fellow outside who has important friends. This letter carries the joint signatures of people like Quintilius Varus, Cornelius Gallus and Asinius

Pollio, no less…" then he motioned to the slave to bring in the petitioner.

While they waited, the Etruscan looked fondly his two friends. He had met them three years earlier during the War of Modena, one a foot soldier, the other an optio in the army of Mark Antony, who at the time had been against Octavian. And though he had always remained on excellent terms and in constant contact with Plotius Tucca, he had been forced to chase Horace. The two had met only occasionally and their encounters had not always been pleasant. To be honest, it had taken a long time to overcome Horace's diffidence, but then Horace had saved his life at Philippi and something had begun to change between them. Maecenas had not yet dared to declare to him in so many words that he felt much more than simple affection and friendship for him, and nominally continued to court him purely to encourage his poetry, which Plotius insisted was the expression of a superior talent. But Horace, certainly aware of what the Etruscan felt for him and perhaps not even entirely repulsed by it, seemed to enjoy keeping him on tenterhooks, certain that he still had him where he wanted him.

There appeared before them a man of about thirty with a prominent nose set amongst features which were otherwise delicate, a frightened expression on his face and a resigned attitude. He remained silent while Maecenas looked him over and had Plotius pass him the documents relating to Mantua. Without speaking, the Etruscan examined the map of the area around the city, marked up with the plots allocated to veterans and those which had been left to their original owners. He decided that the assignments needed to be formalised and sighed, before turning to speak to the petitioner. “So, Publius Vergilius Maro… You apparently have some very influential friends,” he said. “It seems that we will have to revise our decision. It says here that you’re a lawyer and that you’ve practiced in Rome, though you can’t be a particularly good one, because I have never heard of you. But you must have been lucky while you were defending someone high up to have managed to rally all these illustrious personages to your assistance… It asks here for your family’s vast estates to be left untouched.” The man looked embarrassed, then tried to assume a dignified demeanour and cleared his throat. No, thought Maecenas, he really didn’t look like a Cicero, and it was impossible to imagine him giving a vehement harangue in court.

“Erm, well, sir… it’s more to do with my father than with me,” he replied in a shaky voice that the Etruscan hoped he didn’t use in court. “His honey is very popular and many prominent personalities here in Rome have always been supplied by him. When I came here to study and practice law I had the opportunity to meet his most prestigious clients, to whom I sometimes make deliveries myself, and have been fortunate enough to speak to. Every now and then they have even invited me to dinner, where I have entertained them with… "

"All right, all right," said Horace unceremoniously. "We understand. We will review your petition and by tomorrow we will let you know. You can go."

The man looked somewhat puzzled, and glanced at Maecenas who nodded, then bowed his head in thanks, turned and left the room.

"Why did you throw him out so rudely?" asked Maecenas, turning to Horace. "I would have given him a little more time."

"These daddy's boys make me sick, that's all," said Horace. "He will manage to avoid the confiscations not on his own merits but on those of his father. Didn't you see? Why I doubt he's actually capable of practicing law, and he lives like a parasite, scraping together the odd dinner now and then in the company of the powerful."

IX

As soon as he found himself standing in front of Clodia Pulchra, Octavian's wife, Maecenas realised that he had given little thought to what he was actually going to say to her.. He'd known that what he'd been given to do was rather unpleasant but only now did he realise that he had been too hasty in offering to help his friend out of a potentially embarrassing situation.

"Well, dear Maecenas, do you bring me news of my beloved husband?" the lady asked, as gentle and sweet as her mother Fulvia was perfidious and cruel. Any other husband would have considered her a precious jewel to be guarded with the greatest care, but not Octavian, who had never known what to do with her.

According to Octavian, he had never touched her nor even lain a finger on her since he had taken her in marriage to seal the alliance with Mark Antony three years earlier. He had refrained from any kind of physical contact, not because he did not find her appealing – the young woman was so desirable that she aroused something even in the Etruscan, whose principal interest was boys. No, Octavian had found the strength to remain unmoved by her charms simply because he knew that it would be useful when the eventual breakdown of his truce with her stepfather Antony forced him to leave her.

Everyone had known it would happen sooner or later. Fulvia's excesses, which included causing a war simply to satisfy her lust for power, had only hastened events, and Antony's ambiguous behaviour during the Battle of Perugia had made it clear that he could not be trusted. With the latent conflict with Sextus Pompey at stake they could no longer afford to worry about appearances as well. For that reason Octavian had finally broken through his inertia and had decided he must get his hands on the Gallic troops Rufus had assumed command of after the unexpected death of Calenus. It was not simply a way to safeguard themselves against the threat the pirate posed, it was also a way of forcing Antony to finally come out into the open.

And Antony had, in fact, made his counter move, to judge by the news coming from across the Adriatic, by starting negotiations for a separate peace with Sextus Pompey.

So now the ball had passed back into Octavian's court and Maecenas had devised a plan to give him an advantage. And that was why he was now in the triumvir's house.

"Indeed, yes, I bring you news of him, Clodia Pulchra," he replied, attempting to hide his discomfort. "He apologises for not being here in person, but as you know, at the moment he is dealing with the discontent caused by the grain blockade put in place by Sextus Pompey as well as many other burdens on the State..."

"I understand, I understand..." she nodded, docile and sympathetic. By the gods, why did she have to make everything so difficult? If she'd had a character like that of her mother or if she had become aggressive, he would have had no problem getting rid of her. "I know that being the wife of the most important man in Rome entails sacrifices and above all that of having to give up the idea of seeing him for much of the time. But I'll get used to it, though it costs me dear not to be with the man who has made me so happy by choosing me as his bride."

Maecenas wanted to leave. The girl was pretty much confirming what Octavian had already told him – that they had never been intimate. Yet she loved him and still had hope. It would be like sticking a knife in her back, the Etruscan thought to himself, as he cleared his throat. "You are right, dear Clodia, it means great sacrifices. And now I am going to ask you to make the greatest sacrifice of them all."

The girl looked at him intently with her childlike eyes, in which he saw curiosity but also, he thought, fear.

"I know that he is making great sacrifices for the state and I cannot allow myself to do any less. Tell me, dear friend," she replied proudly.

"Very well. You know that the situation with your stepfather is fraught with many unknown dangers. And your mother has created a multitude of problems for Caesar Octavian, as you know, and in some ways it is rather... *inconvenient* that he is still married to her daughter. And then, for the good of Rome, he has to find a way to mitigate the threat of Pompey. And if Octavian were free of marital obligations, we might succeed..." he said in one breath, leaving the girl a moment to take in and fully realise the significance of his words.

She was naive, but not stupid. It didn't take her long to understand what was going on.

"Are you telling me that Octavian wants to divorce me?"

Maecenas nodded, with a heavy heart. It was he who had orchestrated the whole thing and yet now he felt like a worm, hurting this poor girl in that way. To convince himself that he was doing the right thing – the right thing for her too – he reminded her that Octavian had never loved her and if they had stayed together he would doubtless have sentenced her to some unhappy fate. At least in this way Clodia could rebuild her life alongside a man who would respect and love her, as a girl like her who promised to become an exemplary matron deserved and no doubt would. Clodia did not shout, or cry or let herself go. Only her eyes grew moist and her body stiffened, held in a tight grip of obvious pain. She stood for a moment in silence, as tears began to trickle down her pale, rouged cheeks, and then she said, in a trembling voice, "On... on what grounds can he ask for a divorce? I have done him no wrong."

"The marriage has not been consummated. That is what he will say," he replied firmly.

"But... that is not my fault," she feebly tried to protest.

"That is irrelevant. As I said, there are the needs and of the state and opportunities which cannot be neglected."

That was that. Part of his job was done. The most unpleasant part. Suddenly, he was in a hurry to get out of that house. He took leave of Clodia, without approaching her, bidding her only a hasty farewell, while she, no longer caring about maintaining her demeanour, collapsed onto the sofa and wept bitterly. The Etruscan left the house and climbed into his litter, ordering his servants to proceed quickly to their next destination. He banished from his mind the image of Clodia devastated by sorrow and focused on his next steps. The cult of Mars Ultor found itself in a very delicate position at that moment – perhaps one of the most decisive of its brief but intense existence. There was the risk of war not only against Sextus Pompey, but against both him and Mark Antony. Nor did he know what Lepidus would do, as he had legitimate grievances with both Antony and Octavian. Lepidus had been given Africa and sent there immediately to get him out of the way. Then there were Antony's generals, who had left Italy and joined their leader after the defeat of Lucius. Of the thirteen legions that they had commanded, Agrippa had managed to take command of only a few in time – those of Munatius Plancus.

Now that Rufus had taken over Calenus's units in Gaul, Octavian had forty legions, a good number but still insufficient for a war against several armies. If Antony and Pompey allied, they would have access not only to the troops of the First legion and its generals, but also to the resources of the kingdom of Egypt, which the triumvir clearly now controlled, and above all, a fleet of more than five hundred ships with such overwhelming superiority as to be able to isolate and starve Italy.

In short, the prospect of war had too many dangerous variables and the only way to avoid it now was to induce Antony and Sextus Pompey to break off negotiations before they formalised a true alliance at Octavian's expense. When he was announced at the home of Lucius Scribonius Libo, Sextus

Pompey's father-in-law and one of the leading exponents of the pirate's cause, Maecenas knew that he was expected and exactly what to say. He had prepared for that meeting with extreme care and all that was left to do was formalise their verbal agreements. He was taken into the tablinum of the owner of the house, who rose from his chair and approached him amicably, greeting him with enthusiasm.

"So, Libo, I hope you have not changed your mind,"Maecenas said. "And above all, that your sister has not changed hers."

His host smiled at him. "Of course not. I talked to Scribonia and she is well pleased to accept Caesar Octavian as her husband," he said with satisfaction.

*

Octavian hoped it was worth it. Laying immobile on the bed with a blank expression on his face, he stared at Scribonia while she undressed – without him having asked her to. Suddenly, a smile appeared on his face.

"What is it, do you find me ridiculous?" said his wife, clutching the tunic that she had just removed to her breast, a mortified look on her face.

"Not at all. You are very sensual," said Octavian, hoping to have sounded sufficiently enthusiastic.

"You are very beautiful, too. Please, continue, I am enjoying watching you."

Scribonia hesitated for a moment, not entirely convinced by her husband's words. She had celebrated their sumptuous wedding just that day. She took off her robe slowly, swaying as though attempting to confirm what Octavian had just said.

In fact, the young man was smiling not at her but at the paradoxical situation in which he found himself. Maecenas's idea to marry him off to the sister of the father-in-law of his worst enemy might bring good results, that was undeniable. But it was ironic, as well as a paradox, that, for political purposes, he was now about to make love to a woman much older than himself and he had been forced to give up the graces of a beautiful young girl, Clodia Pulchra, who was genuinely in love with him. Scribonia was thirty years old and on her third marriage. She was by no means an unpleasant looking woman, but you could tell that she was equipped with a strong will, a far cry from the submissive sweetness of his previous spouse. Octavian could not help but smile as he observed the awkwardness and imperfections of his new wife as she tried to seduce him, her breasts, which had begun to sag, her wobbly thighs, the hint of a belly, and then compared her to what little he had seen of Clodia the only time she suddenly came into his room and began to get undressed. He had managed to stop her, saying he was too tired and worried about the current wars to appreciate her offer. Clodia had stood before him in her thong and *strophium*, revealing her sublime body, her smooth, velvety skin and a grace so rare that for a moment it had left him shaken. He'd had to muster all of his willpower to reject her, remembering that failure could jeopardize his plans – and he was not the kind of person to mess things up for a fuck.

But this time he had to have sex with his wife. Libo and Pompey would not take it well if they discovered that it was only a marriage of convenience.

If he had been a normal man, he would not have had such problems, he said to himself, as he watched a half naked Scribonia approach the bed. But the gods, and Caesar, had made him special, and if this was the price to pay, he accepted it willingly.

"Well really! I violate all the rules of decency by behaving like a prostitute, letting myself be seen by the lamplight and by taking the lead, instead of hiding my body and waiting for you, and you just lie there like a dead fish? Do you want to at least remove your loincloth?" complained Scribonia in that commanding manner he had become accustomed to since the ceremony, where she commanded almost all the participants to sit and behave as she so desired.

"You must excuse me, my wife, but a man in my position has a thousand things to think about and sometimes is not as responsive as he should be…" he said, rising from the pillow and holding out his hands to Scribonia, who in the meantime had reclined on the bed. He did as his wife had asked him, but felt no impulse to do more. He limited himself to caressing and admiring her long bare thighs, and wondered if he would ever feel pleasure with a woman like her.

"Having had two husbands, I have learned that the only way to stop men taking lovers is to behave in this way. This is how you like it. But bear in mind the fact that I would be very annoyed if you betrayed me, my dear husband. *Very* annoyed," she repeated, in a way that Octavian had already begun to find hateful. The woman did not realise that it was precisely by acting like that she would induce him to betray her but he could not argue with her on their wedding night, nor the night after – and then at least not until the situation with Sextus Pompey had been clarified. Scribonia seemed convinced that she could push him around simply because she was older than him, it was unfortunate that she was not in awe of him. Usually people feared him, even people of rank, and with others it was always he who was in charge.

Apparently, however, he had taken a wife who had no idea that it might be dangerous to try to dominate him. Well, he would make Maecenas – who had intrigued to get her to divorce her previous husband, Cornelius Scipio Salvito – pay for this. And Scribonia would pay for it too, one day…

But for the moment, he had to give in. "I agree with you," he said eventually, slipping his fingers between her legs and starting to caress her with all his skill. "If a woman knows how to be as lovely and sensual as you do, what need would a man have to go and seek pleasure elsewhere?"

She seemed happy and immediately followed suit, lifting her tunic and removing her thong, then grabbed his still limp member and handled it with expertise. Octavian had to admit she knew what she was doing. Before long, she realised that he was ready to possess her and sat astride him, doing everything herself, her hands flat on her husband's chest. She was panting, Octavian noticed. He was unable to entirely surrender himself to making love, a part of his mind always remained alert and clear. For some time he had known that even in those circumstances a part of him still ruminated on issues that most interested him. By now he was resigned to the idea that no woman was capable of involving him completely in intimacy and making him forget the mission for which he had been born. Nor was he looking for one. Those who had been charged with the task of saving the empire could not be swayed by pleasures of the flesh.

When it was over, he decided he was not sorry that he had made love to her. But then, when the woman began to speak without interruption immediately afterwards rather than leave him alone, he judged her totally unsuited to him. He would release himself from Scribonia as soon as he no longer had need of her – and, of course, before she became too old even to provide him with this pleasure.

He listened to her as she talked of the changes she intended to make in the house, the bad habits of her previous husbands, the credit she attributed to herself for having improved them, the children she wanted to give him, the people she could exert some influence over, her father, her mother, the granddaughter of Pompey the Great and of Sulla, her brother, who she wanted him to make a consul as soon as possible… until someone started knocking on the door. A slave entered and handed him a letter, he said, from Apulia. His wife's words ringing in his ears, he read it, and knew that the next few days would be decisive. Mark Antony had appeared in the waters off Brindisi and, as per the instructions received from Rome, Popilius Laenas with his five garrison cohorts and the city decurions, had forbidden them to land, using the pretext that he was escorted by the fleet of Domitius Ahenobarbus, an exile who had created a lot of problems for their convoys during the campaign of Philippi.

Octavian would never have believed that he could have been so happy to receive such bad news.

*

"I'm not going!" shouted one of the settlers.

"Neither am I! Why should I fight the general who led me to victory and allowed me to earn this piece of land?" shouted another.

"Fight your own battles! I've finished my service and now I'm enjoying what I deserve!" added yet another to the chorus of protests.

"I say that it was Caesar Octavian who let me have this piece of land! So it is right to help him again if he needs me!" cried a voice in his favour. But it was one of the few. The triumvir spotted him in the crowd and beckoned him to come forward, whilst his more agitated companions jostled and insulted him. A few other veterans who had been given land to settle on in the colonies of southern Italy had agreed to return to duty, but in their march from the city, Octavian and his staff had obtained very little support for the prospect of fighting Antony which the triumvir had not foreseen when he deliberately caused his return to Italy. The further one went south and away from Rome, the fewer people agreed to join them and the ranks remained thinner than he had expected. There in Canusio the support was virtually nil and he could expect no more in the towns the army would reach in the following days.

Octavian looked towards Maecenas, Ortwin and Veleda and shook his head. This time he really seemed to have miscalculated. His marriage to Scribonia had not yet sufficed to stop Sextus Pompey, who was encouraged by Antony to harry the Italian coasts and he, who was in charge of defence, had made himself look like an imbecile. The soldiers, even those who had fought so hard to earn their farms, antagonising the Senate and the civilian population, showed no interest in fighting Antony, whose fame as the victor at Philippi still guaranteed their respect.

Octavian had left Rome counting on forcing the other triumvir to surrender, which he had assumed would happen purely on the basis of his numerical superiority, but things were threatening to go awry. Antony had cut off Brindisi with a moat and a rampart on the mainland and a fleet of two hundred ships at anchor in front of the port, isolating it and holding it under siege. He had also been sanguine enough to send forces to besiege Sipontum. Meanwhile, Sextus Pompey had sent his freedmen, all experienced admirals, to besiege Turi and Cosenza. The boot of Italy now seemed lost, and what was worse, Octavian was giving them the impression he was unable to do anything about it.

"I reckon we won't collect even a hundred men here…" said Ortwin.

"And it seems that things are not going much better with Agrippa," said Maecenas. Agrippa had taken a legion to Sipontum in an attempt to liberate them from the siege. "A message has just arrived from him. It seems that the settlers who join his army sneak off and desert during the night. Among the soldiers there is a genuine desire for peace – and in any case, they have no intention of fighting Antony."

"We risk a colossal fiasco, this time," said Octavian bitterly. "The situation promises to be even more difficult than the war of Perugia. Then we had Italy against us but all the soldiers were on our side. Now I have all these units I can't fully rely on and two fearsome enemies who have a strategic advantage… Maybe I shouldn't have provoked Antony by commandeering the Gallic legions. But how could I have known that Calenus would die? I was planning on buying him so that the whole thing would look like his idea!"

"You could not have done otherwise," Ortwin consoled him. "Those legions were standing idle and Pompey was threatening an invasion at any moment.

It was your right to take them and after Perugia, Antony was likely to react in one way or another. That is why he joined forces with Ahenobarbus and Pompey.... "

"But now he is playing the victim and making *me* look like the aggressor... He goes around saying that I have not allowed him to land in Italy and that I stole his legions... Meanwhile Pompey sets me against the entire population with his blockades along the coast." Octavian was overcome by one of his moments of despair, when all his defences came down and his weakness, usually held in check by his determination and ambition, gained the upper hand. He began to cough more violently and frequently than usual.

Maecenas encircled his waist with one arm in an attempt to calm him. "Fear not, we have got ourselves out of worse situations. Antony cannot afford to declare war against us either, and the negotiation phase has only just begun. However we must start from a position of strength which is more consolidated than our position today. Let's just hope that Agrippa manages to prevail."

"But how can he? He will arrive in Sipontum without enough soldiers to chase away Antony's troops."

"Agrippa is resourceful, as you know," continued Maecenas. "And then, Antony knows we have ample reserves on the other side of the Alps, with all the legions Rufus has taken command of. He also knows that Sextus Pompey cannot trust everyone and that we will do everything possible to prevent them from consolidating their alliance. Don't worry, at the end of the day that pirate will amount to little more than an irritation. Now that he is his ally, perhaps Antony will prevent him from starving Italy, otherwise he might be considered equally responsible." "

"I doubt it. It is his chance to get rid of me once and for all. And he will make use of any means available, even starving the population, if necessary," said Octavian between bouts of coughing. There were tears in his eyes, from the coughing as well as from his despair.

"You forget that you were the one to award the land to the veterans. The soldiers have no more wish to fight you than they do to fight him. I remain convinced that we will reach an agreement."

At that moment, a mounted messenger pushed his way through the crowd of settlers who had gathered and paused before Octavian. He was about to hand him a letter but, on seeing his expression, passed it to Maecenas. The Etruscan took the tablet from the bag and read it, suddenly turning white.

"What's the matter?" asked Octavian, even more desperate now.

"Perhaps it would be better for you to go and rest now. You're not at all well. I will call your doctor immediately," said Maecenas.

Octavian gathered his remaining strength. "I want to know what the problem is!" he shouted, but his voice almost died in his throat.

Maecenas took a deep breath. "Perhaps the situation is more serious than I thought. Menodorus, one of Sextus Pompey's freedmen, has occupied Sardinia and captured our troops who were stationed on the island."

Octavian felt all his strength vanish. Wracked by coughing, he sank into the strong arms of Ortwin, wanting only to lie down on a bed.

*

There were too many of them for his meagre forces. Agrippa observed the enemy troops standing around the walls of Sipontum, which they had surrounded with fortifications, cutting it off from the mainland. He had left Octavian's army with one legion and now he found himself commanding a total of only six or seven cohorts. He estimated there were four or five thousand men – at least a full legion – before him and realised that to attack them would be suicide. He could not risk a clash. Octavian's situation was already difficult since Antony had landed in the area of Brindisi and if things went wrong in Sipontum it would fatally compromise the action, delivering him to the mercies of the enemy.

Conversely, a victory would allow Octavian to approach the positions of Antony's troops with his prestige at least partially restored and on an equal footing. So he had to find a way to win at all costs. The whole campaign depended on it. As, once again, did the survival of the sect of Mars Ultor.

He rode further, climbing higher so that he could see beyond the city. He peered at the harbour and saw that Antony's forces had not cut it off – having control of the seas, it did not occur to them that one of Octavian's ships might succeed in providing support to the garrison. The oversight offered him an opportunity and he wasted no time in taking advantage of it. On the way to Sipontum he had passed another port, which still seemed to be operating normally. He said to the centurion beside him, "Go to Manfredonia with two cohorts. Commandeer eight cargo ships, large ones if possible. Get the soldiers aboard them, but concentrate your forces mainly in two of them, and then sail to Sipontum and cast anchor near the point where the enemy fortifications meet the sea. Try and find a way through in that area, which will be less guarded, and have the soldiers leave the first ship and then the second in successive waves. You must give the impression that you have only used a part of your actual manpower so that the enemy think the vessels contain large numbers of legionaries. When I see you coming, I'll start an attack on the land front. Is everything clear?"

"All clear, *legatus*. I'll go immediately!" answered the soldier, turning his horse and trotting off towards the ranks.

Agrippa returned to the remaining troops, and told them to make camp half a mile away from the enemy rampart. The enemy would think that these few cohorts were there to keep an eye on them and to prevent them from pressing on to other coastal towns. But it was necessary that his subordinate acted swiftly. Antony or Pompey's ships could easily turn up near the port, preventing the pincer movement he had planned, or the enemy could take advantage of its numerical superiority, which was now more evident than ever, and attack him. Or, even worse, the enemy could conquer the city, thereby making themselves impregnable to any assault. In short, the possibility that the whole thing would be a disaster was incredibly high, but he had no choice – his was the only viable strategy.

He was very late to bed, estimating that the naval contingent would appear near the town in the middle of the following day, and on rising after just a few hours of sleep he went to scrutinise the horizon himself, beset by anxiety at the risk he was running. The hours passed in frustrating inertia, while his eyes went from the sea to the walls and then back from the walls to the sea in a continuous rhythm dictated by the beating of his heart. His soldiers, meanwhile, were hard at work preparing ladders and platforms with which to scale the fortifications. But the situation made Agrippa recognise once again that this was the kind of tension he enjoyed having in his life – one that he found far more intoxicating than the yearning passions of love. He wanted to be victorious, and to keep on having similar sensations for the rest of his life.

By mid-afternoon no ships had appeared on the horizon and the enemy forces had managed to push a battering ram up to Sipontum's main gate. He hoped that the soldiers up in the city's battlements would find a way to destroy it, but the incendiary projectiles they fired at the machinery from above were ineffective for it was covered in fleeces soaked in water. After an hour, there was still nothing to be seen on the horizon but the iron head of the ram had begun its inexorable work. Agrippa was tempted to send a column of troops to attack the men working the ram. If he could remove them, he could buy himself at least another day with the help of the impending darkness. But he would also condemn to death any of his soldiers left behind enemy lines and he could not afford to lose any men if he wanted his pincer movement to succeed.

He got as close as he dared to the rampart and saw exactly what he had been dreading: the city gates were cracking and the rampart's foundations were starting to crumble. He was filled with despair. It was all over. Suddenly, a gap appeared between the doors, and Agrippa gasped. But they had not been smashed open, nor had they opened up completely – the defenders had evidently built a wall of earth and debris just behind them. It was a nifty trick, but it would only suffice to buy a little more time. The ram continued its inexorable swinging. They would probably manage to break their way through the mound in the hour and a half before nightfall.

"The legions are coming! They're coming!"

Then he heard the words he had been waiting for all afternoon. Together with the messenger who had given him the news, he rode down to the shoreline and counted eight ships sailing rapidly across the water. He told the messenger to inform him the moment the legionaries landed, then rode back to the camp, urging the officers to deploy the units for the attack and prepare the necessary equipment. He waited impatiently for the legionaries to take their positions in tight ranks and then ordered a slow paced advance. He rode at their head until he was close to the enemy battlements, and then paused, waiting just beyond the range of enemy arrows.

He waited for the messenger. He could not see what was happening around the gate from where he was. Over half an hour had passed since they had first broken through them and by now they might be inside. But maybe there was still hope – he could surprise them inside the walls during the raid.

The messenger galloped towards him. "They've landed! The battle has begun!" cried the soldier and Agrippa gave the order to attack. He rode at the flank of the front line, where every eighth legionary was equipped with a ladder and each centurion drove a wagon pulled by a mule and filled to the brim with stones and debris. The enemy battlements suddenly filled up with soldiers, but there were not enough to man every sector. As Agrippa had hoped, they were all concentrating on the imminent conquest of the city and had already started to flock to the area under attack from the sea.

The shield wall of the legionaries in the front row minimised the effect of the arrows of the few archers on the ramparts, and the soldiers managed to empty the contents of the carts into the moat, creating makeshift bridges under the light rain of arrows and spears and placing the first ladders against the embankment and the platforms. Soon the legionaries were at the top of the palisade and were waging a savage battle with the enemy soldiers. Agrippa urged his men on, waiting for an opening to appear so that he could make his way through. The first men to reach the ramparts fell like sacks, but those behind them on the ladders managed to eliminate a few enemy soldiers. A legionary cleanly severed the hand of an enemy swordsman who fled from the fence, screaming and crashing into a comrade who lost his balance and exposed his chest to another aggressor. In an instant, an opening was created and Agrippa's men took advantage of the situation to rush up onto the stands. The first to arrive was run through by a pair of swords, but the second avenged him and paved the way for two of his fellows, who opened up the bridgehead.

Agrippa decided it was time to intervene. He gestured to his bodyguards and went over to the ladder under the opening. He stopped the soldier who was about to climb up it, waited for those already climbing to reach the stands, and then went up himself, followed by his bodyguards. He arrived at the summit, jumped over the side and stood on the walkway. From there he had a better, more complete view of the battleground – and he realised that there was, in fact, no second wall like the one he and Octavian had built in Perugia.

He saw that the embankment behind the front gate of the town had given way and that some legionaries were scrambling over the rubble and debris to get inside. Yet they had opposition and were not helped by the comrades behind them, who were confused by the new enemy offensive and didn't know what to do. But what was even more encouraging was that the contingent from the sea had already broken through and its column was heading straight for the gate of Sipontum, sweeping away all the enemy soldiers who found themselves between the fortifications and the walls without orders. Many were trying to get to the fence to climb over it and throw themselves down below in an attempt to escape what had now become a trap.

His men were increasingly taking possession of the battlements, so Agrippa climbed back down and ordered the rapid formation of a column. Once there were enough legionaries behind him, he felt ready to charge the enemy forces still grouped together in front of the damaged entrance.

He raised his sword and shouted, "For Rome! For Caesar Octavian!" before charging forwards, mowing down with his sword whoever got in his way.

X

"Caesar, Mark Antony surprised Servilius and captured the whole column that he was bringing you as reinforcements!" cried the messenger, arriving in the camp constructed by Octavian near Brindisi, a short distance from the enemy.

"You mean the *whole* column?" asked the young man, horrified. "All fifteen hundred cavalry?"

"All of them, triumvir," confirmed the soldier.

For a moment, the young commander slumped on the platform steps in front of the drill field before realising that he was in full view of all the men training. They already seemed listless and were uncomfortable with the conflict between the two triumvirs. It would not take much to induce them to desert and join Antony after seeing their commander's despair.

That accursed man was humiliating him in front of everyone, but Octavian blamed himself for having got them into this nightmarish situation. He wished he were a hundred miles away, or in Rome, rather than within walking distance of the seemingly unassailable Mark Antony, who was about to attack Brindisi. His men indicated that his adversary had now finished building the siege machines and by the next day at the latest he would start the siege operation. He wanted to punish the people of Brindisi for not allowing him to enter the harbour and to embarrass his younger colleague by making him a helpless witness to their surrender.

It was all pure insanity. The ruler of Italy forced to stand and watch from a short distance away the fall of one of the cities that he was supposed to have been protecting. He couldn't imagine anything worse. He felt absolutely ridiculous, and what was worse, it seemed that even the soldiers thought the same thing.

"They don't even deign to look at me, now," he complained to Maecenas, who was standing beside him and had probably sensed his mood. "They have no confidence in me."

"No, that is not so," his friend tried to reassure him. "They simply do not want to fight. They are here and they followed you here because they expected you to come to some kind of agreement, as in the past."

"But as long as I continue to receive bad news, I doubt that Antony will want to come to *any* sort of agreement, unless from a position of strength that would reduce me to the same level as Lepidus. Meaning that all of this will have been in vain," groaned Octavian. "And now there is this business of Servilius too… I should bring back Agrippa from

Sipontum to give me more men, but if I bring him here before he has managed to conquer it that will look as though he is retreating, and people will think it is another failure."

"Do you want me to try and arrange a meeting with Antony? But this time, perhaps we will have to make some sacrifices to rectify the situation..."

Octavian jumped up. "I'm not going back on my word! Never! My divine father never did it. I haven't come this far just to give up!"

"We are only talking about playing for time," said Maecenas, "until we have more influence."

"We will never have more influence if I humiliate myself in that way, outclassed by Antony and pushed around by my own soldiers."

There was a thud in the distance, then another and a group of legionaries approached.

"Go and talk to noble Mark Antony, Caesar!" shouted one of the soldiers. "Do you want him to destroy the city that has been exposed to his revenge simply because it obeyed your order to prevent him from entering its harbour? Are you so ungrateful to those who respect you?"

"Antony is the greatest general in the empire," said another. "Anyone would want him on their side. Can it be possible that you two cannot manage to get along?"

"You even fought together at Philippi!" added a third. "Why are you arguing now?"

Above the soldiers' increasingly insistent cries, more loud thuds were heard. There was no need to ask what they were – the attack on the walls of Brindisi had begun, and his legionaries were crowding in front of him not to ask him to render assistance to the city but to demand that he implore Antony to stop.

He could not imagine a more unpleasant situation.

He had been pushed aside by his rival on the battlefield at Philippi. That victory was thanks to Antony, and although the propaganda orchestrated by Maecenas emphasised his role and convinced ordinary people that both triumvirs had contributed equally to the triumph, the soldiers knew what had really happened. And now he was in danger of falling behind his colleague on a political level too, an area in which he had always thought he was more capable. No, he could not lose now, otherwise he would become an unworthy heir to Caesar in the eyes of all.

But what could he do? Everyone was against him – not just Antony but also Sextus Pompey, and the Senate, who were exasperated by his land seizures, and even the soldiers, who had always been his strongest allies.

"All that's left for me to do is attack. That way I will make those who don't follow me ashamed, and perhaps those who remain faithful to me will finally unite," he said to Maecenas eventually, as though seeking his consent.

But the Etruscan opposed him firmly.

"That is madness! They'll end up trying to stop each other and fighting, and then you'll be defeated and that will make the situation hopeless!" he protested. "And you don't have enough troops to get over his fortifications! You don't have a hope in hell."

"I won't if I just wait for things to happen. Right now I'm too weak and if I show myself to be irresolute, even the soldiers will want my blood!"

"Trust Agrippa;" insisted Maecenas. "Hold on and wait for news of him. I'm sure that, as always, he will not disappoint you."

"I wish I could believe that, but time is running out and Turi and Cosenza are under siege too, as everyone knows… I'm losing everything without doing anything except standing here watching. Antony and Sextus Pompey are bleeding me, and the soldiers are deserting me."

"You have to rely on the fact that Antony's legions don't want to fight another civil war either. Hold on, I say!"

"I cannot. I am going to give the order to attack," he said, then tried to raise his arm to draw the attention of the tribunes.

But Maecenas stopped him. "No! Do you not see that the soldiers are still protesting? If they don't obey you – which is likely – you will be further discredited!" he hissed. "And anyway, Popilius Laenas knows what he's doing in there," he added, pointing to Brindisi. "He knows how to put up a fight, fear not."

Octavian gave him a withering look. He owed Maecenas so much, but he could not tolerate being opposed by him like that. Perhaps he had started to believe that he was the leader of the sect? Or the state, perhaps? He could barely contain his anger. At Philippi, he had not given his friend due credit, and had even reached the point of almost killing him with his sword. He forced himself to calm down, but he could not restrain himself from threatening him.

"So be it. We will do as you say. But if everything goes down the drain, you will pay the consequences," he snapped, with the fiercest glare that he could muster. Maecenas turned away and said nothing. It was clear, Octavian thought to himself, that his friend considered him ungrateful, but by now the young man considered his friends and close associates almost part of himself – extensions of his being which compensated for what he lacked himself:

one man with a multi-faceted personality and many talents. He felt entitled to treat them with the severity he treated himself. Only in this way could he achieve the great goals that he had set himself when he decided to accept the inheritance of Caesar.

Maecenas began to address the soldiers, standing on the platform and inviting them to return to their duties and let the commanders do their jobs. Because the commanders knew what they were doing, he said. Octavian wished that it were so, for in reality they were desperately groping in the dark. But Maecenas's efforts were interrupted by the arrival of a new messenger, who demanded Octavian's attention and shouted out to him, "Triumvir, your *legatus* Agrippa sent me. I come to tell you that he has freed Sipontum from the siege and has sent a contingent to liberate Turi!"

Octavian and Maecenas's eyes met, and a few moments later the soldiers were cheering and shouting Agrippa's praises and chanting the name of Caesar Octavian as word spread amongst them. At the same time, the war cries coming from Brindisi and the roar of the siege engines ceased.

Antony must have heard what had happened as well.

*

Maecenas realised that the atmosphere he breathed in the enemy camp must be the same as the one in their own. As he had hypothesised, the soldiers there too, had no desire to fight against the other triumvir, and if they held Brindisi in check by threatening to destroy the city walls it was only because they had sensed that a few warning shots from the catapults would encourage Octavian to negotiate.

The arrival of the Etruscan had been warmly welcomed by the legionaries, who knew him as the right hand man of Caesar's son and saw in his presence at their camp a sign of a willingness to negotiate. Never before, said Maecenas to himself, had soldiers been so instrumental in determining the destiny of the empire. Octavian had been forced to accept how much the other triumvir still enjoyed the prestige gained at Philippi. It was too early to hope to get rid of him, that was now clear, and the veneration the legionaries had for him – all the legionaries, on both sides – meant that he was still unassailable. It would take years to undermine his status and detach him from the army, but Maecenas had no doubt that a bon vivant like Antony – inconsistent Antony – would give them a hand by being careless and making mistakes the cult of Mars Ultor could take advantage of. The man did not have the unbridled determination and ambition of Octavian, nor the same motivation, and he would eventually lose.

But not now. For now he was too strong, Maecenas said to himself, as he listened to the exhortations of the soldiers to bring the two triumvirs to some agreement, and prepared to enter the praetorium of his enemy.

*

Perhaps it was not surprising that an emissary of Antony's presented himself at the gates of the camp, Octavian thought to himself, when it was announced that Lucius Pinarius wanted to talk to him. Still, it was incredible – no one would have expected such a sudden change of approach by the other triumvir simply because of Agrippa's victories. Evidently, the soldiers had exerted pressure on him too, just as the Etruscan had said.

Lucius Pinarius was a good man, and no doubt Antony had sent him because he had a good relationship with both of them and believed that Octavian would listen to him. But Octavian did not intend to be conciliatory. The situation, in everyone's eyes, had him at a disadvantage, and he did not want to reveal himself to be too eager to make a deal, but rather hoped to make it look like a concession on his part for the good of the state. He had learnt long ago that in politics, appearance was more important than substance. It was always necessary to give people the impression you were in control of the situation and able to resolve every problem – much more necessary than actually resolving them. There was always time to fulfil a promise and you might even convince people that it was not possible to meet their needs, there was always some obstacle that could be used as an excuse, but at all times they must feel confident that they are dealing with someone who knows what he is about. Woe to any who show insecurity and doubt, or bow their heads before their adversaries, even at the risk of appearing presumptuous. And it was this lesson, more than any other, that he had learnt from Caesar – the people much preferred the arrogant to the uncertain. In their eyes, the former were winners and the latter, losers.

"Triumvir," said Ortwin, rushing into his tent. "I must warn you that the arrival of Lucius Pinarius was accompanied by the advance of many of Antony's soldiers behind our fortifications."

"Are they attacking us?" he asked anxiously.

"For a moment we thought they were. But then we saw that they just wanted to reconcile. They're shouting to our men to persuade you to make peace, they are reproaching them for not joining Antony in Brindisi and in forcing him to fight, they are asking us to join them... that sort of thing. They do not seem dangerous."

"Keep an eye on them, though," he said. "Actually, I have an idea, send off a thousand of our men as well, as soon as they leave. They can go over to the enemy fortifications and reproach Antony's legions for besieging Brindisi and for being allied with that scoundrel Sextus Pompey. Give the order."

Ortwin nodded and left the tent and Octavian took the opportunity to reflect for a moment before Lucius Pinarius entered. The game had only just begun, and it would be played on different levels.

*

Antony received Maecenas with his elbows on the table and his head in his hands. The Etruscan had not seen him for a while, and found him much aged. All that revelry with Cleopatra couldn't have been doing him much good.

"Sit down, equestrian," said the triumvir when he became aware of his presence. "I'm glad to finally have the opportunity to talk to someone who knows what goes on in that twisted mind of Octavian's."

Maecenas sat on the bench, while Antony rose from his desk and went to lie down on the couch in front of him.

"I'm glad you agreed to see me, triumvir," he said. "We will finally have the opportunity to put an end to all the speculation that has arisen because of your lack of communication. I am sure that a healthy dialogue will put all to rights and the relationship between you both will return to being as fond and harmonious as it was immediately after Philippi."

"There has never been any fondness or harmony between me and that snake," Antony replied. "Yet I have tried to work with him for the good of the state. But that lad is never satisfied. He always wants more… Sometimes I have the feeling that by eliminating Brutus and Cassius at Philippi, I did more of a favour to him than I did to myself. Perhaps it would have been better to ally with them instead of becoming his servant, as he seems to expect I will. He wants me to enjoy the same fate as Lepidus, that is now clear."

All of Antony's complaints had some basis in fact. And in fact, he had unwittingly described the strategy that the sect had devised to bring Octavian to supreme power. But everything had to be denied, of course. "No, nothing like that, I assure you. You must admit that he faced great difficulties in Italy and that your taking a clear position would have been opportune, since you were dealing with your brother and your wife. But that didn't happen and this fuelled misunderstandings and suspicions…" was all he said.

"But I didn't know anything about it! How could I have when I was in Egypt and was always travelling in the eastern provinces? The messengers who were sent to me only found me when it was all over and I couldn't do anything to prevent what had happened. But I assure you, when I met Fulvia in Athens, I gave her a piece of my mind. In fact, I may have even gone a little too far..." he added, with a grimace of regret, or even pain.

Maecenas did not believe for even a moment that he had not known anything about what was happening in Italy. It was clear that he had only waited to see what would happen so that he could then act accordingly. Now that the revolt had failed, he could put it all behind him and say that he had always respected the triumviral pacts.

"Gone too far? If you really didn't agree with what they did in the Peninsula, I doubt that any reprimand could be considered going too far..."

"Well, as shortly after my reproach she was left to die along with her Manius, I would say that was more than enough of a punishment. You know, for a while I loved that woman," he said, visibly upset. "It was impossible not to let yourself become entangled in her webs..."

Maecenas barely held back a gasp of surprise. Fulvia was dead, then. Good – that was one less enemy for them to take revenge on. He couldn't help wondering, though, whether Antony had reproached her for having sparked a revolt or for not having been successful…

*

Octavian forced himself to receive Lucius Pinarius cordially. He had ample grievance against the man, but he must show everyone that his going over to Antony's side had somehow been agreed, and he couldn't mistreat his rival's envoy without putting himself in the wrong. It was probably for this reason that Pinarius had consented to act as mediator, knowing that he didn't risk becoming the victim of a vendetta.

"Dear Lucius," he greeted him, holding out his hand and inviting him to sit down, "I'm glad to see you, even if I'd rather have seen you in a less… *uncomfortable* situation."

"You're right, Caesar," replied Pinarius. "The situation has got out of hand for everyone. I am sure that neither you nor Antony wanted it to get to this point."

In reality, thought Octavian, he had done practically everything he felt was necessary to get to that point, and he was only unhappy about the way he'd had to do it."Yes, you're right, I'm sure," he said instead. "Unfortunately, physical distance created much confusion and caused an infinity of misunderstandings, of which our common enemies took advantage of to sow discord. With responsibilities as great as ours, though, we cannot afford to act lightly and we must take everything seriously. A civil war in Italy against his brother and his wife, without him giving any indication of interceding, you must admit creates many doubts about his intentions, and some suspicion on my part is legitimate…"

"Just as your commandeering eleven legions provoked some suspicion on the other side…" said Pinarius.

"I had to," replied Octavian. "With Pompey threatening Italy, it was pointless to leave them languishing in Gaul, where they could have ended up in the hands of anyone if I had not appropriated them on behalf of the triumvirate. Antony should have approved, instead of taking on so – at the end of the day, Pompey is our common enemy and I was assigned the thankless task of defending Italy against him, while Antony is off enjoying himself with the queen of Egypt."

"But it would have been appropriate of you to have asked his permission."

"There was no time. I would have done so, but here in Italy I have a lot of problems and he should understand that. In the East, there are not the same sort of problems that I face here. He should have written to me and not reacted immediately by resorting to an alliance with the man who is starving Italy and against whom I am at war."

"But you sought an alliance with Pompey by marrying the sister of Scribonius Libo," objected Lucius Pinarius, "isn't that so?"

"I had to look out for myself! I only did it when I heard that Antony had been in touch with him!"

"Being in touch doesn't mean making an alliance but only trying to reason with that pirate, since it seemed that you were unable to. And then, when he saw what you were doing, maybe it became something more… You see how ambiguous it all is?"

"Should I pretend to believe you? I can do, for the good of the state and because the soldiers have asked me to."

"Then that will mean that he too will pretend to believe that you took over the legions of Calenus for the triumvirate, isn't that so? Or those of Plancus, after the war of Perugia."

Octavian ignored that last sentence. "But he let himself be escorted by Domitius Ahenobarbus! That murderer! Yet we drew up the list of the Assassins of Julius Caesar together and it was Ahenobarbus, along with Staius Murcus, who hindered him when he sailed for Greece at the Battle of Philippi. How can I trust a man who can change sides so easily?"

"Ahenobarbus was not one of Caesar's murderers. You only put him on the list because he was a friend of Brutus's, as you did many others. It's about time you put aside these recriminations: I believe he doesn't get on well with Sextus Pompey, and sooner or later his skills could come in handy in for the triumvirate. If that really was the reason why Antony was prohibited from docking at Brindisi as an enemy, I would say that it's an easily surmountable excuse, right? If we cannot forgive Ahenobarbus, then we will end up being the enemies of everyone, sooner or later and for one reason or another."

"Ahenobarbus does not deserve forgiveness given his obstinacy in supporting these killers."

"But we cannot keep looking for war against anyone who is guilty of misconduct. The empire will suffer and we will all feel it. Don't you think that – given the naval superiority which Antony now possesses with his agreement with Pompey – he will be able to exert even more pressure on Italy, continuously attacking the undefended coasts and forcing you to surrender?"

It was true, unfortunately, Octavian acknowledged to himself.

"The fact remains that Antony cannot be trusted – he lets women twist him around their little fingers," he stated, sounding deliberately stubborn. "Cleopatra in the East, Fulvia here. Who can assure me that he will not let himself get carried away again by that woman's greed?"

Lucius Pinarius cleared his throat. "Don't you know? Fulvia is dead, neglected by Antony who had ignored her in Athens. I would say that the only thing to do now is for you both to express your mutual suspicions. Why don't you write to him? You're younger and you should make the first gesture towards an older man..."

Octavian breathed a sigh of relief upon hearing of the death of that pernicious woman. He knew that Maecenas, had he been present, would have strongly supported accepting the proposal. After all, he thought, he didn't have to adopt a conciliatory tone... However, there was one thing that he just couldn't ignore.

"I've been having this idea that the younger man must respect the older one repeated to me ever since I arrived in Rome, shortly after the Ides of March four years ago, to ask for the attention of the famous and powerful Antony. *You of all people should know that better than anyone*," he said. "A lot of water has passed under the bridge since then, and we are now on the same level."

Pinarius looked down, embarrassed at last. After a moment's hesitation, he said, his voice breaking, "Know that I have not betrayed you, Octavian. Only, I chose the empire. Not you, not the sect, and not even Antony, but the empire. I think I have more worth than you have ever acknowledged, and if these agreements are successful it will be proof that I can help even by being with Antony. At least as regards the part about your intentions to reform the empire, which exclude your personal ambitions. I will never be able to forget that you considered me capable of betraying you: I never have, and I never will. But I do not wish to work exclusively for you."

Octavian cursed himself for having misjudged Pinarius and wondered what he should do with his cousin in the future. He concluded that he would think about it – for the moment, he had more pressing problems to solve and more dangerous people who needed to be put out of action. As with Marcellus, there was always time later for revenge. He nodded, smiling, then put his hand on his shoulder. "Do not worry, Pinarius, I understand you, and I do not expect you to forgive me. I was wrong, and maybe I too would have acted like you. I just hope that our plans for the empire always coincide, my dear cousin."

*

"Your alliance with Sextus Pompey and Domitius Ahenobarbus is a source of great embarrassment to Caesar Octavian," Maecenas reminded Antony. "It looks as though you do not take avenging Julius Caesar seriously, although you solemnly swore before the senate to do this when you drew up the list of outlaws."

"What are you talking about?" Antony said. "I would do anything for the memory of Caesar and I amply demonstrated that at Philippi! Much more than Octavian, who is only able to send assassins to stab whoever killed him on the Ides of March in the back. I faced them in battle, openly, directly challenging them, and I've eliminated most of them. I have nothing left to prove in this matter now."

"However that may be, you are in the wrong now and you cannot deny it," insisted the Etruscan. "Octavian fought a war to apply the provisions for the veterans that you had agreed upon together. You did not help at all, whether you realised it or not, and now you have allied yourself with those you should be pursuing and fighting. Italy is struggling because of Sextus Pompey and by remaining with him against the defender of the Peninsula you will lose the support of the ordinary people and perhaps of the senators, who are as angry with you as they are with Octavian, both because of the absolute judiciary you have set up and for damaging their property and their clientele by the confiscations in favour of the veterans. So it is in your own interest to make an agreement with him."

To Maecenas, Antony looked tired, and the Etruscan was convinced that it would only need a convincing pretext to convince him to make peace. Something that would save his wounded pride. It was worth pushing for, he said to himself.

Antony shook his head and immediately confirmed his assumption.

"Problems, always problems… But why can't we just have a quiet life and work for the empire?" he groaned. "In the East there is much to do, don't you think? The Parthians have invaded Syria, and my legions have failed to repel their attacks. I will have to intervene, sooner or later, because Quintus Labienus, who is now one of the leaders of their armies, is carving out a private potentate within the Roman territories. Now that we have eliminated all the principal assassins of Julius Caesar, no one would hinder us if Octavian and I worked together to build a better empire. There is still Sextus Pompey, of course, who has raised discontent against the triumvirate, but at the end of the day he only wants to have his privileges reinstated. Once satisfied, I'm sure he will no longer have any interest in playing the champion of all those who believe they have been wronged by us."

"So you see that there *is* a mutual benefit in joining forces?" said Maecenas enthusiastically. "Otherwise you will only be playing the game of those who are trying to take the control of the empire away from you – those like Quintus Labienus and Sextus Pompey, and perhaps even Lepidus, who are just waiting for an opportunity to come between the two of you and thereby return to power."

Antony said nothing, but nodded gravely. It was time for the two to prepare to meet.

*

Ortwin and Veleda, along with their German soldiers, formed a semicircle behind their leader, who was sitting in front of Antony in a pavilion set up for the occasion in front of Brindisi. The other triumvir was in turn protected by a semicircle of guards, equivalent in number. It all made for an extremely crowded tent. The leather roof echoed the patter of the rain which had necessitated the hasty erection of the tent in which to hold the meeting both armies had been waiting for.

The two triumvirs had been facing each other for half an hour and it seemed that neither of them wanted to deal with the problems that had caused their differences. They spoke with mutual distrust and recrimination on their respective responsibilities, it seemed to Veleda, without actually resolving the issues that the mediators had worked so hard on over the last few days.

“Don’t tell me you weren’t off having a great time with Cleopatra, in the East,” protested Octavian. “Otherwise, how could the king of Parthia’s son and Quintus Labienus have penetrated Syria, defeated your Decidius Saxa’s legion and settled in the province? You know, at least, that Pacorus is still in the Asian provinces and is running about undisturbed in the South, while Labienus took possession of the West Bank and is continuing to expand his territory. At this rate, he will become more powerful than you and we will have to accept him as the third triumvir, because of your idleness…”

“If you keep on stealing legions from me, how do you expect me to stop my officers from being defeated? You demanded troops to fight Sextus Pompey before we discovered the threat posed by the Parthians and Labienus,” spluttered Antony. “I, too, should be able to enrol men in Italy.”

“Very well, if that is what is necessary to make the Eastern borders more stable,” agreed Octavian. “But that means that you must take charge of the war against the Parthians, with no excuses.”

“Just as you will have to take charge of the war against Pompey, if we cannot make an agreement with him. And I don’t see how you have the right to accuse me of having unstable borders,” said Antony, "when yours are no better, especially at this moment in time."

"If you would deign to order Pompey to return to Sicily rather than encouraging him, I would be able to stabilise the borders. And while we're at it, get rid of Ahenobarbus, if you really don't want to execute him – knowing that I could bump into him somewhere offends me."

"I've already thought about that. I'll send him to govern Bithynia, and as for Pompey, I will tell him that there is no need to continue to attack the coasts and that we will try to meet his demands."

"That's fine by me. But now we need to clarify once and for all who governs what," said Octavian. "The division established along the Adriatic does not sit well with me. I let Africa go to Lepidus, and I cannot take it away now without giving the impression that the triumvirate has become a diarchy, and so I have less territory than you, especially considering that you reserve the right to enlist troops in Italy."

Antony pulled the map that was on the table towards him, upon which he had drawn a demarcation line that divided the empire into two almost equal halves, running along the coasts of the Ionian and Adriatic seas and bisecting Illyria. "But you have Gaul, now, too. And all the legions that you have stolen from me," he protested, "I think it's a more than adequate compensation. You see? Scodra is right in the middle of the Adriatic Gulf, and that seems to me to be the ideal boundary. What are you complaining about? Everything to the west of the ocean is yours and what's on the east towards the Euphrates, is mine. You should also consider that you have all the provinces and possibilities of expansion in Germany whilst I am blocked by the Parthian empire, and many of my territories are not actually provinces but semi autonomous satellite kingdoms, such as Egypt."

"But they are rich kingdoms, from which you claim tax without restraint. I have provinces which have been bled dry by civil wars and Pompey's raids! You are practically a monarch, over there, while I'm just a consul, here!"

"Rubbish! You're just trying to twist everything to your own ends, and you know it," said Antony. "Once the matter of Sextus Pompey is resolved, one way or another, you will be the absolute master of the West. That pirate is a problem that will be resolved, sooner or later, while the Parthians can only be held off and will always be a thorn in our side. At least until I set off on the campaign to recover the insignia lost at Carre by Crassus that Caesar was about to undertake. I want to do it to seal my reputation as a leader, and I need peace in the West. You must guarantee me this, Octavian – you're the only one who has the authority to do so, and I have to be able to count on you, no matter what. Do not make me regret it. I'm going to entrust to Ventidius Bassus the task of driving Pacorus beyond the boundaries and of teaching Labienus a lesson. Not to mention the murderers of Julius Caesar who are still wandering undisturbed around the East. And once the frontiers have been secured, I will counter attack and I will need troops, a lot of troops, and I will only have them if the two of us agree – otherwise I will be forced to reduce the area that I can control. And remember that my victory over the Parthians would also be *your* victory."

"In the same way that the consolidation of the borders in the West, over the Alps, Spain and the Rhine would be a victory for you. The triumvirate should appear to the Romans as a single entity," specified Octavian.

Antony nodded. "Exactly. We must work together, it is in our common interest as well as in that of Rome. Come," he said, "if we can reach an agreement, I will reveal a secret that could be very useful to you..."

It seemed to Veleda that Antony wanted peace more than Octavian did. On the other hand, she already knew enough about her commander to know that he would never stop until he was the absolute master of the empire, just like Caesar. But those continual references to Labienus had brought to mind the suffering that despicable individual had caused her. He still appeared in her nightmares, standing between her and the man she had chosen in his place, and suddenly she decided that she and Ortwin had to do away with him once and for all if they really wanted to leave the past behind. As long as Labienus was still alive and able to harm them and the sect, she would never really know just how much she loved her man. She decided to seek an opportunity to propose her idea favourably to Octavian. She knew she had to wait until the meeting was over, but she was driven by an uncontrollable impulse to act. After a few moments, she took advantage of a moment of silence between the two rivals and approached the triumvir. Ignoring Ortwin's bewilderment at her breaking protocol and Octavian's angry expression when she took him by the arm and asked him for permission to talk to him for a moment, the woman waited with determination for the young man to answer her.

Octavian let out a sigh, but not so loud as to give the impression of not being in complete control of his bodyguards. Veleda took a deep breath and whispered quickly, "Triumvir, forgive me for this interruption, but in the past Ortwin and I have shown you that we are able to act just as well as assassins in the East as we are in the West. Why not send us to stop Labienus, in order to be sure that all of us wreak vengeance? There are many more of Julius Caesar's assassins out there than there are here. We would get rid of others who are more than likely with him. You can always tell Mark Antony that we will be your liaison officers with him, joining the general staff of Ventidius Bassus. You are in a position to demand that, are you not?"

Octavian gave her an intense look and slowly the fire in his eyes dimmed, giving way to the depths of reflection. He said nothing, he merely nodded for her to return to her place, where she was glared at by Ortwin. However, her suggestion was the first thing Octavian mentioned when he spoke to Antony again, and he did not object. Ortwin looked at her with surprise and admiration, and her chest swelled with pride.

"I think we have gone over everything," said Antony at the end of the conversation, which had gradually become more convivial in tone. He rose to offer his hand to Octavian, who took it after a moment's hesitation.

"We can go and make the announcement to the troops, then, and inform them of the new constraints established by the mediators," said Octavian, also rising to his feet. Now, as Veleda knew only too well, it was all just theatre. The guards emerged from the tent, forming two rows and a corridor for the triumvirs, who walked down it until the end and stopped a little way beyond. Before them, a crowd of soldiers, soaked from the rain, waited anxiously to hear what had been decided, ready to pay homage to them in the event of an agreement, and voice their displeasure if not.

There was a tense silence, Antony embraced Octavian and then they raised their arms in the air, and immediately there was such a cry that it frustrated all his attempts to make the announcement. He had to wait until the legions had grown hoarse before he could begin. It was up to him, as the senior of the two, to address the troops.

"Legionaries!" he shouted. "Rome is again united under the command of the men who saved it from the decline of the civil wars! The triumvirate is more powerful and cohesive than ever, and I guarantee that now, once again, your objective will be to fight Rome's external enemies as well as whoever threatens peace! Mark Antony and Caesar Octavian have resolved their misunderstandings, which other men and women, driven by their own lust for power, have used for their own ends, and now we will work together for the glory of Rome! From now on, Caesar and I will no longer be only allies, but also brothers. You must know that in order to consolidate our relationship, I will happily end my widowhood by marrying the sister of my distinguished colleague, who is also widowed: the sweet, beautiful and exemplary Octavia, who I am proud to take as my wife!"

The ovation that followed was even louder than the previous one. While the two triumvirs saluted the crowd, Octavian asked Antony, "What was the secret you wanted to tell me?"

The other smiled and invited him back into the tent, and Veleda, Ortwin and the other guards followed them. Once inside, Antony put his arm around Octavian's shoulders and said, "You have bred a serpent in your bosom, my dear brother-in-law. Things with Calenus did not go as you were told they did. I believe that he was murdered by Rufus, and that the proofs of his agreements with Pompey were the invention of your friend. And Pompey has confirmed to me that he has never had anything to do with the legions in Gaul."

Octavian stiffened. "Are you accusing me of…"

Antony leaned back and shook his head.

"No, no – you would never be so stupid. Probably all you said to Rufus was to bribe him and anyway, I have proof that you were not involved."

Octavian waited.

"Rufus has written to me putting himself at my disposal. He wants to join me, and even declares himself willing to do me the favour of killing you, if necessary." He immediately pulled out an envelope from under his toga, which he gave to him. "This is the letter that he sent to me, if you do not believe me. You will recognise his handwriting, I expect," he said, while Octavian hastened to read it, looking more and more bewildered as he read the flowing lines.

After a moment of stunned silence, Octavian asked, "Why… did you not take advantage of his offer? To kill me, I mean…"

"I told you. I have concluded that you are the only one who can watch my back while I conquer with glory that which Caesar coveted. Without you, I could never leave Rome to these hordes of hungry predators. They are almost all like Rufus, don't you think?"

"But why did you not take him with you? Like Pinarius?"

"I trust Pinarius," Antony said. "He's a good man, who immediately told me that he would never do anything to harm you or your family. I don't trust Rufus. Pinarius himself told me that he is a creature without scruples. I am sure he would stab me in the back as soon as I gave him the opportunity to do so, just as he has stabbed you in the back. He is trying to climb over both of us. The man only looks after himself, and I would always have to watch my back with him at my side."

Octavian was appalled. "And… and now? What do I do?"

Antony smiled, then patted him on the shoulder. "That I will let you decide," he said. "I have given you the information. Use it as you see fit."

XI

Octavia couldn't believe it was actually happening. She had given birth just a few days earlier and was only barely able to stand when she had been catapulted into the middle of a ceremony in which she was the protagonist. Or she and Mark Antony, to be precise. The man whom her brother had in the past poured rivers of scorn upon until she too had begun to hate him for all the obstacles he had put in Octavian's way on his rise to power. For the last two months, however, he had done nothing but tell her how flattering it would be to be the wife of the greatest leader that Rome had ever known – after Julius Caesar of course – and what a famous lover he was. He eulogised Antony's eternal youth, his generosity, his political acumen, the valuable contribution he made to the cause of the Mars Ultor sect and his personal ascent, his wise dissociation from the exploits of Fulvia… until almost without realising it, Octavia found herself engaged to Antony with the wedding date already fixed and all of Rome gossiping about the wedding of the century.

She was well aware that Octavian did not really think all the things he was saying to her and she knew her brother well enough to know that he had in no way changed his mind about Antony, whom he still considered the main obstacle standing in the way of his own greatness. An obstacle to be removed sooner or later – and what would happen to her then? It annoyed her to find that her brother still continued to use her as a political pawn, keeping her unaware of his true intentions and telling her tales just as he did with any other stranger, even forcing her to have two children with a husband she hated before killing him before her very eyes without even bothering to warn her beforehand. She realised now, more than ever, that she was barely taken into consideration by the other members of the sect and that her brother had only allowed her to join so that he could use her, and actually lacked any esteem for her. The words that Octavian kept repeating to her were completely empty. He reminded her how valuable her contribution to the campaign of Philippi had been, saving them by sending Chaerea over with vital information. In reality, however, he considered her so dispensable that he had decided to dispose of her to his real, ultimate enemy.

She looked around again, hardly able to take in what was going on. It seemed to her that she was wrapped in a thick fog, from which familiar faces occasionally appeared. Everyone was there, including Octavian. Her stepfather Marcius Philippus, Maecenas, Agrippa, even Salvidienus Rufus had returned from Spain for the occasion, many senators and equestrians, many of their clientele, and all of Rome cheering her name and that of Antony with hymns of joy that echoed along the slopes of the Palatine. Every now and then some outcry of protest arose about the famine caused by Sextus Pompey's blockade, the protests had become more vehement recently and there was more and more anger with Octavian for refusing to ratify the agreement Antony had proposed with the outlaws.

But everyone and everything seemed blurred, as though Octavia was dreaming about them. The walls of her house swayed, the voices of those present were subdued and muffled, distant just like those of the people who thronged the streets outside her home. The only tangible things were the tears that streamed down her cheeks, fortunately hidden by the orange *flammeum* veil covering her face. She could still smell the roasted sheep, whose sacrifice opened the ceremony. She saw the huge silhouette of Mark Antony approaching her, with whom she'd had no opportunity to speak in the previous days. In fact, she had only received a congratulatory message when little Marcella Minor, her second daughter, was born.

For a moment, it seemed that the profile was that of Gaius Chaerea, made whole again and able to walk, finally free from his constraints and so risen in rank for his merits that he could take a patrician in marriage. The fantasies of a frustrated and unhappy little woman, Octavia immediately told herself, driving away her ghosts and focusing on Antony's radiant smile. He grasped her hands firmly and approached the table where the marriage contracts – the *tabulae nuptialis* – lay. She saw him put his signature on the document and a voice asked her to do the same. She realised that those papers were not only a contract of marriage but also a contract of political alliance, the most important between Romans for a long time. Her head weighed more than ever. She wanted to get rid of the elaborate bridal hairstyle her slaves had prepared for her, with her locks divided into six braids wrapped in wool and gathered on top of her head.

She thought she saw the ten witnesses required by law parade before the *tabulae*, but she was unable to recognise them all. Some were probably acquaintances and associates of her new husband. The *pronuba* took her hand for the fateful moment and she felt a mixture of conflicting feelings mount inside her: fear, anger, bitterness, loneliness. Antony was perhaps whispering reassuring words, but she barely understood any of what he said. Then she heard herself being urged to utter the ritual verse and the rising tide of emotion grew even more overwhelming. She tried to speak but nothing came out. She felt Antony's caresses again, and he seemed to have the same icy gaze as Octavian and she became afraid of disappointing him. She heard, from far away, her own trembling voice saying: "*Ubi ti Gaius, ego Gaia.*" Then, when the *pronuba* brought her right hand to join it with that of Antony, she learned that she was married again. Another marriage destined to create unhappiness.

She felt her husband embracing her, and he lifted her veil. She felt herself being kissed and could not help but notice that her new husband smelt good and that being touched by him did not seem as bad as she had thought it would be. Then Antony made room for all those who wanted to congratulate the bride, an endless line of people, relatives, acquaintances, people of rank and *clientes* who, in the end, must all have rubbed the *galbeata* toga, the yellow cloak she was wearing, and even the *recta* tunic, the ritual white petticoat worn for the occasion.

Octavian came to her last of all, as everyone else was entering the triclinium for the wedding feast. He took her aside, held her hand and said, "I'm proud of you, sister. You are a valuable asset to the sect. Now more than ever. You can imagine what I expect from you from now on. I doubt that your husband will share his most hidden intentions with you, but in any case it is up to you to refer to me by letter, wherever you go, all your impressions on his movements. Try to steal every plan you have the opportunity to and communicate it to me. Probe his intentions discreetly, without ever seeming more than a devoted and affectionate wife – indeed, one who is in love. Get him to trust you in every way possible until he consider you as much a companion as a wife. And remember that before being his wife you are my sister and a member of the sect of Mars Ultor. The god is watching you, always. It is to us you must dedicate yourself before him, is that clear?" What could she say? His voice was mellifluous, but his attitude peremptory. She nodded.

"Another thing," Octavian continued. "Always remember that Antony is sensitive to the graces of women. Very sensitive. So make sure that he doesn't start missing Cleopatra and all the whores he spends so much time enjoying himself with. Make sure that he does not get tired of you. If necessary, engage a prostitute and learn a few tricks, if you see that he is not enjoying himself in bed with you. We do not want him to abandon you and return to the Egyptian or his revels before he has served us, do we? Keep in mind what we want, and keep him as occupied as Cleopatra did, distracting him so that he neglects his duties and, especially, our activities, and leaves us in peace to make our plans without getting in our way."

Octavia nodded again, feeling exhausted.

A whore. Her brother wanted her to become a whore.

*

Popilius Laenas, who had been promoted to tribune just three months earlier, found it hard to contain his euphoria. Octavian had just explained what he expected of him and he was flattered. But not only that, he now saw before him an open road that could lead to him becoming one of the most important men in Rome, now that Caesar's heir had restricted the number of people he could count on. The fact that he had convened with him before any other member of the sect was clear testimony to the confidence he had in him – and he the most recently consecrated member of the sect of Mars Ultor.

Octavian also told him to call the others. Laenas stepped out of the *tablinium* and waved to Maecenas, Agrippa, Rufus, Ortwin, Veleda and Octavia, fresh from her wedding night with Antony, to come over. He wondered how she was faring with the triumvir, although he doubted that, given her recent confinement, she'd been able to enjoy herself much, and he pitied Antony. But then, he said to himself, Antony would certainly know who to enjoy himself with in the meantime.

They entered one at a time, silently. The atmosphere was tense and heavy. Everyone knew what the topic on the agenda would be, more or less, except for the individual concerned and, perhaps

Octavia, and several of them were pained by it. But not Laenas. In fact, he was relishing the opportunity to be in the limelight again. They sat in a semicircle on chairs placed in front of Octavian's desk, and Octavian, after waiting for them all to take their places,said, "Well, friends, it's been a long time since the sect last met. Once, these meetings were more frequent, but now we have grown and each of us has clearly defined roles in the institutions which have not allowed us to meet often. Today, for example, we salute our precious fellow members Ortwin and Veleda, who are preparing to leave tomorrow for the East, where they will join Ventidius Bassus's army against the Parthian invasion and eliminate once and for all the threat of Quintus Labienus, who, as you know, killed my cousin Quintus Pedius and my mother, in addition to seriously injuring Ortwin himself at Philippi, and who has caused us so much trouble. I think I can say that he is one of the most dangerous of Julius Caesar's murderers, so I really hope that the sacrifice of my two precious friends and bodyguards will be rewarded by the elimination of that accursed man."

He paused for a moment, and Rufus jumped in. "Well said, Caesar," he commented. "We all have institutional roles that keep us busy with our commitments, so I hope you did not call me here to Rome just to say goodbye to Ortwin and Veleda. As you know, the Lusitanians are causing problems in the Spanish provinces, and the Gallic legions need my presence. You will understand that I need to return as soon as possible."

Octavian grimaced. "I understand, of course, Rufus, and fear not, I did not ask you come all the way here just to make you say goodbye to our two friends, but for another reason – a much more serious reason," he said, and then he fell silent.

Rufus looked at him quizzically, expecting him to continue, while the others simply waited in anticipation.

"Well?" Rufus asked. Octavian took from the table a letter, which he handed to Rufus. "In fact, I called you here to show you this."

Intrigued, Rufus stood up and took the document, which he immediately began to read. A moment later, his face went white and he dropped into his chair. "Who… who gave it to you?" he murmured.

"Antony. Who else? It was meant for him, wasn't it?" asked Octavian, his tone of voice suddenly changing and becoming inquisitorial and hard.

"It's not true. It's not true… none of it," protested Rufus. "It's one of Antony's plots to set us against each other. You'll see, he will do the same thing next with Agrippa or Maecenas…"

"Rufus, you have disappointed me greatly," said the head of the sect.

"Be careful what you do! Once before you misjudged Maecenas, and Pinarius too! And now it's my turn, I see…" Rufus was returning to his normal self and seemed determined to deny everything.

"Antony could have no way of knowing your handwriting so well as to be able to duplicate it. This was written by your hand."

"He must have found a way to retrieve a document written by me…"

"I've given you all my trust over the years. I made you my right-hand man, I made you proconsul and next year you would have been consul… Why? What could Antony have given you that I haven't?" Octavian asked him. "But instead, you took advantage of your power to plot against me and to do exactly what you wanted. Do you think that I do not know you killed Calenus? Nevertheless, I would have forgiven you if Antony had not presented me with the evidence of your treachery…"

"You really don't want to believe me, do you?" whined Rufus. "You are willing to believe everything they say about me while you'd probably give no credit to somebody saying the same things about Agrippa…"

Octavian did not answer. The others had concentrated their gazes on the accused: Ortwin and

Veleda both wore contemptuous expressions on their faces, Agrippa looked disappointed, Maecenas looked on in disapproval and Octavia simply stared in resigned disbelief. The triumvir, however, had no expression on his face – he just nodded to Laenas, who knew he had to act now.

"So all I can do now is to go to Antony, since you do not want me any more," said Rufus looking deeply offended. "Just as Pinarius did. I see that you are back on good terms with him and maybe in the future it will be like that again for us. But for the moment, of course, I'm outraged and I do not want to have any more to do with you for now. I do not want to leave, but you are forcing me to with your absurd accusations. Too bad for you. I…"

He did not have time to finish the sentence. Laenas had rapidly moved behind him, pulled a dagger from under his gown and stabbed him just below the sternum, as instructed by Octavian. It was meant to be a crippling blow, but not a fatal one.

Rufus slumped in his chair, grasping the tribune's arm, while he pulled out the dagger and released a gush of blood. Laenas pulled himself free, and Rufus fell to the floor, rolling around in his own blood. Gasping, he dragged himself almost to Octavian's feet. Laenas, meanwhile, still following his instructions, handed the bloody dagger to Ortwin, telling him: "Now it's your turn. But let him live. And the rest of you must do the same."

The German did not show any emotion. He took the dagger, stood up, towering over the agonised man, and aimed a blow at his collarbone, from whence yet more blood gushed out. Rufus moaned while Ortwin passed the weapon to Veleda. The woman didn't hesitate for a moment, and plunged the dagger into his thigh, just under his groin. The victim groaned again and the dagger passed into the hands of Octavia who initially pushed it away in horror. "Do it, sister," said Octavian, icily, and then, trembling, she took the weapon, approached Rufus, leant over him and nicked the skin on his forearm. "Do it, I said!" commanded her brother, raising his voice. Weeping, the woman aimed a more powerful blow in the same place, then closed her eyes and stabbed again, and again, crying out desperately. Veleda took the dagger from her, handing it to Maecenas while she tried to console the woman, who was visibly upset. The Etruscan seemed to hesitate too, then he gathered up his strength and determination and plunged the dagger into Rufus's hip, cutting his skin without going too deeply into the flesh.

It was now Agrippa's turn. He took the dagger and looked at his friend for a long moment – Rufus, even in that situation, found the strength to give him a look of hate as he clutched at his deepest wounds. Agrippa shook his head and then plunged the dagger into his collarbone, which was still intact. Rufus's body was completely covered in blood by the time the dagger reached Octavian. The young triumvir rose from the table and stood staring at the traitor for a long time, while the bloodied form on the floor reached out to him.

Suddenly, Octavian gripped the handle of the weapon tighter. "You are not even worthy of sharing the same fate as Caesar..." he whispered, and stabbed him in the throat. "Throw him into the street tonight. We will say that he was attacked by some bandit," he said, thus declaring the meeting at an end.

*

"There's revolt in the air, triumvir," said Popilius Laenas as he greeted Octavian at the Senate. "It would be a good idea to avoid the Forum – people are ripping down the texts of the edict you've just released from the walls. A lot of people have gathered and there are protests."

Caesar's heir looked at the senators with him, and one of them did not hesitate to say, "Do you see that we are not the only ones protesting? Did you think that you would only affect us, the rich, by imposing taxes on the owners of slaves and estates? Have you any idea how many ordinary people possess slaves and homes?"

Octavian made an irritated gesture. "And how exactly do you think I should fund the war against Sextus Pompey?" he answered. "Should I have made new proscriptions to procure money?"

"Then seek peace instead of war. As the illustrious Antony has repeatedly suggested. You cannot further harass people who are already starving from Pompey's blockade after having already subjected them to confiscations in favour of the veterans and, before that, with taxes for the civil war against the assassins of Julius Caesar and the proscriptions. All you have done since you took power is suck money from our purses!"

If they had been alone, Octavian would have forced those words back down his throat, and maybe he would have disappeared just like Rufus. But they were surrounded by too many others and so he could not behave like a tyrant, crushing the man the way he deserved. His popularity was at its lowest ebb and he needed the support of the senators – or at least some of them.

"My dear friend," he said finally, "I cannot make peace with Pompey, who took Sardinia from us after I returned to Rome. If he was going to enter into any agreement, he would have shown himself to be more accommodating when he saw the consolidation of the triumvirate."

"But you haven't even tried to talk to him!" protested another senator, who had evidently drawn courage from the determination of his colleague. "Do you realise that people are starving and that trade is at a complete standstill? The Eastern merchants no longer take to the sea to come to Italy because they know they might be attacked by Pompey's pirates in Sicily, and those of the West are just as unwilling for fear of being attacked in Sardinia and Corsica! Meanwhile no grain has arrived in Rome for months! What little remains sells for its weight in gold!"

"Yes, because you landowners, who have your own reserves of grain, are exploiting the situation for your own financial benefit!" an annoyed Octavian retorted. But he immediately repented. He must not show any weakness in this type of situation – he already seemed practically helpless in the face of events, and that damned pirate was really making him look foolish, because now responsibility for the grain supply fell to him, as head of the West and of Italy and Rome. Antony was free to play an easy game by simply doing nothing or by continuing to suggest seeking a peace which in reality was impossible to achieve. And now, all regretted the fact that it was not the other triumvir who was leading Rome.

"Even assuming that were true, what would you have us do?" the second senator asked him. "Would you have us distribute what little grain we still have among the population? And in any case, this would only delay the problem. It is you who are afraid of Pompey and all you do is make excuses for not standing up to him!" The other senators looked uncomfortable. No doubt they shared the views of those who had spoken, but lacked the courage to express them out loud.

Octavian memorised the names of the two troublemakers and made a mental note to pay them back when the waters had subsided. "I am not afraid of anything. If I have managed to get to where I am in just four years, it means that I will stop at nothing, and now I will go to the Forum myself to quell the riots. You will see that when I speak to them in person, the people will calm down," he said almost instinctively, annoyed by the accusations of cowardice that were particularly hurtful because they were so close to the truth. He immediately regretted his impulsive reaction, but now it was too late to turn back. Laenas looked at him incredulously.

"But… are you sure, Triumvir?" he murmured. "I mean… you have only the sergeants and an escort of twenty men with you… It seems unwise."

"I am absolutely sure," he replied firmly. "The people trust me, and I run no risk in my own city. In fact, I am so certain of that fact that we will take along with us these two friends of ours." He looked with pleasure at the terrified expressions on the faces of the two senators who had dared to challenge him. The two men could not escape and followed him with bowed heads when he set off, ordering his bodyguard to surround them and the lictors to precede him.

He did not know what he would actually do or say once he was there among the people. In the Senate, he had used the force of his constitutional position to face down the widespread discontent over the recent edict, at the same time reassuring the conscript's fathers that the war would soon begin. But he realised that the senators were afraid of him, especially now that Antony seemed to be supporting him, while the people were not. The common people were starving and believed they had nothing more to lose. It seemed such a long time ago that they had welcomed the young heir of Caesar as the champion of the oppressed against the privileges of the aristocracy. He desperately wanted to return to being their champion, the man who would make them proud to be Roman citizens, but first it was necessary for them to go through a long series of hardships to enable him to act freely, without obstacles or enemies, in their interests. But he couldn't delude them with promises like that. Not after what he had continuously subjected them to over the last two years. He would have to use the fact that he too was a victim of the situation.

When he arrived at the Forum his men forced the crowd to make way so that he could reach the tribune of the Rostra. He took the stage, visibly distressed by the looks of hatred he encountered, the insults he heard shouted at him and the cries urging him to make an agreement with Pompey. He raised his hands in an attempt to silence at least those nearby, while the guards stood around the grandstand. With him there were the senators, who were now looking absolutely terrified. "Let's get out while we can! It was madness to come here!" exclaimed one of them anxiously as he gazed down at the angry faces below.

"That is no longer possible. We cannot leave now with our tails between our legs," said Octavian, trying to display courage he didn't have. Meanwhile, the noise showed no sign of abating. There were even women holding up their small, malnourished children, heedless of the crowd that might crush them at any moment.

Octavian tried to open his mouth to begin his speech in the hope that the people would be curious and quieten down so as to hear him, but a stone hit him on the shoulder, causing him to falter. The lictors hastened to close ranks around him just in time to prevent various kinds of other projectiles hitting him, but they began to rain down on the Forum and the unfortunate senators. The guards below thrust their spears forward, injuring some of the more excited people in the crowd, but the people grew even more exasperated, and they seemed to be edging nearer and nearer to him.

"Enough wars for your interests at the expense of the poor people!"

"You don't give a damn about us! All you care about is glory, you swine!"

"You're nothing like Caesar! You're just an opportunist, Octavian!"

"We've been hungry for years! What more do you want? Our blood and the blood of our children?"

"You lot have plundered the provinces and Italy just so you could fight one another!"

Octavian trembled. Yes, everything had changed since he had first made his appearance, convinced that he could follow in the footsteps of Caesar and put an end to all this injustice.

Now it was he who was perpetrating the injustices. Now he was the tyrant, he thought, as he watched as some of his guards were overwhelmed by the fury of the masses.

Within moments they would be on him. Popilius Laenas thought that slitting the throats of a couple of them would induce the others to retreat or perhaps even to run away. He drew his sword and struck out, but a stone hit his helmet, leaving him momentarily dazed and a man in the crowd took the opportunity to attack him, slamming him against the Rostra. Behind him, others advanced, but two soldiers blocked them with their lances. Meanwhile, Laenas had recovered and backhanded his aggressor, pushing him backwards, and then brought his sword down on the man's head, splitting it in two. He saw the people around him shrink back in horror, some covered in the brains of his victim, and enjoyed the terror he had sown. But it lasted only a moment. The crowd's reaction was not long in coming, and the boldest threw themselves upon him and the soldiers, regardless of the lances pointed at them, dragging the mob behind them. In an instant, a surging human tide swept over the guards, who ended up pressed flat against the Rostra.

Laenas felt as if he was on the battlefield. He began hacking away blindly, but didn't have enough space to accomplish much. His career was over and Octavian was practically dead, he said to himself desperately.

"Antony! Mark Antony is here!" he heard several voices suddenly cry out, and instantly the pressure on the soldiers eased.

"Let's ask him to make peace!" shouted the people. "That's what he wants! He wants us to eat!"

"He has soldiers! Loads of soldiers! Let's get out of here!" shouted others who were closer to the Via Sacra, from whence the triumvir seemed to be arriving.

"No! Let's talk! You can reason with him!"

Laenas could not see Antony – the crowd around him was still too dense. He tried to pull himself up onto the Rostra to reach the grandstand. He scratched his hands and tore open his thigh, but he ended up in mid-air, unable to climb over the railing. He saw a man who had managed to get over it about to pounce on Octavian. He drew back his arm and threw his sword, which struck the man in the chest. The man collapsed at the foot of the triumvir, who looked at his subordinate with gratitude. Laenas finally managed to get onto the platform and squeezed himself in next to Octavian, while the pressure on his men seemed to be ease as the crowd's attention turned to Antony.

The tribune could see the triumvir in the middle of the Via Sacra trying to calm the people pushing against the line of legionaries surrounding him. He appeared to be talking to some of the citizens, and initially the situation seemed amicable, but suddenly stones began to rain down in his direction too. Antony's attitude changed instantly – he gave the soldiers an order and his legionaries formed a phalanx with tight shields and spears at the ready and then charged the demonstrators. The civilians under attack tried to retreat down the slope of the Via Sacra, but many fell to the ground and were trampled upon, first by their fellow protestors, then by the soldiers who continued to advance.

In seconds, a human tide began to flow between the buildings, seeking escape through the alleys, but Laenas saw that the people trying to escape were now faced with a new wall. Two squads of legionaries had just arrived, taken positions along the sides of the Forum and were advancing towards the Rostra. Many of the citizens did not know where to go and so remained in the area between the Rostra and the Via Sacra, continuing to protest. The soldiers could not advance further without charging again. And when the order came from Antony and Octavian, they did not hesitate to do so, cutting down anyone who got in their way and leaving few routes of escape for the tightly wedged in crowd, shoving and trampling each other in their efforts to escape.

Laenas breathed a sigh of relief. Now he wanted his share of revenge on those animals who tried to lynch him. He left the grandstand and gathered the guards together, placed himself at the head of the small column and began to clear a path to allow the army to spread out and surround the rostra. He abandoned himself to an orgy of blood that sent waves of pleasure washing over him, until he saw nothing but severed heads and limbs, viscera flying through the air, crimson fountains and faces distorted with pain. He stopped only when he could find no more bodies to cut into, and actually took a few steps forward in search of more. But by now they had all disappeared. He returned to Octavian just as Antony joined him.

"It seems that I owe you my life," were the first words Octavian said to the other triumvir. He did not seem too happy about having to admit it.

"I told you. As long as you behave yourself, as long as we are brothers-in-law, and as long as you prove yourself capable, you are very precious to me," replied Antony. "It is handy having the legions just outside the walls of the City. We should think about a law regarding this. But you must make a decision about Sextus Pompey, you cannot go on like this. The citizens are right – you must go to war or make peace..."

"We'll see," said Octavian. "Now, though, we have a more pressing problem that needs to be resolved. Look around you."

Antony did so, as did Laenas, and what he saw amazed even the tribune, who had seen dozens of battlefields. The Forum was covered with corpses, drowned in a lake of blood, dismembered, stacked one upon the other, crushed. There were bodies of women and even children and the fact that none of them had any military equipment, armour or weapons threw an even more sinister light on the scene, enough to shake even a seasoned roughneck like Laenas. He had not realised what he was doing, he had just advanced, mowing down anyone who came within range.

"By the gods..." murmured Antony, who was visibly shocked. "It's a massacre."

"This will not make a good impression upon the Romans who were not here today. Nor upon those who were," said Octavian, who was the first to recover from the shock of that awful sight.

"What do you mean?"

"We must get rid of them right away. We will order the soldiers to throw them into the Tiber immediately. Tomorrow morning there must be no trace of even a drop of blood here and in the future we must deny that this was anything other than the work of a few fanatics."

Antony nodded. "You see? That's why I need you. You're practical, more than I could ever be. Get it done, then."

Octavian ordered Laenas to begin clearing away the piles of bodies, Antony did the same with his men and before long hundreds of legionaries were busy dragging or carrying what was left of the Roman citizens who had dared to protest against the triumvirate to the river. For days afterwards the

Tiber would regurgitate their bodies, but the important thing was that they didn't all appear at the same time.

While directing a group of soldiers, Laenas noticed one of them peering under the toga of one of the dead, pulling out a purse and emptying its contents into the palm of his hand. There was gold.

The man realised that his superior had seen him. "Tribune… I don't know what came over me…" he stuttered, in an attempt to justify himself.

"You are a despicable individual, soldier. That money will go to the women who were widowed today. I'll take care of the matter personally," said Laenas peremptorily, holding out his hand. "Give me that."

The mortified man put the gold back in the purse and handed it to him, then picked up the body and moved towards the river. Laenas looked around and saw that almost all the legionaries were too far away to be able to see an officer rummaging among the clothing of the dead. There was nothing wrong with it, he said to himself, and knelt down next to another corpse, looking for loot.

After all, he had done it often enough on the battlefield.

XII

"I find all this humiliating," said Octavian to Antony as he tried to keep his balance on the walkway that had been built across the water.

"A fact you've been reminding me of ever since we arranged this meeting," snorted Antony. "And now we are here. You see? He's coming down from that monstrous ship of his."

But Octavian kept complaining. Trying to keep his precarious balance on those improvised catwalks did little to improve his mood, nor his uncertain health. "Showing off his hexaremes yesterday wasn't enough for him – no, now he has to rub my face in it as though he were the master of the world, one who deigns to confer with his subordinates! Well in any case," he continued, "I'm certain we'll resolve nothing, not with someone like him..."

"But we must. You don't have the means to go to war with him and he will not want to lose the favour of the plebeians. I would say that this is one of the rare occasions in the history of Rome in which the populace has forced the powerful to make a decision that they themselves had no desire to take," Antony reminded him, and Octavian nodded bitterly as he stared at the rival who had made him a hostage of the common people, who had brought him to the point of exasperation. Octavian hated him, and he hated his own people too, because now it was he that they hated, and not that damn pirate who had starved them for months on end. Sextus Pompey was climbing onto the outside walkway of the port of Dicearchia, near Capo Misenum, and was about to reach the point where the two triumvirs had stopped on the inner wharf.

It was a peculiar, inconvenient meeting place, thought Octavian, but then they had no choice. Pompey did not trust them and refused to go ashore and the triumvirs had no wish to climb aboard his ship, so therefore, since the previous night, teams of men from both sides had been sinking sharpened stakes into the seabed along the bay in two parallel rows, which had then been covered with wooden planking so the participants could talk to one another from their own walkways without shouting and without the risk of having to shake hands.

"I will do the talking, agreed?" whispered Antony as the pirate approached them followed by Scribonius Libo, Octavian's father-in-law, who would act as mediator for the meeting. "You are too agitated, and I wouldn't want you to accidentally provoke him."

Caesar's heir looked at him askance. "Do you think I do not know how to behave?" he replied testily. "Would I be your colleague now if I didn't?"

Antony raised his eyes to the heavens a moment before Pompey came within earshot. "What an honour, finally!" exclaimed the pirate in a mocking tone that, if it were possible, irritated Octavian even more. "The two triumvirs finally deign to meet an exile!"

"We are happy that this meeting can take place, noble Pompey," said Antony. "And to finally have the opportunity to resolve out mutual misunderstandings and, perhaps, to remedy the possible wrongs that have been done you in the past."

Bristling with irritation, Octavian nodded a greeting to his father-in-law. That certainly was not how *he* would have begun the conversation. Too conciliatory. He eyed Sextus Pompey, trying to conceal his hatred for the man who had made him look ridiculous in the eyes of the world and who, like the assassins of Julius Caesar, he would therefore never forgive. Pompey was four years younger than Octavian, but his face bore such an indolent expression that it made him look older than he was. He was a libidinous pleasure seeker, and cruel to boot, the young triumvir remembered. He had recently received news that, at the instigation of his freedman Menodorus, he had killed Staius Murcus after Murcus had chosen to join him. And even Domitius Ahenobarbus, moreover, after having joined him for a time, had chosen Antony. Sextus tolerated only his freedmen as subordinates, not valid admirals of noble extraction who might challenge his decisions, and therefore only the assassins of Julius Caesar and other outlaws who had no great aspirations remained with him.

"Of course wrongs have been done to me," said Pompey. "Everything was taken away from me because of my name, even before I had admitted to being responsible for anything. The Senate had appointed me to certain positions after the death of Caesar."

"My dear fellow, a man is, above all, what he represents. And you, as the son of Pompey the Great, represent a reference point for those who never loved Julius Caesar and those who have defended his memory," said Antony.

"Anyway," Octavian pointed out, "later you were guilty of terrible crimes against Rome and the state, persecuting and starving even the ordinary people who had done you no wrong."

"Is that not what you have done too, with all the wars that you have fought in your lust for power, sending thousands to die on battlefields or in hardship, and forcing them to pay crippling taxes?"

Pompey had a long, sharp tongue. Antony put his hand on Octavian's wrist, fearing that he would react rashly. "Let us try to be a little more constructive," he said quickly. "We are here to resolve our problems, not to recriminate against one another. We would like you to be able to return to being an esteemed citizen of Rome, with legitimate property and a status worthy of the noble birth of your family. Is it not time to put an end to your exile?"

Pompey smiled. "More than anything else, it is time to restore dignity to the triumvirate by replacing Lepidus, who you only need now to safeguard the judiciary, with someone who *actually* possesses a third of the empire – me!"

This time it was Antony who smiled. "The current appointments last until next year. They were sanctioned by senatorial laws and decrees galore. You would not want me to subvert the state just to please you, would you?" Antony responded. "Lepidus is still the third triumvir, and in any case, the people would find it outrageous to find from one day to the next that they are now governed by those who have starved them."

"But all you have done since you created the triumvirate is starve and kill people!" cried Pompey. "I have more power than Lepidus at this moment in time, and it is time that the fact was acknowledged!"

"If you have come here with the hope of becoming a triumvir, you will be disappointed," said Octavian. "Be content with no longer being an exile and an outcast. This is what we are offering, nothing more."

Pompey waved his arm in so violent a gesture of contempt that it almost made him lose his balance. "If you have not come to suggest sharing the empire with me, there is no point to us having this meeting. Go back to Rome and explain to the people who are starving that you do not want to share your power with anyone. Not even with those who could defeat you, if only they wanted to," he cried, then turned and walked away angrily, followed by Libo.

*

"I convinced him to moderate his demands. And the outlaws who are with him will also urge him to find an agreement. I am confident," whispered Scribonius Libo, who had come to welcome Maecenas onto Pompey's hexareme. It was already the third time the two had met over the last two days in search of a solution that would allow the two triumvirs and Pompey to come to an agreement which was satisfactory for all parties and would put an end to the conflict between them. But they had always previously met on land, where Libo had come, willingly and contributing enthusiastically. Maecenas appreciated his efforts – he had known it was a good idea to marry Octavian to Scribonia, and now he was going to reap the benefits.

"Have they accepted the restitution of a fourth part of their property?" asked the Etruscan, following Pompey's father-in-law towards the cabin where his son-in-law was awaiting them. Meanwhile, he looked around and was not at all reassured by the sight of all the soldiers dressed for battle. Finding himself for the first time in the lions' den, without any protection or guarantee of being able to return to land safely, made him feel deeply uneasy. Only now did it come to his mind how unpredictable Sextus Pompey was and he chided himself for not having thought of that before offering himself to Octavian and Antony as a mediator.

"With some caveats," Libo replied. "Many expect that the state – that is, you – should confiscate the part that they are due from those who took their places after the proscriptions. Those involved in the murder of Caesar have no great demands, but the others find that having a quarter of their property returned is an injustice."

"The triumvirate cannot go back on their decisions, you have to understand that," said Maecenas, feeling more and more nervous as they approached Pompey. "If they allow such a thing, they will have to make it look like a gesture of magnanimity, not a change of policy. You know that in this, as almost always in politics, it is all a matter of prestige."

"I do not doubt it," said Libo. "But Pompey also has his own prestige to safeguard – especially with all those who took refuge with him and elected him as their defender. He has already cast himself in a somewhat questionable light with this matter of Staius Murcus… A foolish move, in my opinion."

"You can say that again," agreed Maecenas an instant before entering Pompey's cabin, where he was sitting behind his desk waiting for them. The pirate gave him a nod and invited him to sit down, while the slaves offered them something to drink. But against the walls, as immobile as statues, their eyes staring into space, were two soldiers holding spears, and the Etruscan felt a trickle of sweat slide down one temple.

"So? What are we to do with these exiles?" he asked his guest unceremoniously.

Maecenas tried to explain the triumvirate's point of view. "Libo informed me of your needs and the needs of those under your protection, Admiral," he said. "You have to understand that at the time many of them were sentenced to death. They should be pleased that, thanks to you, they have kept their lives. I don't think it is permissible to ask for more than that. The assassins of Julius Caesar will be pardoned, and those who supported them will regain a fourth part of their property from the current owners, who will have to sell it to them for next to nothing."

"And I'm supposed to be satisfied with that?" snapped Pompey. "And what about how your friends regard *me*? As an outlaw like the others who will be content to beg for a fourth part of his properties? Well I'm no beggar! I demand! I want not a quarter, but a third. And not just of my property – of the empire!"

Maecenas sighed, realising that the faith he had up until that point in the successful outcome of the negotiations was far from well placed. "Admiral, it is evident that there will be special treatment, institutional offices and properties for you... All done with discretion to avoid giving the impression that there is any favouritism. But there can be no change in the current structure of the triumvirate."

Pompey stood up and slammed his fist down on the table. "In that case there is nothing more to discuss!" he shouted, his face red with anger. "Those two will not give up any of what they have. *They* are the real thieves who have robbed me with their proscriptions and robbed half the Senate too, and now they don't want to give any of it back, nor lose the clientele they have acquired, practically giving away our properties to their friends! After all I have suffered I have the right to get back what I lost, with interest! And I also want a part of the empire! And you, you ridiculous little man, you dare to humiliate me like this on my own ship? Octavian doesn't give a damn about anyone, all he cares about is accumulating more power. Shall we wager that if I keep you prisoner here, he won't pay anything to save you?"

"You're wrong… Octavian cares deeply about the empire and all its citizens…" stammered Maecenas. He had been in a similar situation during the campaign at Philippi. Held prisoner in Brutus's camp and at the mercy of the murderers of Caesar. But he had never really been particularly scared on that occasion, because Brutus was a mild and measured man – just, even in his convictions. Pompey, however, was angry and impulsive. And much, much crueller.

"You – take him and put him in the hold to row with the others," the admiral told the two guards, who immediately surrounded Maecenas, pointing their spears at him when they saw him trying to rush towards the door. But just then, several men burst into the room. They wore togas which bore purple stripes along the hems – exiled senators, without a doubt. "Pompey, if you disrupt the negotiations, what will become of us and our families? We'll be outcasts forever!" said one of them, who Maecenas recognised as Tiberius Claudius Nero, the man who had fomented the uprising of the slaves in Campania. "If I set foot in Italy I will be executed, do you realise that? And simply because you want the empire! If you come to an agreement, I can go back to being a free man, at least able to walk the streets without having to watch for assassins," cried another, approaching Pompey until the guards blocked him by thrusting their spears at him.

"A quarter of my wealth might not make me rich again, but at least it will give me enough to live with dignity on. Not like now, where I have to eke out a living, hoping for your generosity while I watch you carry out raids against my own people!" said another still.

"Oh, really?" responded Pompey, taking a step forward and shouting in the face of the last man to have spoken. "If you are not happy with what I have done for you, you are free to leave now. I have fought, I have made sacrifices, I have fed you with what I obtained from what you call 'raids', but apparently you do not feel that I deserve any gratitude. Indeed, now you even expect to give me orders!" He grabbed the man's toga and tore it away, and then he began to pull at his tunic too. "What else do you want from me, you parasites? Who can I ever trust, if not my freedmen? Why isn't Menodorus here, the only one who still believes in me? You have betrayed me, you cowards! So be it. Therefore, I will continue the negotiations, since you leave me with no choice. I should throw you into the sea with all your families, but that is something that a man of honour such as I could never do. Thank the gods that you found refuge with the son of Pompey the Great, and not with some nobody like yourself!"

He motioned for the guards to release Maecenas and invited him to sit down again. The Etruscan breathed a sigh of relief and gave a wry smile at the thought that he had been saved by the very people he had helped to condemn. But he was certain that Octavian would not be grateful to them.

*

"I want it known that I do this only for those who have given themselves unto me in order that I protect them," said Sextus Pompey as soon as he reached them. His ship, surrounded by the rest of his fleet, was waiting for him nearby, while in the port of Dicearchia there was the more modest fleet of Antony and Octavian's ships. The two triumvirs had been waiting on the dock for a while, and the younger of the two had begun to get impatient.

"And seeing as we are speaking bluntly, I want to make it very clear that I am only doing this for the good of the state and the citizens who have been oppressed and hungry for years," replied Octavian bitterly, gesturing to the scribes not to write anything down.

"Very good, very good," said Antony in an attempt to ease the tension. "So, I take it that we are all here against our will and only for the sake of the people for whom we are responsible – shall we proceed?"

"Of course, I have come for precisely that reason," said Pompey, looking askance at Octavian. "And to collect what is mine, as compensation for all the unjust persecution that I have suffered in recent years."

"As long as there is an end to the attacks on the Italian peninsula and the provinces and an end to the state of belligerency between us, by land and by sea, and that trade is not impeded anywhere," stated Antony. "All acts of piracy must end, once and for all."

"And that you remove the garrisons in Italy and the naval blockades along the coast. And accept no more runaway slaves," said Octavian.

"In exchange for my part of the empire," insisted Pompey.

"The part you took by force, yes?"Octavian pointed out. "Sicily, Sardinia and Corsica."

"Your Etruscan friend accepted my request for the Peloponnese, although I would once again request the whole of Greece."

"We said the Peloponnese," interrupted Antony. "And it will cost me – the place gives me a good income. In fact, all the taxes that they owe me, you must now pay."

"Absolutely not!" said Pompey "You leave, and from that moment on it is all mine."

"Well then, there is nothing more to discuss. No Peloponnese."

Octavian had an idea. "Pompey, why don't you give him six months to collect his arrears and then take over?" he suggested.

Both of them made as though to argue with his proposal, but then fell silent and reflected for a few moments, each evaluating whether and how Octavian's proposal could benefit them.

"That's fine by me," said Antony eventually. The other triumvir had had no doubt that he would be the first to accept.

"Three months," said Pompey.

"Four," replied Antony.

"Very well, four it is!" said Octavian. "That seems a fair compromise," and the others nodded, despite grimacing slightly. The youngest triumvir struggled to hold back an expression of satisfaction. The agreement was in his favour. He had proposed it because, knowing Antony, he knew that he would try to cheat Pompey by bleeding the Peloponnese dry before leaving. Relations between the two would go back to being tense and when he wanted to resume the war, Antony would not prevent him.

"Well then," he said. "Pompey will have the islands and the Peloponnese, the latter in four months."

"In practical terms, less than even Lepidus, who also no longer has any power. But in any case, it must be specified that my domains are tied to yours, and that they will last as long as the triumvirate does," Pompey demanded.

"It has been so established, has it not?" said Octavian – who, however, had other ideas about it. "Always on condition that you resume sending wheat from the islands."

"You'll also have the consulate in six years and become a member of the priesthood immediately," declared Antony.

"I contest that. Why in six years? Why do I have to wait so long? I already told that Etruscan that it does not sit well with me."

"Because then you'll be of the constitutional age to take the position," Antony pointed out.

"You are trying to make a mockery of me!" protested Pompey, pointing to Octavian. "This man here was younger than me when he did it four years ago!"

"Those were special circumstances," said Antony, half-heartedly. "There was an institutional vacuum and both the consuls were dead. There was a civil war..."

"And wouldn't there be a civil war now if we weren't here to reach an agreement in order to prevent it?"

Pompey did not seem to want to give in.

"I held that position for only a few months," said Octavian, trying to defend himself.

"Of course. Just long enough to become the equivalent of a dictator immediately afterwards..." said Pompey.

The three were silent for a moment. They seemed to have come to a stalemate, despite everything having been prepared beforehand. Octavian was eager to close the matter and get on with spreading Maecenas's propaganda, which would make him appear as the artisan of peace. He decided it was time to finish these skirmishes.

"What is done is done. There are already three rulers of the empire now, and no room for any more," he said. "Considering the circumstances and the need that we all have to put an end to this conflict, you can consider yourself lucky to be reinstated in Roman civil life and to hold a fourth part of its dominions."

Pompey reflected. "It's still too little. I hope at least that those under my protection derive advantages from this, because I certainly will not," he complained. Octavian struggled to contain his anger – that pirate was practically extorting a quarter of the empire from them and he still wasn't happy. If anything, he seemed to have decided to demand even more.

"I would say so," repeated Antony, reading the informal notes that had flowed from the contacts among the mediators in the previous days. "They will all be allowed to return from exile, except those convicted by vote and sentence…"

"And that too does not sit well with me," Pompey interrupted him. "You said that the amnesty would be valid for the assassins of Julius Caesar as well."

"Impossible. Not while I'm alive!" declared Octavian firmly.

"That was only a hypothesis, but an impractical one, given the situation," said Antony.

"And now what am I supposed to say?" Pompey protested.

"You have many good reasons to rid yourself of them. You will save almost all the outlaws except for the very few who have committed crimes too serious to allow any form of forgiveness," urged Antony.

"Come on, they can be counted on the fingers of one hand…"

Pompey grimaced. But possession of a quarter of the empire was worth more than a handful of murderers, and so he was silent.

"To all those whose properties were taken away by violence or seized by others because they had fled in fear, their properties will be returned to them, but not the furniture," Antony went on, reading from the notes. "All those who fought for you, Pompey, shall be rewarded. The slaves will be set free and at the end of their service, the others will have the same rewards as our soldiers. And with that, that is all, for now."

Pompey nodded, but then added, "No, that is not all. We still have to determine the next magistracy and, if I may say so, agree to strengthen our bonds."

The idea of bonds, even bonds of kinship, had been expressed by Maecenas, who had been pleased by the role played by Libo in the negotiations; that was easy for him to say, thought Octavian to himself, when he did not have to put up with Scribonia's annoying personality.

"We can define these things on a more convivial occasion," he suggested.

"We could spend the next three days each as guests of one of the other two, in rotation," offered Pompey. "What do you say?"

Antony looked at Octavian and nodded. “Good idea,” he said. “It will give the impression that we are united, and that is what the people want.”

“Good! So tomorrow you will be guests aboard my ship!” exclaimed Pompey, jovially.

“I think it would be better if we draw lots on the order, don’t you agree?” said Octavian.

The pirate grimaced and hesitated a moment, then nodded. “So be it.” He called over one of his freedmen secretaries, who were stationed at a respectful distance from them, telling him, “Break one stylus into two pieces of different lengths and then offer it to us with a whole one in your fist, leaving only one end of each sticking out.”

The man quickly proceeded to carry out the order, and offered his clenched fist to the three.

“Please,” said Pompey, gesturing to Octavian to extract one. “Whoever pulls out the whole one will be the first to offer his hospitality.”

The young man looked fearfully at the three styluses, then told himself that he must not appear hesitant and took one.

It was the shortest.

He tried not to express his disappointment and merely hoped that Antony would choose the whole one. But the triumvir found the other broken one in his hands.

Pompey looked happily at the unbroken stylus which his secretary had handed to him. "Apparently, the gods have welcomed my suggestion," he said.

Octavian felt a chill run down his spine. But he could not refuse the invitation without offending him and compromising the agreements.

*

It was hard to tolerate the chatter of the diners. As he had settled onto his triclinium with Maecenas, he had realised that his host could have had his throat cut at any time by one of the many armed men who filled his vast hexareme, and that the knife which he kept hidden under the *vestis cœnatoria*, the green silk robe that he had been made to wear for the dinner in accordance with the rules of high society, would be useless. He himself would have been tempted, had he been the host. The chance to become the master of the world with two simple crimes was too tempting to be stopped by considerations of honour or anything similar. Even Antony, Octavian knew well, kept a dagger with him and he was certain that Pompey had taken his own precautions too. None of the three trusted each other and if he felt reasonably sure of the other triumvir at that particular moment, he was aware that with regards to the pirate it was only a truce. He only hoped that it was not going to be too brief.

The ship was surrounded by sentinels belonging to all three of them, and a tiny spark would be sufficient to ignite a blazing struggle and unleash a massacre. There was a tense moment when Pompey, before taking his place, seemed to have argued briefly with Menodorus. Octavian and Antony had looked at each other and instinctively placed their hands on their daggers, but then their host had relaxed, lying down next to them and the freedman had vanished.

Octavian was distracted by the women's table just behind him, where Pompey's wife as well as the wives of the exiles were to be found. Their host had decided that they too should attend the dinner and many of them were anxious, he said, to thank the triumvirs in person for their forgiveness. One girl in particular caught his attention – there was something familiar about her, he said to himself when his eyes fell on that elegant figure, before realising that she looked like him, with the same delicate features, sharp, intelligent eyes and a small nose. Her face was only slightly more florid than his own, which was not difficult, given the delicate nature of the triumvir's health.

Maecenas, who never missed anything, said, "You like that woman, eh? That doesn't surprise me – she looks more like your sister than Octavia does, and thinking about the high opinion you have of yourself, how could you *not* like a woman who looks like you…"

Octavian gave him a contemptuous smile. "Instead of talking such nonsense, find out who she is," he replied. "I see that she also has a small child in tow." As soon as the Etruscan rose from the couch to make enquiries with his usual discretion, one of the outlaws took advantage of the space beside Octavian to approach the triumvir.

"Caesar, I would like to take advantage of this occasion to thank you for your noble gesture in welcoming us back home, even those like me who in despair at having lost everything perhaps over reacted," he said, and Octavian recognised him as Tiberius Claudius Nero.

"Ah!" he exclaimed. "You are the one who believed himself to be the new Spartacus… Not really very noble coming from an aristocratic descendant of one of the oldest and most prestigious families."

Mortified, Nero bowed his head. "I told you, Caesar. At times, despair leads to madness. Between the proscriptions and confiscations I had hardly anything left… But now I realise my mistake and am ready to serve you faithfully."

"It's not me you have to serve, but Rome," said Octavian. "I am not the master of the city but only an executor of the will of the Senate and the people, who have placed in me, Antony and Lepidus their trust to ensure we put in order a state divided by too many civil wars and revolts. And yours, I hope, was the last."

He knew it was not so, and that he would never trust Nero. He would not make the same mistake as Caesar: forgiving traitors and making them your lieutenants, as his father had done with the likes of Brutus and Cassius, could be fatal. And anyway, unlike Caesar, he would never forgive, and sooner or later he would make them pay for the trouble they had caused. But not now.

"Nonetheless, I gladly welcome your words. We need the assistance of all to return Rome to the glory that belongs to her, and we will certainly find a way to put your skills to use," he added.

Nero thanked him just as Maecenas was returning. The outlaw politely stepped aside, surrendering his place to the Etruscan. "By a strange coincidence, the woman you were looking at is the wife of the man you were talking to. She is called Livia Drusilla and she's nineteen. The child is called Tiberius and he is almost three," was his exhaustive reply.

Octavian found the surprise rather pleasant and smiled. An idea had already come to his mind about a way to use the abilities – or rather the resources – of the man with whom he had just been speaking. He stared for a few moments at the girl, turning away when she noticed: it was not good manners to stare at other people's wives at the table. Then he chose from the plate of appetisers, taking hard-boiled eggs with fish, and turned his attention to the main banquet. But he could not resist the temptation to look round again.

And realised that she was watching him.

Yes, the vendetta against Tiberius Claudius Nero would begin soon, he told himself as he received the copy of the agreement from Antony, on which only his signature was required before it could be sent to Rome and kept in the house of the Vestals. He read it through one last time and then signed it, giving it to his brother-in-law Libo, who was instructed to take it back to the city immediately.

"We said that we would talk about strengthening your bonds, did we not?" Libo said. "Between you and Pompey, Octavian, I would say that we already have one – your happy marriage to my sister, which the gods have blessed with a pregnancy, is an excellent omen for a strong and lasting alliance. Now I believe we must do the same between my son-in-law and you, Mark Antony. Pompey has given me a lovely granddaughter, who would be a perfect match for one of your two sons, do you not think?"

Octavian studied Antony. The triumvir had two sons by Fulvia, Antyllus and Iullus, and had already made Octavia pregnant. He wondered how his fellow triumvir, who never revealed much of his true intentions, would react. Several times Octavian had sought to understand how transitory he considered the agreements with Pompey. Caesar's heir was champing at the bit for a showdown and had never thought even for a moment that the alliance with that pirate would last – he just needed to consolidate his power on the part of the empire that was due to him and which had been affected by the war of Perugia and create a viable fleet with which to face the enemy. But he also needed Antony's support to avoid the risk of a conflict on two fronts. However, the other man always responded to his inquiries with vague platitudes, the same way he replied to anyone who expected declarations of peace from him. But facts were what counted in politics, and now he would see what Antony really meant to do.

"Dear Libo," said Antony, a grave expression on his face, "it really is an honour for me to join my line with that of your family. But I feel that my sons are too old for your granddaughter and they have already been promised to other noblewomen. You will understand that I cannot annoy important senators. I need their support, I cannot go back on my word. However… because I believe this bond would be valuable and necessary, I could see a possible engagement between your granddaughter and my stepson Marcellus."

Libo had to make the best of a bad job, and so did Sextus Pompey. But they both understood exactly what Octavian had. Antony did not want such close ties with them for he wanted it to be easy for him to sever them at any time he wished.

The youngest triumvir felt a thrill of satisfaction – his colleague would let him have his way when the time was right.

And he had no intention of waiting long.

XIII

Octavia looked almost disbelievingly at the baby girl the midwife placed in her arms. She could still feel the excruciating pain between her legs, but that little bundle she held made her forget instantly the agonies of labour she had endured to give birth to her. She was her fifth. The first, though, to come from an incredibly happy relationship. When she had Marcus, her son by Gaius Chaerea who was born when she was still a teenager, she had felt frightened, alone and reproached by her family, who had immediately rejected him. Then, three children with Marcellus. The first, Marcella Major, was born without love, the other two, Marcellus and Marcella Minor, had been born in an atmosphere of contempt and coercion.

This time it was different.

She was looking forward to Antony being allowed to come and see his daughter. His first daughter. Those ten months of marriage had been a pleasant surprise for her and she was happy that they had been followed by the birth of a child. Initially the prospect of a marriage to the man who appeared to be her brother's biggest rival had frightened her, and on the day of the ceremony she had been genuinely terrified. Her legs had trembled as she faced the ordeal and in the evening when Antony had taken her home and picked her up to carry her across the threshold, she had felt lost, as though imprisoned in a nightmare. That first night, she had been so rigid with terror that her new husband was unable to make her his without forcing her. She had wanted to give herself to him, but her fear paralysed her. She had expected Antony to be angry and take what was by rights his by force – after all, he had a reputation as a lover and had hundreds of women in his lifetime, and she was sure that such a man would not waste time with pleasantries and coaxing. Instead he showed himself to be patient, considerate, sweet and even tender, and had not insisted. He had limited himself to caressing her and whispering reassuring words that evening. The following night she had wanted to please him but she was as rigid as a tree trunk, expecting, this time, an outburst from her husband. But Antony was again sympathetic and continued to be so for the next three nights until she finally relaxed, allowing him to break through her defences.

It was the beginning of a new, wonderful discovery for her. Over time, she had let her memories of her time as a young girl with Gaius Chaerea grow out of all proportion, becoming so intense that they eclipsed those experienced with her first husband, Marcellus. She had always thought that no man could make her feel like she had with the centurion, but instead, as she felt Antony inside her, she savoured his expert caresses and kisses, both gentle and vigorous at the same time. His movements were never violent or mechanical, his timing was perfect in every moment of their intercourse and she realised that what she was feeling was a faithful reproduction of what she had imagined she had experienced with Gaius.

It had been wonderful, and afterwards she found herself covering her husband with kisses like an enthusiastic child, barely aware of what she was doing. He was touched, and they did it again, and then again. Since then, they had made love most nights with an intensity that she would not have imagined possible for her body and its needs, until the size of her belly prevented this. She discovered that she had a much more physical attitude towards love than she thought. Led by an expert hand, she was finally able to let herself go in ways she never had with Marcellus or Gaius, and this was a joyous discovery. It was incredible, she kept saying to herself. Before marrying Antony, she had been convinced that she was condemned to a desolate life, and finding herself wed to a man notoriously addicted to debauchery and bad company, a slave to the lowly prostitutes of the Suburra and to the exclusive ones like Cleopatra, experts in the sexual arts, she assumed that her husband would ignore her, betray her in front of everyone and humiliate and torment her with his infidelities. She had thought he would treat her badly simply to spite Octavian, whom Octavia knew her new husband would never be able to get along with.

None of that happened, though. Antony was proving to be a faithful, caring and affectionate husband, and he really seemed reconciled with his brother-in-law. Sextus Pompey appeared to have calmed down, apparently satisfied with what he had obtained with the treaty at Misenum in the spring, and in Rome, finally, peace prevailed. People had started to look favourably to the future, and the triumvirs were again hailed as the saviours of the State – those who had put an end to the infighting, the sending of children to war, the revolts of the slaves, the looting of the fields and starvation.

Yes, she could actually say that she was happy for the first time in a long while. It was true that she still thought fondly of Gaius Chaerea, and wondered if he, too, was happy with his family. But her love for Antony had allowed her to set aside the pain of rejection and missing her son Marcus. It would have entailed explaining far too much to her new husband if she dared to go to the Suburra just once. Moreover, the long arm of Octavian was now everywhere, and

Octavia was afraid of her brother's reaction if he knew of her past connection to Chaerea. His first victim would probably be Gaius himself, but the ruthless and vindictive triumvir would hardly have stopped there.

Once Antony was authorised by the midwife and the doctor to enter, Octavia was suddenly seized by the fear of not pleasing him. He had known many beautiful, alluring and provocative women, and she always feared she was dull in comparison. At that moment in time, exhausted by childbirth, she felt truly ugly. She had always spent a lot of time perfecting her makeup and doing her hair nicely so as to be worthy of his affection and she feared losing all that she had gained in an instant.

"You look beautiful, my beloved wife, and our child is beautiful too," Antony said, instantly dispelling her fears and reassuring her. He caressed her and kissed her sweaty forehead gently, then took the little girl tenderly in his arms. He lifted her up and with that gesture he recognised her as his daughter. There was no need to choose her name – it was Antonia, and it could not be otherwise.

"I'm proud of you, Octavia. You've given birth to a lovely daughter, of whom I am already so proud," Antony then said, turning back to his wife. He handed the little one to the midwife, who laid her in the crib where the little girl, who up until then had been quiet, began to whimper. The woman clapped her hands and called for the wet nurse, who settled down beside the cradle and offered one of her ample breasts to Antonia. It did not take the baby girl long to learn how to feed herself, and she soon seemed satisfied with her first great discovery in the world.

Octavia and Antony were left to contemplate her while she drank her fill. Octavia gave her hand to her husband, who squeezed it gently, while they continued to admire the small masterpiece they had generated.

"Antony," Octavia suddenly asked her husband, "how is it that you know how to make me so happy? I mean... I'm not the most beautiful woman, or the most interesting or the most sensual that you've ever known..."

He turned to her in surprise and his face took on an expression of amusement, as he thought of an answer to give her. "Maybe because I had never met a woman like you and it is a welcome change. It makes me feel – or perhaps I should say, be – a different person..." he said finally.

"And what about when I am no longer a novelty?" Octavia asked herself, silently.

*

Octavian would never have believed he could find a woman who was five months pregnant, a woman who was now dancing naked on top of him whilst he lay on the bed, so alluring. He tried for a moment to imagine his wife in the same position. Scribonia was pregnant too, and in her eighth month, and he had not touched her for a long time, disgusted not only by her awkward and clumsy movements but also by her flaccid skin and suffocating personality.

With Livia it was completely different. It had always been that way, since the first time they had made love a few weeks after the Treaty of Misenum. On that occasion, he had seen her and he had liked her right away, but no more than other girls who had been brought to his bed to satisfy the impulses that assailed him from time to time. He had her brought secretly to one of his residences, and she had gone there without resistance. Neither had she resisted when he had openly displayed his attraction to her, and had granted him what he desired without delay. It had been a joyful, intense encounter, and having originally invited her purely out of lust and a desire to spite Tiberius Claudius Nero, he discovered that he wanted to see her again immediately and realised that he actually really liked the girl.

He had realised this while making love to her for the first time. Previously, with any woman he had been with, his mind had never stopped working, not even during intercourse, but with Livia he was momentarily released and able to lose himself. He thought of nothing except her gorgeous body wrapped around his, her intoxicating scent and the taste of her which he lapped up greedily, and he found the feeling so pleasant he wanted to repeat it immediately.

They discovered that her husband had made her pregnant for the second time just a few days before the beginning of their relationship and he had seen her belly grow week after week, and with every encounter he had discovered other qualities in her, even more extraordinary than those he enjoyed while they made love.

Livia moaned, and began to move more urgently, and he realised that she was approaching the apex of her pleasure. Octavian indulged her and intensified his own movements, becoming totally lost in the vortex of pleasure which brought them both to orgasm, and after which they both collapsed exhausted onto the bed next to each other.

They were silent for a while, in a tender half-sleep lulled by their laboured gasps, until their breathing slowed enough for speech. With Livia, there was always time to talk and such was the lucidity of her intelligence Octavian regretted that he could not be completely open with her.

"Has my pregnancy ever bothered you, Caesar?" she asked, propping herself up on one elbow and looking at him, a slight smile on her radiant face. "Everyone will think that the child is yours once our relationship becomes public knowledge. If it isn't already, of course…"

Octavian smiled and caressed her face. The tenderness between them was natural, but was something he had never felt with any woman before. Livia's concern was well-founded, but it was precisely upon that fact that he based his strategy to humiliate and punish Nero. Although… the more he got to know the girl, the more he wanted to develop their relationship.

"There were people who doubted that Marcus Brutus was the son of Caesar and Servilia, just imagine…" he said. "And I don't think that the sky fell down because of the gossip. They loved each other in secret for years and years and everyone knew it, but that never stopped them. Or at least, not until Caesar considered her too old, and Cleopatra entered his life."

"Well, you too will consider me too old one day, then," she replied with a mock pout, tickling him.

"May I remind you that Servilia was older than Caesar, and that you're a lot younger than me."

"So you too will expand your territories until you meet Cleopatra and then it will be over for me," continued Livia, teasing him. Octavian gave a dismissive laugh. "I am impervious to the charms of that Egyptian whore! Antony fell for her, though his dedication to my sister has put him back on the right track… Far more so than I would ever have imagined, quite frankly, Anyway, the East is his concern, so if there is anyone who might fall for her, it will be him."

Livia looked at him intently, but said nothing.

"What's the matter?" he asked her.

"Nothing. It's just that I thought that sooner or later *you* would arrive in the East."

Octavian propped himself up on his elbows and asked in surprise, "What makes you say that?"

"I'd be surprised if you stopped at the West. From what I understand of you, the Misenum treaty… the agreements with Antony… the things you've given Lepidus to keep him happy… they are all just steps towards world domination."

Octavian felt a chill run down his spine. The woman was reading his thoughts. And it had always been a source of pride for him that he was able to hide his feelings. "You're wrong. I have great respect for the institutions and for the Republic," he said brusquely.

"Yes, of course" she smiled. "But anyway, I would find nothing wrong with that. In fact, I think that we need someone who can bring order to the chaos that Rome has become for quite some time now."

There it was, one of the many qualities he valued in Livia. She was lucid and analytical and she had an open and ambitious mind. She spoke with political acuity and this led him, during their meetings, to open up beyond what was acceptable. And now, she even seemed to share his grand vision.

"And do you think this person could be me?" he found himself asking her.

She thought about it for a moment, then said, "You conquered the consulate when you were only nineteen years old. You took Antony and the Senate down a peg or two, you formed a triumvirate and then you reduced it to a diarchy. You made sure that Antony would win for you in Philippi and you have eliminated much of your opposition. You have managed to surround yourself with brilliant, talented staff, while your rivals love to use slaves and freedmen – especially ones who flatter and admire them. Didn't you send Agrippa to Gaul to consolidate the boundaries and suppress the riots? Didn't you entrust Maecenas with the task of creating propaganda? Did you not send your bodyguards to handle the Parthian invasion? And did you not marry your own sister to the only man who can contest you for absolute power? And are you not dealing with the city's administrative needs, in order to make it the true capital of the known world? Yes, if there is anyone who can make a real empire of Rome, you are the one, Octavian! You have a grander, more forward looking vision than anyone else. In comparison with you, everyone, even Antony, appears sluggish, dull and narrow minded. I am sure that the current tetrarchy – Antony to the east, Lepidus to the south and Pompey to the west with the islands, is closing in on you and this is nothing more than a prelude to new wars. This peace is only a temporary illusion. But one day you'll make it permanent," she concluded solemnly, before immediately giving him a kiss which left him no chance of replying.

Octavian was speechless. A woman like that could not be only his mistress, he told himself as he indulged her embrace.

*

The warrior rode almost up to the Roman lines. He was impressive looking, despite the simplicity of his armament, which consisted of a wire mesh, an oval helmet with a plume and cheekpieces and a long spear. Agrippa could easily distinguish his proud features, the defiance and determination – these people would not surrender easily. Then, taking a better look, he noticed the small bags hanging from four points on his saddle.

No, they were not bags, they were heads. No doubt belonging to Roman citizens who had settled in Burdigala following Julius Caesar's conquest, which was supposed to have been absolute.

Absolute! The rebellion in Aquitaine had assumed massive proportions, enough to necessitate Agrippa to rally the garrison legions, originally Calenus's and then Rufus's, and scattered all over Gaul, and concentrate them in the region. Then he began marching all five legionary units along the Garonne to restore Roman rule to those towns that had fallen into the hands of insurgents. But the Gallic warriors were elusive. The wars with Caesar had taught them not to attack the Romans on the battlefield, where the legionaries' superior discipline and training were always most evident. Nor did they barricade themselves inside the cities, which Caesar, with the conquest of Avaricum and Alesia, had shown were highly vulnerable to the advanced techniques of a Roman siege. Even the most powerful walls had been unable to protect the cities from the Roman's massacres and looting, after which the soldiers had abandoned them.

No, in the cities, now, they left only the old men, women and children, while all the men old enough to go to war had disappeared, as they had from the farms scattered about the countryside too. The warriors were waiting for him somewhere, waiting to ambush him – that much was clear. There would be many of them. All the Aquitaine tribes had risen up and as yet they had not come across a single rebel in the territories of Bituriges, the Vasati, the Cocosates or even the Sotiates. Even in the Pyrenees there were almost no adult men. It was unthinkable that the Tarbelli, the Suburates and the Bigerriones had joined the common cause and were in hiding in the mountains. But he would deal with them later. Now he intended to bring the tribes of the Garonne to heel.

And the time for that had probably just arrived. The man before him, just out of the reach of the archer's arrows, was certainly a leader who had come to lure him into a trap. A forest loomed behind him, and it was easy to guess that the Gauls had chosen this place to concentrate their men for an attack on the Roman flanks. The dense vegetation and supplies the Romans were carrying would force them to move slowly and spread out, making it difficult for them to see the enemy hidden by the bushes, until they found themselves suddenly under attack. The guide with Agrippa had described the ground ahead. The forest was about a mile in length and about two in width, and this allowed him to work out a plan.

The horseman shouted what presumably were insults, spitting and waving his spear, which he ended up throwing to the ground a short distance from him. Behind him, the group of tribesmen from which he had emerged remained in a line along the edge of the forest, ready to welcome him back into their ranks and disappear as soon as the Romans made a move.

Because that was what they expected. That Agrippa would follow them into the forest, convinced that there were but a handful of them, and expose himself to an ambush. The proconsul decided to give the impression that he had taken the bait. He did not know how many more opportunities he would have to take the rebels on in the field and win a clear victory and he did not want to miss one, even if there was a risk of defeat. The alternative was a long drawn out war of exhausting chases and marches, burning territories that were just recovering from the devastation to which Julius Caesar had subjected them. Octavian wanted to make a second Italy of Gaul, a new centre of the future empire, and he had to give those regions the opportunity to thrive under the protective wing of Rome. Therefore, a pitched battle was the only viable solution, and now he had the opportunity.

He told one of his tribunes to keep a legion at the ready. Then he waited for the rider to turn his horse round and return to his companions. He then gave his lieutenant the signal for the unit to move off quickly in pursuit of the Gauls, who would believe that the Romans had taken the bait. Then he called the tribunes of one of the two remaining legions.

"Take five cohorts each and march briskly," he commanded, "one of you on the right flank and one on the left flank of our vanguard column. Jump on the Gauls as soon as they attack our men." In a few moments, the legion was split into two equal halves, which set off in an oblique direction towards the edge of the forest and then penetrated it at points far from the main column.

There was one legion left. It might not be needed, but if the Gauls had actually become as smart as he feared they had, he would serve up the rebels the same kind of surprise that Caesar had reserved for Pompey the Great at Pharsalia – that of keeping a double reserve. As cunning as they might be, it was a trick that the barbarians would not know.

He ordered the remaining legion to follow him, urged his horse on and rode to the far left of the forest, where the cover was sparser. He demanded absolute silence from his men. The enemy had to be afraid of the cohorts he had sent from the flank of the main body and not have the slightest idea that an additional contingent was waiting a little further away.

He hoped he wouldn't hear war cries.

He hoped he wouldn't hear the clang of metal on metal, the cries of pain, the thuds of bodies as they slumped to the ground.

He had used the main army as bait, but he hoped that the Gauls, on seeing the two units, would hesitate to attack, giving him time to circumvent them altogether and cut them off. As they ventured into the forest, he realised he had taken a real gamble. He wondered if Octavian would criticise him, knowing that he had put the troops entrusted to him at risk, but it was the only way to pacify these places and prevent them from turning into a new Iberian Peninsula. For almost two centuries the Romans had been unable to govern there effectively because of the Celtiberians continuing insurgence.

Octavian had grand ideas for the provinces and he was there to lay the foundations to enable them to be realised. In order to bring civilisation to regions so far from the city, and to civilise them to Roman standards with spas, town halls, amphitheatres and aqueducts, it was necessary to eradicate all forms of resistance and convince the population that the empire had something to offer them. Without the tension created by guerrillas and rebels, people would understand that the Roman way of life was easier, for it brought order, safety, comfort and entertainment. They would not care much about the loss of their freedom – people generally opt for comfort over principles.

But then came the cries. Far away, echoing in the forest, accompanied by the sounds of startled animals. Now he had to hurry.

"Do you hear them, proconsul? Let's get over there to help them quickly!" said one of the tribunes.

"No, we will proceed as agreed. Only, give orders to advance at a run, in so far as the vegetation allows. But be careful not to lose contact between units," he said firmly. The other looked at him incredulously. Agrippa, however, had his subordinates used to total discipline, so the man made no objection. The speed of their progress increased. The legionaries were aware that their fellow soldiers were in danger and did not spare themselves. Arriving on the opposite side of the forest to where they had entered, Agrippa gave orders to stop. He let the soldiers catch their breath for a moment, waited for the ranks to recover, then commanded them to resume marching, silently heading into the woods. As they advanced, the sounds of battle grew more distinct. When he saw the first shadows darting between one trunk and another, he sent scouts forward to inform their comrades of his arrival, then halted the column.

But when the scouts returned, they gave him unexpected news. The shadows he had glimpsed were not Romans.

They were Gauls.

The Aquitanians had been smarter than he thought. They too had a reserve, ready to surprise them behind the Roman flanks sent by Agrippa to threaten the attackers of the main column from behind.

He now had three contingents to save – the central column and the ones on the sides.

*

Four months of peace. Maecenas couldn't remember such an occurrence, but he decided to take the opportunity to start working on his idea, which concurred with Octavian's as regards positive propaganda. The people had to know that they were in good hands and that those who governed them enjoyed the favour of the gods. They had to be convinced that only Octavian, with his capable staff chosen by divine inspiration, could allow the Romans to live with dignity, enjoying the privileges that belonged to the chosen race.

He wasn't sure exactly when the idea had come to him. Maecenas had been trying for a long time to find talented people who could give the empire a cultural direction. Rome had fed off Greek culture since coming into contact with the Hellenic world, taking responsibility for its protection and for freeing it from Macedonian rule. He was convinced that Rome had to produce its own culture instead of simply repeating or copying that of the Greeks or producing crude low quality creations which were adequate for the common people but not for the more educated and upper classes. He himself had tried to create works comparable with Hellenic ones, but he soon realised that he lacked the necessary talent. He was more skilled as a politician and administrator than as a poet and this was the reasoning behind his project. He wanted to *produce* culture. He was skilled at handling politics, but he was also good at finding talent and was more than happy to let his protégés express themselves.

Well then, he would create a culture of propaganda.

He had been cultivating the idea for a long time, but he always to put aside his own plans for the needs of the sect, and without which he would not have been able to fulfil his wishes anyway. Now, finally, he had time to look around him and lay the foundations of his project.

However, he did not have much at his disposal. Only large amounts of capital to invest, the certain and malleable talent of Plotius Tucca, who was happy to celebrate the rise of Octavian's present and future Rome, and the alleged talents of Horace, who still refused to show him his compositions. But he knew where it was possible to tap into new resources.

"Are you sure that we are welcome here?" Plotius asked him again, while preparing to be received at the palatial home of Pomponius Atticus, the so-called *domus Tanfiliana* on the Quirinal hill. "I still find it hard to believe that such a dear friend of Cicero would be keen to maintain relations with those who had him killed."

"Yes, yes… but it's not the first time I've been to his house and he has always been very friendly," explained Maecenas. "Pomponius has no great interest in politics and has always been a friend to everyone. In the past, he lent money to both Fulvia *and* Brutus, and that was why Antony crossed him off the list of outlaws. He is a true Epicurean who takes the separation of politics and the practice of an active literary *otium* very seriously, and when I wrote to him, he confirmed that he would be happy to meet people 'who are dedicated to culture in these times of iron and fire.' In fact, he told me that he wanted to introduce to me his own talented people who seek the triumvir's favour."

"I don't like these people who want to suck up to the powerful at all. How can they be really creative if their art is addressed to a specific purpose? They're nothing more than craftsmen…" complained Horace, whom Maecenas had persuaded to come along in spite of his aversion to worldly social occasions.

And nothing was more worldly than an invitation from Pomponius Atticus, as was clear as soon as they entered his triclinium, where he found his host already in the company of a group of people. The décor confirmed Pomponius's moderation in all things and his elegant but restrained tastes, beautiful without ever being ostentatious or excessive. Surrounded by gleaming walls of coloured marble, decorated with rectangles of various sizes in the Greek style, a woman and two men were lying on sofas upholstered in orange silk arranged around a dinner table upon which was placed a large basket of fruit. A slave, one of the many supremely learned servants that Pomponius kept at his home, interrupted the reading of a text when she saw the visitors.

The host rose to his feet, ready to receive Maecenas, who shook his hand warmly. He was a gentleman of well over sixty with a warm and harmonious voice which put his guests at ease. The Etruscan introduced his two friends and politely inquired about the progress of his work. "Dear Pomponius, which family are you working on now? The last time I saw you, you were on the *gens Fabia*. Who is now lucky enough to receive your precious attentions?"

Pomponius invited them to take a seat. "At the moment, I am working on the *gens Aemilia*, and I am rather distressed, I must confess. I have discovered reports that their founder, Mamercus, is the son of the philosopher Pythagoras, but others claim that he was the son of King Numa Pompilius. Then I found an Emilio who was the son of Ascanius and therefore the grandson of Aeneas, and even an Emilia who was the daughter of Aeneas and Lavinia. Imagine that even the Aemili, who commissioned the work, tell me that they have no idea what the truth is. But since Mamercus comes from Mamers, who was the Oscan god of war, in my opinion the Aemili have Sabine origins..."

"Ah, really?" said Maecenas. "I don't envy you having to inform the Aemili of *that* – I doubt they will be very happy to be deprived of their descent from Aeneas..."

"Precisely. I can just imagine the reaction of your dear friend Octavian if you suggested that he and his father are descended from Venus..." interjected Horace with his usual sharpness.

After a moment of general embarrassment, Pomponius spoke again. "It is a theory, in fact, that I have not discussed with them. But you must excuse me, in my enthusiasm to greet you, Maecenas, I forgot to introduce my daughter, who perhaps you have not met before, and my guest ... Here is my jewel, Caecilia Pomponia," he said, indicating the woman sitting on the triclinium who rose politely, bowing her head in greeting. Maecenas found her to be very pretty and certainly as accomplished and intelligent as one might expect the daughter of Titus Pomponius Atticus to be. But it was on one of Pomponi's two guests that the Etruscan concentrated his attention. He thought he recognised him. Pomponius introduced him to the other guest. "Meet Lucius Varius Rufus. He is writing a tragedy on the character of Thyestes that, I assure you, will be a masterpiece. He is a fervent admirer of Caesar Octavian and also of his right hand man Agrippa."

"I am delighted to meet you, Maecenas. I was anxious to have the opportunity to talk to such a clever man, and one so close to Caesar Octavian. I have taken the liberty of bringing with me a small sample of my work in the hope that you will appreciate it and bring it to the attention of the triumvir," said Varius, handing him a scroll which Maecenas accepted gracefully, passing it to Plotius and reassuring him that he would read it as soon as possible.

"This is the man I wanted you to meet," replied the host, indicating the other guest. "We were just reading a most agreeable piece he has written in hexameters – an eclogue which celebrates the peace established after the Misenum treaty between Caesar,

Antony and Sextus Pompey. His name is Publius Vergilius Maro, and in my humble opinion we have a new Theocritus. A Roman Theocritus, in fact, who started with the Syracusan poet's style, but has taken the form much further. There is none of the detachment that we find in the work of Theocritus, but instead an intense emotional involvement, which vibrates the strings of the soul."

Maecenas remembered where he had seen him before and, casting a glance at his two companions, realised that they too had recognised him. It was that annoying lawyer who had come to claim the restitution of his family's property at the time of the confiscations, boasting of powerful friends. No wonder he was at the home of one of the most important men in Rome. He thought it unseemly to mention it before the other guests, though, and hoped that Horace would feel the same way.

He hoped in vain.

"Well, well, look who's here! Did you manage to get back all that you lost, Virgil?" asked his friend.

"Do you two already know each other?" asked Pomponius Atticus.

Maecenas glared at Horace. "We met in a rather… particular situation, yes… But Virgil, I am truly interested in your work," he said, mostly to change the subject from that embarrassing topic. "It seems to me an excellent idea to celebrate the current peace. The triumvirs would certainly appreciate it, if they knew of it..."

"What was I saying earlier about people sucking up to the powerful?" whispered Horace in his ear. Meanwhile Plotius Tucca, who had started reading Varius's work, was tugging at his friend's sleeve.

"I hope then that they may become aware of my work, sir," said Virgil, with the resigned air that made Maecenas and his friends smile when they met him, imagining him dealing with lost causes in the Forum. "But it is only a modest work on a pastoral theme. I wrote the fourth eclogue just under a year ago, in truth, on the wave of enthusiasm we all experienced at the time of the Brindisi agreements between Caesar and Antony and after learning that Antony's new wife and Caesar's sister were pregnant. Peace came only a few months later, when Sextus Pompey also became involved in the agreements, but by then the groundwork had been laid."

"Very well. Let us hear this eclogue, then," Maecenas said, more intrigued by Pomponius's evident esteem than by Virgil's own presentation. Meanwhile, Horace and Plotius were showing great interest in Varius's text. Plotius caught the Etruscan's eye and made an eloquent gesture with his hand to show him that it was good stuff.

Pomponius nodded and motioned to the slave to resume the reading. The man approached the lectern and began to declaim:

For thee, O boy,
First shall the earth, untilled, pour freely forth
Her childish gifts, the gadding ivy-spray
With foxglove and Egyptian bean-flower mixed,
And laughing-eyed acanthus. Of themselves,
Untended, will the she-goats then bring home
Their udders swollen with milk, while flocks afield
Shall of the monstrous lion have no fear.
Thy very cradle shall pour forth for thee
Caressing flowers. The serpent too shall die,
Die shall the treacherous poison-plant, and far
And wide Assyrian spices spring. But soon
As thou hast skill to read of heroes' fame,
And of thy father's deeds, and learn
What virtue is, the plain by slow degrees
With waving corn-crops shall to golden grow,
From the wild briar shall hang the blushing grape,
And stubborn oaks sweat honey-dew. Nevertheless
Yet shall there lurk within of ancient wrong
Some traces, bidding tempt the deep with ships,
Gird towns with walls, with furrows cleave the earth.
Therewith a second Tiphys shall there be,
Her hero-freight a second Argo bear;
New wars too shall arise, and once again

Some great Achilles to some Troy be sent.
Then, when the mellowing years have made thee man,
No more shall mariner sail, nor pine-tree bark
Ply traffic on the sea, but every…[1]

With each new hexameter Maecenas felt increasingly overcome with emotion, and after a few moments he realised that the apparently insignificant man sitting next to him was the personification of all that he had hoped to find since he had begun his cultural project. His talent was immense, his enthusiasm for Octavian's government sincere and convincing, and the two together created an overwhelming effect which showed how powerful that poem could be if it were given the proper direction and support.

He decided that the project could never be fully realised without the contribution of Publius Vergilius Maro.

Whilst all were voicing their praise, he looked over tot Horace and Plotius Tucca and saw that the text had made an impression on them too. Plotius showered Vergilius with compliments, Horace, however, looked troubled, and seemed even to be trembling. It was clear that he was trying to hide the powerful effect that the verses had on him.

Suddenly, he asked for silence and said, "It has been a long time since I have heard such well-fashioned hexameters." And it was obvious that it cost him to admit it. "A very, very fine style, really. Elegant and sensitive, and since we are among people who appreciate good poetry, I would like to take this opportunity to declaim a poem of my own. I'd like to improvise, if you don't mind, and see if others are able to do the same."

Without waiting for the host's consent, Horace rose from the couch and stood beside the slave, who he motioned to leave.

And while Pomponius gestured to him to continue, Maecenas looked at his friend and asked himself, incredulously, what had moved him to finally reveal his art, which in one way or another he had always refused to let the Etruscan see, limiting himself to an audience of one, Plotius.

Now I return to myself, who am descended from a freedman; whom every body nibbles at, as being descended from a freedman. Now, because, Maecenas, I am a constant guest of yours; but formerly, because a Roman legion was under my command, as being a military tribune. This latter case is different from the former: for, though any person perhaps might justly envy me that post of honour, yet could he not do so with regard to your being my friend! especially as you are cautious to admit such as are worthy; and are far from having any sinister ambitious views. I can not reckon myself a lucky fellow on this account, as if it were by accident that I got you for my friend; for no kind of accident threw you in my way. That best of men, Virgil, long ago, and after him, Varius, told you what I was. When first I came into your presence, I spoke a few words in a broken manner (for childish bashfulness hindered me from speaking more); I did not tell you that I was the issue of an illustrious father: I did not claim to ride about the country on a Satureian horse, but plainly what I really was; you answer, as your custom is, a few words: I depart: and you re-invite me after the ninth month, and command me to be in the number of your friends. I esteem it a great thing that I pleased you, who distinguish probity from baseness, not by the illustriousness of a father, but by the purity of heart and feelings.[2]

While the audience applauded, Maecenas was overcome by another wave of emotion – not simply because Horace had finally decided to display his extraordinary talent to him, but also because he understood why he had decided now to reveal what he was capable of. He had noticed how impressed Maecenas had been by Virgil's hexameters as well as by Varius's work and had feared that he would lose his attention.

Now the Etruscan was certain that – albeit in his own way – Horace shared his feelings.

In a sense, it was true: it had been Virgil and Varius who had allowed him to actually understand him. Without them, he would never have known the man who was beside him.

*

A central column of Romans attacked on its flanks by two contingents of Gauls who, in turn, were being attacked from behind by Roman cohorts, who were in turn under threat of other barbarian attacks. Agrippa could never have imagined ending up in such a complicated situation when he conceived of his plan to surprise the Aquitanians. Now more than ever, everything depended on him. He had no way of seeing how they were faring in the centre and could only hope that they were managing to organise an effective defence, otherwise, his manoeuvre would fail – he would have no chance of achieving a decisive victory, and the price would be the loss of an entire legion.

His original plan was to deploy troops in a line along the edge of the forest and move forward, raking out all the Gauls fleeing from the attack from the flanks, but the appearance of enemy reserves had forced him to change his strategy. Now there was no alternative but to join the battle while keeping the column in formation and focus on a specific area to break through and assist the central legion in the hope that it was still in one piece. He explained to the tribune what was expected from the unit and remained at the head of the formation. Then they advanced.

The forest did not allow the Romans to keep close ranks, but their discipline helped them remain focused. The Gauls had already noticed them and tried to set up a defensive wall with shields and spears, but they were pre-occupied with their attack on the Roman flanks. When Agrippa and his men engaged in battle with them, many Gauls were trapped between the Roman units.

Agrippa had to dismount to get through the dense forest, and progress was made even harder by the presence of dead bodies underfoot and groups of soldiers fighting one another. He cleared his path by cutting down branches and weeds, as well as any enemy arms, legs and heads that almost spontaneously offered themselves to his sword. In fact, several times, after eliminating one, he would find a Roman from the flank behind him who would just manage to avoid being stabbed in the back by another Gaul. The central Roman column must be behind him but Agrippa still couldn't see it.

"Join us! Merge into this column!" Agrippa cried out to anyone within earshot, gradually advancing. Those who were able to did, swelling the ranks of his legion, which was becoming increasingly more capable of overwhelming the enemy front line, which had now been broken by the double offensive. But behind them there were more Gauls and when Agrippa came into contact with them, he found much tougher resistance. He had to slow down the advance and wait for his troops to tighten their formation, but the density of undergrowth and warriors made it impossible. The whole thing was chaos but the high number of barbarian warriors he encountered made him realise that they had concentrated their forces there to inflict a mortal blow to the Roman army. Now was the day of reckoning – he would destroy them, or they would be destroyed, and if he lost, all of Gaul, and not just Aquitaine, would rise up, creating even more difficulties for Octavian than he had faced in the past. The triumvir would not have the resources to conquer it again and Sextus Pompey would take the opportunity to start forcing his hand, and Antony might take over and their dream would vanish.

He had to win at all costs.

He urged his men to greater efforts, although he knew that they were doing all they could. At the head of their respective units, the centurions exhorted their men onwards, and the Gauls ended up crushed under their feet, slashed by dozens of swords, and stunned by the impact of their shields. Their colourful clothing, pale skin adorned by countless tattoos and elaborately decorated shields, everything was blended into a mixture of mud, sweat and blood. Agrippa's progress was almost rhythmic, mechanical even, swings of his sword alternating with shoves with his shield and blows with his elbows and knees. For every fallen Roman soldier, he counted at least twenty barbarians collapsing under the blows of the legionaries, unstoppable in their combination of compact size and brute strength.

He split open the head of yet another Gaul who appeared before him and then had to halt another swing of his blade in mid-air for the central column appeared in front of him, arranged in an approximate square, with their shields and swords pointing outwards on all four sides. Their lines were interspersed with a few fallen men, but overall Agrippa thought that the formation was still solid. The soldiers of the central column gave cries of joy at the sight of their comrades, and Agrippa shouted greetings to them. But it was not over yet. Now there was the other side of the central column to deal with before the Gauls engaged there were able to escape to fight another day.

"Everyone with me! March on!" he shouted and in a few moments his column had almost doubled in size, turning into a human tide that swept away everything in its path. The barbarians attacking the square formation from the opposite side were the first to be overrun. One moment they brandished their swords above their helmets, their eyes blazing with elation and blood lust, their war cries resounding through the forest and their shields well-placed in front of them. A moment later they were trampled into the mud by hundreds of feet, their ravaged bodies lying in pools of blood and viscera, their bones crushed and twisted and their armour dented and bent.

The five cohorts that were themselves caught between the two warring flanks joined the human tide. They were on their last legs. A moment later and Agrippa would have found only corpses, reduced to the condition of those of the Gauls they had just passed over. But even they retained enough discipline to merge into the ranks of the advancing army. Even the wounded, many of them barely able to walk, bent double, limping and unable to even hold their shields up, looked for a place to give one final blow to the enemy.

Now there was nothing behind the last line of barbarians. They could run away and escape if the Romans weren't sufficiently rapid in their pursuit. And that mustn't happen. None of them must remain free to return and be a threat to the empire. Agrippa urged his soldiers to run. It now no longer mattered whether they kept the ranks tight or not, because the numerical superiority of the Romans was overwhelming.

He was no longer facing the wild screams and grinning faces of the barbarian warriors, but was looking at their retreating backs. The Gauls' only thought now was of escape and many had cast aside their shields in order to run faster. But the thick vegetation into which they had lured the Romans to hinder their proverbial cohesion now hindered them in turn, slowing them down, forcing them to veer through the undergrowth and making them, sooner or later, fall victim to a converging legionary arriving from the right or the left. Agrippa breathed a sigh of relief. He had seen and experienced enough battles to know that this one was won.

Now he could start thinking about building bridges, roads and aqueducts with which to convince the Gallic population that life would be better under Roman rule.

1. Translation taken from http://classics.mit.edu/Virgil/eclogue.4.iv.html

2. Translation taken from http://www.authorama.com/works-of-horace-6.html

XIV

"Are you sure that he is still in there?" Ortwin asked Ventidius Bassus.

"No doubt about it," replied the general. "He'll be waiting for his Parthian friends to come to his assistance... *Imperator* and *parthicus* he calls himself... Hah! As soon as I get hold of that renegade, I'll make him pay for the death of poor Decidius Saxa. A Roman who sides with the city's worst enemies to kill his fellow citizens deserves no mercy. And to think that he is from the Picenum region, just like me!"

"Do not underestimate him, General," insisted Ortwin. "He is clever – very clever. I have known him for many years and he has never been outwitted."

"Well, he has allowed us to get here to Attalea without doing anything to hinder our progress through his dominions," continued Bassus. "This means that his potentate is unstable and that we will take it back before the Parthians get here. He managed to conquer Syria and Cilicia and get to Lycia because Saxa's soldiers fought with him, taking advantage of the shortage of garrisons, but now things have changed and he will have to face a real army."

Ortwin looked at Veleda and grimaced. Ventidius Bassus was a fine general, he said to himself, but he lacked imagination – and like many before him, he tended to underestimate Quintus Labienus. The ruthlessness of the traitor was inexhaustible and his resourcefulness had grown over the years, you needed to be equipped with a healthy dose of imagination to anticipate his moves. In the past, Ortwin could never have imagined him going to the Parthians and convincing them to give him the command of an army to make a sortie against his own people, just as he could never have imagined him capable of the massacres at Alabanda and Mylasa against those who had tried to resist his attacks. As soon as he had stormed their walls, he had put the whole city to the sword, allowing his soldiers to vent their basest instincts on the unfortunate populations, then he had drained the Cilician cities of all the money they possessed, and because of him, Pacorus, the son of King Orodes, had taken possession of Syria and Judea, which had been Roman territories in all but name since the days of Pompey the Great.

Ortwin did not tell Bassus that it was Labienus who had murdered Quintus Pedius, Octavian's mother and Etain, all of whom were protected and even hidden. Nor that it was Labienus who had injured him so badly at Philippi, or that he had sacrificed the life of Cassius, his supreme commander, to save himself.

No, Quintus Labienus was a man to be reckoned with. He was capable of all kinds of wickedness.

"In any case, at this point we should attack the city," suggested Ortwin. "If we wait, the Parthians might arrive from Syria."

"Listen, German, it is not up to you to tell me what I should do," said Bassus, icily. "I was told to treat you with respect and I will, but always remember that it is I who make the decisions here, is that clear? And I prefer to wait until the legions arrive before I give the order to start the assault. With only these auxiliary units at my disposal, I risk looking a fool. Do you see those scorpios in the stands? They are just waiting for us to try to make a move against the walls..."

Ortwin bowed his head and nodded. He could have continued to argue, saying that it would be wise in the meantime to encircle the city with ditches and embankments, cutting them off and trying to starve them into surrender, but there was no point. Bassus was not the kind of general who listened to the opinions of his subordinates and he did not consider the light infantry with whom he had come this far capable of building strong fortifications like those of the heavy infantry.

They spent two more days there before the other legionaries arrived and the excavation work to encircle the city began. Two days during which Ortwin twitched with impatience as he waited to come face to face with his old enemy again. He had the man within reach once again, yet he was helpless, waiting for the decisions of the commander in chief. He had crossed the sea to meet him and end to their feud once and for all, and he wanted to approach the walls and call out to him in a loud voice, inviting him to come out and challenge him to a duel.

But he knew that Labienus would never do that. He had never been a man of honour and as long as he had any chance of survivial he would do whatever he could to avoid confrontation of any kind.

There was also Veleda to consider. An eerie silence had fallen between them since they had arrived in Asia – a constant tension caused by this latest chapter in their pursuit of the man who had scarred their lives, and they could not talk about it. Ortwin had never been entirely sure of Veleda's feelings towards Labienus and now, as he approached a new showdown, the German, though hoping that this would be the decisive one, feared more strongly than ever that his wife would hesitate. Despite everything the man had done to her, she was not indifferent to nor did she hate him as she should have done, and that was something he could not stand. She had encountered him again when he had gone on the raid in which Octavian's mother had died. Veleda confessed to Ortwin that she was unable to kill Labienus even as she held a dagger at his throat because the lives of Octavia and her daughter had been at stake, and then Labienus had managed to escape. But Ortwin hadn't been there, so how could he know that things had really gone as she said? What if she had forgiven him? What if she hadn't killed him even though she'd had the opportunity? Or even worse, what if she actually didn't want to kill him?

It was Veleda who had wanted to spare him when, after Munda, the German had defeated him in a duel, and the man had come back again and again to haunt them in Rome, in the East, in Philippi. But this time he would do anything to put an end to this persecution and to prevent Labienus from continuing to come between them and causing mistrust between them. He watched Veleda during the long hours of waiting in front of the city walls, trying to understand her emotions yet not daring to speak about them. He did not expect her to tell him the truth so he didn't ask any questions. Ortwin thought that perhaps even she did not exactly know what she still felt for Labienus. Even killing him would not completely sever the bond that had formed between the woman and her jailer and tormentor. Assuming that the German actually did manage to kill him. The last time they met, at Philippi, it had been Labienus who had prevailed, and if he hadn't finished him off it was only because he had immediately been forced to flee.

The proverbial Roman efficiency allowed Ventidius Bassus to get his fortifications completed in just two days. No one could enter or leave the city without the permission of the Capitoline troops. Bassus's legions, which had continued to flow there, were now all present. An increasingly impatient Ortwin went to see the commander in his praetorium and, putting aside all pleasantries, asked him directly, "What do you intend doing, general? Would you mind telling me?" It wasn't like him to be disrespectful towards a superior – not even to that imbecile Dolabella the last time he was in Asia – but now that he was faced with the prospect of fighting Labienus, he could no longer control himself.

Bassus frowned at him. He knew that Ortwin enjoyed protection in high places and that he could not put him in his place as he would have wished to. "I was just about to give the order. Will you come with me?" he said simply, while leaving the tent. The German followed him in silence until they reached the area where the onagers and ballistas were. Bassus had ordered them from Europe for he was certain that the Asian campaign would be based primarily on the need to deprive the Parthians of the conquered cities. "Move them into range!" he ordered, and soon the crews were busy shifting the machines towards the walls. Veleda appeared alongside Ortwin and the two Germans looked at each other in silence. They both knew that the moment of truth had arrived.

The weapons had been arrayed across a wide arc in order to be able to target a large section of the walls, all of them at the same distance, at the point which had been calculated as ideal for the attack.

"Load up! Let's fire before they have time to think!" ordered Bassus, standing behind the closest onager.

The crew loaded a boulder into the sling at the end of the shooting arm and then, by means of the winch on the left, they lowered the beam until it touched the frame. Bassus moved to one side to avoid the recoil, raised his arm, and then suddenly brought it down. The crew released the sling, which collided violently against the cushion positioned at the top of the structure to interrupt the movement, and the boulder was thrown towards its target with incredible force, sending the machine recoiling violently backwards and reminding Ortwin of the wild animal from which it took its name.

The stone struck the walls with a deafening crash which was immediately followed by many others. The enemy artillery also started firing.

Bassus ordered a second bombardment, and then a third, and boulders began to rain down almost continuously against the city walls. He was about to order the fourth when someone pointed out to him that the gate was opening. Ortwin peered at it with his one eye and saw some civilians emerging with their arms aloft. Bassus froze as they approached. The gate closed behind them, and the general ordered some legionaries to escort them.

When they were finally in front of him, Ortwin and Veleda were at his side. Labienus, of course, was not among them. "General, we ask you to suspend the attack," began the one who looked like the leader, a fat man dripping with sweat who was clearly very frightened. "The city is yours and we are willing to open up the gates, if you promise not to harm us."

"I doubt Quintus Labienus will have agreed to this. Why has he allowed you to come out?" asked Bassus.

"Quintus Labienus is no longer here, general," said the man, to Ortwin's dismay. "He decided that he had insufficient manpower to resist your attack and went to Syria before you built the fortifications, taking with him almost the entire garrison of soldiers and two outlaws, the Bucolianus brothers... you know, the ones who killed Caesar, who are part of his staff. He left a few soldiers with scorpios and ordered them to remain in the stands to give the impression that the city was being defended and to gain an advantage over you. He also ordered us to resist the siege, but we of the city senate consulted and decided that it was not worth risking our lives for a man who had left and who had extorted all our riches. Riches which, incidentally, he took with him…"

Bassus glanced at Ortwin and then quickly looked away, in a clumsy attempt to conceal his embarrassment at his own misjudgment.

*

"There he is! It's him, I can see him!" said Veleda, seeing the silhouettes of a column of legionaries at the top of the pass. They were little more than dark spots surrounded by gleaming snow. "How do you know it's him?" answered Ortwin, at the head of a group of scouts preceding Ventidius Bassus's column.

"Do you think I can't recognise him from afar? I tell you, he is among those soldiers," said Veleda resentfully, realising an instant too late that she had offended her man. But she didn't apologise. She never apologised.

Ortwin winced. That was the most that he allowed himself to express disapproval or displeasure. "Even if he is there, how can we stop him?" he protested. "We might be able to reach him on horses, but there are too few of us to take him on. According to what that man from Attalea said, he took at least five hundred men with him, there are only thirty of us."

The woman turned to their guide, who they had brought with them from Attalea. "Is there another way to get to the pass?" she asked him.

The man thought for a moment, then answered by pointing to the right of the crossing point, where the Taurus Mountains continued, creating a barrier between Pamphylia and Cilicia. "There is another pass that is closer and more difficult. It is very steep and dangerous, but it's quicker. The fugitives have not taken it because there are many of them and they have carts, which would struggle in all that snow."

Veleda made a gesture of triumph. "The greed of Labienus has betrayed him," she said. "Those carts are all full of the riches he plundered in Lycia and Pamphylia and mean that he has to take the long way round. We will take advantage of that. Ortwin, leave the men with me and go and tell Bassus to hasten his march."

The German was startled. "What in Wotan's name are you going to do?"

"Simple. I'll take the shortest route and blockade the road. When he sees us waiting for him he will have to stop in the pass, allowing the general to catch up with him," she replied confidently.

"Are you joking? There are only thirty of you. He will wipe you out in an instant," the man protested.

"Not if we have him believe that there are more of us than there actually are. Our men are all archers are they not? So it can be done. If anything, send me some reinforcements when you and Bassus arrive just to be on the safe side."

Ortwin pondered for a moment. He knew that when Veleda got an idea in her head it was impossible to get her to change her mind. "Very well. But you go to Bassus. I will remain here on the Taurus."

"No. I will go."

"Why?"

Veleda had no ready answer. She only knew that she felt great pleasure at the idea of being the one to block off Labienus's escape route. "Because I have decided that it shall be so," she said regally, just as she did when she didn't actually have an argument, and putting her trust in the fact that once, long ago, Ortwin had served her and her father.

It always worked. A little of the awe that a warrior of a royal *comitatus* held towards his sovereign's family still remained in him, and Veleda did not fail to take advantage of the fact.

As she expected, Ortwin nodded, turned his horse round and set off towards the army of Ventidius Bassus, who – once again – had brought only light infantry. Then Veleda gestured to their guide, and they set off briskly until the land began to rise and become rocky. They had to proceed more slowly, but Veleda refused to let the men dismount, despite being aware of the risk of stumbling. She continued to push on her mount, leaving the others, who found her hard to keep up with, behind. Even the guide. But she neither turned nor stopped to wait for them, facing the icy wind that reddened her face, the bright light which reflected off the snow and the thin air of the high mountains with a fierce frown and grim determination.

Once on the pass, however, she had to stop and wait for the guide, at whom she shouted insults because he was, in her opinion, going too slowly. He indicated the route and she started to trot, hearing him yelling from behind her that the descent was, if anything, more dangerous than the climb up. She ignored him and continued her mad rush until her horse stumbled on a rock jutting out of the snow, and fell forward, catapulting her into the white snow. She felt no pain. Perhaps she was hurt, perhaps not, but the intense cold, together with her frenzy for the job at hand, made her unaware of the messages from her body. She waited for one of her warriors to arrive and commandeered his horse before remounting and continuing to descend the slope. She realised that arriving there alone would pointless, but she was also convinced that by following her lead, her men would go faster.

She only stopped when she came to a fork where her road met one coming down from the peaks. She waited for the guide to catch up with her and asked, "Does this road lead to the pass the fugitives took?"

"Yes. We can wait for them here, where the rocks are bigger," said the man, pointing to a group of boulders a few steps away.

Veleda nodded, moving towards the boulders, studying the terrain and mentally positioning her forces. The position was a good one, she decided. There was enough cover to hide in, for as well as the rocks there were plenty of oaks and junipers, full of snowy branches. She heard a noise and was about to come out of her hiding place to call her men, but on realising that it had not come from the road she had just travelled, she went back behind the rock, indicating to the guide to do the same and watched the scene. Soon afterwards, two horsemen appeared on the other path – no doubt they were Labienus's scouts.

They mustn't see that she was alone. Or rather, their leader was not to know that the blockade was so flimsy it was barely there at all. The two stopped and looked around. This was the moment. Watched by the terrified guide, she drew her sword and rode close to the rocks until she was forced to come out into the open. But by now she was close to the enemy soldiers, who saw her suddenly come at them. The first did not even have time to lift his spear before she slashed his neck wide open, he fell from his saddle, his head lolling to the side like a sack. The other tried to take aim with his javelin, but Veleda threw herself and her sword at him, striking him in the chest and piercing his leather armour.

Just then the first of her soldiers arrived.

"Finally!" she gasped, then distributed her men as they arrived behind rocks and trees which allowed them to target the road. She also gave orders to leave the two bodies where they were. That would make the enemy hesitate, giving them just enough time for Ortwin to send reinforcements.

When everyone was in place, she saw the head of Labienus's column appear. As expected, the soldiers stopped suddenly when they noticed the two bodies in the road, but they noticed them only at the last moment, because the wind had risen and had already partially covered them with snow. She ordered her men to get their arrows ready and then to fire, and an instant later, seven men fell to the ground with arrows in their chests. The rest of the column immediately drew back, even though some tried to retrieve their wounded comrades. But a second burst dissuaded even the most willing, who vanished round the first corner.

It was done. Now they just had to wait for Ortwin and Bassus.

*

There was no way to attack Labienus. Realising that they had blocked the road at both ends of the pass, he had entrenched himself at the top in an almost impregnable position. As long as he had provisions, it was impossible to flush him out with the few men they had available. Veleda – as Ortwin never missed an opportunity to remind Ventidius Bassus – had done a great job of making the German think that he could go no further in Cilicia, and soon the blockade hastily set up by the German had widened to become a robust barrier.

But neither Bassus nor Ortwin intended to simply wait for Labienus to surrender, or for him to launch a desperate attack to try and force the blockade. After what had happened in the city, the German had convinced the general that the Roman was unpredictable and that he would be planning some surprise of his own. Bassus had ended up agreeing to call up his heavy infantry, in addition to the light infantry he had sent in pursuit of the traitor, to launch an attack on the enemy position.

Ortwin's morale had finally picked up. Persuaded by the determination with which Veleda had blocked

Labienus's escape route, he now had more confidence in his woman's feelings, though he still continued to nurture some fear for the final outcome. It was then that he would really see where her sentiments lay, behind the rationality that would guide her until she found herself face to face with him.

After a week, the reinforcements' scouts finally appeared to announce their arrival, and Ortwin went to Bassus. "General, we can attack, they're here!" he announced, with the agitation he always had when his old rival was involved.

"Well, let them rest for a day at least," said Bassus with a smile. "May I remind you that they will have to climb a mountain in the cold and the snow, and that if they do it immediately after their long march they will not be at their best. We will attack the day after tomorrow. After all, he is trapped."

Ortwin could not deny that there was something in the commander's words. "How are you going to proceed?" he asked finally.

"We will send a legion over to Veleda on the other side to launch a diversion from the ground while the majority of our men we will go up this slope," Bassus explained. "He is done for, and there's a good chance that he will surrender without even fighting back."

"I wouldn't count on it," Ortwin replied. "He will do anything to avoid giving in."

He left the general and the camp to go and await the troops, only occasionally returning to his tent to warm himself, but after a few hours, he heard a loud bang from the camp. He rushed down the valley and stopped a soldier.

"What happened?"

The man didn't have time to answer, but suddenly Ventidius Bassus appeared in his place. "The Parthians! That was what Labienus was waiting for, damn it! He must have warned them when we arrived in Attalea. From Veleda's end they reported that they have started to come up – and our men, obviously, being totally outnumbered, our men have hidden. It seems that there are a lot of them."

Ortwin was dismayed. "And now?"

"Things look bad. We're probably going to have to engage in an equally matched battle. I doubt they have come up here in such great numbers just to save Labienus. They must have sensed an opportunity to inflict another Carre on us. But I'm no Crassus, you can bet on that!" Bassus shouted. "I'm in an advantageous position and I am certainly not going to go down there to the plain to make things easy for their cavalry."

"So we will wait for them?"

"It's the only sensible thing to do. I'll wait for all the legionaries to get up here, then if the enemy attack, I'll know how to deal with them," he replied firmly, heading toward the camp.

They did not have to wait long. The first Parthian horsemen appeared at the base of the slopes within an hour and soon, ranks of riders had formed a line along the slopes. But in the meantime, the legionaries had started ascending the opposite slope, on the side towards Pamphylia.

Battle formation.

"They want to attack us right away!" cried Bassus as he watched their manoeuvres.

"Labienus must have told them that we are without heavy infantry," said Ortwin. "But they don't know that it is on its way," Ortwin intervened.

"Well, we'll show them that there aren't just a few of us and we'll go and attack them," said Bassus.

"Perhaps it would be better not to let them see that, general."

Bassus looked at him suspiciously, but he had learned to respect him, and so he motioned to him to speak.

"Let them believe, instead, that there are only a few of us," explained Ortwin. "If they haven't seen the legionaries yet, let's line up our forces at the head of the valley and wait for them to attack, and in the meantime, tell the legions to move around the slope and cross it on the side. And they will attack them when they are busy fighting us."

Bassus weighed up the idea. “It might just work,” he declared, then immediately gave orders for everything to be prepared just as Ortwin had suggested. Shortly afterwards, the Roman auxiliaries were deployed in front of the rampart, with Bassus and Ortwin at the head, while the enemy ranks were getting into formation just below.

The German observed the famous horsemen who had inflicted the most dramatic defeats on the Romans in recent years. What made them deadly was their impressive combination of the heavy cavalry of the cataphracts, completely covered in metal plates from the riders’ heads to the horses’ legs and holding long lances in both hands, and the light cavalry, which consisted of skilled archers capable of emptying a quiver in a short time with frightening precision and who were always in motion. They were enough to frighten even an experienced warrior like him. In all his many campaigns, he had never had dealings with them, and he did not feel as confident as he usually did. Fortunately, he reflected, Veleda was with another contingent and would not be participating in the battle.

“They are managing to climb even loaded down like that – look,” said Bassus, pointing to some horsemen who had already departed for the attack without waiting for their fellow soldiers. “They must have a very poor opinion of the Romans after defeating them in Carre and having won half of Asia with such ridiculous ease…"

"And we're giving them confirmation that we are unwary," replied Ortwin, "by leaving the entrenchment rather than waiting for them there. They will be on top of us in a moment."

"Exactly," said Bassus, then turned to his soldiers. "They will shower you with arrows then move aside to make way for the heavy cavalry. Form a roof of shields and then when they get close to you, throw yourselves to the ground and aim to cut the horses legs!"

As soon as he had finished speaking, the Parthians came in range and the sky was suddenly streaked with a myriad of arrows. But however skilled the archers were, firing uphill whilst in motion was not conducive to accuracy and only a few arrows hit the Roman line, most of which were stopped by the shields. They barely had time to fire a second volley before the shiny metal monsters placed themselves between them and the enemy soldiers, preventing them from firing again.

"Remember, go for the legs under the edge of the armour!" shouted Bassus.

In a few moments, the long enemy lances smashed into the troops, some hitting their targets. Ortwin saw the man next to him attempt to block a lance with his shield, which, however, shattered upon impact with the tip, which went on to pierce his chest. Immediately afterwards, the horseman rode over his victim, trampling him to a pulp and then stopping so as not to fall into the ditch in front of the rampart of the camp. It was then that Ortwin lunged at the horse's legs, severing the two front ones in one single blow. The beast slumped forward, ending up right in the ditch along with the knight.

Ortwin saw another cataphract trying to remove his spear from an auxiliary soldier, and he took the opportunity to roll under the horse's belly. He lashed out with his sword and found himself on the opposite side of the animal when it hit the ground. He had narrowly missed being crushed beneath it. He saw that a fellow soldier had not been so lucky – he had managed to cut one of horse's legs, but had been trapped underneath the fallen animal and had already suffocated. Not so her rider, who was on his feet and had drawn his sword to deal with the nearest enemy soldier: Ortwin. His armour was heavy, though, and it hindered his movement, so it was easy for the German to wait until he could see the only part of his body that was unprotected – the lower part of his face – and ram his sword into the man's mouth. Just then the pressure eased and the enemy's cavalry ranks began to thin out. Ortwin looked at the sides. The columns of legionaries had entered the fray, engaging with both the cataphracts and the archers of the light cavalry waiting behind them to finish the Romans off.

Before long, though, it was they who were finished off by the Romans.

XV

"I would say that we can be satisfied. Antony behaved exactly as we expected," said Maecenas as he left the Senate, where he had just attended a sitting. One finally without Antony, who had left with Octavia and the children for Athens, for he had chosen to administer his part of the empire and prepare for the forthcoming war against the Parthians from there. Octavian had breathed a sigh of relief: although relations between them had improved, the man's presence in Rome was a real burden, and in his heart, he had hoped he would go away as soon as possible. This had been one of the first meetings of the Senate chaired by him alone, and it had been a different kettle of fish altogether.

After the news from Sextus Pompey, he could actually sleep in peace. The admiral had written to protest about Antony's behaviour in the Peloponnese. Before handing it over to Pompey, in fact, the triumvir – just as Octavian had anticipated – had stripped it to the bone, going far beyond what he was actually due in back taxes and leaving Pompey with a province that was practically bankrupt – and in which he would need to invest a great deal in order to make it flourish again.

But that was not what they had discussed in the Senate. The consolidation of power was something that only concerned the cult of Mars Ultor and Octavian kept only the cult's members informed of its progress. With the other representatives of the institutions, the triumvir discussed the drafts of laws for improving the lives of the citizens of the empire and of Rome in particular: a more extensive road network, a state postal system, a military code, expeditions along borders to consolidate them, just administration of the provinces, efficient taxation… In a nutshell, all the things required to make Rome a better place to live, with rules to control construction and renovation work, improved lighting at night, a regular flow of clean water to the capital through the construction of new aqueducts, improvements to the sewerage system and a consistent and plentiful grain supply for its citizens. And in addition, entertainment provided by state events of various kinds, from conventional gladiator fights and the hunting of wild animals to chariot races and the naval battles which Caesar had started and to which he intended to give a special space by constructing a basin specifically for that purpose. And he had shown that he intended to dedicate a great deal of energy to restoring patriotic customs and ancestral rites and to promoting the building of places of worship wherever his empire extended.

But he found opposition to his innovations in the Senate. Perhaps partly due to the senators themselves, who were conservative and narrow minded, and attached to their privileges which they considered the only things that needed defending. They had nether the desire nor the imagination to initiate new reforms, and because he was not the supreme ruler of the empire the senators least willing to go along with his program of renewal used the pretext of needing to hear the opinions of the other rulers to hinder any progress. Until the sect had eliminated all those who were opposed to Caesar and his projects and brought their leader to the very highest position in the state, overcoming all opposition, any reform would be limited. Like the senators, Antony, Lepidus and Pompey were only interested in preserving the order that had brought them to power, or – in the best case – their own personal glory. For this reason, Octavian never ceased to think about how to get rid of them all and remain the only repository of power in Rome – to really turn it into an empire.

"Antony's behaviour attests to the fact that he wouldn't be entirely opposed to a war," said Octavian in response to his friend, "although, of course, if he wants to defeat the Parthians he will need peace in the West and will want to make it look as though war is the last thing he wants. We'll have to present him with a fait accompli."

"And have you any idea how we might do that?" the Etruscan asked.

"Of course. There's something I haven't told you, my friend. I was afraid that you would tell me that it was inappropriate and premature."

Maecenas looked surprised and then disappointed. Octavian smiled. "Don't worry. I have yet to act and I would like to know what you think."

This seemed to cheer the Etruscan up. "What does it concern?" he asked.

"It is Menodorus, Pompey's freedman."

"You have corrupted him?" said Maecenas immediately.

"If anything, it was him that contacted *me*, and I have no intention of letting this opportunity slip away. At the end of the Misenum meetings, he approached me, candidly confessing that he had suggested to his master, when we were guests in Pompey's hexareme, killing both me and Antony and taking the whole empire."

Maecenas blanched. "By the gods! And he actually *told* you that? But Pompey refused, right?"

"Pompey chided him for not having done so directly without saying anything, specifying that his honour prevented him from accepting such an immoral plan."

"It's very fortunate for us, then, that after all he is a man of honour," said Maecenas.

"Yes, but I have no intention of thanking him for it," Octavian continued. "My honour forces me to consider the good of Rome and it is a bad thing for Rome that he is still around. Menodorus told me that he was disgusted by his lack of determination, which he seems to feel I have in great measure. For this reason, he has offered to put himself at my service... Considering that Pompey has entrusted Sardinia and Corsica to him, he would be a great asset for us, and us for him too: we will have to pay him more than Pompey did."

"And you didn't want to take advantage of his offer until you'd seen relations between Antony and Pompey break down."

"Yes, but now it feels as though the time is right. I am going to write to Menodorus. I'll send someone to take delivery of his islands and not only that, he will have to help ensure that the responsibility for the resumption of hostilities falls squarely on Pompey's shoulders."

Maecenas held his hands up. "It seems to me that your ideas are clear. Do you want my approval?"

"Well, I would like you to tell me if there is a flaw in my plan."

"I think there is. Antony. You said yourself that he may not agree."

"It's true, he may not," answered Octavian. "And what do you suggest I do about it?"

"Hmm... Now you are going to call him back to Italy to agree on the war, right?"

"That's right. But there is a danger that he will want peace and will refuse to give me the ships to fight Pompey."

"Hmm... I might have a solution. Let's go to your house and write him a nice letter inviting him to meet us in Brindisi..."

"And then what?"

"And then... We will talk about it over a glass of *Falernum* in your *triclinium*," said Maecenas with a smile, deliberately being mysterious in revenge for Octavian's silence about the project. His friend smiled and pressed him no further. Moreover, he also had a more urgent task to carry out.

"Good idea," he concluded jovially. "Come to my house so you can see what is going to happen. I have been wanting to make changes at home for a long time, and this news makes me realise that the time has come..."

*

From one end of Gaul to the other, and beyond. From the maritime Gauls to the Germans of the Central European forests, Agrippa had restored

Roman rule within a few months. During the struggle for supremacy in Italy the territories beyond the Alps had been governed half-heartedly. But the shortage of troops and infrastructure meant there was always the threat of some widespread new uprising, just like in the times of Alesia, when the Germans penetrated up to the west of the Rhine and imposed their sovereignty close to the river tribes. Just as had happened in the time of Ariovistus, where Ortwin had fought almost two decades before. He would have been really useful to him now, that brave German, along with his woman, Veleda, Agrippa said to himself as he advanced through the remains of the village that his Suebi had razed to the ground. Burning debris smouldered around him, long flowing lines of prisoners with bowed heads filed between soldiers who poked maliciously at them with swords and piles of corpses lay stacked up in the streets. He was marching against the people of Ortwin's fellow initiate in German territory, but Agrippa had no doubt that Ortwin would have behaved impeccably if he were here. If anything, it would be Veleda who would have worried him. Agrippa knew the woman's desire to resume playing a leading role among her countrymen, reclaiming the inheritance her father Ariovistus had left her, and he had sometimes thought to himself that when Octavian's rise to power was complete, it wouldn't be a bad idea to help the two Germans conquer a kingdom that could become a client state of Rome, ensuring tranquillity along its borders for the empire. Better to have the Suebi controlled by Ortwin and Veleda, in fact, than have the Germans divided into myriad tribes ready at any moment to raid the frontiers.

He made a mental note to talk to Octavian about it one day. But only when they no longer needed them, which seemed unlikely in the near future.

On the other hand, it was to put an end to the raids that he had crossed the Rhine, only the second Roman commander after Caesar to dare try it. The Ubii, whose elders marched at his side in the punitive expedition, had asked him to. Caesar had made them allies of Rome, creating the buffer state just beyond the Rhine that Agrippa would have gladly given to Ortwin, but they were a rather weak people who had soon been over-run by the neighbouring Suebi. And some Ubii had rebelled against the inconsistent Roman sovereignty and joined the other barbarian tribes, extending their raids to the west of the Rhine.

Having quelled the rebellion at Aquitaine, Agrippa had then been forced to delay the constructive phase of his proconsulship to rush to the Rhine and fight back the raiders. But he hadn't stopped there. The Ubii had made it clear to him that the Suebi would return if he did not teach them a harsh lesson, and so he continued further into the German forests and swamps into which the enemy had retreated, and as they crept deeper into hostile territory he realised how difficult it would be for Rome to extend its sovereignty across the Rhine. Maybe it should do so, because there was always the risk of an unknown danger to the empire emerging from those woods, but the river certainly seemed a natural boundary to all that the city could realistically dominate without risking a continuous attrition of its troops and resources in areas that were all too mysterious and free of any form of civilisation.

His soldiers were ill at ease in those unknown lands – not like Ortwin would have been had he accompanied him. In that village they had gone far beyond what he had ordered them to and had apparently vented their frustration at the fear they felt, and continued to feel, whilst marching through the wilderness in search of an elusive enemy.

Like the Gauls in Aquitaine, in fact, the Suebi warriors had evaded the battle by taking advantage of the cover the forests and swamps could offer them, so Agrippa had ordered his men to destroy their bases and capture their wives and children to force them to come out. It was not the type of warfare he preferred, but it was necessary to protect the allies of Rome and thus demonstrate that the empire could be trusted and was to be feared, thereby inducing others to acquiesce to Rome's rule as the Ubii had. At least until the Rhine was equipped with an outer belt of allied nations and an internal one of forts and fortifications.

Within days, he had seen dozens of villages reduced to the same state and yet he still hadn't managed to provoke a fight with the Suebi. Those warriors preferred to watch their relatives taken into slavery rather than intervene to spare them that sad fate. But he had concluded that with all that there was to be done in Gaul, he could not spend too much time on the border. He called a tribune and said, "Gather the cavalry on the flanks and position them behind us, giving the impression that they are withdrawing, then leave the men free to plunder."

The junior soldier looked at him for a long time, astonished and perplexed by that sudden neglect of foresight and discipline. Until that moment, in fact, while advancing into enemy territory, the proconsul had taken all the necessary measures never to expose them to ambushes, and it was this which had prompted the enemy to stay away, thought Agrippa, while the officer carried out his orders. In a short time, the cavalry pulled back and the soldiers fanned out in search of anything worth recovering amongst the debris. The proconsul then summoned the commanders of the five cohorts he had brought with him and said, “Make sure you only give the impression that your men are scattered, but make sure that you actually keep them all together without mixing up the units so that they are ready to go into action when they attack. Because they will attack, that is certain, if they are around. The soldiers immediately disappeared in different directions, vanishing between the trees and the burning huts.

And he prepared to wait for the enemy, who would think that the Romans were not alert, to attack them.

*

As they climbed the Palatine hill to Octavian’s house, Maecenas reflected on how delicate this time was for the Mars Ultor sect. The triumvir was starting to outline his reform program and he was finally beginning to lay the groundwork for the regime’s propaganda. This was to go hand in hand with the business of the government to help the population accept the idea that there was someone predestined to lead Rome regardless of the institutions. Agrippa, meanwhile, was in charge of consolidating the empire and of ‘romanising’ the most recently acquired provinces. But the three of them were too few to address the enormous problems that the rise to power entailed, and other members of the sect were not, nor would they ever be, as capable as they. The sect of Mars Ultor, by now, consisted of just the three of them, and it was unfortunate that Rufus had turned out to be a disappointment. If only he had been reliable, another member would have been useful, especially at a juncture when alliances were precarious and their enemies numerous and diverse.

Octavian had never once mentioned Rufus after having him killed. Never a word about him, and he glared at anyone who dared even say his name. He had put all thoughts of his one-time friend in a tightly locked *damnatio memoriae*, as though Rufus had never been in the sect at all, perhaps to avoid having to admit to himself that he had made the mistake of giving him too much credit. But now his plans required tireless activity in two directions: the reforms and achieving absolute power. They needed new members or a dense network of matrimonial alliances and patronage that tied people of importance to their cause, whether they knew it or not. In kingdoms, to give stability to the throne, they usually entrusted the most important roles to family members, and so, with a view to ruling in the future, it would be appropriate to create and extend ties with those who could provide concrete support for the consolidation of power.

A court. A court was needed for the future king, which would be such in fact if not in name. A court made up of children and heirs, singers and poets, relatives and friends willing to do anything for the extended family that revolved around those chosen by the gods.

"Let us hope that the son to whom Scribonia is about to give birth proves able to support you in your work when it is his turn. We need new blood," he said, expressing out loud his thoughts to his friend. "The challenges that still lie ahead are endless."

"Yes, let's hope so," replied Octavian. "But he will have to do it without his mother. The two of us are about to announce that I'm going to divorce her." Maecenas took a moment to absorb the news, then added, "Well, I'd be lying if I said that I hadn't been expecting it. Now that you're going to reveal your real intentions towards Pompey it no longer makes much sense, and I suppose that it would be a good idea for you to look for a more suitable marriage to a woman whose family can actually support you instead of one who would be an obstacle to your career," he added, more and more convinced of his own vision.

"And as it happens, I have an idea in that regard..." said Octavian, but at that point they had reached the top of the slope, and a slave came running towards them. "*Dominus, Dominus...*" he shouted, "the matron has given birth! It is a beautiful baby girl!" He shouted.

"And with that, your dreams of glory vanish like smoke," said the triumvir to Maecenas. "Scribonia had only one chance to give me an heir, and she has failed."

The Etruscan couldn't help but smile. "Well then, maybe it's time that I was heading off," he said. "This is a bad time. You'll be wanting to be alone with the child ..."

"Not at all," said Octavian. "There is no time to waste. We must now write letters to Menodorus and Antony and I have to send a clear message to Pompey with my divorce from Scribonia."

"But... you want a divorce *now*?" his friend asked incredulously.

"Why not? I assure you Scribonia is not the kind of person who deserves pity," said the triumvir, entering the house.

"Perhaps it would be better to postpone it," suggested the Etruscan, mostly to avoid the embarrassment of having to witness the pitiful scene first-hand.

But Octavian did not answer, so Maecenas followed him docilely to his wife's room where they found the woman still sitting in the delivery seat, the doctor intent on checking her health, while the midwife cleaned the baby girl and placed her in the cradle. The slaves, meanwhile, gathered up the sheets that were wet with blood. Seeing them enter, Scribonia hastily covered herself and cast a suspicious glance at Maecenas, and the midwife proffered the crying new-born baby to its father.He looked at the little girl and casually greeted the doctor, who hastened to confirm that mother and daughter were in good health. Tradition stated that the father should pick up the child in order to recognise her as his daughter, and this he did.

"The daughter of Gaius Julius Caesar Octavian can only be called Giulia, like the daughter of Gaius Julius Caesar," he declared solemnly and then returned her immediately to the midwife.

"I approve of your choice, my husband. A name worthy of its lineage. I'm sorry I gave you a daughter, but I'm still happy. But you'll see, the next one will be a boy… in fact, the next ones!" muttered the visibly tired Scribonia, who was breathless, sweaty and pale with sunken, dull eyes.

"There will not be any others," said Octavian. "I intend to request a divorce, Scribonia. Immediately."

The woman's sunken eyes rolled in her head and she seemed on the verge of fainting. The midwife rushed to support her and wiped her forehead with a wet rag.

"But… be-because I gave you a girl in-instead of a boy?" stammered Scribonia.

"No, even if you had given me a son, it would not have made any difference," said Octavian, then took an embarrassed Maecenas by the arm and left the room.

"You're the one who saddled me with that unbearable woman," said the triumvir once they were inside his study, "and so I thought it was only fair that you should be present at the precise moment I finally freed myself from her..."

*

There was a tense, nerve-wracking wait. Soon it would be completely dark and another day would have passed without any action. The soldiers did not know what to raid by now, but they had been ordered to walk round all day, without wandering too far away, to show that they were not in formation. Some were lazily playing astragals with small bones they had found, others chatting, and other still were dozing, but always with their equipment to hand, while the centurions roamed between their units quietly admonishing everyone to be careful.

But nobody believed the barbarians would attack that day, everyone said they wouldn't and Agrippa was beginning to believe it himself. This meant repeating the process the following day, but a little further away from the Rhine, trying to find other villages to sack and thus exposing themselves to greater danger. Apparently he was stuck in a quagmire. There was no way to establish what scope for these punitive expeditions was left to the east of the Rhine, and he had no wish to wear down his troops with a ghost hunt.

He was still mulling over his thoughts when he heard a cry, then another, followed by the hiss of arrows. He felt a jolt of excitement vibrate through his entire body, then he screamed at the messenger next to him, "Go!"

The rider galloped off, disappearing among the trees in the direction of the rear. Agrippa looked in the direction the cries had come, but in the meantime heard sounds of battle coming from a different direction. The Suebi seemed to have surrounded the village to launch an attack from several directions. When he arrived in the area that had been attacked first, Agrippa saw that the legionaries were at the ready. They were already deployed in line with their shields tightly packed together, even though they were in groups and not in a single formation. The barbarians were swarming into their ranks trying to penetrate and wedge themselves into the gaps. They brandished their swords with feral screams, their tattooed chests naked despite the bitter cold, their heads bare and their hair tied up in Suebian knots, with multi-coloured hexagonal shields in their hands.

Only some were heavily armed, and Agrippa thanked the gods for that. All the others together didn't have the power to break a legion, even if it was scattered across the battlefield, and what mattered was to hold out for a while. After a day of waiting, he felt frustrated by not fighting and although Octavian had told him not to take risks in skirmishes, he needed to use his hands. Along with his personal shieldsmen, he went to tackle one of the groups of Suebi, and in the meantime the other legionaries flocked to the front line, their centurions shouting deployment orders to them as they arrived.

Agrippa attacked an enemy soldier who was more resourceful than the others and, having managed to slip in between the two sides, was about to strike down a legionary engaged with another, in the back. The proconsul slashed the man's bare hip and watched him fall at his feet, but immediately behind the warrior another appeared and this one was clearly after his blood. The proconsul deflected the swings of the man's sword with his shield, which vibrated violently, while his bodyguards tried to stay close to him, one on his right and one on his left, to create a kind of phalanx. But their presence hindered him and prevented him from fighting as he was accustomed to, so instead of remaining with them, he suddenly raced forward a few steps and pushed into the enemy, finding himself engaged in a personal duel.

"Stop!" he cried, blocking the advance of his aides while his blade clanged against that of the barbarian. But the Suebian was pressed forward by his companions and Agrippa felt legionaries who had just arrived pushing him from behind too. He found himself face to face with a Suebian, his face an inch away from his enemy's, and he didn't hesitate to headbutt him, the edge of his helmet producing the desired effect on the man's bare head, sending him crashing unconscious to the ground. Agrippa finished him off by slamming down the edge of his shield on him and then immediately thrusting his sword forward and piercing the throat of the next Suebian. The battle raged, but the break in the line was no more and it looked as though the Romans would be able to hold formation.

Then he heard the sound of thundering hooves on the ground and soon afterwards glimpsed the outlines of the Roman and Gallic cavalry that had been lurking in the rear. Fanning out along what remained of the Suebian village, the reinforcements did not even need to attack the barbarians. Disheartened at seeing themselves surrounded, they threw down their weapons and surrendered. They had thought that they would surprise the Romans with their rear unprotected but instead they had been trapped. Satisfied, Agrippa ordered the nearest tribune to ensure that they were bound and then rushed to another area where the fighting continued. But then he realised that there too, the barbarians had been disheartened by the appearance of the cavalry, the only difference being that, without him being there to stop them, the Romans were throwing themselves into massacring their now innocuous enemies.

The same thing was happening in another area: the situation was under control. As he made the rounds of the village, he tried to estimate how many enemy soldiers he had lured into the trap and he was disappointed when he realised that it was a band of only a few hundred warriors. He sighed – it would take dozens, perhaps hundreds of days like this, to eradicate the Suebi resistance and convince them to renounce attacking the friends of Rome once and for all.

XVI

Just as they had come, they went away. The Parthians had vanished after a battle that had lasted a couple of hours and was already over before mid-morning – and until the afternoon there had only been a chase: a manhunt through the mountains, getting closer and closer to Labienus's camp. Even Veleda had taken part in the hunt, guiding part of her column in the round-up of the enemies who kept appearing from between rocks as they fled the victorious Romans. She had killed several of them herself, and each time had hoped to find that it was Labienus she had run through with her sword: if she was able to kill him before finding out his identity, it would be easier. That way, there would be no moral conflict, no doubt, nor uncertainties, fears, or crises of conscience.

But that hadn't happened. And so, sated from the bloodshed, she had crossed the mountain and gone to meet Ortwin, because now that battle was won they had to deal with Labienus.

"Some Parthians tried to escape to his camp, but he didn't let them in," Ortwin told her, observing the enemy position a little higher up. "That coward foresees a siege and doesn't want to share resources with those who've come to help him."

"He has done exactly what you would expect from him," answered Veleda sharply. "He has always thought only of himself. What is Bassus going to do now?"

"We're going to attack," Ortwin said firmly. "They are disheartened and we must take advantage of the fact – not immediately, of course, as the soldiers are tired from the march and the battle and it's getting dark to boot. But tomorrow at dawn, Labienus will finally be ours."

"I wish I could believe it," the woman answered with a sigh. "When he's involved, you can never know."

"He's done for, Veleda. Done for. I just hope he won't commit suicide or anything like that and that Bassus will leave him to me, as we agreed."

The German woman nodded, not fully persuaded.

"In fact," Ortwin resumed, "do you know what I'll do? I'll go and challenge him: he has nothing to lose, and I'll spare his life if he can beat me," he concluded and headed towards the fortress.

"Are you crazy?" cried Veleda as she followed him. "Don't you remember that he almost *killed* you last time? Do you want to leave him this way out?"

"I will win this time, you can be sure of it."

Veleda wasn't sure of it at all. Ortwin hated Labienus so much that he could no longer fight him with a clear head, but she also knew that she couldn't force her man to give up his honour. There were many reasons why Ortwin wanted to fight the Roman, and the principal one was herself.

They came close to the fortress and stopped at a safe distance.

"Labienus! Quintus Labienus!" shouted Ortwin. "Come to the bastions to meet an old friend! You – call that coward of your commander!" he cried out to one of the guards on the battlements.

He kept calling until the commander eventually appeared. The sun was setting and they could only barely make out his silhouette.

After a few moments of silence, during which the two rivals squared up at each other, Labienus spoke. "So, you persecute me even here, one-eye. It seems I will never be rid of you. And I see that there's always our Veleda at your side…"

"Yes, and you're lucky that I'm here this time. You're done for and you know it, but I'll offer you a way out," said Ortwin. His voice, the woman noticed, was trembling.

"And why would you of all people offer me a way out?" scoffed Labienus.

"Because I'm a man of honour. And I want to have the satisfaction of killing you myself, in a fair duel."

"Do you mean like the one in Philippi where I spared you?"

"No. Like the one in Munda, where I spared you. Which won't happen this time."

"Those are big words for an old, ailing warrior… So you propose a duel? When and where do you want to have it?"

"Here, and now."

"Even if I won, Bassus would never let me go."

"He would if I told him to."

"Hmmm… Give me some time. I must consult my men. I do have some responsibilities, you know. I've made a career and ruled over two Roman provinces and led great armies while you were falling into the abyss and becoming a money-hungry assassin."

Ortwin kept calm and didn't respond to the provocation. "Well, tomorrow at dawn, this camp will be swept away by our troops. We've just defeated thousands of Parthians, do you think we won't overwhelm a little gang of desperate wretches like you? So you'll have nothing to lose if you accept my challenge now."

Labienus nodded thoughtfully and disappeared behind the palisade. Ortwin and Veleda prepared themselves to wait in tense silence. Meanwhile, other soldiers had arrived after hearing the dialogue and were spreading the news. Within an hour, a large crowd of curious people had gathered to witness the duel. Somebody brought torches to provide light and heat, and the space in front of the fortress was turned into an almost gladiatorial arena. Another hour passed without anything happening, and Ortwin was beginning to lose his patience when several men suddenly climbed down the palisade. But it didn't seem to Veleda that Labienus was among them. Two of them ran over to Ortwin.

"We want to surrender, barbarian."

"All right, all right… But where's Labienus?" replied Ortwin, impatiently.

"He's left with his general staff. He's abandoned us. We've just realised it, all of us: he must have got changed, disguised himself and…"

"Where has he gone? The way down is barricaded!"

"He's taken the road between the mountains. It's tough and risky, and few would be able to manage it. We've been studying it carefully over the past few days, in case things went badly…"

Ortwin grabbed him by the hem of his tunic. "Take me to him! Take me to him immediately or I will kill you!"

Then the German turned to the soldiers around him, and said, "Whoever wants a reward of money from Caesar, join me for this night hunt!"

He waited just a few moments, during which only a dozen legionaries, and of course Veleda, came forward. Then, Ortwin urged the soldier to guide him, and the man took him around the fort. It was a clear night and the sky was full of stars which seemed to the woman to be very close. Up there, the night was not so dark. They climbed between rocky outcrops, exposed to the icy wind of the night, their breath almost freezing on their lips, clutching their torches for a bit of warmth. But Ortwin never slowed, and he was always the first in the line, forcing the soldier that guided him to keep up with his relentless pace. Veleda began to think that it was madness: once the torches burnt out, they would find themselves lost in the dark in an unknown place and would risk freezing to death despite the furs they had put on after the battle. Suddenly they saw some winking points of light ahead of them: their quarry must be just behind the outcrops of rock ahead.

"Lower your torches!" hissed Ortwin, moving even faster. They drew nearer to the lights and Veleda could just make out a dozen silhouettes. "Don't let them get away!" cried the German. "Spread out!"

Sword in hand, he sprang upon the nearest fugitive. He cut him down with his first swing, and then like a fury, set about the one immediately behind him who, instead of facing him, tried to escape, thus ending up with a sword between his shoulder blades. Wanting to help her man, Veleda tackled another of the fugitives. He didn't look like Labienus to her, but she was no longer sure of anything in that surreal battle against shadows carried out in a brooding silence broken only by the sound of boots scuffling in the snow and against the rocks, by the clanging of the swords and by the heavy breathing of the combatants.

The fugitives didn't put up much resistance. After having exchanged a few blows with her opponent, Veleda finally realised that he wasn't Labienus, and as she dealt with the man she wondered whether he would be the next, and whether she or Ortwin would face him. If she was honest, she didn't know which she preferred. Meanwhile, she continued to swing her sword at her opponent, pushing him up against a rocky wall where she slashed at him repeatedly until she managed to hit his thigh. The man collapsed to his knees and surrendered. Veleda looked around and saw that it was all over. Six bodies lay on the ground. Three more had surrendered.

Ortwin was bending over one of them. She came up to him: he was still alive, but it was clear he wouldn't be for long. He had a slash in his stomach and a rivulet of blood ran from his mouth down his chin.

"You are Cecilius Bucolianus, one of Caesar's murderers," said Ortwin. "I recognise you. But I don't see Labienus. Where is he?"

"He… left us shortly after we left… the fort… Now I understand."

"What? What do you understand?" said Ortwin, shaking him to get an answer.

"He used us… this time too. He knew… that you would follow him and… he left us behind… to distract you," the murderer muttered.

The German looked at the three survivors, who nodded. Then, he raised his sword and delivered a powerful blow to the man's throat that completely severed his head. He did the same to the other murderer, who lay already dead further away. Afterwards, he took the tunic from a corpse and wrapped the two trophies up in it. "Let's get back. We have finished here."

These were the last words he uttered until they got back to the fortress where, in the meantime, the soldiers had opened the gates and let Ventidius Bassus in, before handing themselves over to him.

No one, not even Veleda, had dared approach Ortwin during the return journey, and his face was dark and tormented. But Bassus didn't hesitate to approach him as soon as he was told that he was back.

"They've told me about your act of bravado, barbarian. I would remind you once again that, in spite of everything, you are under my command and cannot simply do as you please."

"Not any more," said Ortwin, without even looking him in the face.

"What?"

"I said that I am no longer under your command. From now on, we part ways."

That was news even to Veleda, who gave her man a startled look.

"Are you joking?" Bassus protested. "I don't see Labienus with you. You have achieved nothing and we must continue to look for him."

Ortwin pulled the two heads out of the bag. "So I've achieved nothing, have I? These are the two criminals we were looking for. As regards Labienus, I will keep looking for him while you go and liberate Syria. He's alone and on the run now, and my woman and I are more likely to find him on our own than your whole army. I'll move faster and catch him in Cilicia before he gets to Syria, where I won't be able to track him any more. She and I will set off tomorrow at dawn. And that's an end to it," he said, walking away and leaving Bassus standing there.

*

Veleda didn't have the courage to tell Ortwin that she could no longer stand it. It was clear that Labienus was shrewder than they were. In three weeks of search and pursuit, they had always arrived a few hours or even a few days later at the place where the fugitive had found shelter. And the traitor left behind himself a network of connivance through corruption or threats, and in some cases even some deaths. He had nothing with him except his own sword, but his name instilled fear and respect for what he had accomplished in the past two years, and people felt compelled to do as he said for fear of retaliation from his allies, the Parthians, who were a much closer, more tangible threat than the Romans, who by then were largely absent in those parts.

The people that Ortwin and Veleda forced by hook or crook to speak revealed the details of Labienus's journey only under the threat of being punished as collaborators by Ventidius Bassus's army. The two Germans went from inn to inn or to the local worthies, bribing people with the money provided by Octavian for this purpose or threatening them with the heads of the two criminals they had killed. Eventually, they always found someone willing to reveal when Labienus had been there and where he was going afterwards.

And yet the Roman was so elusive. Ortwin seemed to have no intention of giving up, though, and he continued every interrogation with the same determination as the previous one, becoming increasingly aggressive towards those whom he chose to question. They then arrived in Tarsus – closer and closer to the border with Syria, beyond which Labienus would be unassailable among his friends, the Parthians. Fortunately, Labienus was forced to take the most indirect and difficult route to the border to avoid them, and it was only thanks to this that they were still on his tail.

Tarsus was a populous city near the coast of Cilicia, on the Berdan river, and a commercial hub of primary importance for the routes between the East and the West. To Veleda's eyes, it looked like one of the greatest and most thriving cities of the Roman world. Mark Antony had rewarded its citizens with Roman citizenship and had taken it under his protection, but not even that had made him feel any real obligation to do something concrete when Tarsus fell into the hands of the Parthians and Labienus. The story went that the triumvir had set off to liberate the city but had turned back at a short distance from the harbour after realising that the undertaking was beyond him.

Nonetheless, there were still many people who owed Antony and the triumvirate a favour, in particular many of his clients. After collecting some information, Ortwin had chosen to talk to a man named Demetrius, a freedman who ran a thriving textile business that had made him rich and powerful. The German had made him believe that his business would be ruined if Octavian – once he had conquered Cilicia again, as Bassus was about to do – found out that he had refused to help them. And the freedman, frightened at the prospect of becoming poor again, had asked for a day to find news and had given them an appointment for the following night.

When they entered his sumptuous study, furnished in the style typical of those who wanted to flaunt recently acquired wealth, with statues at every corner and abundant, gaudy coloured decorations on the walls, Veleda was expecting to hear once again that Labienus had set off for the oriental border.

"And what if I told you that the man you are looking for is still in the city?" began Demetrius.

Ortwin's eyes lit up. "Where?"

"He is a guest at the residence of a member of the Senate who collaborates with the Parthians," their guest explained. "But I know that he's heading inland tomorrow, to Adana."

"Take me there immediately," the German snapped, his whole body suddenly tense. Veleda could see that he had already begun preparing for the duel he was expecting to fight in the near future.

"On one condition."

Ortwin glared at him and approached him threateningly.

"You dare make conditions?" he hissed.

"Only one – I would like people to say that I was the one who caught him. My business will benefit from it when the regions go back to normal administration. That would be a victory for me, and the triumvirs wouldn't need to reward me further."

Ortwin relaxed. "That is acceptable for me. Now take me to him."

Demetrius nodded and called a slave, to whom he gave orders to take them to Labienus, and then wished his two visitors farewell and good luck. Ortwin and Veleda found themselves walking the city streets behind their guide. Both were silent, but she knew well what was going on in her man's mind, and she took his hand. They walked like that, hand in hand, until the slave pointed at a house.

"Knock on the door and ask for the *dominus*. Say you come on behalf of your master, who would like to make an appointment with the senator to discuss a business matter," Ortwin ordered the man.

The slave gave him a puzzled look but the German's expression didn't allow for any discussion, so he did as he was told. In the meantime, Ortwin whispered to Veleda, "Labienus must have done this to slip into Quintus Pedius's house and into Octavia and Atia's. Finally, we will give him a taste of his own medicine."

"Yes," she said, feeling obliged to add, "but be careful. Keep in mind that he's dangerous."

The German nodded, and kept a short distance behind the slave as he asked the house keeper for the master. As soon as the latter, a fat, middle-aged man, appeared on the threshold, Ortwin launched himself at him and put a dagger at his throat. "Where's Labienus?" he asked him. "And don't dare scream."

"What are you talking about?" the terrified man said. He was no hero, and that was a good sign, Veleda thought. The house keeper and the slave stood paralysed in terror.

"You know very well, since you're the one who's hiding him. So where is he?" Ortwin insisted, starting to push the tip of the blade into the man's throat, which began to bleed.

"He'll kill me if I speak," he stammered.

"And I will kill you if you don't. And General Ventidius Bassus will strip your family of all your belongings and rights and label you as collaborators."

The senator hesitated for a few moments, during which the blade pressed even harder into his flabby throat, then gave in. "We were having dinner – my daughters are there too, and..."

"Show us the way. And remember that my knife will always be on your back. And you, Veleda, check that these two don't call anyone," he added, pointing to the house keeper and the slave.

They walked along the vestibule until they came to the atrium, passed through the impluvium and, when the man was on the threshold of what must be the triclinium, he stopped. "He's here, please… my wife, my daughters…"

Ortwin almost flung him to one side, then kicked the door open and stormed into the room alone, while Veleda remained with the others, but she could see what was going on inside. Around the dining room there was a woman, two girls, one very small, and him.

"Quintus Labienus," the German announced. "On behalf of the Senate and the Roman people, and on behalf of the triumvirate who sent me, I am here to carry out your death sentence!"

Then, he moved towards his enemy, who in the meantime had sat down. Veleda saw her old lover instinctively go to take the weapon from his belt, but he didn't have one, so he took hold of the little girl sitting next to him, stood up and held her in front of his chest, clutching her throat.

"I'll kill her if you dare try, my friend," said Labienus. "You don't want to have her on your conscience, do you? After so many years spent at the service of Rome, you're no longer the fierce, brutal barbarian that Caesar took away from Ariovistus. Even you have feelings…"

Ortwin trembled and froze. The senator began to weep. "I told you…" he murmured.

"Hush!" Veleda ordered him. "I can see another entrance to the room behind Labienus. Take me there instead of whining!"

The man didn't hesitate to do her bidding, guiding her along a corridor until they came to a door. The woman pulled the dagger from her belt, gently opened the door and saw exactly the same scene she had just witnessed moments before, but this time from the opposite side of the room. Now she was behind Labienus, who hadn't realised she was there. Ortwin had. His one eye followed her movement, but Labienus noticed and realised what was happening. The Roman spun round, but it was too late: Veleda already had her dagger at his throat, and Ortwin leapt forward as well, pointing his at Labienus's back.

Labienus sighed and let the little girl go, and she ran into her mother's arms, crying.

"Well, you've managed it, Ortwin," said the Roman at last, turning to the German. "Kill me and let's get this over with. But I'm sure you won't enjoy it, because Veleda won't forgive you in her heart."

Ortwin looked into his woman's eyes and she gave a mocking gesture of denial and then a reassuring one of assent. More reassuring than she actually felt. She realised that in a state of panic, as though she was aware that she, or at least a part of her, was about to die.

The German moved away from Labienus and addressed the master of the house. "Senator, bring a sword for this man."

Their eyes wide, Veleda and the Roman stared at him, and they asked the same question at almost exactly the same time: "Why are you doing this?"

"Because, unlike you, I am a man of honour, Labienus. And for another reason as well."

Veleda thought she knew what it was. He wanted to prove to her once and for all that he was the better man.

But there was also a chance he might lose. And Labienus, who was aware of this, smiled mischievously.

*

Ortwin waited for the sword to be given to Labienus, shifting his eye only momentarily from his rival, so as not to lose sight of him, to Veleda, to see what effect his decision to give Labienus a chance to defend himself had upon her. He was about to take up two simultaneous challenges: one against his long-time enemy and the other against his idea that his woman had of him. And he had to win both of them. Winning one made no sense if he didn't win the other too. He hoped that he had done the right thing, and when Labienus had the sword in his hands, he prepared himself to face him. He reminded himself not to let himself be overwhelmed by his passions as he had done the last time, three years earlier, when he had almost lost his life.

With this in mind, he let his opponent make the first move. The Roman darted forward and took a slash at Ortwin that he easily avoided by stepping aside, trying to hit his opponent's side, which he had exposed. But Labienus avoided him in turn, diving forward onto one of the couches in the dining room. Meanwhile, all the onlookers, whom Veleda had ordered to stay in the room so as to keep an eye on them, flattened themselves against the walls.

The Roman got to his feet before Ortwin could thrust at him, and then kicked the triclinium at his opponent, trying to make him lose his balance. Ortwin managed to get one leg out of the way, but not the other, which took the brunt of the impact and made him stagger forward.

Towards Labienus's sword.

Veleda gave a scream. The German tried to dodge sideways, and the blade of his opponent grazed him, tearing his tunic at the shoulder and scratching his flesh. As he hit the floor, he rolled and leapt swiftly back to his feet, succeeding perfectly, and stood up just in time to cross blades with the Roman who, on seeing him close to the wall, began to swing manically at him in an attempt to corner him. Behind him, Ortwin heard screams and people panting as they tried to get out of the way. He was forced to retreat until his back was actually touching the wall. Now he had less room to manoeuvre and ward off the blows raining down on him. And Labienus was fast. Their swords crossed again and again, with greater and greater violence, sending out sprays of sparks. In the room, they could hear the crowd muttering, the clanging of the blades and the increasingly heavy breathing of the two combatants.

A particularly powerful blow from Labienus sent Ortwin's hand slamming into the wall, and the impact made him lose his grip on his sword, which fell to the floor. The German hastened to catch it before it touched the floor, reaching out with his left arm and grabbing it with his left hand, giving Labienus the opportunity to strike him again right in the chest. As he dived, though, Ortwin twisted, offering his enemy his thigh instead of his breastbone, and it was there that the Roman's sword struck him, slashing open his flesh. Labienus's cry of victory drowned out Veleda's horrified shriek. Limping, the German got to his feet and went to the centre of the room, where the table was still laid for dinner.

Labienus chased him, and Ortwin tried to avoid him by jumping on the table, amidst trays, dishes and bowls of all kinds. The smell of spicy food blended with the smell of his own blood, and the burning sensation in his thigh grew stronger. He feared that he was losing his lucidity and tried to clear his mind. He was playing the role of prey for the hunter, and unless he was able to reverse those roles, he wouldn't stand a chance. He shifted backward, dragging all the dishes with him, while, a grin of satisfaction on his face, Labienus repeatedly struck the table with his sword, and each step backwards Ortwin took, the blade struck the wood a hand's span from his foot.

Ortwin jumped down to the floor and, in spite of the pain, willed his legs to hold him up, then grabbed the edge of the table and lifted it, slamming it into the approaching Labienus just as he swung his sword. The blade got momentarily jammed in the wood, giving the German just enough time to get round the table and counter attack his opponent.

He struck him in the side, though only grazing him, because Labienus managed to dodge it. However, he noticed that he had ripped the Roman's tunic and flesh. Now both of them were bleeding profusely and had exposed skin. As though in tacit agreement, the two warriors took a moment to catch their breath, moving from side to side, their swords held in front of them and their eyes staring into one another's.

"Come on then, you one-eyed bastard!" cried Labienus suddenly, putting an end to the momentary truce. Ortwin saw that the floor was now scattered with broken dishes and food, meaning that it would be very easy to slip, and he told himself to be very careful. But he was hindered by having only one eye, which restricted his view of both his opponent and the surroundings.

He saw that part of the floor was covered in shards of pottery, and the idea of pushing Labienus onto it suddenly struck him, but he would have to stop being on the defensive, as he had been until then.

That, however, was easier said than done with the wound he could feel throbbing in his thigh. He forced himself to press Labienus and managed to take the offensive, moving in such a way as to force Labienus in the desired direction. But the wound in his leg was sapping his strength and he wasn't able to harry him as he had wished. Labienus too had lost some of the impetus he had previously, but he managed to put up solid resistance, and forced Ortwin backwards, spoiling his plan, and in fact, it was the German who ended up stepping on a broken pot. Inevitably, he slipped and fell, crashing down to the floor on his back. Labienus lunged at him with his sword, but Ortwin rolled to one side and managed to avoid the thrust, though a burning sensation in his shoulder told him the blade had made contact. He kept rolling out of the way of Labienus's attacks until he was forced to parry one with his sword one just a few inches from his face. Labienus continued to attack fiercely, the German continued to parry, and the swords now met an inch from his nose.

He continued to defend himself, but he began to feel as though he was already done for. And the Roman understood it too.

"Die, blind man! Make your mind up and die, once and for all!" he hissed in Ortwin's face. Ortwin held his muscles firm, but knew was becoming weaker. He looked around and saw Veleda take a step towards them, her sword in her hand. He shook his head: he could never have borne being defeated by Labienus for a second time and being saved by her. He didn't want her pity, only to be sure of her love. Then, he realised that he had ended up near the shards of pot. It was his last chance.

He roared in his opponent's face to summon up all his remaining strength and, both hands on the handle of his sword, pushed away Labienus's blade, knocking him off balance. The floor under the

Roman's feet was littered with detritus, and he lost his footing, falling backwards. Ortwin didn't stand up, but scrambled over his opponent, and, holding his sword as though it were a dagger, sank the blade straight down into his chest. Labienus tried to twist out of the way, but failed to avoid the blow, which penetrated between his arm and his right shoulder, tearing through his tendons and bones and forcing him to release the hilt of his sword.

Ortwin took a deep breath and then pulled the blade out, he remained kneeling, waiting a few moments until his breathing had calmed down before standing up.

Absolute silence fell over the room. Only Labienus's panting and rattling was to be heard. He looked at Ortwin with hatred.

"Are you… are you *happy* now, barbarian?" the Roman rasped. "You've finally… finally killed your enemy."

"I see no enemies," replied Ortwin, observing the wounds he had inflicted on Labienus and the blood that was gushing out of the most recent one.

"And what do you see? A man who… who claims his superior right over the woman you believe is yours?"

Ortwin said nothing.

"So? What are you waiting for?" gasped Laenas. "Finish me off!"

Yes, Ortwin said to himself. Yes, now Veleda could kill him. In fact, it had to be her who killed him, to prove to him once and for all which of the two she had chosen. He turned to the woman and offered her his sword.

Veleda hesitated a moment, and then understood what he wanted. She took the weapon, already dripping with her old lover's blood. She looked at him for a long time, and Labienus began to speak once more. "My… my little German girl. Do you know… yes, do you know you've always been the only one… for me?"

"Unfortunately, I do. And it has been a persecution," replied Veleda, kneeling down to lift Labienus's head slightly with her stump before raising her arm and bringing down her sword on the Roman's neck, cleanly severing his head, which rolled across the floor until it was stopped by the remains of a roast suckling pig.

Ortwin shouted in triumph – a barbaric shout of triumph like the ones he used to give in the forest when he was young, back in the days when he used to fight with his people under Veleda's father. It was a double triumph for him: he had finally defeated his rival and he had conquered his woman's heart for good.

He embraced her tightly and wept. And Veleda did the same.

XVII

Octavian's home was illuminated by the numerous torches set around it. Livia Drusilla stopped on the threshold and looked at the torch-bearers, flautists, friends and relatives around her before walking to the nearest crossroads a few yards away and, as tradition demanded, throwing a coin against the wall of the building that loomed over the road, then she turned to watch her new husband spreading nuts around the doorway while his friends gently mocked him for following the ritual, which was said to favour the bride's fertility. Twice now, the girl had heard somebody say the same thing she had heard in her own house at the crowded wedding banquet: "What a fertile marriage – the bride is already pregnant!"

Well, she should have expected it, she thought, as she went back inside her new home and asked the slave for the woollen ribbons to adorn the door. Octavian hadn't waited until she had given birth and she'd had nothing against getting married immediately after his divorce from his wife Scribonia. Curiously, her husband, Tiberius Claudius Nero, had nothing against it either – or at least had not objected, neither to Octavian himself, nor to her. Indeed, he had even accompanied her to the ceremony and performed the duties which would usually have fallen upon her father to guarantee a perfect marriage *cum manus* in which the woman passed from *patria potestas* to her husband's property.

Clearly, Octavian must have been very persuasive if, immediately after being summoned to the triumvir's residence, Nero had returned home announcing that he was going to divorce her and take her to marry the head of the Roman world. Livia had wondered if her husband had been so amenable because Octavian had threatened him somehow or whether it was just because he was nauseated by the rumours about the pair of them. However, she had stopped asking herself questions soon enough – after all, she didn't really care why her husband had raised no objection. She wanted to marry Octavian, the man she had been sleeping with for months and who would make her the most powerful woman in Rome.

He finished decorating the door and then was given some oil and lard to grease the door jambs as tradition commanded. And her new husband seemed to care a great deal about traditions. Livia asked herself if she really loved him. Not her old husband, no – she had never loved him, though she had been as devoted to him as a Roman *matrona* of high birth had to be, following him even in the misfortunes of exile and defeat. Certainly, she felt something more, much more, for her new spouse, but she couldn't tell if it was love. Nor could she really say whether Octavian actually felt anything for her. He was certainly very taken with her, and it was clear that they both wanted to be together. But love was something that didn't seem to be meant for them.

She looked at her new husband and sensed the power that emanated from him, his unrestrained ambition, his determination to pursue his goals, his conviction that he had been chosen by the gods to save Rome from decline, the lucid intelligence which shone in his eyes, and she knew that it was exactly all this which she liked. Because she felt the same way. Seemingly more than any other, Octavian embodied all those qualities and therefore there was no other she liked more than him. And she would stay by his side for as long as he proved to be thus. It was her way of loving, and if anyone had told her that it wasn't love, well, she didn't mind. Livia knew that it was the same for him: he wanted her because they were alike. He liked making love to her, of course, but he also, and perhaps above all, liked the conversations they had, her ability to express her political opinions and her perceptive remarks. And Livia was satisfied with that. They would be a happy couple – far happier than many others who declared themselves to be in love.

She suddenly felt herself being lifted off the ground. Two young senators had picked her up and were now carrying her over the threshold, surrounded by the cheering crowd that had followed them from the house she'd shared with Nero and where they had held the ceremony and banquet. Inside, she found the *pronuba* who had assisted her during the wedding ritual and Octavian, who hurried to join them, greeting the guests left outside.

Her husband took her by the hand and led her to the fireplace, around which effigies of *Lares* and *Penates* and Julius Caesar were displayed. Next to it, there was a basin of water, in which Livia was required to wash. After rinsing her hands, the girl pulled out another coin from the bag she had with her and threw it into the fire to gain favour with the Lares of her new home. Finally, the *pronuba* led them into the atrium.

They were alone, finally. Simultaneously, both of them gave a sigh of relief and collapsed onto the bed, exhausted by the fatigue of the arduous day: it was as if the whole of Rome had attended the wedding, and of course Octavian had felt obliged to invite anyone who counted for anything in the city. As a result, she had had to greet hundreds, perhaps thousands of people, whose embraces and kisses had forced her to change her wedding gown several times and spend hours repeating pleasantries despite how far on her pregnancy was. And even with the help of the nomenclator provided by her husband, remembering the names of the guests had also been quite an undertaking.

They looked at each other and smiled, aware that they were thinking the same things. They kissed passionately, but Livia hoped that Octavian would not want to immediately claim his husband's rights. After all, he had exercised them abundantly when they were lovers and he could grant her some rest for that night at least.

As if he had read her mind, her spouse pulled away from her, saying, "I'd say that we can do without that for tonight. Especially because I'm going to have you spend your wedding night in a rather singular way."

Livia became curious. "Really? I'm looking forward to seeing what you've prepared…" she said excitedly.

"There's something I have to do, but I'd like to involve you in it," he explained. "My hope is that you will take part in my activities. I respect your opinion very much and I'd like you to share my projects."

"I'm delighted to be part of your world and I hope I'll be worthy of your high opinion of me," she replied sincerely. She was excited by the idea of climbing the pyramid of power at his side, but she was also afraid of disappointing him.

"I am certain that you will be. I'm always good at judging people," said Octavian, taking her by the hand again. He rose and told a slave to prepare a litter. Livia was surprised that she had to go out again, and called for her slave to fix her make up, but Octavian stopped her, saying, "There's no need, I can assure you that where we're going they won't care about that."

They left the house and got into the litter. It was the dead of night, and Livia dared not ask her new husband any questions during the journey. Octavian talked to her about everything and anything until he eventually picked up the topic that interested him most at that time, as she had realised the many times they had met as lovers.

"I have sent one of my freedmen to take control of Sardinia, Corsica, three legions and various *auxilia* so now I can tell you that Sextus Pompey's chief admiral Menodorus has come over to my side," he explained. "Pompey doesn't know it yet, however, and I want to pre-empt him in preparations for war. Agrippa has sent me troops from Gaul: he has quelled the riots there and he's going to mount an offensive in Germany, so he can do without some legions now."

"But you must be outnumbered at sea," interrupted Livia. "What will you do with the fleet?"

"I've been secretly having quadriremes built in Ravenna and Ostia for months," he replied. "And now I'm going to send some ships from the port of Ravenna to have them ready in Brindisi and Dicearchia. I'm going to attack Sicily from both seas while Pompey's not yet expecting it and I'll make up for my numerical inferiority with surprise. In any case, I've summoned Antony to Brindisi, and if he gives me his support I will also have his ships. I'll march to the straits myself as soon as possible. Since Agrippa is on the other side of the Alps, this is a war I intend to lead myself. It's time for me to gain credibility as a general, otherwise I'll never live up to the reputation of my father and the soldiers will always prefer Antony over me."

Livia didn't ask him how, given his weak health, he was planning to cope with all that, and merely nodded consensually. Over time, she thought, she would learn to speak more freely. In the meantime, they had reached their destination. They got out of the litter and entered a building that she recognised as the Tullian prison. Once they crossed the threshold, Livia was struck by a blast of foul air that made her eyes water but she forced herself to be strong. She didn't want to disappoint Octavian by behaving like some fearful, spoilt little woman.

A tribune came to meet them. His tunic was smeared with blood and it was evident that he had just rinsed his face before meeting them.

"Hail Caesar, I wasn't expecting you today… We're keeping them down below and we've already achieved some good results. Do you want to see them?"

"Of course, Laenas, let's go down. You lead the way."

The officer made to go, but then stopped to cast a questioning glance at Livia.

"Yes, she's coming too," Octavian said, without asking his wife's opinion. The officer's face briefly registered surprise, then he nodded and led the way. He slipped through a trap door which led to a ladder. Livia followed her husband, who went down before her and helped her down on the awkward rungs. As soon as she got below the level of the trapdoor, the blast of rank air that struck her made her almost long for the one on the upper floor. For a moment she felt like fainting, but fortunately her husband was supporting her and didn't realise that she had swayed.

She found herself in a cramped, damp cave, three quarters of which was of a circular shape and which was dimly lit by sparse torches. Still dazed by the overwhelming stench of urine, excrement, sweat, blood, mould and damp – it took a few moments for her eyes to adjust to the semi-darkness. And when they did, she shuddered at the sight of the demonic faces she saw, like spirits floating in the darkness. Faces with empty sockets instead of eyes, mouths with no teeth, temples with no ears, faces with no noses… all dripping with blood. When her eyes finally grew further accustomed to the gloom, she began to see hands with no fingers and bodies covered with wounds, cuts and burns. Weak moans and guttural sounds accompanied those spectral visions.

She felt the bile inside her stomach rise. But no, she couldn't vomit – Octavian was testing her to see if she had what it took, just like him. Otherwise he wouldn't have dragged her into that hellhole on the very night of their wedding and with her in an advanced stage of pregnancy. She instinctively covered her mouth with her hand and forced herself to keep everything inside. Her mouth filled with bile which she forced back down while wiping away the tears that kept coming to her eyes.

"We have their confessions," said Laenas. "Sextus Pompey sent them to plunder Italy despite the treaty and the peace in force."

Octavian turned to Livia and whispered: "Actually, Menodorus sent them to implicate Pompey. We agreed for him to send them to a certain place along the coast of Campania where we were waiting and caught them."

Then he looked at her for a long time, with the obvious intention of analysing her reactions thoroughly. Livia tried to assume a neutral, unflustered expression and to stand up straight, then she nodded and said, "An excellent idea, my husband."

Octavian smiled at her, looked at her again, reached for her arm and took her hand.

And Livia was sure she had passed the test.

*

No Agrippa, who was busy on the Rhine. No Maecenas, who was engaged in governing the city of Rome. No Popilius Laenas, who was stationed with the other fleet. Not even Rufus, who had turned out to be a traitor, or Gaius Chaerea, who had long been out of the picture after losing his leg at Philippi. Not to mention Pinarius, who had gone over to Antony's side, and Quintus Pedius, who had been killed by Quintus Labienus. Ortwin and Veleda were also still away in the East with Ventidius Bassus. And not even Antony was there to compensate for his shortcomings as a commander, as had been the case at Philippi.

This time, Octavian was alone, completely alone, with subordinates he didn't fully trust, none of whom were as brilliant as the men he had chosen in the past to help raise him to the summit of the world. Suddenly, the young triumvir wondered whether he had been right to march against Sextus Pompey in a campaign that was going to be difficult, perhaps long and wearying, and opposed by everyone. He would have preferred to have some of the members of the sect of Mars Ultor with him, even just for comfort, in the face of the task awaiting him: a victory against his opponent at land and sea might indeed prove to be an endeavour beyond his abilities.

But he couldn't retreat now without risking looking a fool and losing his credibility. In his position, it always came down to the same thing: it was a matter of prestige, and once you began something you had better go through with it. A defeat would perhaps be remediable, but surrender would condemn him to public ridicule.

Yet Antony's behaviour had startled him. The triumvir had arrived in Brindisi on the day agreed for the meeting, but Octavian, waylaid by the need to gather together troops in Etruria for the upcoming campaign, had been delayed. He'd known very well that Antony would reproach him for denying him the opportunity to recruit troops in Italy, and in truth he'd made little effort to be on time for the meeting, but after all, *he* needed those men, *now*, and he wasn't going to do without them. In the meantime, Menodorus had come over to his side, and to reward him, the young triumvir had appointed him second in command of the fleet. Not supreme commander, though: Menodorus might be an experienced seaman but all the same, he was a freedman. And what with Agrippa not being there and Rufus being no more, he'd had to choose a senator to please the others at a time when the disapproval of the war he had waged was widespread. There were none skilled in warfare, so he had appointed Gaius Calvisius Sabinus, one of only two senators who had tried to defend Caesar on the ides of March six years ago, as prefect of the fleet and the equestrian Lucius Cornificius as vice-prefect.

Afterwards, Octavian had moved to Taranto, where he was preparing to march with the army to Reggio so as to attack Sicily while Cornificius was steering the fleet from Ravenna with the flagship on which he would go into battle, and Calvisius and Menodorus were sailing from Etruria for the island that was still Pompey's stronghold.

But he wouldn't receive any further help. Antony was offended because he hadn't showed up in Brindisi, and instead of waiting for him he had immediately returned to Athens to resume doing what seemed to interest him most of late: getting

Octavia pregnant. However, before that he had publicly protested and written him an outrageous letter in which he not only accused him of deliberately not coming but had also warned him against continuing with the preparations for war and urging him to respect the deal with Pompey while he was busy dealing with the Parthians in the East.

Antony's admonitions had heartened all those who'd had enough of war. The confessions extracted from pirates under torture hadn't been enough to persuade people that Pompey was threatening the Italian coasts again, and many *municipia* were protesting openly against what they considered a breach of the covenant.

"Caesar," announced his attendant to him when he entered the *praetorium* of his camp near Taranto, "the troops don't want to go. They're saying that this isn't a just war."

Octavian rolled his eyes: he had known that this would happen even before he came to Reggio. The centurions had repeatedly told him of the discontent among the soldiers, many of whom had previously fought under Antony and thought that if *he* didn't regard this war as just then it was not. Octavian tried to keep the despair lurking in his mind under control, and began to fear that he might fall prey to one of his attacks of phthisis. Since he was afraid of coming down with any kind of illness during the campaign he always had his doctor at his side, wrapped himself up in half a dozen tunics, avoided being outdoors in bad weather as well as making too much effort and overeating.

He was well aware that he wasn't exactly a model commander so he felt it was necessary to compensate for the fact by giving an authoritative speech that would convince the troops of the rightness of his cause. He ordered his attendant to summon the soldiers to the exercise field close to the provisional camp, and then he set off calmly in that direction, accompanied by an escort of his Praetorian guard.

When he reached the grandstand, hundreds of soldiers had already gathered in front of him. The agitation in the ranks was tangible and many were looking at him with mistrust: nothing he couldn't overcome with his proven oratory ability, he said to himself to steel his nerves. After all, several of them owed what little wealth they could count on to him.

His heralds demanded silence, and only when there was no more noise did he begin to speak.

"Soldiers," he began. "There is no war juster than one fought to save our families from hunger and enemy aggression. Mark Antony believes I have waged it unfairly, but he is comfortable in Athens, far away from the oppression that Pompey is inflicting upon Italy, so what does he know about it? And what is more, he himself refused to hand the Peloponnese over to that pirate as was agreed in the pacts, thus recognising that it was Pompey who broke the agreements as soon as he resumed his raids, which has been confirmed by the pirates we have captured. And if Antony isn't taking part in this conflict, it is only because he must focus on the eastern border where the Parthians are becoming an increasingly serious threat to us."

He paused for a moment to get his breath back and saw the troops muttering. There were hints of approval, though – that was clear from the expressions on the soldiers' faces. Good, he was winning them over, as usual.

"You also know," he went on, more confidently, "that even Pompey's chief admiral, Menodorus, has come over to the state's side, denouncing the wrongdoings of his supreme commander. Therefore, it is my duty – indeed, it is *our* duty, mine and yours – to punish those who have broken the agreements and deprive them of all that we rewarded them with so many months ago, giving them more credit and trust than they deserved. And so I say that this war is legitimate and blessed by the gods! The gods don't want Rome to suffer any more abuse from that pirate who, remember, has already tried to starve our fellow citizens. And we must prevent that from happening again, otherwise what will happen to your children, to your parents, to your women?"

At that point, the cheering of the soldiers forced him to stop, and soon afterwards, the isolated cries had turned into a roar of collective acclaim. Yes, he had won them over, he said to himself as he made to leave the stage.

But at that very moment his attendant caught his attention and brought a dispatch courier over to him, who had to shout into his ear to make himself heard over the bedlam. Octavian had to have the man repeat his words several times in the vain hope that he had misunderstood.

"Caesar, Cornificius's fleet ran into a storm and dropped anchor near Picenum. That's why it's late. There was no significant damage, except..."

The soldier hesitated.

"Except?" Ottaviano urged him.

"One ship was sunk. It was your flagship, Caesar. I'm sorry."

He heard these last words distinctly, because in the meantime the soldier's cheers had ceased and the hostile muttering had resumed. The news must have spread through the troops as well, and everyone knew what it meant.

They had lost the flagship. *Only the flagship*.

There could be no worse omen for a campaign that had barely begun.

XVIII

Another violent impact rocked the trireme. No longer able to contain his agitation, Popilius Laenas leaned over the bulwark and peered down at the hull below. "No damage this time either," he cried to Menodorus, "but if we keep on like this, we'll end up smashing into the rocks! We must get out onto the open sea!"

The admiral, who had chosen to side with Octavian after deserting Sextus Pompey, listened without responding. He was staring towards the bow, keeping an eye on his main opponent, Menecrates, who had been chosen by the pirate to head the fleet after discovering his desertion. "It's the only way we can win. We must lure them here. Out there in the open sea, their numerical superiority will allow them to prevail. Menecrates must come closer," he said vindictively. "Only then will we be fighting on an even footing, and I can teach him the lesson he deserves for having tarnished my name with Pompey."

"But this way you risk doing him a favour!" said an increasingly frightened Laenas. "You'll kill us all without even getting close to him!"

"We can only hope that Calvisius has enough courage to attack his flank and force him towards us," replied Menodorus. "Menecrates wants me, and he might fall for it. But first, Calvisius must wake up."

Why had he done it? Laenas asked himself. He was a soldier, and the idea of fighting on a ship without solid ground under his feet scared him, but when Octavian had told him to board the flagship and keep an eye on Menodorus to make sure that he didn't double-cross them and that he respected their agreement while they travelled south from Etruria to join the triumvir's fleet he had been unable to refuse. Laenas would have liked to answer that Calvisius alone would be sufficient, as he would be following with his ships, almost doubling the number of vessels.

Right from the start, he had done nothing but fight off seasickness and look for places where he could vomit overboard without being noticed by the crew. Once, when he had realised that a sailor had seen him while he was retching into the sea, he had wiped his mouth with his forearm and grabbed the poor man, threatening to throw him overboard if he dared reveal what he had seen. He kept stumbling and tripping on the sails, and was sure that at least on one occasion he had made a fool of himself by falling over the ropes right in front of the crew – for he had heard their sniggers and sarcastic comments. It was a nightmare for him, and it had got even worse when they spotted a fleet near Cumae which Menodorus recognised as that of his personal nemesis, Menecrates.

No one, not even Octavian, had imagined that Pompey would react to the triumvir's pincer movement offensive by deciding to counter attack and eliminating one of the two aggressors before both could close in on him. The numerical superiority of Menecrates' fleet had forced Menodorus and Calvisius to take refuge in the Gulf of Cumae, where they had spent the night, but then they'd been forced to resume the journey in order to prevent Pompey from attacking Octavian with another of his fleets in the meantime. Once they had set off, however, they'd had to sail along the coast in order to avoid risking a battle with an uncertain outcome. And not only was the pace too slow to provide Octavian with the necessary support in time, there was also the risk of losing ships because of their proximity to the rocky shore.

Another loud crash confirmed Laenas's fears. Just ahead, a vessel was taking on water after it had apparently run aground on a partially submerged rock. They would have to let it sink and take the crew aboard. It was already the third since dawn.

"Don't you see that we're doing ourselves in?" he shouted to Menodorus. "Gods, it was an unlucky day for Caesar when he decided to enlist *you*!"

"Shut up!" the admiral replied, without looking at him.

Laenas couldn't tolerate being treated like that. After all, he was a tribune and the representative of the triumvir while Menodorus was just a freedman. Impulsively, he set off towards him, but the other pointed to Calvisius.

"Look! He's finally moving!"

Laenas observed the coast behind them and saw that, yes, the other admiral's ships *were* actually rowing towards Menecrates' flank, which was deployed in a semicircle to block them. He observed their movements carefully as they came closer to Menecrates' ships and began attacking the edge of the formation. That was where the battle started, and in the meantime, the enemy fleet, harried on its flank, instinctively moved forward, coming closer to Menodorus's ships.

"You see?" the admiral exclaimed with satisfaction. "Now we can fight!"

Laenas asked himself if he was supposed to be happy about that. He had hoped that in the end, Menecrates would grow weary of waiting and simply leave, abandoning the battle and resigning himself to joining his commander. The prospect of fighting on land excited the tribune, but battles at sea just made him nervous. He feared his reactions might be too slow in the event of a boarding and that his head would spin while his opponents were attacking him. He was aware that on deck he wasn't as lucid and ruthless as usual: on land, he fought with no hesitation, but here… here he was frightened.

"Well now that he is surrounded, he might decide not to engage and prefer to flee, mightn't he?" he said hopefully to Menodorus. "Even if he does outnumber us, he's at a tactical disadvantage now."

"Absolutely not – he wants me, and I won't back down. He won't go back to Pompey without my head," replied the admiral, as he continued to scrutinise the enemy ships in search of the one carrying his opponent, with whom there was evidently fierce rivalry.

He ordered the ship to advance a little and to signal to the others to do the same to prevent Menecrates' fleet from pushing them onto the rocks when the battle began.

It wasn't long before the two fleets came into close contact. Directly in line with their flagship, a trireme was heading in their direction with the obvious intention of ramming them. Its oars moved rhythmically and powerfully, thrusting the ship forward at maximum speed, but Menodorus seemed unconcerned, and soon afterwards Laenas understood the reason.

"There he is! He's mine!" cried out the admiral, looking in another direction entirely and telling the helmsman to steer to port just as the trireme was approaching their flank, thus exposing themselves to its ram.

"Have you lost your mind?" protested Laenas. "Don't you see that they're coming at us? You're showing them our flank!"

"Not if we advance as quickly as them. *That's* the prey I'm interested in," he said, pointing to a quadrireme in the centre of the enemy fleet.

"Menecrates?" asked the tribune.

"Exactly – a direct confrontation between me and him is worth an entire battle, and whoever wins it will prevail. And you'll see – it will be us."

"Are you joking? His ship is bigger than ours!" Laenas protested again. "You'd be able to take on a trireme like this, but you're going to attack a taller, more powerful ship full of soldiers?"

"So I can prove that I'm better than him," snapped Menodorus.

Laenas felt a wave of panic wash over him. Not only was there no guarantee that they would survive being rammed by the approaching trireme, his commander was also going to engage them in what was effectively a personal duel against a much better-equipped opponent.

And he would have to fight in even worse conditions.

*

The trireme which had targetted the flank of Menodorus's flagship only grazed them, sending Popilius Laenas staggering across the deck and slightly altering their course but the only damage was some scraping along the stern where the ships had made contact. But when the tribune went back to observe his commander's target, he realised that their trireme was no longer heading towards the flank of Menecrates' quadrireme.

Now it was Menecrates' quadrireme which was aiming its ram at their flank.

"Damn it!" he shouted in terror at Menodorus. "We're done for, you blunderer!"

The admiral gave him an irritated look, then told the helmsman to turn their bow towards the enemy. The man protested that there wasn't time for the manoeuvre but Menodorus insisted. The other soldiers on deck were fretting as much as Laenas was, frightened by the prospect of a collision with a much larger ship, and the tribune knew that, as the highest-ranking officer of the land forces present, he should discipline and encourage them, but all he could think about was the risk to his own life from Menodorus's insane manoeuvre as he neglected his duty to Caesar in the name of petty personal revenge.

As the two ships drew closer, he couldn't see how a collision could be avoided. The helmsman had just managed to straighten the trireme's course, but their only hope of survival – avoiding the enemy's ram – was simply impossible: at best, the two ships would collide bow to bow, and you didn't have to be a sailor to work out which of the two would come off best.

A moment before the impact, he gasped the bulwark tightly, as did all other soldiers, some of whom even sat down to avoid being thrown overboard. Menodorus, on the other hand, stood proudly in the bow: that madman would be the first victim, Laenas said to himself.

The impact was like an earthquake which shook the deck and almost flung the tribune overboard, and the air was filled with a roar as loud as a collapsing building and the screams of dozens of men.

The ship rolled violently. Laenas looked over at the main mast and saw that it hadn't broken, and that the trireme still seemed to be well above the water. He looked over at Menodorus and saw him peering over the side to check the damage to their bow and to the enemy quadrireme. The waves raised by the impact pushed the two ships apart and then brought them crashing back together again in a series of increasingly less dramatic collisions. The admiral turned round and shouted, "They've broken our ram but the planking of the hull is intact. They've lost their rudder, though, so they can't steer! They're ours! Use the grappling poles, and you, tribune, get your men ready for boarding, and watch out for enemy fire!"

The sailors raced over to take the long poles stacked along the bulwark, each with a wide hook at the end. They hoisted them over the side, waited for the sea to push the quadrireme closer again, then reached out with the poles and attempted to hook the enemy ship. The crew of the quadrireme were doing exactly the same thing at exactly the same time, however, and soon the two ships sides met and they looked like a single vessel, divided only by the bulwarks and the height difference.

When the enemy troops appeared on the bulwark, Laenas realised that coming alongside had provided their opponents a platform from which to board them by exploiting the advantage of their greater height. And they outnumbered them, to boot! That lunatic Menodorus had really dropped them in it, but there was no time for recriminations and so he ordered his men to get into formation immediately and to form a shield wall: the enemy had already begun hailing down spears, rocks and arrows on them, and to judge from the screams of pain he heard, he had waited too long to act.

His shield was struck by a boulder that forced him to momentarily lower his guard, but out of a reflexive instinct of pure self-preservation, he brought it back up just in time to block an arrow that almost struck him an instant later. He wondered what to do: on land, he would have known, but here? Here, he could only adopt a defensive strategy and await the inevitability of an enemy boarding.

"Launch the boarding ramp!" Menodorus shouted. "We'll board them! I want to face that fool in person!"

"Are you crazy?" cried Laenas. "You'll just be doing them a favour! We'll have to climb up, and they'll be coming down!"

But a moment later, it ceased to matter: Menecrates' men, protected by the covering fire of their fellow soldiers, were already throwing down their boarding ramps.

"Come on, then," Menodorus shouted, "let's stop them before they can get onto our deck!"

Hesitantly, Laenas ordered his men to advance, fearful of being even more exposed to the hail of projectiles that continued to fall onto the deck. Given his uncertainty, the men reached the bulwark out of formation, in a ragged line. "Try to push the gangways off!" the tribune shouted, hoping to prevent the boarding, then made to move forward, but Menodorus stopped him.

"No! Come here, Menecrates, come here and face me, if you have the courage!" he shouted, wielding his sword and holding out his shield, which was immediately struck by an arrow. "Come and fight me!"

"You idiot, you'll get us all killed!" cried Laenas, pushing him out of the way and dashing over to the gangway where some of the enemy troops had begun to descend. But the hail of arrows was unrelenting, and one hit Menodorus in the forearm after Laenas's shove had forced aside his shield. The admiral cried out in pain and dropped his sword, finding time to give the tribune a glare of hatred.

There was a cry of triumph from the deck of the other ship. A man came across the boarding ramp and stopped at the near end while the soldiers who had already crossed it tried to climb aboard the trireme, but were being thrown overboard by Laenas's soldiers.

"Not so boastful now, eh, Menodorus? Come on, come and get me if you can!" shouted a man who Laenas presumed must be Menecrates. Instinctively, Laenas grabbed a steel *soliferrum* spear from one of the auxiliaries on deck and promptly hurled it at the enemy admiral. It struck Menecrates in the thigh, and Laenas gave a cry of triumph which was instantly echoed by Menodorus, whose wound was far less serious than his opponent's. Menecrates now had a jagged javelin sticking out of his flesh which wouldn't be easy to remove.

Menecrates' soldiers looked at their injured commander in shock, and no more of them dared cross the gangways. As they attempted to understand their commander's condition, Menodorus was quick to take advantage of their hesitation.

"Go on, attack them! Now! Let's take the ship!" he ordered, and all the soldiers who had not been killed, wounded or stunned by the projectiles fired from the enemy vessel began swarming over the bulwarks and stormed onto the gangways. Meanwhile, Menecrates' men carried their leader to the stern, with Menecrates still shouting orders to his men to repel the assault. They did their best, but the uncoordinated nature of the defence gave Menodorus's soldiers time to climb over the enemy bulwarks.

Now full of the reassuring fervour of war, Laenas too went aboard the enemy ship, and vented all the frustration he had accumulated at sea by immediately severing the first arm that dared raise a sword against him, following it with an oblique swing at the man who came at him immediately afterwards which slashed open his chest. The blood spraying over him only increased his enthusiasm, and he decided to go and look for Menecrates to settle things once and for all. After that, the enemy soldiers would surely surrender.

He spotted him leaning against the opposite bulwark, clearly in pain but still able to shout orders, whilst a man had just finished pulling the *soliferrum* from his leg and was beginning to bandage his wound. He ran towards him, but was stopped by a wall of enemy soldiers. With the help of his men, he set about trying to overcome them, engaging in a battle that, apart from the rolling of the ship, was no different from one on land.

He shoved with his shield and swung his sword again and again, inflicting deep and deadly wounds, but even though the enemy line grew narrower with every victim, it held – and when he did finally manage to open a breach, he saw that Menecrates had gone. He ran to the bulwark and looked out to sea, where he spotted him on a boat with several others, far out of range even of a spear. He groaned with frustration, and then he noticed what was happening in the background.

Calvisius was withdrawing to the Gulf of Cumae, leaving several of his ships behind in flames.

He grasped the bulwark until his palms hurt.

They had captured the flagship of the enemy fleet. But the battle was lost.

*

"Triumvir, the rearguard has been attacked!"

They were the words Octavian had been afraid of hearing since setting off across the strait with his fleet.

Together with his flagship, he had almost reached the sea between Calabria and Sicily and was about to head towards Scilla. To his lieutenants who had wanted to engage in battle immediately, he had scornfully replied that he didn't want to risk a fight without the assistance of Calvisius and Menodorus and not even Pompey would dream of attacking him without the support of his freedman. Once he had heard about the battle in the waters off Cumae, he had decided to unite the fleet as soon as possible, rushing from the Ionian Sea to the Tyrrhenian to meet his lieutenants.

But he hadn't taken into consideration that while he crossed the strait he would be vulnerable to attacks from enemy ships, and would thus be a very tempting target for his enemies. And just when he thought he had got away with it, Pompey had attacked. And now he was in serious trouble.

"What?" he asked, mainly to play for time while he tried to think of a course of action that wouldn't make him look incompetent.

"We are under attack, Caesar," said the man who had received the communication passed from one vessel in the column to another. "The ships at the rear have been attacked by ships sailing from the port of Messina, their flanks are exposed to the enemy rams."

This meant condemning at least one third of the fleet to its doom, and thereby losing any advantage to be gained by joining Calvisius. He had to do something, Octavian said to himself, barely managing to suppress the panic he felt rising inside him.

"We have to… we have to go back and help them," he ordered unwillingly.

The man looked at him uncertainly and waited for him to repeat the order, which he had given with such little conviction.

"Yes, we'll turn around and attack the pirates' ships ourselves," he repeated, a lump in his throat. He didn't feel ready for undertaking a battle without anyone who was an expert in naval tactics by his side.

It took some time for the ships to change course. The rowers had to work flat out as the drum beat provided them with the rhythm for their strokes and the soldiers prepared to board.

Soon, Octavian reached the place where the battle had begun. The stretch of sea along the Sicilian coast was teeming with enemy ships, making it impossible to surround them in the middle of the channel. He signalled to the rest of the fleet to continue sailing along the coast of the peninsula, but as soon as he saw how they were wedged in between the enemy's fleet and the mainland, he realised that he had made another mistake. He was forcing them to fight in a much smaller space, with their hulls almost touching the rocks.

The image of a humiliating defeat appeared before him. He had noticed that some of his rearguard ships were burning, set on fire by incendiary projectiles from Pompey's ships, while those closer to him began to crash into one another during the confusing manoeuvres, and oars were broken.

He stood there watching, in the hope that Pompey would content himself with preventing him from joining Calvisius and would return to Messina, but as time passed, it became clear that his opponent was aware of his difficulties and had no intention of leaving without inflicting serious damage. And his ships kept on pushing both the rearguard and the ships that had gone to help them towards the coast.

With a feeling of nausea, Octavian was forced to return with his fleet to the coast they had departed from but a few hours earlier. It was a blow, but at least it would mean avoiding a total defeat. Then, when Calvisius's remaining ships arrived, he would decide what to do. But after giving the command – the third in a matter of minutes – he immediately realised that carrying it out would present serious difficulties for at least a part of his fleet: many of them were already struggling, and others soon would be too if they didn't get to a mooring place right away. There was no time to get back to port, they would just have to drop anchor wherever they could.

Some triremes had already been wrecked, and they hindered the passage of the others, and the fires were spreading from one ship to another, but at least most of the fleet would be able to retreat undisturbed. Pompey, however, had no intention of easing the pressure and stayed close to the ships he had already attacked, preventing them from manoeuvring and rowing away. In the meantime, the vessel carrying the impotent triumvir approached the coast while just a short distance from his flagship the air above the masts was filled with projectiles of all sorts fired by both sides. Grappling poles were held out over the bulwarks and rams struck from every direction, but Octavian's ships were all on the defensive while the enemy vessels were on the attack.

One after the other, the triremes dropped anchor off the coast, but at a prudent distance from the rocks, hoping the shallow water would dissuade the enemy quadriremes from approaching them. Some, harried by their adversaries, were wrecked upon the rocks, but most of them managed to drop anchor with their bows towards the enemy, forming a sort of fishbone deployment along the coast. The enemy ships slowed as they approached, stopping close enough to the triremes to fire arrows and bolts from the scorpios mounted on their turrets. Some of them, though, did not stop in time and ended up colliding with the ships in front of them, their larger size devastating the smaller vessels. Octavian saw one sinking not far from where his flagship was anchored, its hull devastated by the enemy ram, and watched men leaping into the water to try and reach the shore. But the soldiers on the quadriremes targeted the survivors, and many got no more than a few yards before they went under, killed by an arrow or a spear.

Other ships, targeted by the hail of projectiles and fearful of meeting the same fate, began to pull back to put more distance between themselves and their opponents, but soon the sound of arrows and scorpio bolts was drowned out by the creaking of planking as it smashed on impact with jagged spikes of rock emerging from the sea. Captains ordered their crews to throw the boats into the sea and abandon ship, but the ocean, made turbulent by the battle, capsized the boats as they hit the water. Soldiers then climbed onto the rocks to escape, but many were hit by arrows and scorpio bolts.

Octavian cursed himself for his impotence. He must at least show that he was trying to do something to help them. He ordered a boat lowered into the water and, accompanied by his bodyguards, went to the shore, where, his clothes drenched and gasping for breath, he climbed onto the rocks to assist the men who were helping their companions climb ashore. Several times he risked falling into the water himself, dragged down by the weight of the soldiers struggling amidst the waves, and had to be saved by his bodyguards, who grabbed him by the arm and pulled him to safety. Many of those who managed to make it up onto the rocks did not recognise him, and some made mocking comments about the abilities of their supreme commander.

Many arrived with cuts and slashes, their bodies pierced by arrows, and were held afloat until they reached the shore by their brave fellow soldiers. He tried to comfort them when they were rescued, giving orders for a makeshift shelter to be built for the wounded and telling them that the day of their vengeance would soon arrive. Meanwhile, however, he noticed that some of his ships had raised anchor and were beginning to advance towards the enemy. It looked as if it was the flank led by Cornificius. What was that idiot doing? Was he trying to make this disaster even worse? He stared in disbelief as the smaller ships slipped between the enemy vessels and engaged in battle again. The exchange of projectiles and the battles between ships immediately concentrated themselves in that area, and he thought he saw boardings taking place.

The men around him watched the scene too, and began to shout praise for Cornificius when they saw a quadrireme catch fire. Apparently, Cornificius's initiative was succeeding. A boat arrived on shore and a man climbed out and started frantically trying to attract the attention of the triumvir.

"Caesar, vice-prefect Cornificius wishes to inform you that he has decided to die fighting rather than stand waiting for death to come to him!"

The troops around him stared at the man, and Octavian felt a shiver of shame. With his courage, Cornificius had highlighted the incompetence of his supreme commander.

And when he saw that Cornificius's ship had rammed what appeared to be the admiral's flagship and that his men were streaming onto its deck to capture it, he realised that with a little more courage he could have saved himself this humiliation.

He detested Cornificius for the embarrassment he was causing him. But he could never punish him for doing what he had not dared to.

XIX

Ortwin accelerated his step as he saw the distant flickering of the fires in the gaps between the rocks. He ordered the commanding officer of the XIIIth legion to follow suit and hasten the progress of the troops, and together they traversed the rough land leading to the sea. When he reached the top of the hills overlooking the coast, he peered down at the scene below him: the faint light of the stars and the fires burning on the coast allowed him to make out the silhouettes of ships moored near the shore and boats crowding along the rocks on the waterfront. He also made out moving figures going back and forth near the shore. He feared they had arrived too late and gave Veleda a worried look, clutching the sack he kept the gifts for Octavian in.

He had returned to Italy and landed in Brindisi, anxious to communicate to his commander the success of his mission, only to discover that Octavian was now at war with Sextus Pompey and was already in the Strait awaiting battle. He had therefore decided not to go to Rome and headed south, with news of the increasingly dramatic developments reaching him only intermittently. On the way, he had met the XIIIth legion, who had been told to go to the tip of the country to wait for embarkation in view of the invasion of Sicily, and had joined them. Then, news had arrived of an enemy victory at Cumae which had deprived Octavian's lieutenants of several ships and delayed their joining the triumvir's fleet. And finally, just when he was near the Straits at Hipponium he had learned from the locals of the battle fought off the headland of Scylleum, where the triumvir had come off worst. They were saying that no one even knew if he was still alive.

He went down the slope, followed by Veleda and the others, and as he approached the coast he could see the scene he had only glimpsed from above in more detail. He soon found himself amongst hundreds of soldiers lying scattered over the rocks, many of whom were wounded and roughly bandaged. Men shouted for a doctor or for someone to attend to their wounds, while from the water there came cries for help, though in the darkness it was hard to tell exactly where from. Some soldiers wandered about distributing supplies, others called for water and others still cursed their commanders for their ineptness. There was a line of fires along the shore to guide the men still in the water to dry land and around them men shouted to help guide their less fortunate companions to safety.

In the water, a ragged row of ships was at anchor, but the area between the triremes and the coast was dotted with partially submerged wrecks. Hanging onto them were men who lacked the strength or courage to swim the last stretch to the shore.

It was the image of a defeat.

"We have to look for Octavian, Ortwin," said Veleda and the German asked the first soldier he passed while the rest of the XIIIth arrived and scattered in search of a place to store supplies and erect a makeshift camp. One of the tribunes, however, joined him in the search.

"He's around, I don't know where," the legionary replied laconically. At least he was alive, if nothing else, said Ortwin to himself, as he continued to ask each man he passed who was in a condition to speak. Eventually, somebody pointed him out, and Ortwin rushed over. He found the triumvir amongst a group of injured men, offering one of his comrades water and talking to another officer of the XIIIth who had found him before they had.

"Caesar, Caesar!" he called out, reassured to see that he was unharmed. But when he met his eyes, he saw that his pride was hurt, and for Octavian, that was probably even worse than a physical injury.

However, as soon as he recognised him, the triumvir started and relief spread over his face. He went over to Ortwin, Veleda and the officer, and grasped the hands of all three, then he turned to the officer. "Tribune, I am glad that you of the XIIIth

have arrived! If nothing else, it will prevent Pompey from taking advantage of our difficulties to disembark his troops and attack us for the moment!"

"How many ships have you lost, Caesar?" asked the officer.

"We don't know yet," answered Octavian. "We will count them tomorrow. But it wasn't a total defeat. By the end, we were making progress and we captured the enemy flagship – the one belonging to Democarus, another of Pompey's freedman admirals. And while we were gaining back some ground, the enemy suddenly retreated – for reasons which are still unclear, because they had blockaded most of our fleet against the shore."

Above all, Ortwin was worried about his leader's condition. Knowing his ill health, he feared he might have one of his attacks, which could jeopardise the entire campaign. "But you're all wet, Caesar," he said. "At this time of night you should be in your tent!"

"Unfortunately, it is absolute chaos here," said Octavian. "I haven't even managed to find my servants to put my tent up. And to tell the truth, I do not even know where our stores have ended up."

"Come with us, Caesar," said the tribune. "Every officer in the XIIIth legion will be proud to give you his tent!"

Octavian hesitated for a moment, then nodded, eliciting a sigh of relief from Ortwin. The tribune led them to the camp, while Octavian whispered to the German, "So? How did it go?"

"I have something to show you as soon as we're alone," he replied, holding the sack tight.

The officer reached the area where soldiers were busy erecting tents in a manner which bore no resemblance to the usual orderly, square provisional camps of the Roman legions. There were no protective ditches or embankments, which were impossible to build given the harsh nature of the terrain. He found his assistants and, after waiting for them to put up his tent and equip it with the essentials, he offered it to Octavian, who thanked him and invited Ortwin and Veleda in.

"I cannot tell you how happy I am to see you again," began the heir of Caesar as soon as they were alone while, with the assistance of one of the tribune's slaves, he began to take off his wet clothes and put on his tunic and toga. "It has been my first campaign without any members of the sect with me, and it has been hard. I really hope that being deprived of you for all these months has served some purpose."

He was obviously glad to see them, thought Ortwin, as he was being much more affable than usual with them. He must have really felt alone. But there was always the hint of a latent threat in his voice, which made him hope that he never disappointed him. Fortunately, this time there was no risk of that.

Ortwin offered him the sack, which Octavian, still half-dressed, grabbed. He opened it and peered inside. His face showed no surprise or change of expression when he took out one of the three trophies.

"And what are these?"

Ortwin immediately recognised the relic, which by now was practically nothing more than a bare skull. It was his most recent – and most gratifying – victim.

"I got the man you sent me to kill, Caesar."

A smile appeared on Octavian's tired face. "Quintus Labienus? My mother and my cousin are avenged, then." He looked back inside the bag. "And what about the other two?"

"Two pleasant surprises, I had the chance to cross other names from our list. They are the Bucolianus brothers. They were Labienus's lieutenants in Lycia."

Visibly satisfied, Octavian addressed Ortwin and Veleda. "If it weren't for you two, there would still be a gang of Caesar's murderers walking free. When all this is finally over, you can ask me for anything."

Ortwin felt the eyes of his woman upon him, and knew only too well what it was she would ask for.

"Unfortunately, it is still far from being over," Octavian continued. "It's true, the XIIIth has arrived, but..."

A soldier appeared outside the entrance to the tent, calling for the triumvir's attention. The head of the sect motioned for him to enter.

"Caesar, we know why the enemy fleet interrupted the battle this afternoon," said the man.

"Well?" Octavian prompted him.

"Calvisius arrived in the afternoon. He was behind them, so they rushed to Messina."

The triumvir gave a sigh of relief and dismissed the soldier. Then he turned to Ortwin and Veleda. "First the XIIIth, then you two with this wonderful gift of the heads of three of the assassins and now the arrival of Calvisius. Things will go much better tomorrow!" he exclaimed enthusiastically.

Ortwin would have liked to have felt the same way. Without a more capable leader than Octavian in command, he could not feel equally confident.

*

"The wind is rising, Caesar," said Veleda, worried by the sudden change in the weather. The horizon was covered with clouds and the surface of the ocean increasingly disturbed by the wind which also moved the flotsam, jetsam and men floating there. The fires still burning on the ships offshore danced in the air as though sucked up towards the heavens and the ragged outline of the coast looked like so many claws poised to attack the survivors on the rocks.

"It's normal here, or so they tell me. It'll be over soon," said the triumvir, who was busy managing the recovery of damaged boats he was trying to repair. A team of men under his command were carrying a new mast for a ship moored just a short distance from the rocks, replacing the one which had been broken the previous day in battle. The entire sector looked like an improvised shipyard, where vessels under repair floated next to others now reduced to disintegrating wrecks whose planks, rigging and sails continued to wash up on the rocks. The area before Veleda's eyes had become a huge open-air dump where there were also human remains.

"But Pompey could take advantage of our hardships to attack us now… he also has the wind in his favour: it's blowing towards us," she objected again.

"That's why I ordered Calvisius to create a protective cordon with his ships," said Octavian confidently, pointing to the deployment of triremes arranged parallel to the coast by his admiral to form a seamless barrier.

But those ships too rocked dangerously under the force of the rising wind, and risked damaging each other. Veleda was not heartened by her commander's answer, and her fears were soon confirmed by a further worsening of the situation. The scaffold erected on the deck of a trireme to erect the mast collapsed in a clear sign that it was no longer possible to carry on the work of restoring the damaged ships. The beams fell, crushing the workmen under them, and a chorus of screams could be heard from beneath the bundle of sails, poles and rigging that had fallen onto the deck. Then the newly erected mast came down too, crushing the balustrade, with a roar that was almost lost in the rising howl of the storm. Men threw themselves into the water to avoid being crushed, but in a few moments, most of them had either disappeared beneath the waves, been thrown violently against the devastated hull, or pounded mercilessly against the shore. Octavian watched a body thrown like a toy against the rock with horror and the shock made him lose his balance. It was only the speed with which Veleda threw her arms around him and pulled him back from the edge of the shore that stopped him from falling into the sea.

He looked at her without understanding what had happened, but the intensity of the storm was increasing by the moment. Some men shouted to their fellows on the boats and the ships to return to the shore, but their cries were lost in the wind. Chaos reigned on the decks of the ships: the sailors could no longer hear each other and the depleted crews were unable to control the vessels. The southern wind began to push the ships and the wrecks towards the coast of the peninsular, and some collided with each other, causing new breaches in their hulls. The anchors broke and no boat managed to stay in position. In front of Veleda, one trireme accidentally rammed another. The damaged ship keeled over to one side and its stern began to sink, forcing soldiers and crew to leap into the water, where the swell erased all trace of them.

More and more ships were being pushing towards the rocks. She could see men on board fending off other vessels with long poles over the balustrade but most of the time the poles broke when they made contact with each others hulls. Some ships, amongst which Veleda noticed Menodorus' flagship, began to move towards the open sea to escape carnage along the coast.

"Where are they going, those cowards?" cried Octavian, who seemed almost out of his mind with frustration.

"Caesar, they are saving themselves. If they stay here, too many ships will end up being destroyed!" Veleda tried to explain. Even though she was not entirely convinced that they would withstand the storm out there, where they were completely exposed to it.

"They are cowards! They are abandoning me because they think I no longer have the favour of the gods! They are going to Pompey, who is safe with his ships in the port of Messina!" the triumvir continued to yell until seized by one of his violent coughing fits.

Veleda realised that he was having one of his acute attacks. She looked around her for Ortwin, but couldn't see him in the chaotic rush of people trying to salvage equipment and supplies piled up along the rocks, which were now threatened by the fury of the storm. Octavian suddenly collapsed but she caught him and slowed his fall. He had lost consciousness and was drenched in sweat and struggling to breathe. The woman summoned up all her strength, then heaved him up onto her shoulders and went looking for his doctor, heading toward the praetorian tent that the XIIIth had made available to the triumvir.

But when she got to where it had been, she discovered that the wind had blown it away.

*

Octavian came back to himself just before dawn, with his doctor, Veleda and Ortwin nearby. He saw the concerned faces of his friends around him, the darkness lifted slightly by torches flickering in the force of the wind. He could still hear the crash of the waves, screams of terror and pain and the splintering sound of colliding ships. Then he realised they were real sounds which were happening in that very moment, and despair washed over him once more.

"Are the gods so set against me, then?" he asked, in a voice that, after a night of cold air and coughing, he did not recognise.

"The troops haven't yet had time to think about it, Caesar," replied Ortwin. "They are too busy facing the storm."

"But there is no doubt that they will soon enough, though," said Octavian. "I have to remedy all this."

"I do not see how. The storm is dying down, but the locals say there hasn't been one like it since time immemorial," said the doctor.

"And apparently, Pompey managed to avoid it and keep his ships safe," muttered Ortwin. "While ours..."

The triumvir tried to get to his feet to see for himself what was happening, but his head started to spin and he was forced to lie down again. In his head, he could still hear those cries in the darkness. They were frightening, like ghosts which lurked beneath him, waiting for a chance to get him on his own and punish him for his arrogance.

"Stay... stay with me... please," he muttered, before falling asleep.

*

When he awakened again, it was day. The doctor was still with him, and so was Veleda, but there was no sign of Ortwin. "Where is he?" he asked when he eventually felt able to express himself.

"He went to help," his woman answered. "The storm is over and there is much to do, Caesar. According to the commanders, we have lost at least half of the ships, including Calvisius and Menodorus's fleets, and the remaining ones need repairing."

"Now Sextus Pompey will attack us..." murmured Octavian, realising that this was the most likely hypothesis.

"Perhaps, and perhaps not. The sea is full of wrecks and debris, and it would be difficult for him to advance on us without an accident."

"And he could send legions to attack the coastal towns, knowing that I am in trouble and am stuck here."

"Perhaps."

"And perhaps someone in Rome will take advantage of my disgrace to carry out a plot against me and get me out of the way."

"One of your enemies might take advantage of it, yes."

"And the population might rebel because it believes that I have unjustly begun this war again and have been punished by the gods."

"Perhaps."

"Even the soldiers, seeing that by myself I am unable to win a battle while Antony, who wisely kept out of it and is now preparing for a triumphant campaign against the Parthians, might abandon me. They will choose him now."

This time Veleda had the good sense to stay silent.

Octavian felt overwhelmed by despair. With great difficulty, he got to his feet, and the woman went to support him. "Take me to the rocks," he ordered, and she did as he said. He contemplated the scene before his eyes, finally visible in the clear light of day with a full and warm sun and without the powerful wind which had made everything blurry and indistinct.

The double defeat he had suffered – from the enemy and from the weather – was revealed to him in all its brutal horror, and there was no way of denying it. Even Maecenas's best propaganda would be unable to mitigate the effects of the disaster to which he had condemned the fleet with his obstinacy. And the fact that even the gods had been against him also put him, in the eyes of the people, unequivocally in the wrong. He could make no excuses in the face of the terrible sight of hundreds of wrecks floating in the water and perhaps thousands of drowned soldier's bodies banging against rocks and detritus, and all that devastation without even engaging with the enemy.

When he had begun his adventure as the heir to Caesar, he would never have imagined that the man who, above all, hindered him from attaining his goals would be Sextus Pompey, the most insignificant of Pompey the Great's sons. He had faced much more imposing enemies and obstacles, and had resigned himself to the idea of having to sweep them all away sooner or later in order to achieve supreme power and pursue without bounds the reforming work of his august predecessor. But never as now had he been forced to admit his own limits as a commander and as a man, and the impossibility of managing without his friends, who he had, in fact, chosen precisely for their ability to compensate for his shortcomings.

It was all over now, unless he decided to change tack and put aside his pride. But it was worth making one last attempt before throwing away six years of superhuman efforts to save Rome from herself.

"Give the order to the praetorian court to prepare to depart. We are going to Hipponium. We will leave the rest of the legion to help Calvisius and Menodorus," he said to Veleda. "I will write to the decurions of the coastal towns to warn them against pirate attacks. And to Agrippa, too, to tell him he must return from Gaul. And to Maecenas, to strengthen surveillance on Rome and watch out for any conspiracies."

"Very well, Caesar. And then?" the woman asked.

"And then… Then, I will have to ask our worthy Etruscan to do something for me," he replied, reflecting on just how much pride he would have to set aside to send his friend to Athens.

XX

Maecenas was to come here, as was the excellent Cocceius, both sent ambassadors on matters of great importance; having been accustomed to reconcile friends at variance. Here, having got sore eyes, I was obliged to use the black ointment. In the meantime came Maecenas and Cocceius, and Fonteius Capito along with them, a man of perfect polish, and intimate with Mark Antony, no man more so. (…) The next day arises, by much the most agreeable to all: for Plotius, and Varius, and Virgil met us at Sinuessa; souls more candid ones than which the world never produced, nor is there a person in the world more bound to them than myself. Oh what embraces, and what transports were there! While I am in my senses, nothing can I prefer to a pleasant friend.[3]

"I am glad that you, at least, find all this so amusing," said Maecenas in the atrium of Antony's house in Athens, while Horace read him his latest piece. "One would need to possess your philosophy on life to be able to joke about the journey we had to make to get here and the meetings we have had to have with Antony's emissaries to define the agreements with the triumvir. Unlike you, however, I am exhausted, and truly hope that we manage to finally conclude something."

"Well you cannot deny that the company relieved your sufferings on the way from Brindisi," said Horace. "You must be proud of having assembled such an impressive group of talented artists."

"Perhaps, but I feel that I have not yet done enough to permit your talents to make their best possible contribution. Unfortunately, as long as we are at war, we have other priorities…"

"Sometimes I doubt we will ever see the end of these civil wars," said Horace. "Do you think he is so stupid he doesn't realise that once the one with Pompey is over, there will immediately be another – an even greater and more destructive one?"

Maecenas motioned to him to silence his now proverbial impertinence. They were right inside the wolf's den and if Antony was deliberately making them wait – probably with the aim of humiliating his brother-in-law, just as Octavian had once made Antony wait in vain in Brindisi – he couldn't rule out that he was hiding somewhere and listening in on their conversation. "Don't make me regret having brought you with me," he answered sternly.

"You didn't seem to be regretting it last night aboard the ship…" said his friend mischievously.

Maecenas sighed and raised his eyes to the heavens. He considered it a great victory to have conquered Horace and to have won him over to Octavian's cause, but he certainly shouldn't fool himself that he was going to be able to change his character.

Eventually, after subjecting them to an offensively long wait, Mark Antony appeared.

"Please forgive me, my dear equestrian," he began, ignoring Horace completely and immediately underlining the difference in rank between himself and Maecenas, "but my dear Octavia, who is pregnant, isn't feeling at all well, and so I preferred to make sure she fell asleep quietly before I left her on her own."

Maecenas stifled a sarcastic smirk. It was said that in recent times Antony was no longer the dedicated husband and citizen of Rome he had striven to be in the early days of his marriage. He seemed to spend a lot of time with young wrestlers and presiding over gymnastic competitions without even taking with him the paraphernalia of his triumviral position. The apparel he wore to receive them, on the other hand, spoke volumes: a Greek cape with white sandals that would have been unlikely to make anybody think that he was a Roman.

He looked, Maecenas said to himself, like anything but a general who was in the process of setting off on a major campaign like the conquest of the Parthian empire.

"I am pleased to hear that your wife's pregnancy is going well. I'm sure she will be glad of a bit more serenity, if we can only manage to come to some sort of agreement," said Maecenas, who could not help but notice how their their host had not accommodated them in his *triclinium*. It was a beautiful spring day, that was true, but standing in the atrium beside the humidity of the *impluvio* was not exactly his idea of a summit meeting to define the destiny of the empire. He was sorry that Antony's mediators were not present: for the triumvir would have been compelled to make everyone comfortable, if only out of respect for his close associates.

At that moment, a secretary came into the room and handed several wax tablets to Antony, Maecenas had the impression that the scene had been planned so as to coincide with their encounter. The triumvir excused himself from his guests and carefully read the documents, and a gratified look appeared on his face.

"Well, Publius Ventidius is giving me a lot of satisfaction. He forced his way into Syria, defeated the Parthians in battle in Cirrestica and killed Pacorus, the son of the king," he said as if speaking to an audience. "It is the third battle he has won under my aegis, and now it seems that the Parthians are pulling back to their own borders with their tails between their legs. I will have to stop him before he steals all the glory," he concluded with a smile, "otherwise what is the point in me going to Parthia at all?"

His intention was clearly that of showing off his achievements, especially given the poor results Octavian had obtained in the west. It was a way to remind them that the young triumvir was always a step below him.

"I can only rejoice, like all of Rome, for these victories," commented Maecenas, cautiously. "Now we must also provide stability in the west, though, if you wish to have your back guarded for your glorious new undertaking, which will certainly consecrate you to posterity as the greatest Roman leader of all time – greater than Crassus who allowed himself to be defeated and greater even than Caesar, who never managed to get there. If I were you, I wouldn't leave any loose ends..."

"And in fact I have absolutely no intention of leaving any problems behind me," said Antony, his mood suddenly changing. "Even though Octavian keeps on creating them for me whenever he can! The lad absolutely refuses to try and get along with me, and as far as I can tell, he never honours the agreements we make and is always lacking in respect. And now, after the way he treats me, he sends me his errand boys to beg for help!"

"But that was just a series of misunderstandings," said Maecenas, trying to calm Antony down, "caused by the fact that you were so far away from one another and by the great responsibilities that weigh upon both your shoulders, but..."

"What do you mean, '*misunderstandings*'? We had clearly established the rules, and he systematically violated them! Do you think that I haven't left for the East because I *enjoy* being here doing nothing? The truth is that, regardless of the division of the territories, we had agreed that we would both recruit soldiers in Italy so that I would have the necessary troops to invade Parthia. And instead it seems that what is on Italian soil all belongs to him, and he will not allow my men to recruit for my armies."

"On the other hand, he needs ships to fight Pompey, and he says that you have failed to provide them," pointed out Maecenas. "So you both have good reasons to find a way to come to a new agreement, don't you think?"

"And what is the point in giving them to him, if he lets them all be destroyed by storms and pirates? It's a waste! I've heard say that thanks to all his victories, Pompey now actually considers himself Neptune!"

"Octavian is currently preparing a fleet of unimaginable proportions and this time he will see things through right to the end without leaving anything to chance. If and when you come to Italy, you will have the opportunity to see what is being built in the place where you last met Caesar and Sextus Pompey."

"*If* I come to Italy…"

Maecenas had expected objections from Antony, whom he feared was less than willing to return to support Octavian. Perhaps, in spite of the problems it would create for his campaign, he would be happier to see the young triumvir struggling with Pompey and the discontent of the citizens.

"I understand your point of view…" he said eventually, "and that is why I have devised a solution that would save the dignity of both of you and offer the people a concrete reason for wanting peace between the triumvirs," he concluded, hoping that he sounded convincing.

*

When the commanding officer of her escort informed her that he had sighted the squadron of lictors, Octavia leaned out of the covered carriage to look for her brother, who she had not seen for almost two years. She saw him standing like a god in a sort of temple, between columns made up from bundles of poles culminating in the dark, double-headed axes called *bipennes* and she had no doubt that this was an artfully studied backdrop, perhaps devised by Maecenas, to impress her and induce her to report her impressions to her husband. And when she saw that the Etruscan was standing beside her brother, and beside him was the massive frame of Agrippa, she was certain of it. All the members of the sect were awaiting her.

It was her chance to return to playing a role in her brother's political adventures, but she wasn't actually sure that she wanted to. She didn't even know if she should consider herself simply a tool in the hands of powerful men like her husband and Octavian or an actual asset whose participation was of importance in the future development of their alliance. She didn't know whether everything had already been decided and she was simply playing a role in a piece of theatre or if she really had a chance of influencing their reconciliation.

She also feared that her brother was angry with her. Octavia had never understood whether he'd given her to Antony to get her out of the way or to spy on her husband's activities and plans. In any case, even though he treated her with respect, affection and even love, he had never shown her that he trusted her completely and had never revealed anything to her except his most widely known plans and ideas, and therefore, she had never had anything significant to report to her brother. Perhaps Octavian now thought she was of no more use to the sect. In any case, Octavia couldn't help agreeing with her husband when he complained about Octavian's unwillingness to comply with their agreements, and if she hadn't been so afraid of her brother, she would have written to ask him to be more conciliatory. In her eyes Octavian was in the wrong, and it seemed to her that he was the one who had gone looking for trouble.

But she had decided not to, deliberately choosing to enjoy the period of inner peace that her unexpectedly happy marriage was giving her, far away from Italy, the sect of Mars Ultor and the memory of Chaerea's atrocious rejection, which still burned inside her.

She had become progressively more attached to Antony, the only one of them all who seemed not to have abandoned her, and to the numerous children she was bringing up – those Antony had with Fulvia and those that Octavia had in her first marriage, namely the two Marcellas and Marcellus, and their own children, Antonia and the child in her womb. It was, finally, the peace she had been seeking since she was a girl – and after all the suffering she had endured and the sacrifices she had made, she appreciated it even more.

As soon as they stopped, the slaves helped her to out. Holding her belly, in which the movements of her unborn child grew increasingly stronger, she carefully placed her foot on the pedestal and looked at her brother, who came to greet her with open arms and an ecstatic expression on his face, followed by his two friends. He seemed to have changed enormously. He was only twenty-six, but over the last two years he seemed to have aged a decade. She studied him more closely: no, he hadn't aged, he had simply lost his youthful look and become a man – not robust, but charismatic. His features had hardened and there was no longer any trace of naivety or purity in his eyes.

A man to be afraid of, she concluded immediately.

"My sweet sister! If you only knew how happy I am to see you again!" Octavian greeted her, and his exclamations of joy were immediately followed by those of Maecenas and Agrippa.

"Apparently, I owe this meeting to you, Maecenas," said Octavia when they had concluded their greetings and she had been accommodated on one of the couches in the triclinium of the country villa where Octavian was being hosted.

"Your husband thought it was a good idea," replied the Etruscan, sitting on the couch next to hers. "How is he anyway? Is he staying in Taranto or is he off travelling around Italy?"

It was a rhetorical question, obviously. The sect was perfectly well aware of Antony's movements since he had arrived in Apulia.

"He's fine, but of course he's worried. He managed to get a glimpse of how much the famine caused by Pompey's blockades is poisoning Italy."

"Is that why he brought three hundred ships with him?" asked her brother bitterly. "To put an end to this hunger?"

"Actually, those ships are for you, if you manage to come to some sort of agreement," she replied timidly. And if you think that you owe him something too."

Even her brother's voice had changed. It was harsher, empty, devoid of inflexion.

"I heard that he came with that fleet still undecided about who to give it to, to tell the truth," Octavian replied, studying her diffidently. "And I know that he has sent his freedman Callia to Lepidus, certainly to plot against me!"

"No, my dear brother," Octavia said patiently. "He sent him to organise our daughter's wedding to Lepidus's son to strengthen the triumvirate."

"I don't understand whether you actually believe what you're saying or whether at this point you've totally gone over to your husband's side," he burst out. "It seems that you agree with everything he does against me now!"

“Well you must understand that he too feels that he has been wronged by you and wants his help to be recognised as important,” she said, hoping not to annoy him.

But she realised immediately that she had said the wrong thing.

“Wronged? So I have wronged *him*, have I?” protested Octavian. “He left me to fight that pirate on my own simply for the pleasure of being able to pick up my mortal remains. And not because he was busy with the Parthians – he got his generals to do all that while he spent his time having fun in Athens! Well I am sorry for the pair of you, but I am still here – bowed but not defeated and ready to fight back! Thank goodness that you were working *for* me! You have betrayed the oath you made to the sect of Mars Ultor,” he concluded contemptuously, “just like Rufus, and like our cousin Pinarius!”

Octavia was devastated, and was not consoled by seeing how Maecenas and Agrippa took her brother by the arms and tried to calm him. She felt the tears running down her face and hated herself for not being able to show the fortitude that everyone expected of her. It was clear that, just as she had feared, Octavian detested her. Perhaps he even considered her a traitor, and it was useless to try and explain to him that she was grateful to Antony, even in love with him, because he had given her the serenity she had been seeking for so long. But in her brother's unbridled ambition there was no place for that kind of sentiment.

She decided to speak her mind.

"How can you accuse me, dear Octavian, of having failed in my duties?" she said, her voice breaking with emotion. "I who more than any other suffer for this disagreement between the two of you. If there is war between my brother and my husband, there will be misery and misfortune for me whoever wins, don't you think? Is it my fault that I care for both of you and wish that you would get along? Do you not think it natural that I love my husband too and that he has been able to make me happy? I am here because I truly hope that you can once again come to some sort of agreement, so I ask you to make a genuine effort not to turn me from the happiest woman into the unhappiest. This problem of Pompey has been dragging on for years – you will only be able to solve it with Antony's help, and he will only be able to solve the problem of the Parthians with your help. So why can't you arrange to meet again?"

Octavian was about to reply, but his words died on his lips. Octavia saw Maecenas and Agrippa nodding, and watched the expression on her brother's face attentively, as it seemed to finally relax. A slight smile appeared on his lips, and Octavian reached out his hands, rose from his couch and came over to embrace her, squeezing her tightly and whispering to her that she was right.

But Octavia wondered if she had really convinced him or whether that man, whom she hardly recognised as her own brother, already had a plan of his own about what was going to happen.

*

Octavian listened to Antony speaking beside him in the triumvir's carriage and could not believe his ears. The young man had said to Octavia that he would meet Antony between Taranto and Metapontum, but he would never have imagined that his fellow triumvir would have behaved so affably. Evidently, his sister had been doing a good job and he had been wrong to accuse her of failing in her duties. She had obviously persuaded her husband to be helpful – so much so that nothing could have surprised him more than his brother-in-law's behaviour when the two had seen one another from the opposite banks of the Metapontum river. Octavian had expected to have to argue with his rival about which shore to hold the meeting on after a long discussion of guarantees and protections. Instead, Antony had simply jumped down from his chariot, had a boat lowered into the water and had started rowing towards him, stopping in the middle of the river.

Alone.

Both shores were packed with soldiers but there were also many simple peasants who had been attracted by the news of their encounter which had spread throughout the entire area over the previous days. As Octavian was in full view of so many eyes, Maecenas had suggested that it would be inappropriate to refuse to accept Antony's conciliatory gesture, and so he had found himself on a small boat in the middle of the river, persuaded by his Etruscan friend to outdo his brother-in-law's zeal and to propose, once they were within speaking distance, going together to Taranto to visit Octavia.

Antony had felt obliged to up the stakes even more, offering to come over to the shore of his younger colleague, and their dispute had taken a turn for the paradoxical: a sort of competition to see who could demonstrate more trust in the other for the benefit of the public, with the certainty that, what with so many people watching, neither of them would be able to go back on their word once it was given.

In the end, the idea of visiting Octavia had won out, and Antony had agreed to take his brother-in-law with him to Taranto, but without an escort: his men, he said, would handle Octavian's safety. They had even agreed that his brother-in-law would spend the night in their villa. Octavian had climbed into his chariot with a last glance at his general staff on the other shore, hoping that he would see them again soon.

In the meantime, however, Antony wouldn't stop talking.

"… The Parthians have grown weak and I intend to take advantage of the fact. They are weaker than they were when Caesar wanted to attack them, so perhaps I will need a few units less than your father had planned to take. And I hear that there is a civil war between King Orodes and his son Phraates, and in fact it is true that no one went to aid Pacorus when Ventidius Bassus defeated him several times. While the sovereigns are busy with their problems, my generals and I will get to work. Bassus has restored the borders of Syria, and now Canidius Crassus has the order to occupy Armenia, to prevent that serpent of King Artabasdos from playing any tricks on us, like he did on Crassus before Carre. Then I will occupy the territories around the Caspian Sea so the Parthians can only flee to the east to avoid my troops. I have almost finished collecting troops from allied kings, and I count on receiving at least thirty thousand. Added to the sixteen or eighteen legions I intend to take with me, that gives me an army of at least one hundred thousand men. I will set off from the Euphrates, so the Parthians can face me in battle. They will end up retreating into their strongholds. That's why I want to take at least three hundred war machines with me – it will be a siege campaign, this one!"

"If I were you, I wouldn't take the unpreparedness of the Parthians for granted," Octavian finally managed to say. "You've been talking about this campaign for two years now: they know that you intend to attack them, and they will have taken their countermeasures by now."

Antony took advantage of Octavian's words to immediately raise the stakes.

"That's why I need more legions. I can't get to a hundred thousand men without getting rid of the borders unless you give me some of yours. I don't have any more time to recruit. And anyway, you don't need legionaries: your only enemy is on the sea now. Lepidus has his own legions, and he can make them available to you if you need them."

"Of course I need them! What do you think I'm going to invade Sicily with? I don't want to have to ask Lepidus: he will certainly start demanding the triumviral rights he has been denied and I will have to give him something – now, when we had got him out of the way..."

"My friend," said Antony, still pretending to be jovial, "one always has to give something to get something in return. Do you want to launch a concentric attack on Sicily from Italy and from Africa? Then you must involve Lepidus. Do you want your ships to defeat Sextus Pompey's fleet? Then you must give me some legions. You are not the only lord of the Roman world, though sometimes you tend to forget it," he said, though without the arrogance and scorn he had always displayed in their previous meetings after the death of Caesar.

"Take the legions from Lepidus, then," answered Octavian finally. "He has more than he needs for his purposes..."

"He would never send me them, even if he did agree to," said Antony with conviction. "Oh, he might *say* he would – but can you imagine me going to get them from Africa? Pah! The way things stand, the only way to use his legions is to involve him as second commander. He would never allow you to have them unless he were personally involved, because he knows that otherwise he would never get them back. And in any case, we also need to renew the triumvirate. The five year mandate has just expired, and I wouldn't want anyone to think that we no longer represent the state. We cannot afford to anger Lepidus too much: we need him now to save appearances and to continue the magistrature. As long as we renew it quietly, the Romans will accept it – by now, they are used to it. But if we turn it into an actual diarchy, we will create new enemies, So, no demands for troops from Lepidus, just a sincere prayer for his collaboration in the war."

With a smile on his face, this talkative version of Antony was putting his back to the wall, thought Octavian. However, the young man reflected, if Lepidus could go back on his word, there was no reason he couldn't too.

"So how many legions would you like?" he asked after a long pause.

"Well, at least three!" replied his brother-in-law with conviction.

Octavian burst into laughter. "Three? I can't give you three even in return for all three hundred of the ships you have brought from Greece. I can't risk losing against Pompey just to guarantee your success against the Parthians. We must each guarantee the other significant reinforcements."

"I need the ships too," said Antony. "I can give you seventy, at most, in exchange for at least two legions."

"For seventy ships, I could give you a legion, at most. And they must be big ships, like the ones Agrippa is building for me."

"I need at least two legions, ten thousand men. Less than that and you might as well not have given me any at all."

"Two hundred ships, then," said Octavian.

"One hundred."

"One hundred and fifty."

"One hundred and thirty," said Antony with a gesture of his hand that suggested it was his final offer.

Octavian reflected for a moment. He would have liked more, but then he would have to promise more legions, and the failure to respect the agreements would be so obvious that it would look bad.

"Very well – one hundred and thirty ships for two legions. And Lepidus will have to find another fiancée for his son, just so we're clear. I will send you the units when I have trained new ones for myself to replace the veterans I must give you."

"In that case I will give you the ships later too," replied Antony testily.

"No, I need them now. You don't want Pompey to bring Italy to its knees, do you? You've waited this long for your Parthians, you can wait another four months for my recruits to be trained. Denying me expert soldiers at the moment might expose me to a dangerous counterattack," he said, certain that Antony would not be able to argue the point. "You might not be under any pressure, but I am."

And in fact, his fellow triumvir said nothing and simply nodded, a diffident expression on his face, before adding, "You wouldn't play any nasty tricks on your brother-in-law, would you?"

Octavian smiled as pleasantly as he was able. It was a piece of luck that Antony desperately needed those ten thousand men.

"Of course not. I would *never* do that to my brother-in-law."

He did not, though, intend to remain Antony's brother-in-law for much longer.

*

"So, consul? What progress are we making with this port?"

Agrippa heard himself called by that title to which he had not yet grown accustomed. He recognised the voice of Octavian who, together with Maecenas, had come to see him in Misenum, where for the past few months he had been engaged in building a suitable place to host a fleet worthy of an empire.

He left the rowers benches which were stacked up on the steep shores of Lake Arverno and went to meet his two friends, who were escorted by the two faithful Germans and by Popilius Laenas. Apart from Octavia, all the followers of the Mars Ultor sect were present.

"So finally you deign to come and see it," he replied jovially. "We've worked hard these last few months, dear Caesar, and I doubt you will recognise the marshland that used to be beside the port of

Pozzuoli. You have been here often, and many times have gone to relax at the hot springs neat the bay of Baia…"

"Ha!" said Maecenas, embracing him. "As the consul is busy with other matters, someone has to stay in Rome to deal with the administration of the city and the provisioning, which is growing more and more difficult to manage thanks to the famine forced on us by Pompey and by the threats of part of the Senate."

"By the way," Octavian added, "I haven't yet had the opportunity to thank you for turning down the triumph I had conferred on you by the Senate for your victories in Aquitaine and Germany…"

"I never had any doubt about that, Caesar," said Agrippa. "It was an immense honour, but it didn't seem appropriate to me to celebrate them in the midst of a war and in view of the difficulties you were facing."

And, he wisely avoided adding, given Octavian's military failures, which would have been even more evident in comparison with his own successes.

An embarrassed Octavian quickly changed the subject. "Well, my friend, explain to me instead what you've been doing here! When do you think we will be able to bring the ships that Antony has given us and the ones we've had built in Ravenna? Only then can we really launch the offensive against Sextus Pompey."

Agrippa led his comrades to the new port, whose state-of-the-art jetty was still being built.

"I expect that it will take another three months, at least, Caesar, if not more, to get it finished," he explained. "Lake Arverno was the marshland furthest inland from the sea, and now I use it to train the rowers: we need expert crew to go up against Pompey's veteran sailors, and I don't want to send our men off into action too early. The Arverno was separated from the other lake which we are now passing by, the Lucrino, and I had to dig the channels you see to connect them and to drain the water. Here I am storing the provisions and materials we need to build the ships and organising an area on the shore to lodge the rowers. All things which are difficult to transport here at the moment, what with Pompey's men in Ischia watching all the routes. But the Lucrino too will become a port in all respects, alongside the external one, which I will now show you."

"Very large-scale earthworks, I see!" said Maecenas, looking at the channels connecting the mirror-like surfaces of the lakes.

"You can say that again," Agrippa said. "I could have only built the outer part – the one that opens out onto the sea – but we are talking about a military port that must provide absolute security. And one day, it will be the central base of the imperial fleet, at least in the Tyrrhenian, and will host hundreds of triremes, liburnas and quadriremes, and perhaps even quinqueremes. If attacked, it must have enough internal space to protect the ships from enemy attack. That's why I had to dredge all three lakes and connect them to each other."

They came to the outer harbour, going around a low promontory and finding themselves in a narrow, jagged inlet, inside which a large basin had been dug which opened onto the gulf. Next to it was a strip of land longer than any of the other surrounding bluffs, and the land and water around them hummed with activity. On the slope down to the sea, many buildings and warehouses were being constructed and large parts of the jetty had been completed, some boats were already moored there. It was a warm, sunny September day, and the view was clear wherever the eye looked. From there, one could see the entire bay of Naples, with Cumae and Vesuvius further inland, Procida and Ischia in front, the active port of Pozzuoli nearby and immediately behind it the Sorrento peninsula flanking the opposite side of the gulf, with Capri a little further behind.

"It is a splendid place for a military port," said Octavian with satisfaction. "We will call it Portus Julius, in honour of my divine father, and one day our enemies on the seas will tremble at the sound of its name as our enemies on dry land tremble when they hear the name of Rome!"

They all nodded with conviction. But then Octavian suddenly frowned.

"Conqueror *and* builder..." he murmured, visibly amazed by his friend's work. "It seems that everything you do is a success, Agrippa. I consider it a privilege to know you and to enjoy your friendship. And if that remains the case, nothing will ever be denied you, I swear it to you on Mars Ultor himself."

Agrippa swallowed. He was always aware of the need to remain one step behind the leader of the sect, despite the temptation to outshine him and take his place at centre stage, but unlike Rufus, he was also aware of Octavian's qualities, his connections, and his foresight – none of which he would ever possess. He had faltered under the weight of his passion for Fulvia, but that would not happen again. Now he knew what was best for him.

"It is your light that has made me so, Caesar, and I will never forget it. Whatever undertakings I succeed in, it will only be because you have put me in a position to. If it is true that you need my help, I need yours too, and it will ever be thus," he replied with sincerity, and his words seemed to please Octavian, who patted him on his robust shoulders.

"Of course! The consulship is only the beginning for you!" Octavian replied cheerfully, turning to the Etruscan. "You're not like Maecenas here, who never wants official posts, are you?"

"I prefer not to attract too much attention, as you know," Maecenas replied. "I work better in the shadows. For example, Agrippa, now that you are a consul and a victor, it is time that you found a wife for yourself. And I'm busy trying to help you out in that regard, my dear friend."

Agrippa was taken aback. Since Fulvia's time, he hadn't thought seriously about a woman.

"Now you even have to choose my wife for me? What am I, a child who can't do it on his own?" he said, sounding more amused than scandalised.

"You are a man of action, Agrippa," the Etruscan explained. "We handle the politics, and we need a nice marriage with someone who can support us. Titus Pomponius Atticus has a lovely intelligent daughter, and his circle is precisely what we need to clearly outline our reform plans for the Republic. You will like her, you'll see."

"It would appear that our principal activity at the moment is procuring wives while we prepare to wage war," cut in Octavian. "I have also thought of one for you, Maecenas. I told you that sooner or later I would take my revenge for your marrying me off to Scribonia, and I think I have found someone with whom to pay you back. The *gens Terenti* are a useful bunch, and we must bind them to us as soon as possible. The good offices of my wife Livia have already produced interesting results."

Agrippa and Octavian enjoyed the awkward expression which appeared on their friend's face. Agrippa knew very well that the tastes of the Etruscan ran more to slaves and friends than to women. "And very soon we will find one for Mark Antony too..." added the triumvir.

At that point, Agrippa and Maecenas's surprise at his previous announcement were swept away by this even more shocking revelation.

"Antony? But... what about your sister?"

"Her being married to him can only be a hindrance to me – I will now fight Pompey with the ships he lent me. And I need an excuse for not sending him the troops I promised him. I didn't tell you, Maecenas, because I was afraid you would disagree," explained Octavian. "I have an agent in the court of Cleopatra, and he has informed me that the queen still has great power over Antony, in spite of my brother-in-law's attempts to seem a loving and faithful husband. And so, in return for further help, she intends to convince him to go and live in her kingdom before the Parthian campaign begins and to support her demands for autonomy and the extension of the area of Egyptian influence in the East."

"And so?" murmured Agrippa and Maecenas in unison.

"And so… yesterday I received a letter from Alexandria. Antony went to see Cleopatra, and everything has returned to as it was before he married my sister, so now nobody can criticise me if I refuse to send troops to that back-stabber who has violated the sacred bond of kinship and dared to humiliate the second most important woman in Rome after Livia Drusilla."

His two friends said nothing.

"You see?" said Octavian. "*This* is why I will prevail over Antony in the end: he is weak, gullible and easily manipulated, and I am not. And that is why I must be the one to guide and reform the state – not him, who is guided only by his loins and his baser impulses. He will behave exactly like those who preceded him, and will do nothing to save Rome from destruction…" he concluded with a cruel and mocking smile.

XXI

The largest naval undertaking ever attempted, said Octavian to himself as he carried out the final steps of the lustratio classis, the purification ceremony for the fleet in the port of Capo Misenum which was preparing to depart for Sicily. Before him, the crews were lined up along the shore in religious silence, while in the waters of the harbour there were over one hundred warships that the triumvir would take with himself and Agrippa, plus five hundred transport ships to carry the legions. It was the day before the Calends of July – the month whose name Octavian had changed from Quintilis to Iulius in honour of his father, the date he had set for the departure of the three elements of the pincer movement with which he intended to surround Sextus Pompey from the east, from the west and from the south. At that moment, the same ceremony was taking place on the Adriatic coast, in Taranto, where Statilius Taurus, his other admiral, was preparing to set off with the fleet of Antony, and on the African coast, the other triumvir Lepidus was ready to set sail with seventy warships and a thousand transport ships holding twelve legions.

Octavian left one of the altars along the pier, where he had just carried out the sacrifice three times, and, still stained with the blood of his victims, climbed into the small boat to perform the rite of the purification of the fleet together with the priest. Immediately afterwards, Agrippa and the other subordinate commanders did the same, climbing into boats filled with expiatory offerings. Among the admirals there was no Menodorus, who Octavian had persuaded to pretend to desert once again and return to Pompey to take the place of Democarus, who had died after the battle of Cumae nearly two years earlier. The agreement with the ambiguous freeman, of which only the members of the Mars Ultor sect knew, was that he would give false information to Pompey about Octavian's preparations and then return to the triumvir with information about enemy defences. If possible bringing some of the pirate's ships with him.

This time, Octavian intended to silence for good the accusations that he was proud and no longer enjoyed the favour of the gods. He wanted to show everyone that he had very carefully procured divine support, above all that of his august father, by drawing the auspices in the month dedicated to the man who had become a God – the man who had never been defeated.

He climbed aboard his flagship and leant out over the balustrade, waiting for the other commanders to take their places, then covered his head with his toga and nodded to the priest next to him to begin. The man began to loudly proclaim the litany that the other priests immediately intoned in the nearby boats, and the sea around the quadriremes began to fill with raw chunks of the flesh of the animals butchered in the sacrifices carried out earlier.

"We call upon you, Father Neptune, and call upon you, Tranquil Ocean, to favour this noble enterprise and to give your support to the State against the enemies of the sea," declaimed the priest, following exactly the form Octavian had ordered him to use. "And we ask you that every misfortune fall on these offerings we give you and not on the fleet. Oh gods – or whatever name you choose to allow yourselves to be called, you who have the power over the sea and the storms – please, grant success to the undertakings begun under the imperium of the triumvirate. And may Caesar Octavian return victorious," he said, deliberately excluding Lepidus from the formula, "defeat the enemy and do to him what he wished to do to us and has done to the Roman people over these years of suffering to which he has condemned them. Fill our enemies with cowardice, fright and terror. We offer you their bodies, their lives, their goods, their cities and their lands in exchange for the people and the army of Rome!'

The priest waited for his colleagues on the other boats to finish, and a cry of acclamation from the crews followed. Next, Octavian, in accordance with the ritual, touched his chest, bent down and stretched out his arm to include in the ritual his ships and the earth and then raised both arms to the heavens to call on Jupiter, the father of the gods, to witness his commitment. There was silence again, and the ritual began once more, the custom requiring that it be repeated three times, as it had been on the coast.

Octavian felt comforted. He didn't really believe in what he was doing and considered it only for the benefit of the public, but he felt completely confident at last. This time he was with his lieutenants: Agrippa was at his side and would let him command the fleet under his watchful eye, Ortwin, Veleda and Laenas were with the legions, ready to collaborate for the invasion, with the same soldiers who over the course of the last year had threatened to rebel, demanding better pay in the certainty that they would now have to face a new civil war against Antony, who had left for Parthia after abandoning his wife for the Egyptian queen. But they were back with him at last for Octavian had won them over with promises and money, and made them the champions of Octavia's lost honour. And he had provided funds illicitly to the Parthians, large amounts of money to hire more mercenaries to prevent Antony from obtaining victories in the eastern lands so as to tarnish yet further his glory. After Philippi, Antony had appeared to be the saviour of his homeland and Octavian the one basking in the reflected light of success – the former the victor and the latter the defeated. Now it would be the other way round.

Now, he felt protected by the gods and his friends, once more invincible and unassailable by the bad luck which had persecuted him in recent times. And the increasingly loud applause already made him feel as though he were walking on the roof of the world.

*

The wind howled between the flanks of the ships, which were barely able to find shelter from the storm in the Gulf of Velia, near Capo Palinuro. Octavian – remembering what had happened in the previous campaign – had been quick to order the fleet to gather there as soon as the wind had begun to grow stronger, and he had lost one ship, which had been forced onto the rocks of the surrounding promontory. He had resigned himself to waiting for the bad weather to blow over, hoping that Taurus and Lepidus would be as quick to react to the fury of the elements, and had disembarked most of the troops and the horses so they could rest and be refreshed. His only concern was that the two parts of the pincer movement would probably no longer arrive simultaneously – and that, of course, Sextus Pompey would have more time to prepare his defences.

But then the wind had changed direction, and had started blowing ruthlessly from the south into the gulf, which no longer offered protection. And as soon as it began battering the ships anchored along the coast, the spectre of those nightmarish days on the Straits came to Octavian. As he watched the first ships crashing into one another – for the anchors could not hold them fast – he blamed himself for not having thought to equip them with poles to hold them apart from one another and for not leaving more men on board to handle them.

But above all, he was terrified of the idea that even that undertaking was cursed. Because the others, at least, would see it as such after a beginning like that. He commanded the crews to get into the sea and to make their way to the decks of their ships to get them under control, but the powerful wind blew in the face of the men in the boats, forcing them back and smashing the vessels against the rocks. By now most of the crews were isolated from the ships.

His men, fallen from the boats or the rocks, were drowning in the water, pushed under by the debris that in the space of a few moments had filled the water around the ships. The screams of pain and cries for help that had rent the air that tragic night almost two years earlier returned to his mind, together with the nervous and physical breakdown he had suffered because of his impotence in the face of such adversity, and he wondered how he could face that experience again. It seemed as though Sextus Pompey was actually protected by the god of the sea, and if that was the case, there was nothing he could do. He would never have thought that the real nemesis among his many opponents on the difficult path to power would have been that insignificant man.

The men sought comfort and guidancce from him, but Octavian felt paralysed and was afraid of sending them off to face new disasters. Without conviction, he ordered the trierarchs to return to their ships, but they pointed out to him that it was impossible. And in the meantime, right in front of his eyes, the sides of two liburnas – the lightest and most manoeuvrable vessels – were smashed in and turned into wrecks. Dismay overwhelmed him. What could he do if the gods showed their preference for Pompey? What did he possibly have that could defend against that?

Then he saw Agrippa. He was arriving at speed with a group of soldiers carrying tree trunks and ropes. He looked at him incomprehendingly. His friend made a reassuring gesture and Octavian immediately felt better, without understanding why. Agrippa had the men join three or four trunks together with nails and other pieces of wood to create long poles that they lowered into the sea with ropes. Once the poles were in the water, they continued to add pieces to the nearest ends until they became long enough to reach the moored ships.

Before long, several gangways to the boats had been created, each consisting of a long beam, attached at the opposite end to the keels of the ships. Then the men began to walk along them, after having tied around themselves the ropes they had used earlier, which were held by their comrades on the rocks. Grasping the trunks so as to withstand the powerful motion of the waves, large numbers of them began crawling towards the ships, eventually reaching their sides. The sailors on board pulled them up, and shortly thereafter, an uninterrupted flow of soldiers began to reach the ships and regain control of them. Agrippa signalled with a torch and the boats began to remove the poles. They pulled them up onto their decks and began cutting them to the lengths they needed to hold each vessel from each other and the rocks.

In the meantime, the storm had claimed new victims. More ships had crashed against the rocks, more men had been thrown into the sea, more masts had collapsed. But Agrippa's system seemed to have halted the worst of the damage, and he had apparently given the order to follow suit elsewhere in the gulf, as makeshift bridges had begun to appear along the full length of the line of anchored ships, holding the vessels in their respective positions and saving them from certain destruction.

It was then that Octavian realised who, not what, he had that could go up against Sextus Pompey: Agrippa. Agrippa was the man the gods had sent to defeat his nemesis.

*

"Caesar, the season is too far on, we must give up," protested Valerius Messalla Corvinus, the senator to whom Octavian had assigned the provisional command in the absence of Agrippa, who was currently busy conducting operations to collect timber in preparation for the Sicilian invasion. But he had already regretted his choice. "It took over a month to repair the storm damage to the fleet and now it is the middle of August. We may not have enough time to conclude the campaign, and soon the sea will begin to grow rough. Even if we do manage to invade Sicily, we risk being trapped there at Pompey's mercy!" continued his subordinate.

Octavian paced agitatedly around the desk in his praetorium in the camp he had set up at Hipponium, near the Straits. "We're already in Sicily, by the gods!" he replied, annoyed by his general's doubts. "When the storm appeared, Lepidus managed to land at Marsala with eight of his legions, and now he holds the western part of the island. As far as I am aware, the self-styled 'son of Neptune' hasn't yet driven him out, even though a month should have given him time to do so!"

He preferred not to underline the other triumvir's subsequent failure, when his other four legions on their way from Africa had run into one of Pompey's lieutenants, Papias, who had sunk half of the fleet, costing them at least two units. That was a defeat, too – and a heavy one at that.

Messalla was less tactful.

"Lepidus's morale will be low: he has just lost two legions, no one has come to his aid in a month and, moreover, he makes no attempt to hide his expectation to be treated as of equal rank and command to you. I would not be surprised if he refuses to cooperate and raises the stakes at the crucial moment. In my opinion, he's just waiting for you to need him desperately, and if we attack, that's exactly what he'll have," he said bluntly.

Octavian could not help snorting in disgust at Messalla's defeatism. He missed Agrippa – they understood one another perfectly: he asked no questions and never had any doubts, but simply acted so that the desired outcome was achieved without complaints and without recrimination. "Pulling out now would be like admitting defeat, and I would lose face. I need a victory now, and that's an end to it. Keep quiet, or I will exclude you from any role in the operation!" he concluded angrily.

Messalla grew more conciliatory. "But Menodorus… since he returned to Pompey, he is making us look ridiculous. He captures every isolated transport ship he can find, depriving us of our supplies, he traps our ships to lure us in and then escapes from right under our noses, he takes senators prisoner and then releases them… The men are scared."

Messalla did not know of the agreement with Menodorus, thought Octavian. It was all part of his long-established strategy: the admiral needed to show Pompey his ability so as to be assigned as many ships as possible, but without significantly damaging the leader of the sect of Mars Ultor. And he was going about his job brilliantly. "It doesn't matter. His attacks are nothing more than mosquito bites," he replied. "Now, though, we will establish once and for all how the invasion will proceed. I want you to go to the island to create a beachhead with two legions in support of Lepidus," he ordered, more to get rid of him as soon as possible than anything else. Otherwise, he would have had to put up with him in general staff meetings when Agrippa returned, and that was something he would rather avoid.

"As you wish, triumvir," replied his subordinate in a submissive tone so as not to appear too bold. "But… where should I stop if Lepidus is unable to meet me?"

Octavian showed him the map of Sicily on the desk. "Here in Taormina, on the gulf, which we have to conquer," he said, pointing to the area with his finger. "And anyway, I'll send three legions to Stylis to complete the surveillance of the Straits. Now I will write to Taurus and tell him to set off immediately from Taranto towards Mount Scylaceus so you will have him at your flank. He is capable both on the battlefield and at sea. Meanwhile I will move between the Aeolian Islands with the fleet. In this way, we will threaten Pompey from three directions on land and at sea, and he will be forced to keep all his forces in the Messina area, ready to send them wherever we attack. We know that almost all of his troops are concentrated between Pelorum, Milazzo and Tyndaris, and by doing that he allows us to extend the area under our control, so we can easily conquer much of the island.

And when he attacks a column, we will arrive from behind him, cutting him off from his headquarters."

He had devised the strategy together with Agrippa, who had made his goal of forcing Pompey into a corner of Sicily practicable. And the good thing was that his friend had found a way of advancing their forces in parallel, with the fleet moving forward at the side of the ground troops and vice versa, like the great King Xerxes with his monstrous invasion of Greece in the year of the famous battles of Thermopylae and Salamis.

In the face of his commander's faith, Messalla gave in and stood contemplating the map as a soldier asked for permission to enter the tent and delivered a letter. Octavian read it and smiled.

"But there is still the problem of Menodorus, Caesar," objected Messalla. "We do not know where he is, so far Pompey has given him free rein to attack us and he could arrive from any direction."

Octavian looked at him with compassion. Messalla had been exiled, but since he had donated his fleet to Antony, he had been forgiven and fully rehabilitated. He was a capable man, if not a particularly elastic thinker.

"I doubt that – they have just informed me that he has arrived in the harbour, delivering fifteen ships," he replied, rushing out of the tent to talk to the freedman he had so well employed.

*

"There are only forty ships, Admiral," the lookout shouted to Agrippa, who was standing on the aft turret of his quadrireme, watching the stretch of sea in front of Milazzo, where the fleet of his opponent Papias was deployed.

Agrippa rubbed his hands. It was an excellent opportunity to rob Sextus Pompey of one of his principal lieutenants. After going round the northern coast of Sicily and taking the Aegadian Islands without violence, he had returned to the Messina area and verified for himself that the enemy had fanned out his fleets to cover a greater stretch of coast to hinder the invaders.

"Then we attack!" he ordered the crew. "We clearly outnumber them, and it will be an easy win! Trierarch, give the signal to the other ships and let's get into a line formation. We will ram them and send them to the sea bed!"

He watched as the men cheered enthusiastically and dedicated themselves to their duties: the oarsmen adopted a faster rhythm and made the ship fly across the water and the helmsman was steady on the rudder, the sailors divided themselves into those who had deck duties and those who were required to launch projectiles at the enemy ships, the legionaries formed boarding parties. Soon, the one hundred and twenty ships of his fleet were arrayed in three successive lines, ready to use their momentum to smash into their opponents.

But suddenly the man on the mast cried out to him, "Admiral, ships approaching! It looks like a little less than fifty!"

But now they were moving rapidly towards their seemingly helpless foe. Agrippa squinted and tried to make out the new fleet, which he saw moving towards his flank from another point on the coast. Evidently, Pompey had deployed his units so as to assist one another if they were attacked.

"It doesn't matter! We still outnumber them and we have a more powerful navy! We go on!" he shouted loudly to encourage the men on deck. He was comforted by the fact that he had chosen quadriremes instead of triremes or liburnas: he wasn't planning on fighting in the straits, the way Rufus and Octavian had in the past. In the open sea, these bigger ships had an advantage that he was intent on exploiting to the full.

The ships crashed through the waves like mighty plows, leaving furrows in the rough sea, but a new cry from the mast shook even the admiral's confidence. "On the other side! More ships! There must be at least seventy!"

It didn't take Agrippa long to realise that another column was now converging on Papias's fleet: attacking him head-on, he would find another two contingents on his flanks. He had to decide whether to launch into a battle with an uncertain outcome or to retreat, if it was not already too late: Pompey's triremes and liburnas were faster than his ships, and perhaps would catch up with them if they tried to turn tail.

But the situation, he reflected, could be turned to his advantage by acting cautiously. He gave the order to stop and then cried out, "Call the rest of the ships to Hiera, let Caesar know that almost all of Pompey's fleet is here! Now that we have drawn them out, we have the battle that we were looking for and we can eliminate all his ships in one fell swoop!"

Now he had to play for time. He did not know exactly where between the Aegadians and Milazzo the rest of the fleet of which he was the vanguard was, and he risked having to wait so long that they would end up surrounded. He ordered the ships to divide into two groups and to move outward, so as to widen the formation and avoid ending up in the midst of enemy ships. It was a complex manoeuvre, where they had to coordinate with the opposite flank. And as much as the ships tried to spread out, other vessels were cutting them off at the edges and forcing them to move back in towards the centre.

He had to convince himself that this defensive strategy was only the first phase: with the arrival of the rest of the fleet, he could attack. It was a necessary sacrifice to draw the enemy into battle. He saw one of his outer ships smash into a small liburna that had got too close to the massive quadrireme, and it comforted him: in the crash, the lighter boat lost its oars and a gash opened up along its side. In no time at all, the liburna was a wreck, its remains sinking after the larger ship dragged it in its wake for a short distance. Good, he thought: as long as he kept away from close combat with the fulcrum of the enemy fleet, he could continue to avoid engaging in battle.

He saw a wider formation of liburnas coming up on his flank, accompanied by a trireme: it was clear that Pompey's admirals were trying to provoke him into fighting, even at the cost of losing some ships. He signalled to his subordinate to avoid engaging, and the captain abruptly attempted to widen his course. The other ships continued to follow them, and began to fan out to surround them. Meanwhile, Agrippa and the rest of his ships moved in that direction, while other enemy vessels seemed to be heading towards the area where clashes were beginning to take place.

When he was near the threatened quadrireme, Agrippa overtook it and went even further wide. He was then attacked by the rams of at least four smaller boats which hindered his movements. And from the decks, projectiles began to be fired, taking their first victims on both sides. Agrippa began to see the advantages of the situation: the ship was attracting the attention of the enemy vessels, allowing his other ships to fan out again so as to avoid being surrounded. Or rather, to encircle Pompey's ships, which would no longer be able to avoid the battle.

And if all that happened at the price of one ship, he would put his signature to it immediately. He continued moving forward, parallel to the coast, impotently watching the assault on the quadrireme upon whose deck, in the meantime, fire had broken out. His men fought strenuously, and perhaps their captain had realised the situation because no request for help came. He knew he had to sacrifice himself to save the rest of the fleet. A breach opened in the hull near the stern, created by the ram of one of the ships which had attacked her and, realising that they were lost, the sailors and legionaries on the quadrireme threw down the boarding ramp onto the balustrade of the trireme which had rammed them and, in part to escape the fire which was spreading across the deck, raced across it.

Favoured by the height of their vessel, they poured en masse onto the opposing deck, where they overran the small crew awaiting them with light weapons and the few legionaries aboard. Some even carried the flames from their own ship, wandering like fiery embers among opponents who were shoving them or trying to hit them with their spears. It was a fierce fight, and Agrippa, who was moving further away by the second, could see it less and less clearly. It seemed to him, though, that the trireme was no longer under enemy control. If he had stopped and gone back, he could have captured it, but he could not compromise his manoeuvre. In the end he chose to abandon those valiant soldiers, destined to win their battle on the deck only to be attacked again by the crews of the liburnas which surrounded them. He saw the flanks of the ship were already covered with gangways to allow enemy soldiers to climb aboard. He hoped he wouldn't have to make many choices like that in his career as commander, and prayed that it would help lead them to victory. Meanwhile, he told the majority of the ships in his flank to proceed until he saw more enemy ships blocking their way. Only then did he order them to stop. He peered at the sea around them and saw that the enemy fleet were arrayed at a point not far from his own position. But Pompey's ships did not move. They were afraid of spreading out and becoming detached from the centre, left isolated against the quadriremes, and had resigned themselves to a stalemate.

The manoeuvre had been successful, and he hoped it was the same on the opposite flank. Now it was just a matter of waiting.

*

Agrippa saw the ships of the rest of his fleet line up behind him as they gradually arrived. Now the battle could really begin! He waited for the rest of the morning and the beginning of the afternoon until he decided there were enough of them to engage the enemy fleet in battle. Now he and Pompey were on equal terms, with the difference that – as far as he knew – he was there with his men while his opponent, as usual, must be on one of the promontories overlooking the battlefield giving orders from afar to his admirals. He behaved exactly like the great King Xerxes at Salamis. And he would end up the same way, Agrippa said to himself, to steel his nerve before initiating the attack.

What he had been about to do that morning – charging his mighty quadriremes against the enemy fleet near the coast – was now possible on a greater scale against his opponent's entire deployment. By closing the ranks of his front line, he had created a mighty wall of rams which would sweep everything they encountered out of their way, and the reaction of the enemy vessels quickly proved the intimidating effect that it had had upon them: they advanced towards his fleet at differing speeds, betraying the varying conviction of their captains in the face of the devastating wall poised to overrun them. The only sensible thing for them to do was be already moving at the moment of impact, so as not to be totally overwhelmed.

The two formations came into contact at differing times and in various ways. Some triremes and liburnas were literally smashed in two by the rams of the quadriremes, whose momentum shattered into fragments all those not fast enough to manoeuvre out of their way. Others suffered damage to their hulls, but not enough to sink them. Immediately afterwards, though, from the decks of Agrippa's ships, projectiles of all kinds, some incendiary and some not, were fired at them, and they were harpooned with whatever means came to hand, from grappling hooks to boarding ramps, in order to capture them.

Some managed to squeeze into the gaps between Agrippa's ships, with the aim of breaking the rudder blades and entire rows of oars. Turrets had been installed on even the smallest enemy ships like those on Agrippa's much larger vessels, and a rapid exchange of fire from the scorpios immediately followed. The sea fluttered with the waves raised by the mass of ships in an increasingly restricted space which was fast filling up with debris and bodies. The air, already saturated with smoke from the burning decks, was filled with the hiss of flying arrows which forced the men to keep their shields raised and limited their ability to act. The sound of cracking wood, the bronze rostrums smashing open enemy hulls, the cries of the men engaged in combat, and of those thrown into the water, shouting for the help of their comrades, echoed all around them.

Agrippa's flagship rammed an enemy vessel, sending it crashing into a trireme from his own fleet. The enemy ship started to take on water, blocking the passage of the second, and the sailors rushed to the sides to push it out of the way. But Agrippa was not interested in ships. He had come for Papias, and Papias was the one he wanted to face. He told the lookouts to find out where he was, and when he had spotted him, he gave the order to break the line and head straight for the target. His ships moved out of his way, as much as they were able, and, on seeing him moving at such great speed, the enemy ships, which were too small to be able to stop him, tried to get out of his way so as not to be rammed.

Papias realised his intentions, and began to turn his bow towards him, offering a smaller target to the enemy ram. Agrippa urged the helmsman and the rowers to get to him before he completed his manoeuvre. From the turret, he looked at the opposing deck to see how they were preparing for the now-inevitable impact, and noticed that the scorpios on the turrets were now being utilised. Flaming bolts shot toward them, one passing but a few inches away from his shoulder. He stood at the parapet of the turret without moving a muscle, and told the men beside him to return fire. The men loaded the machine and primed the springs and the darts sped almost in unison in the direction of the target, leaving behind them a trail of fire.

The two ships were so close now that, despite the noise around them, Agrippa thought he heard a soldier's scream of pain as he was hit by a projectile. One bolt fell into the water and the other hit the deck. The wood caught fire, but the crew hurried to extinguish it. Agrippa commanded a second volley: they needed to take advantage of the ships' proximity. Meanwhile, other scorpio bolts, which he ignored, hissed past him, refusing to even crouch down behind the parapet as one of his artillerymen advised him. The men must see that their commander was assured and resolute: only that would inspire in them the courage necessary for what was expected from them. Octavian would never have put himself so much at risk, so it was up to him to provide the example.

Instinctively, he pressed against the parapet, as though he could push the ship forward and increase its speed. The ships' bows approached one another, and with them the rams which cut through the water. The vessels were not yet facing each other directly but at a slightly obtuse angle, his quadrireme still heading for the sides of the enemy ship. Standing in the bow watching the approach of the moment of impact from above, Agrippa could now see Papias in the turret of the trireme: he too stood straight, almost as though trying to outdo him in courage. Agrippa took a firm hold of the balustrade and prepared for the impact, which, when it came a moment later, was extremely violent: a devastating thud echoed through the entire structure of the ship, making the platform on which he stood vibrate so intensely that it threw the scorpios against the parapets and hurled men to the deck. Engulfed in a spray of sea water, the turret creaked as though it would collapse any moment.

Agrippa staggered but remained standing and, as soon as he had recovered his balance despite the rolling of the sea, he leaned out again and looked down. His ram had just managed to penetrate the side of the enemy ship, opening a breach in the keel and breaking off the enemy trireme's ram. The ship was taking on water but the men in the hold were trying to stop up the hole with whatever materials they could lay hands on. Meanwhile, those who had been in the turret had been thrown to the deck, and Agrippa could see a visibly injured Papias getting to his feet and giving orders to the crew.

He noticed also that two liburnas were approaching the sides of his quadrireme, aiming to break their oars to give their admiral the chance to escape. There was no time to waste. "Get the poles out against the liburnas! Archers take aim! Use the boarding ramp and the grappling hooks on the trireme!"

Meanwhile, spears began flying from the decks of all the ships. In the turret he ran less risk than the sailors and soldiers on deck, and could continue to lean out and watch the situation: Papias's trireme was freeing itself. He had no intention of losing it but it seemed to him that his men were taking too long to harpoon it. He climbed down the stairs and went over to help the team working the boarding ramp leant against the main mast. He forced the mechanism and the bridge fell heavily over the parapet, but its hook missed the railing of the enemy vessel by a whisker, and Papias's ship began to pull away.

Furious, Agrippa ordered it pulled back up and shouted to the helmsman to keep the two ships close, then he shouted to the sailors to use grappling poles to capture the trireme. The men held out the long poles tipped with claws over the balustrade, and three of them managed to hook the enemy parapet, but only with the effect of breaking it off: the ship was still moving away. Agrippa gave a gesture of annoyance and told them to try again. The man doing the manoeuvring was hit by an arrow fired from the nearest liburna and dropped his pole and the other two turned out not to be strong enough to hold it.

By now the boarding ramp was ready to be dropped again, and in order to avoid wasting the second attempt, Agrippa waited for the helmsman to bring the two ships closer, rebuking him for this ineptness. The Romans had begun to use the boarding ramp known as the *corvus* in the waters of Milazzo two centuries earlier during the first Punic war, but at this point it seemed to Agrippa completely outdated – it was practically unusable when the waters were agitated and only worked if the ships were already close to one another. It suddenly struck him that the ships could be harpooned more efficiently with hooks which were fired across instead of being dropped from above.

When he judged that the helmsman had got them into position, he gave the order. The ramp slammed down violently, and this time it hooked the enemy deck. A cry of triumph rose from the deck. "Get the other gangways down! Board them!" cried Agrippa, holding up his sword. He waited until the legionaries were gathered behind him, checked that the archers had climbed onto the turrets to provide covering fire, and – when he saw their opponents deployed along the parapet of the trireme which was pulling away in a hail of arrows – he raced over to the boarding ramp and was the first to run across to the enemy ship.

He launched himself at legionary who was holding his shield over his head, shoving him against one of his fellow soldiers who had already been hit by an arrow. He rammed his sword into the collarbone of another soldier who tried to resist, then looked around him for Papias, while the soldiers who had followed him began to overwhelm the disorganised enemy forces. He saw him leaning over the parapet and rushed over to him, but the admiral threw himself overboard along with others. When he reached the side, Agrippa peered down into the sea and saw the enemy commander flailing about in the water along with his men. He summoned his archers and, when they arrived, gave orders to target the men in the water. But in the meantime, a liburna had approached and begun to pick up the survivors, and he was forced to watch helplessly while the enemy admiral climbed up the side of the small ship, thanks to a rope that had been lowered into the water, and he cursed himself for being too slow.

Turrets, grappling hooks, poles and scorpios were not enough to ensure success, he reflected. He had been too slow. And the next time they met, he vowed, his ships would be better equipped.

Agrippa watched the enemy fleet retreat as though at a single command from the coast and he peered along the promontories to see from whence the order came. He seemed to see a canopy surrounded by men on the top of a cliff, but it might easily be something else. In any case, the battle seemed to be won, although not decisively. It had been Pompey who had retreated, not him, and the ships which had been sunk, boarded and captured, or which now drifted like wrecks across the ocean were, for the most part, enemy ones.

"They're getting away, admiral. Shall we give chase?" The question came from his second in command. Agrippa thought for a moment. Octavian desperately needed a victory against Sextus Pompey's fleets. It would have been the first in years of disasters and would serve to reassure him, but if he pushed closer to the coast, he would be playing into the hands of the enemy, who were sheltering in low waters where the smaller ships would have the advantage. If he followed them, he would risk losing everything he had achieved with his wise handling of the battle which had just ended.

And that was not all. It was true that Octavian needed a victory, but not an overwhelming victory achieved by one of his subordinates. For the same reason he had avoided celebrating the triumph of his undertakings in Gaul, for the time being he had to avoid humiliating him by winning a definitive victory. Apart from the friendship that bound them, and the ever present fear that Octavian never forgave those who outshone him, it was in his own interests not to delegitimise his friend if he wanted to remain at his side through his ascent. Otherwise, he would never rise any further.

"No. We will just observe them from afar," he replied finally. "They're not going anywhere, and if we keep them blockaded here, the ground invasion can continue and Caesar can move elsewhere and extend our spheres of influence. We will attack them when it is in our interest to do so, not when they expect it. Tell the men to report their and our losses and count how many ships have been damaged."

"But admiral, they're at our mercy!" said the perplexed lieutenant. The soldiers around them looked at him hopefully: they all seemed determined to continue the battle, despite the fact that some of them were bleeding or could barely stand.

Agrippa stared at him angrily. "That is precisely what they want us to think!" he answered, repeating his command. But he understood why his behaviour might be a source of perplexity: the men did not know that he was behaving thus principally for Octavian. Once they had all gathered in the bow of the ship to listen to him, he called for their attention.

"Soldiers! Today you have been valiant, and you have won an important victory against the one who called himself Neptune's son!" he shouted. "But we must be satisfied with the result that we have achieved without risking further. We have won because we fought in the space I had planned for our fleet: by going to engage them now, we would be taking on desperate men, willing to fight even at night. I know that you burn with the desire to show your worth and I thank you for it in the name of Caesar. But the wind has risen and I do not trust the conditions of the sea. Furthermore, we are all tired after this long day which, remember, started at dawn, and although the temptation to finish our opponents off is strong, we commanders must resist and not be irresponsible, so as to avoid falling into the trap into which they intend to lure their enemies. Do not think that I am happy not to render this victory complete, but there are too many unknowns in the event of our engaging in another battle. There is much to gain, now: with Pompey's fleet concentrated here in front of us, after we have rested we will move along the coast and subdue Tyndaris and other nearby towns. And then we will isolate him in the area of the Straits, where we can fight with some certainty of winning!"

Many soldiers nodded while others acclaimed him as the victor and others still said nothing. He seemed to have convinced them, especially when the details of his victory arrived: the enemy had lost some thirty ships, as well as having retreated with many damaged vessels while he had only lost five quadriremes and had ten or so ships which needed repair. Once again, the men cheered his victory, which now seemed more convincing.

Yes, they were all persuaded. And now, he said, he only had to persuade himself that he had made the right decision.

3. Translation taken from http://www.perseus.tufts.edu/hopper/text?doc=Perseus%3Atext%3A1999.02.0063%3Abook%3D1%3Apoem%3D5

XXII

Octavian contemplated the outline of Taormina, whose walls stood not far from the beach upon which he was about to land. The slight sense of nausea caused by the rocking movement of the boat carrying him from the flagship to the shore made everything around him seem hazy, and he felt sure that he was missing something.

"Do you think that something isn't quite right?" asked Maecenas, who – no less in difficulty than he was – was grasping the side of the boat. Octavian had his friend come down from Rome so that he would have at least one of his men with him, given that Agrippa was too busy on the other front to take part in the vast operation to conquer Sicily.

"You mean apart from the fact that, despite all the legions I've given him, Statilius Taurus appears still not to have conquered the city?" answered Octavian as he attempted to focus.

"Yes, apart from that," agreed the Etruscan, "I can see movement, and it can't be only our men, unless the defenders of the place have made a sortie..."

"We'll find out soon enough," said Octavian, as he waited for the boat to reach the beach. As soon as it landed, he climbed out and jumped down to the shore, but his foot landed awkwardly and he fell, collapsing onto the sand.

"Caesar, wait, let me h…" he heard Maecenas and the *legatus* Cornificius who was with them say as one.

From the ground, Octavian glared at them angrily. "I can do it myself," he snapped, and immediately jumped to his feet, peering around him to try and establish who had seen his accident – that was the type of thing they might take for another bad omen. But then, on the other hand, the same thing had happened to Caesar when he had arrived in Africa for the long campaign that would eventually culminate in the grand victory of Thapsus. He noticed that in addition to the boatmen, some of the soldiers from one of Statilius Taurus's camps were hurrying towards him. In addition, a little further on, other ships from his fleet were bringing the legions he had brought the *legatus* as reinforcements to the shore.

And they had all seen it.

That made his mood even worse, but the episode convinced him that now more than ever, he needed a victory to silence any doubts. Fortunately, Agrippa had defeated and blocked Pompey's fleet in front of Milazzo and so all he had to do now was follow that up with a clear success of his own. And while the soldiers he had brought with him from the fleet began to unload horses and supplies – with the engineers in the lead to determine where to set up the new camp – he headed for the praetorium of Statilius Taurus, anxious to vent his frustrations on the man. He walked briskly so as to recover some self-possession after what had just happened and Maecenas, who struggled to keep up with him, had the good sense to keep quiet.

But the *legatus* was not in his tent. The officers told Octavian that he was at the fortification furthest from the city. Octavian went to him, passing groups of soldiers running towards the battlements, shouting that they were under attack.

"Can you tell me why you have not yet conquered the city, Taurus?" he asked as soon as he reached him, but then, before listening to the answer, he looked out over the palisade and saw an army of cavalry deployed a short distance away.

"Because we are constantly under siege, Caesar, that's why. Look over there." Taurus pointed, for a moment forgetting the deference due to his supreme commander.

Octavian decided not to be intimidated. "You don't dare attack the city because of a handful of cavalry? Well you will do it right away. I have brought you three legions, a thousand light infantry and two thousand new recruits, as well as five hundred horsemen. We have enough troops to sweep away the enemy and conquer Taormina right now."

Taurus looked at him with understanding. "I… don't think so, Caesar," he said. "The troops you see in front of me have only arrived now. If you go over to the other side, you'll see that an entire army of legions threatening our flank has been camping there for the last few days."

Octavian swallowed. By the gods, he needed a victory immediately!

"How many legions are there on the other side?" he asked, trying to sound assured and resolute. He must always remember to seem as sure of himself as Agrippa did.

"At least two, Caesar."

"Well in that case we outnumber them," he urged him, "so let battle commence immediately! We will get into formation and face them all!"

He left Taurus there and walked over to the other side to see the bulk of the enemy army, but on arrival, he realised that the battle had already begun. His soldiers who had just landed between Taurus's defences and the sea had been attacked while trying to erect the camp by some vanguard contingents. Confused skirmishes were already underway, with a narrow line of soldiers defending the engineers who were being increasingly harried by their numerous opponents. There was little space between his men and the sea, and the chaos was total between those who were trying to fight, those who were engaged in the work and those who still had to disembark. The supplies and materials were piled up along the shore, making even more difficult the operations and movements of the troops and any attempts by the officers to compose the units.

"I have to go and lead a counterattack!" cried Octavian, but Maecenas grabbed him by the arm.

"Don't be a lunatic, remember what I've always said to you: a supreme commander should *never* risk his life in the front line," said the Etruscan. "And anyway, we can't counterattack now: it would be the end for us!"

Octavian stared at him for a moment without understanding, but then looked more closely at the chaos that reigned among the lines of his troops and realised that he would never be able to get them into enough of a compact formation to repel the enemy.

"You're right," he admitted. "I think the only thing to do now is to get the camp set up, the priority being to provide the men with protection for the night. And tomorrow we'll see. But I must have the front line strengthened – if that breaks, we're done for."

He went to the camp entrance to the where his squires, along with Ortwin and Veleda, awaited him, motioned for them to follow him, and set off towards the newly dug ditch, where the embankments were began to pile up and numerous bundles of wood for the palisade had been stacked. The soldiers were working like madmen but they also had to worry about the arrows of the light infantry who were firing on them from immediately behind the heavy infantry, who in turn were busy trying to force their way through the line which Octavian's men had formed nearby.

The triumvir looked around, saw a tribune and told him to form a new line to reinforce the front line. The man gestured that he was already doing it, and his response sent Octavian into a rage. He ran over to him, forcing his bodyguards to follow him to protect him with their shields, pushed him aside and began to shout orders to the nearest centurions. His anger frightened the soldiers around him, who hurried to tighten their ranks, but the piles of stores didn't give them much space to get into position. However, as soon as Octavian saw that a basic formation was in place, he commanded the centurion to advance and relieve a sector of the front line that seemed to be about to give way. The officer obeyed and moved ahead with his men, and despite the difficulties caused by the pressure the enemy was putting them under, they managed to relievetheir exhausted comrades.

Octavian felt comforted by the effectiveness of his intervention and tried to identify other units that he could send to attack. But at that moment a courier arrived.

"Caesar," he shouted, "Pompey's fleet is off the coast and is about to attack us! The admirals say that given the situation of our ships they are done for if they don't set off to face him. Some have already sailed!"

Octavian looked incredulously at Maecenas. How had Pompey managed to free himself from Agrippa's pincer movement? How many ships did they have? Now he was in the middle of three enemy contingents – ships, cavalry, and infantry. He was trapped.

He had to get aboard ship as soon as possible and face the enemy fleet as a commander, leaving Taurus and Cornificius to handle the ground forces.

*

It had hardly even been a battle, thought Octavian as he stared into the darkness of the open sea where dozens of fires glowed along the dim horizon – it had been slaughter. And he knew that those flames were his ships which were burning after trying to engage a fleet which was tactically, numerically and strategically superior. Having set sail in haste, the triumvir had not had time to deploy the ships in close formation, and their adversaries had surprised them and surrounded them one by one in small groups, breaking their oars and rudders, setting fire to the decks and capturing the majority of them.

"Caesar, I doubt we will find any survivors. From what I've seen, many of the men who saved themselves by jumping from their burning ships were massacred by Pompey's troops as soon as they had swum to the shore," reported Ortwin, the only shieldsman he had left. The others were scattered in the sea, perhaps drowned, perhaps killed, after the sinking of the liburna into which he had leapt to lead the fleet to a new defeat. Luckily, Veleda had elected to stay on dry land with the army and Popilius Laenas to ensure the safety of Maecenas.

He did not answer Ortwin, nor look at him, but the news threw him into even deeper despair. He was incapable of succeeding in anything, it seemed. It was also likely that many thought him dead. After all, he had barely managed to survive the battle: Ortwin had literally had to throw him into a boat seconds before the fire on deck had reached them, and it was only good luck that they had been close enough to the shore to reach it before some other enemy ship intercepted them. The darkness had favoured them, as the victors were primarily concerned with towing away the captured boats, and they had managed to land at a point not under the control of Pompey's troops.

But Octavian didn't know where he was nor how far they were from the army he had dispersed at various points along the Sicilian Coast and the Straits. He had lost contact with everyone, and had no way of letting anybody know that he had survived.

Survive… For a moment, he wondered if he actually would. Would it not be better to die and avoid the ridicule which now awaited him? In any case, what could he possibly do to remedy this latest defeat? He imagined how he must appear to the only eye of Ortwin, who looked at him without a word. He was soaking wet, with a cut along his thigh and with nothing that showed his rank as commander, at the mercy of anyone who wanted to kill him or make him a prisoner, in territory which was for the most part under enemy control, and without a fleet.

Yes, maybe it would be better to die than to live.

He looked at his belt and saw he was unarmed. His eyes fell on the dagger that Ortwin held at his side. He quickly reached out to take it, but the German had faster reflexes than he, and managed to grab his wrist before he was able to touch the weapon, then put his hand back in place without saying a word.

Octavian put his head in his hands and began to cry.

"Why don't you let me do it?" he asked between sobs. "You're free now, you don't have to protect me any more. It would be better for you to abandon me to my destiny."

"I swore an oath," replied Ortwin, "and not only to you, but to Mars Ultor. And I intend to keep it."

"Then you're a fool. Mars Ultor has obviously abandoned me."

"Let me decide for myself if I am a fool. And no, the god has not abandoned you. Didn't he save you today after this defeat?" the German insisted. "Are not you still here, ready to take up the fight again?"

"Take up the fight again? And who will support me now, after this pathetic defeat?"

Ortwin leaned over, bringing their faces closer together. Octavian had never noticed how intense the look in his only eye was.

"Agrippa has a fleet which is intact, and it is still invincible. Cornificius, Taurus, Messalla and Lepidus have vast numbers of troops on Sicilian soil," he explained. "There is more you can do before you decide to give in – you still have many resources."

At that moment, they heard a noise from above them. Hobnail boots and the rattling of weapons. Ortwin threw himself on top of him and forced him to hide behind a rocky outcrop, where they both huddled on the pebbles. In the shadows, they saw a group of soldiers walking along the beach with torches in hand, and only then did Ortwin lift him to his feet.

"Are you mad?" hissed Octavian. "Do you want us to get caught?"

"They are the men of the XIIIth legion – do not you see their emblem upon their shields?" said Ortwin, reassuring him a little. When the soldiers noticed him, it took them a moment to recognise him, and for a few seconds Octavian feared they would not hesitate to show their contempt for their disgraced commander, but their expressions of joy surprised and comforted him. Noticing that his teeth were chattering from the cold, a couple of them took off their tunics and draped them over his shoulders while others held him up to avoid him tiring himself further.

"Caesar, you're in danger. Enemy boats are scouring the area, we have to get you away from here," said the *optio* who was their commanding officer. "Nearby there is the camp of *legatus* Corvinus, which is a safe place. Let us take you to him."

They put him into a boat and took him to the other side of the coast, where a second boat took charge of him. A little further off, the silhouettes of Pompey's auxiliary ships patrolled the sea. They barely breathed, fearing that even the slightest sound might be heard by their enemies, and the soldiers moved the oars slowly and circumspectly, fearing that they would be noticed.

As they went, Octavian stared at Ortwin, wondering if the German might not be right: he was still alive, in spite of everything. And there had to be a reason that the gods had allowed him to survive his failures and had given him such determined friends.

After a time which to the triumvir seemed to be endless, the boat finally landed and the soldiers told him that the tiny sparkling lights inland were Messalla's camp. And once his feet were back on dry land, Octavian began to feel his confidence returning. Yes, he was alive – and now he must make the fact known to everyone, as soon as possible.

He burst into Messalla's praetorium without even being announced to the *legatus* and went directly to the area where the commander slept and sat himself down upon the bed. Seeing his lieutenant's shocked expression, he ordered him to immediately call in his secretaries to dictate letters, and while he was having food and drink brought for himself and Ortwin, Octavian made a mental note of all those he should inform: Livia, to let her know that she was not a widow; Maecenas, so that he could immediately rush to Rome to quell any attempt to subvert his power; Cornificius and Taurus, who were now isolated and in danger, so that they could march to safer areas; Agrippa, to tell him to reach the land troops and provide them with support; and Gaius Carrinatus, the *legatus* of the three reserve legions still across the straits on the mainland in order to have him transfer his units to the island. That way, together with Lepidus's forces in Sicily, he would have a total of twenty-one legions, twenty thousand horsemen and five thousand light infantrymen: an invasion force that would be difficult to stop.

"It's not over yet," he told Messalla before dictating his messages.

He was still alive, and that meant he really was the one destined to lead the empire.

*

Although he was sorry to abandon Octavian at the decisive moment of the punishing campaign in Sicily, Maecenas could not deny that he had welcomed his friend's proposal to send him back to Rome, even though he was charged with a somewhat unpleasant task: he was always more comfortable in civilian life than on some military campaign. From the very first moment, he had been aware that he had been accompanying Octavian to the South for the sole purpose of providing him with psychological support, but he knew that he would be much more valuable closer to the palaces of politics, where – as he soon realised when he returned to Rome, and as his friend had rightly imagined – plans were afoot to bring about Octavian's downfall.

Those who had confirmed this to Maecenas were certain trusted senators who, however, did not know much more than that: being notoriously faithful to Octavian, they had not been asked to participate in any of the suspicious goings on, and were merely making educated guesses on the basis of certain glances they had seen during the sittings of the senate, the hostility with which certain of the triumvir's law proposals were welcomed and the hesitation there had been before they were approved. It even seemed that some had been happy about his recent defeat, and probably only the news that he was still alive had dissuaded those most hostile to his regime from carrying out an actual coup.

Certainly, Octavian's difficulties had shifted the senators' loyalties towards that minority who had always opposed his policies, and now it was impossible to know how exactly they were preparing for the possibility of a new defeat. Moreover, that year the consuls were, according to the arrangements, two of Antony's men, and so it was pointless to expect them to protect the interests of Caesar's heir. But the Etruscan had learned of an arrival in the city – one which could not be coincidental – and had thought up a way of discovering the conspirators and their intentions.

He went to find Lucius Pinarius immediately after the closing of a Senate sitting, taking with him one of his personal slaves, Gaius Melissus, a strapping lad who had been given to him a few years earlier by his adoptive parents because of the remarkable talent he showed for poetry. Maecenas had set him to studying and had soon seen how great his creative and learning talents were – things which had rapidly turned him into a walking library of Graeco-Roman culture which the Etruscan happily exploited to resolve any doubts he might have or to obtain information he needed regarding authors and works.

When he reached the door of the *domus* of Octavian's cousin, he saw two senators who were known to be supporters of Mark Antony leaving, and he was not surprised: Lucius Pinarius had joined the side of the other triumvir, and so it was natural that he should meet with such characters. But it was also suspicious that he would continue to speak with them in private meetings after the public assemblies in the Senate were concluded.

Pinarius received him with cool friendliness.

"I'm amazed at your visit, dear friend," he welcomed him, inviting him to sit on the triclinium opposite his, a rich basket of seasonal fruit on the low table between them. "I thought Octavian would have ordered you not to have anything to do with a traitor like me."

Maecenas smiled. For what he had in mind, he would have to use all of his charm and powers of persuasion. The only hope for putting down any eventual plots was for him to manage to put pressure on the good-heartedness of Pinarius, who was not Rufus and could therefore be talked into a change of heart. "Octavian is of course sorry about your change of sides, but he realises that he treated you ill once and knows that you would never harm him or his family. So therefore he never gave any such orders."

"I'm glad to hear it. How is the campaign going?" asked Pinarius. "We were all rather afraid for him a few days ago."

"Oh, he is fine, as always, and now is stronger than ever. But tell me, how is Antony getting on with the Parthians?"

Pinarius's face assumed an embarrassed expression.

"I don't really know. When I left, he had gone up the Euphrates and had just entered Parthian territory, heading for Fraaspa. But to increase his speed and reach the capital of Ecbatana, he left behind him the stores and the siege machines, and I do wonder what he intends to do when he gets to those mighty strongholds if he cannot besiege them. Perhaps he will wait for Phraates's army to attack him from behind? When he set off, he didn't even know where the enemy forces were based. Bah… two years to organise the campaign, the groundwork well prepared by Ventidius Bassus and Canidius, and then he goes about it in this superficial way… He is no longer the leader he once was!"

Excellent, Maecenas thought to himself. This outburst boded well.

"And in your opinion what is causing this loss of his talents?" he asked. "Senility?"

"What senility?" snapped Pinarius. "Quite the opposite, he has been acting like a young man ever since he got back together with *her*!"

"Cleopatra, you mean?" The Etruscan's eyes became more penetrating.

"Yes, Cleopatra. He was with her in Antioch for months before he left, and his only thought was of enjoying himself instead of planning the campaign in detail, so when the time came he had to improvise without a clear plan. He reminds me so much of Crassus… and let us hope he doesn't end up the same way."

"So you came back here to Rome… because you don't like the direction things took in the East?"

"Let's just say that I don't like him abandoning my cousin for that queen. I cannot approve of that kind of behaviour."

"So is it simply irritation that brings you here?"

"In a way…"

Maecenas realised that there must be something else: otherwise Pinarius would have been happy to remain in Athens and keep Octavia company. And he gave the senator an intense look to show him that he understood.

They remained silent for a few moments while Pinarius's eyes darted nervously about the room, looking everywhere except into Maecenas's face.

"I'm sure Octavian would gladly take you back into the sect. And at least you would be working in the interests of your cousin, your family, and of Rome, not some Oriental queen," said the Etruscan.

Silence.

Maecenas decided to insist, "How do you think it will be later on when Antony has finished in Parthia? Do you really think he will go back to Octavia?" He had been certain that inducing Antony to leave his wife for Cleopatra would have benefits for the cause of Mars Ultor, and he already saw some of them now with Pinarius. Over time, more and more senators would be disgusted by Antony's sacrilegious fling, which Maecenas would ensure was known to all. "Cleopatra is ambitious and knows how to use her charm on weak men like Antony: she will extort everything from him, and soon we will have a de facto Eastern ruler bearing little resemblance to the Roman magistrate he once was. Always given that he survives the Parthian campaign, which – if things are as you say – seems less than likely."

Pinarius was visibly struggling. Beads of sweat dotted his brow, he twisted his entwined fingers, moved his head continually and fiddled with his thinning hair.

But the Etruscan had no intention of letting up the pressure.

"Tell me the truth – he has sent you to Rome to look after his interests and has taught you how to take advantage of Octavian's difficulties in the war against Pompey, hasn't he? Perhaps he has even given you instructions about what kind of regime to set up while he is not here. And now, you are asking yourself if it is right to support a man who is betraying Rome and showing obvious signs of decline…"

Still silence.

For Maecenas, that was already a form of assent. "What did he tell you to do?" he urged him. "Promote the opposition in the senate? Eliminate Octavian's men from key government posts, abolish their laws and pass others that penalise him? Secretly send help to Pompey?"

Pinarius put his head in his hands and collapsed, weeping. "What do you want from me, Maecenas?" he sobbed.

The Etruscan could barely suppress a smile of triumph.

"I want you to help me get rid of the opposition," he said with satisfaction. "And now I will tell you how."

XXIII

Veleda had never seen terrain like it. Perhaps it was true what the local people had told Lucius Cornificius when he had decided to escape with his troops across that hellish landscape: it was as though torrents of fire had come down from the mountains to dry up any form of life and extinguish every water source. All around her there was nothing but a clay plain, and the soldiers marched more and more wearily through the clouds of ash that the wind and their feet raised from the ground with pitiless consistancy.

Not even Cornificius had bothered counting their losses over those five gruelling days. Before they had entered that deathly valley, the enemy had been tormenting them with continual raids on their flanks that the physically and psychologically exhausted troops had found increasingly difficult to repel. The *legatus* had arrayed the army in two parallel columns, placing the unarmed survivors of the shipwreck which was Octavian's latest disaster and those who were particularly debilitated between them, but the attacks from the sides were so frequent that the wounded had risen by the hour and many pretended to have lost their weapons or to have been injured in order not to run any further risks.

There hadn't been a moment of peace, not even during the night. In the rockier areas, it had been the light infantry who attacked them with arrows and spears, opening up gaps in the ranks. In the plains, squads of cavalry would attack the column in several places at the same time, throwing their spears and then falling back for more before Cornificius's men could react. Veleda had been detached from the light infantry with the mission of protecting those exposed flanks, but when their enemies came at them, they always attacked in such a way that they were backlit against the blinding August sun, making them almost invisible to the defenders' eyes. And Veleda, like all her companions, could do nothing but throw her spear and then take shelter among the columns of the heavy infantry.

Sometimes it was even impossible to collect the wounded, many of whom remained on the ground to be finished off by their opponents right before the eyes of their impotent fellow soldiers. The priority for Cornificius, as per Caesar's orders, was to continue west and to reach Milazzo as soon as they could so as to allow Agrippa, who was besieging Tyndaris, to save as many men as possible. This necessity had led the *legatus* to choose the most direct route on the fourth day of the march, entering that arid desert across which Veleda's feet were now leaving a trail of blood.

The woman was, in fact, one of the many soldiers who had worn out the soles of their shoes. She had wrapped her feet in makeshift bandages, but that cursed earth was so bleak and covered in sharp stones that she was continually having to change them, and had even been reduced to tearing off pieces of her tunic for the purpose. The heat was overwhelming, and her thirst was increasing by the hour. There were no sources of water, their supplies were now finished, and there was no prospect of them obtaining more anytime soon. The guides had told the *legatus* that they always crossed that area by night so as to avoid the blazing sun, but Cornificius hadn't trusted them: he didn't know the road, there was no moon, and he feared ambushes and getting lost, so they had continued to walk in the daytime. Although their enemies had followed them, the suffocating heat that beat down on them was proving to be a far worse danger.

Veleda's lips were dry and cracked, her head pounded, her vision was blurred and she was struggling to keep hold of the sword in her hand, but there were others who were worse off than her. Some had fallen to the ground and their comrades didn't bother to help them but just plodded along dully for as long as their strength held out. The fallen, meanwhile, didn't even try to ask for help – they were so exhausted at this point that they only wanted to slip into unconsciousness and then death. At first she had tried to help some of them to their feet, but many had refused her hand, finding it humiliating to be assisted by a woman, while others had collapsed again shortly afterwards, rendering her efforts in vain, so she too had begun to march onward without looking around her, ignoring the moans and thuds that she heard from behind her from time to time.

A dispatch rider came up to tell them that the gorges which were the way out of that torment were in sight. A little further on, he announced, there was water, but the springs were guarded by the enemy. The few soldiers still able to breathe in that persistent cloud of ash gave a cry of joy, and some began to run on ahead without waiting for an order from the officers. Others soon followed them, breaking the ranks at the head of the column. Cornificius told his centurions to call them back to order, but many had already gone too far ahead to hear. From the rocks emerged groups of horsemen who set about the soldiers who had set off first and began to massacre the lot of them, but the second wave of Cornificius's troops managed to attack the horsemen with enough conviction to force them back. Driven by despair, the legionaries defended themselves from the hooves of the horses with their shields and slashed at the animals' fetlocks with their swords, finishing off the knights who fell to the ground.

At this point the troops surged forward, the horsemen retreated and the vanguard raced into the gorge, Cornificius was unable to do anything to stop the entire column from advancing towards the spring. Fresh water seemed to be at hand now, and Veleda found herself running forward too, her only desire that of throwing herself into that rejuvenating coolness.

*

"Admiral! Cornificius's troops will never make it if we don't go and help them! You must abandon the siege!" one of Agrippa's attendants shouted to him.

The young commander contemplated the impressive double wall of Tyndaris – the city named after the mythical king of Sparta, the father of Helen as well as of Castor and Pollux – with its mighty blocks of square sandstone, and then scrutinised the mountains beyond to see if the pincer movement he had planned was ready to go into action.

"I cannot send forces to assist Cornificius until I have conquered the city," he replied. "With Tyndaris still in the possession of Pompey, we do not have a base on the North Coast that will allow us to restrict his area of influence. I have already had to send a part of the fleet eastward, towards Pelorum, to force him to retreat; if he lands at Tyndaris, it will have been all in vain! This part of the island is where Caesar and Lepidus have to concentrate their forces to blockade Pompey from the rest of Italy!"

The subordinate did not insist. Agrippa had known for some time that he was able to inspire the confidence of his officers and soldiers: he always believed in what he was doing, and perhaps his secret was that he let this belief show. In any case, he would not abandon Cornificius: he was certain that he had devised a decisive manoeuvre which would put an end to a siege that had been dragging on for far too long. He had just been waiting for the right time to concentrate all his available forces, which until now had been split between the various columns on land and in the fleet. With the city surrounded, he could have waited until the inhabitants were starved out – but there was no time for that.

Only now could he carry out the pincer manoeuvre that he had devised to capture the coastal city which was in the hands of Pompey's garrison. Finally, he saw the signal: the troops had made their way onto the mountains above the city and were ready for the attack. In turn, he ordered signals with flags to be sent to the ships, and on each turret the scorpios were loaded with incendiary projectiles. Hundreds of pieces of artillery arranged in a semicircle in the gulf around the promontory upon which the city sat were now ready to fire. When he lowered his arm, the men fired the three scorpios at his side, and three tongues of fire sprang up, hitting the base of the walls overlooking the sea and striking the huge blocks, but without any noticeable effect. Soon afterwards the other bolts too were in the air, and a circle of fire enveloped the walls of Tyndaris, converging, as Agrippa had planned, towards the side opening onto the sea.

It was there, in fact, that he intended to attract the defenders. To keep them busy in that area, he also simulated a few attacks from the water, sending four barges full of legionaries to the promontory with the task of landing and keeping the garrison under pressure while the rest of the enemy troops were busy with the fire, taking advantage of any eventual gaps to penetrate. But Agrippa expected the real breakthrough to take place from the mountain on the opposite side. He was awaiting projectiles to be fired that would add to the curtain of flames rising from the enemy walls and which would be followed by something on the other side. The first contingent, at that point, would begin its assault on the walls.

On the battlements, the defenders were busy trying to extinguish the flames but they were harried by constant artillery fire raining down on them, which Agrippa had told his men to ensure continued.

The contingent which had just landed from the sea had also begun to set up ladders along the walls, even though they were only really there as a threat for as long as the battlements were guarded.

Suddenly, Agrippa saw that there were fewer defenders on the battlements, which were rapidly filling with tongues of flame. The attack on the rear had worked and many soldiers had been forced to rush off to try and fight it off. But they would soon have another unpleasant surprise: the column of two cohorts sent to start the land attack was not the only one, nor was it the largest. It's sole mission was to make all the garrison forces available converge rapidly upon it, at which point, Agrippa would land his ships. He commanded the helmsman to bring the flagship to the shore, then he jumped into a boat and set off for land with his shieldsmen, reaching the men already busy under the burning, but not yet crumbling, walls.

He waited again, trusting in the experience of his subordinates to sense when it was time to launch the second attack. By now, almost all the garrison, apart from the few who were engaged in extinguishing the flames, must have gathered at the assault point, and when he heard shouts ringing out from the city, he realised that the second offensive had begun. Right from the first moment, it was clear that the defenders would never be able to repel it: the garrison simply did not have enough men to defend all of the three points that were threatened.

This was confirmed soon afterwards when the men on the battlements started to signal their surrender. It was what he had expected. There was no point fighting when there was no hope of winning and no civilian population to safeguard. He looked at his attendant and said, "Our work here is done. Tell the two legions to disembark right away. We go to assist Cornificius!"

*

"And so, as I understand it, you are apparently a new Theocritus," said the senator, flaunting his learning in front of Virgil. "Or at least that is what my friend Pomponius Atticus tells me. I have read his idylls without translation, in the Doric dialect, and I prefer them to his epyllions, although the one about the Dioscuri has a tragic mood about it which struck me quite powerfully."

Pinarius waited for Virgil to reply, giving him time to work out how best to respond. In spite of Maecenas's instructions, the man still hesitated, apparently from fear of being branded a villain by the Senate. Eventually, the Etruscan's poet friend spoke, in the same the timid voice with which he had presented himself.

"I prefer the Talisies, especially in the way Likidas sings of the pastoral world…"

But the senator immediately interrupted him: he had not yet finished demonstrating his education.

"It is fortunate that you do not like Simichidas, who celebrates ephebic love! However, the style of that Sicilian poet is truly inimitable in its simplicity. He really makes you want to go to the countryside…"

Pinarius saw an opening and immediately took it.

"Of course, Sicily is a somewhat delicate topic at the present time…"

He saw the face of their host Pomponius Atticus assume an embarrassed expression. Maecenas had persuaded him to hold that meeting in his home on the pretext of offering a convivial dinner to some senators and presenting to them the new poets who were part of his circle: Plotius Tucca, Horace, Virgil, Lucius Varius Rufus and a dear friend of Horace who recently joined them, the great tragedy writer Aristius Fuscus, but without their patron Maecenas. The presence of the Etruscan, who was widely known to be Octavian's man, might have made the guests uncomfortable – they wanted to feel as though they were among friends and to talk freely once the artists, who were there as a pretext to disguise a seditious meeting, had left them. Pomponius Atticus, for his part, was famous for his impartiality, and no prominent figure in Rome refused an invitation to his famous house on the Esquiline, which was among the city's most exclusive and elite circles.

Their host was unaware of the machinations of Maecenas, and if he had known, he would probably have refused to take part. The Etruscan had led him to believe the same thing as the other guests: that they were there so that his protégés could meet important senators who could promote their works. But it all depended on Pinarius: it was down to him to induce the three senators who had been invited to open up and reveal what exactly they were planning. Until that time, the opposition had only contacted him to ask him to convince those senators most faithful to Octavian to abandon him when, after the triumvir's subsequent defeat, the two consuls announced his removal from office. They had also talked to him of a large consignment of gold leaving for Sicily to assist with Pompey's resources, and Maecenas wanted him to discover where it was.

"Yes, you are right," commented another senator. "At the moment, Sicily certainly is something of a delicate topic. Let us hope the situation is soon resolved for the best."

"The best for who?" Pinarius asked him. As per Maecenas's instructions, the poets had gone to sit in the next room and had begun arguing animatedly with one another to give the impression that they were no longer listening. Meanwhile, their host had been forced to leave them to answer somebody who had appeared at the door. It was Maecenas, who had come to pull him discreetly out of the trap and inform him of how they had used him, confiding that the marriage of his daughter to Agrippa in the near future would force him to support them.

"You know that very well, Pinarius. That is why you're here," the third senator whispered. "We have to hope that this oppressive regime will finally suffer the ultimate defeat."

"And what are we doing to make that happen, apart from hoping for it?" Pinarius urged him.

The senator looked around, making sure the others were not listening. "You know. The consuls are ready to take power in accordance with the Senate when the news comes, but not before."

"Well, I want guarantees," he insisted. "I will not risk exposing myself without them. You have surely have prepared your coup. I doubt you are just waiting for it to happen, how would you otherwise expect to overturn the institutions from one day to the next?"

"The old consul Nerva is one of those who is very scrupulous about the constitution, and he, as you say, just waits, and will decide what to do afterwards, but Publicola has been busy and has corrupted two tribunes of the praetorian cohort. At the given time, their units will occupy the Senate."

Pinarius nodded. "And are we doing something to help Pompey, apart from simply hoping for Caesar's misfortunes?" he continued. As Antony's representative, he had the right to inquire. And he specified, "Antony does not want a power vacuum in the event of Caesar's fall: he does not entirely trust Sextus Pompey and wants to be sure that in Rome the government remains in the hands of his men, not in the hands of that pirate or some other adventurer who appears at the last minute."

"Don't worry," the first senator reassured him. "There is a nice little cargo of gold ready to sail from Ostia. It should leave tonight: Pompey will build us more ships or engage more troops. In either case, it will give him a great advantage."

He had to know about that ship before he reported them. "But that's dangerous!" he objected. "The ships in Ostia are carefully searched by the harbour guards, especially now: Caesar expressly ordered it because he fears that the opposition might send aid to his enemy!"

"There is nothing to fear in that regard. The ship has been marked with a double eye on the bow. It will be one of the harbour guards in our pay who checks it."

Now he knew all that he needed to know. He stood up and said, "Gentlemen, you will be held here as enemies of the state. Your seditious speeches mark you down as traitors, but I do not intend to publicly denounce you for the time being: it is not in Caesar's interest to reveal that there is dissent. But I will put you in a condition to do no harm: without you, the consuls can do very little."

His voice had been uncertain when he had begun speaking but had grown more secure with each word, as he thought that he must deserve Octavian's forgiveness: he remembered the days when he had been part of the sect and imagined that he was being observed by a god – Mars Ultor – to whom he had made an oath. An oath which also obliged him to protect his cousin. In some way, it had been that which had made him go over to Antony's side, but if he had participated in the coup he would have violated it once and for all, and betrayed his own family to boot. The three looked at him in shock.

"But… what are you talking about? Antony will not take this well…" blurted out one of them. "You… you've betrayed us!"

"No, you have betrayed the state and gone beyond Antony's intentions for your own personal ambitions. He only wanted to prevent the possible fall of Caesar causing further discord. But you wanted to bring down Caesar."

One of the senators found his courage. "You can do nothing to us. We will leave this house and then we will decide how best to deal with you."

"I don't think so," said Pinarius, as Horace and Plotius Tucca appeared behind the three senators with Virgil, Varius Rufus and Aristius Fuscus standing a little further back. Both poets held knives which they had hidden beneath their togas, and they slowly pressed them to the senators' throats.

"I would advise you to be careful. They are all former soldiers and for the moment they will only be hiding you and keeping you under guard… unless you make them angry."

Plotius and Horace tried to assume the fiercest expressions of which they were capable, but Horace almost burst out laughing. At that point, Pinarius left the triclinium, and only then did his legs begin to tremble and a feeling of nausea overcome him. His head spun as he crossed the lobby and walked through the vestibule to reach the exit where he was hoping to find Maecenas, engaged in a conversation with Pomponius Atticus.

They were still there, along with one of Maecenas's slaves, and judging by the host's expression, the Etruscan had already explained everything to him. Atticus looked puzzled and annoyed, if not actually angry. But Pinarius had no time for that.

"Maecenas," he said, going over to him and taking him by the arm.

"There is no time to waste – you have to go to Ostia to prevent the departure of a cargo of gold!"

*

Popilius Laenas was among the first to race towards the water. He had acted out of a pure instinct of self-preservation and, before collapsing on the ground exhausted by thirst and exhaustion, had decided to go all out to try and attack the garrison at the entrance to the gorge, urging the nearest soldiers to follow him. Only after having seen almost all of them fall had he realised that he would have to wait for Agrippa to have any chance of success and to avoid a further waste of human lives. He justified himself by saying that after that hellish march he was no longer particularly lucid, but, paradoxically, as the fighting grew more intense, he felt that he was regaining his strength. And when other soldiers had come to support the shaky line, the horsemen had been forced to pull back.

Now, in front of him, there was a stream of water that opened up in the middle of the gorge into an inviting pool which seemed to be waiting for him to throw himself into for a nice restful bath. But he looked around him. The horsemen seemed to have disappeared, and it was clear that they were hiding. It might well be that there was not just a single squadron of them but that they were the vanguard of a much larger contingent, ready to attack Cornificius's entire, exhausted army. They had left the plain and around Laenas there were high rocks behind which anything could be concealed. The perfect place for an ambush.

But it could well also be that there was no one there at all. He was dying from the desire to slake his thirst, and the same was true for the other soldiers around him, but first he must be sure there was no danger.

"Tribune, I'm going!" said one soldier, who was evidently having the same doubts.

"Me too!"

"And me!"

Other cries announced the advance of the whole group, who Laenas decided not to stop.

"You go, I will stay here. It would be indecorous for an officer to go with you!" he said finally, remaining a little further behind to assess the situation. They would be the bait, he said to himself.

He watched them dive happily into the pool, and in the meantime kept an eye on the landscape around them. There was no one there. Meanwhile, other soldiers began to arrive and, seeing their companions splashing about, they too raced towards the lake, which in no time at all was so full of men that the water seemed to be overflowing its banks.

Laenas still hesitated, and realised he had been wise when he saw something shimmering beside a rock. At that moment, Veleda appeared at his side. "Why do not you enter the water?" the woman asked him, with her usual barbaric disdain.

"It's not decorous for an officer, but you're a wild one. Go, I give you permission," he said. He had already tried to get rid of these two barbarians who polluted the pure Roman blood of the sect at Philippi. After their undertakings in the East, Octavian thought very highly of them, though, and Laenas couldn't stand it. He would have killed them himself if he could, but did not want to put his career in the sect at risk, and so he preferred to let it happen by itself. And now, fate was helping him.

He watched with great pleasure as Veleda walked into the crowd and, at the same time, the glints among the rocks increased. He knew that he should warn the others but he had no intention of ruining his plan and so he remained silent. An instant later, dozens of figures rushed out from behind the rocks and began firing arrows at the pool of water and the stream. Laenas took a step backwards and, with his arms and sword raised, began to hold back the others who were arriving.

At the back of the gorge he saw a heavy infantry formation about to close the way beyond the pool. Apparently, they were trapped in that infernal valley. Meanwhile, the archers continued their lethal work and the soldiers who were their targets cried out as they tried to climb the banks to escape the hail of arrows and the water grew red and jammed with dozens of floating, inert bodies. Many managed to climb out only to be shot in the back while others found their way blocked by the crowd and remained helpless as they were massacred by enemy legionaries who, in the meantime, had approached in compact ranks. Even the soldiers Laenas had stopped stood watching the massacre without knowing what to do, staring at their agonised fellow soldiers, the pierced backs and necks, disappearing into the red water that sucked them down. Then came the enemy infantry, whose troops jumped into the water, killing any who were still alive.

Laenas sought Veleda in the crowd and, not seeing her, was gratified that he had sent her to her death. She was probably already at the bottom of the pool, he thought with satisfaction. He began to evaluate the situation, and in that moment Cornificius arrived.

"What a massacre… are there no other ways out of the valley?" asked the *legatus*, visibly shaken.

"No, sir, not that I know of," the tribune replied. "They've laid a nice little trap for us."

Cornificius shook his head. "We are done for, then," he said. "The only ones here who managed to drink are those who have been killed. We still have thousands of legionaries who are dying of thirst, and a lake full of water that they cannot reach."

In the meantime, the soldiers were beginning to realise what was happening. The rumour that the way was blocked had spread through the ranks, and the legionaries – who had still been clinging to the hope that they would find a way to survive – gave in to desperate tears or threw themselves to the ground in a state of complete physical and mental collapse. Laenas realised that if the enemy attacked them at that moment, they would only need to give them the coup de grâce to finish them off: none of the troops would have the strength or the willpower to put up a fight or even to get into formation.

"Well *I* at least have drunk and am still alive."

The voice of Veleda was the other piece of bad news. The woman appeared beside him, obviously after listening to his conversation with the *legatus*, and regarded him with an expression that seemed almost suspicious. Her tunic was ripped in multiple points, her head was bloodied and she had some scratches here and there, but overall she looked better than she had when he had seen her earlier –

when he had thought this was the perfect opportunity to get rid of her for once and for all.

"You will see that they will waste no time and will try to attack us now that we are tired," said the barbarian woman, addressing the *legatus* directly.

Cornificius nodded. "You are right, we need to set up a line of defence immediately!" he answered.

"Too late," Laenas murmured, as he shifted his gaze to the enemy infantry. They were advancing and, behind the nearest formation, another had appeared. In the background, far beyond, he seemed to see a mass of armed soldiers.

"We might as well just surrender. They won't hurt us if we hand ourselves over to them," said Laenas. "Maybe."

Cornificius gave him a disgusted look, but then a veil of sadness descended over his eyes. "Caesar didn't choose me as his *legatus* just to hand over his legions to the enemy without even trying to fight. We will sell our skin dearly before we give up, I can assure you of that," he said as he watched the enemy advance past the spring.

Under their own initiative, some centurions were already making efforts to get their units ready to fight, but they hadn't managed to assemble anything resembling an orderly formation. The troops nearest to the water were overrun by a dauntingly powerful line of shields and swords, and a second later not one of them was left standing. Cornificius gave the order to retreat out of the gorge, at the mouth of which a temporary line of defence might be set up, but Veleda gestured to him.

"Look down there!" she shouted, pointing to the spring.

Laenas squinted as he tried to make out what was happening behind the enemy formations, where he seemed to see incomprehensible movements of troops. No, they were soldiers who were fighting one another, he realised. Cornificius too had noticed, but in the meantime he had managed to get to the entrance of the gorge. The *legatus* gathered together a handful of men with enough strength remaining to form a barricade – just strong enough to slow down the enemy for a few seconds. But in the meantime, behind the enemy lines the battle seemed to be raging and some of their opponents, hearing the sound of fighting at their backs, turned, disorientated, and remained stationary and watchful.

In a few short instants, the human tide raced back into the gorge. Laenas swallowed, realising that all the others around him were in the same state of extreme tension, and when he saw his opponents throw down their arms and raise their hands, he knew that someone had come to save them.

Shortly afterwards, Agrippa, in full uniform and surrounded by his swordsmen appeared. Laenas had never been happier to see another member of the cult.

XXIV

Maecenas still couldn't believe that he had allowed himself to be talked into it.

After an exhausting ride along the Via Portuensis on a cart, he, Horace, Plotius Tucca and the slave Gaius Melissus – chosen for his imposing size – had rushed to Ostia to stop the ship loaded with gold when the streets were already dark. The only dim light came from the convoys of oxen pulling barges along the Tiber, thus allowing the goods to reach Rome against the current.

"It'll be fun," was all Horace had said when he had originally suggested not mobilising the praetorian guard to carry out the operation, and so they had simply stopped off at one of the civilian houses where the city troops were stationed and left the prisoners temporarily with a trusted tribune before setting off for Ostia. The two ex-soldiers were excited at the prospect of an adventure, but Maecenas could not feel the same way, and his mood darkened further when, after arriving at the pier, they were unable to find the ship with two eyes painted on its side.

“It’s just set sail,” said a longshoremen they asked, pointing to a dark form not far from the mooring, “there she is!”

“Come on, let’s requisition another ship and follow it!” cried Maecenas, but Horace stopped him.

“No – if they realise they’re being followed, the rowers will just row faster and we will never manage to catch up with them – and even if we do, we will have to fight them,” explained his friend, “and I don’t really see how we could win, with a crew that we can’t trust.”

“So should we just let her go, then?”

“I didn’t say that,” replied Horace with a laugh. “Let us just seize the moment without raising our hopes too much, and you will see that all will be well.”

He ran along the pier almost alongside the ship, which was just about to leave the harbour, and jumped into a small boat, gesturing to his friends to join him. “They won’t see us approach and we will be able to take over the ship in less than the blink of an eye,” he said quietly. Maecenas wished that he could be as optimistic, but couldn’t help finding his friend’s confidence infectious. At that point Melissus pulled from his bag a handful of daggers which he then distributed to the boat’s occupants. Horace had got it into his head right from the beginning to enjoy the adventure, and it had in fact been he who had procured the weapons.

"You miss the times when you were a soldier, eh?" the Etruscan asked him in surprise.

"No – but I do miss having fun," replied his friend.

Maecenas, who had taken part in the hard fighting in Sicily, decided that Horace must have a very curious idea of fun.

Having set off from the part of the port closest to the mouth of the harbour, it didn't take them long to reach the barge, whose prow they approached without being seen thanks to the darkness of the night, for the stars were now covered by a veil of clouds. In addition to themselves, there were other small boats roaming the waters of the harbour so no one would have suspected that they were following the cargo ship that had just departed. Melissus, who was the tallest and most robust, threw a grappling hook over the railing, pulled on the rope to check that it held, and then climbed up onto the deck. Once there, he looked around and gestured to the others to follow. Maecenas struggled his way up, pushed by Horace. Then it was Plotius's turn.

They stayed crouching by the parapet, attempting to study the deck and letting their eyes adjust to the darkness. It seemed that those aboard were all gathered towards the stern where the helmsman and captain were using the rudder to steer the ship, while several sailors were undoing the sails on the mast in readiness to set sail as soon as the ship was out of the harbour and into open sea.

"If we can take the captain and the helmsman, the job's done," said Horace.

To do that, though, they would have to get past the sailors working near the mast.

"We'll rush them," said Horace, who seemed to have promoted himself to commander. Maecenas gave him free rein. Horace gave the order and all four of them raced alongside the balustrade towards the ship's bow. Some enemy sailors heard their rapid footsteps, however, and, after a moments hesitation, shouted at them. One threw himself on Horace, grabbing his legs and sending him crashing to the deck. They rolled over together and the other sailors set about the former soldier too. Maecenas and the others hesitated, but Horace shouted, "Go!" so the Etruscan continued running, despite the anguish the situation caused him.

Melissus was the first to throw himself upon the crew. He shouldered the helmsman violently, knocking him to the ground and flung his arms around the captain while Plotius put his knife to the helmsman's throat. Maecenas turned to the rest of the crew.

"Let go of our friend right away, otherwise the captain and the helmsman will come to a bad end," he shouted to the sailors, who looked at him with disorientated expressions.

"Attack them," cried one of the crew, "I command you! I will be the helmsmen."

Behind him, from the hold, the silhouettes of four light infantrymen armed with swords and shields and wearing leather armour and naval helmets appeared.

Maecenas made a gesture of disappointment: he should have known that the senators would never leave a cargo of gold undefended and he cursed himself for having listened to Horace. In addition, they had got it wrong: the man beside the helmsman was not the captain, as the captain was evidently the man who had just spoken. At that moment, he saw Horace take advantage of the distraction and break free, jump on the real captain and throw him overboard. The man's silhouette disappeared over the parapet and immediately afterwards there was a loud splash. Horace ran over to his friends, the two soldiers hard on his heels.

He avoided one slashing blade, then another, while in the meantime Plotius shouted to Maecenas to hold the helmsman and rushed over to help him. All four began fighting while the others watched helplessly. Without the captain, the crew did not seem to know what to do, and the other two soldiers appeared unsure as to whether they should attack Horace and Plotius or Maecenas and Melissus. In the end they opted for the latter: after all, they were the ones who had the helmsman in their hands.

The Etruscan realised that he would have to fight after all: he had left Sicily precisely to avoid having to fight, and now he found himself having to do it in Rome. The two soldiers came at him first, but after stunning the helmsman with a mighty blow, Melissus positioned himself in front of Maecenas, using the body of the other prisoner as a shield against the enemy swords. The slave shoved the man at his opponent, making him lose his balance and then ran him through with his dagger, but in the meantime, the other had gone for Maecenas, who attempted only to avoid his blade. He took refuge behind the rudder bar and tried to push it toward his opponent. Out of the corner of his eye, he saw Horace and Plotius surrounded by the crew but still fighting with the soldiers while the sailors shouted.

Finally, Melissus came to his aid, running Maecenas's opponent through from behind just as the man was about to bring his sword down on him.

"Careful of the helmsman! Make him go back to the port, dominus!" the slave shouted at him as he raced back into the melee to help Plotius and Horace. Maecenas did as he had said and with a few slaps tried to rouse the man, ignoring the fighting that he could hear around him. He managed to bring him round and get him back up on his feet, gesturing to him with his knife to move the rudder and turn the ship around. He had no way of controlling the rowers, but when they saw that their efforts were sending them into the pier, they would stop rowing – he hoped.

The man hesitated, and Maecenas pushed the tip of the dagger into his throat, causing a drop of blood to appear. Resignedly, the helmsman obeyed, and the ship slowly began to change direction while Maecenas, keeping his knife pointed at his hostage's throat, watched the fight on the deck. If all the sailors had joined in to help the soldiers there would have been no hope for his three friends, but the vigour of the three and their skilful, military way of fighting had scared the sailors and kept them at bay. He saw one of the two armed men collapse to the deck, and at that the others threw down their weapons and surrendered.

Melissus and Horace emerged from the crowd, and the latter approached him. His hair was ruffled, he had a scratch on his forehead and there was blood running down his arm, but he did not seem to have lost his good humour. He stared at Maecenas with a smile and said, "See? We seized the moment. And it was fun."

Maecenas could not smile back at him, though: the muscles of his whole body suddenly relaxed and he was overcome by a nausea which sent him racing over to the balustrade to vomit into the water below, much to the amusement of his friend.

"And… And what about Plotius?" he eventually asked, in a fearful voice.

At that moment, Plotius emerged from the hold, saying, "With all the gold below, Pompey could have armed at least two new legions!"

*

Octavian had wanted to publicly thank Agrippa for his conquest of Tyndaris. From the grandstand set up in front of the camp next to the captured city where he had transferred most of his troops, the triumvir had also taken the opportunity to thank his German guard for remaining close to him in the most difficult times and Ortwin had truly appreciated it, although he didn't mention that Ortwin had prevented him from committing suicide. After his words, which were followed by the troops' cheers of acclamation, the barbarian had stared with satisfaction at Popilius Laenas, well aware of how much Octavian's thanks had annoyed him, and the tribune had glared back at him fiercely in a way that made his feelings quite clear.

Ortwin was aware that he had an enemy within the sect, and equally certain that sooner or later the day of reckoning would come, if Octavian allowed it. In some strange way, the triumvir had a great deal of respect for that unpleasant, opportunistic man who would have happily let Veleda and he die in Philippi and who had carried out unheard of atrocities during the proscriptions. And so the tribune was untouchable for the moment. As was he himself, on the other hand.

And anyway, there was a war to win. The biggest he had ever fought under Octavian. The naval operation the triumvir was undertaking was certainly one of the most impressive in history, and a mixture of misfortune, adverse circumstances and, sometimes, incompetence and carelessness had repeatedly complicated things. But now, for the first time after six years of pointless, futile battles, the strategic advantage was with Caesar's heir.

These were the thoughts that filled Ortwin's head as he marched alongside Veleda and Laenas at the head of the column heading from Tyndaris to Messina, where they would join forces with Lepidus. And the manoeuvre was taking place thanks to Agrippa, who not only had conquered Tyndaris, further to the west, but had also made a feint towards Pelorum over to the east, forcing Pompey to decamp in order to avoid being encircled and freeing the gorges he had fortified to prevent access to the Straits.

For this reason, it was a surprise to him when Octavian summoned him to the praetorium with his general staff, of which Cornificius and Taurus were part, and declared, "I have received a message from Lepidus. Pompey has realised that Agrippa's manoeuvre was a feint, and now he is sending an army against us that will attack our flank before we can join Lepidus and Agrippa. We have to meet him and confront him before he attacks us."

The commander pointed to the map on the table. "We will change route," he explained. "We will pass near Etna and surprise the enemy where he does not expect us, even though they tell me that the volcano is currently erupting. But the gods will not be so unfavourable to me as to allow its tongues of fire to overrun my army!"

Seemingly unconvinced, his subordinates nodded. Thanks to Agrippa's victories, Octavian had recovered all his authority, and if anyone had questioned his command skills in the previous few weeks, they were now careful to keep their doubts to themselves, knowing that he would not tolerate any form of defeatism at the point in the campaign where he seemed to have recovered the certainty of divine protection.

The following night, though, Ortwin thought back with a grim smile to that ostentatious confidence Octavian had displayed in the praetorium of the camp, as his teeth chattered with the cold and he crouched under his own shield and Veleda and the other Germans crouched under theirs as they attempted to shelter themselves from the torrential rain in a remote and forgotten place. They had ended up there by accident after having crossed the mountain called Miconius, finding themselves somewhere that no one, not even the guides, could locate on the maps. Meanwhile, in the desperate search for a suitable place to camp – near the volcano which rumbled more and more disturbingly – darkness had fallen, and there had been no way or time to erect fortifications or to put up tents. Everyone had to sleep in the open air in the rain, with only the commanders under shelter thanks to the work of their squires.

If that had been all, Ortwin could have handled it: he had faced even worse in his campaigns with Julius Caesar, who had taken him along with him on his crazed, unceasing manoeuvres to anticipate enemy movements in Germany, Asia and in Africa, often in impossible conditions.

But he had never before had to camp out – at night and in the rain – beside an active volcano.

He had thought that at this point, there was nothing in a military campaign which could make him afraid. He looked worriedly at the summit of the volcano which lit up the night and the rain with its sudden flashes and tongues of fire which flickered upward before cascading down again. But down where? He imagined them sliding down the slope and, in the shadows, enveloping them without them noticing the lava coming until it was actually lapping at their feet. The air was heavy and someone had told him that this was because it was mixed with ash and pumice stone. He felt that his reflexes had slowed and he feared he would be unable to escape or take his commander to safety if the river of fire came to them.

Yet despite feeling extremely unnerved, he tried to keep his fears to himself, as did Veleda. The same could not be said, though, for the other Germans under his command. He'd had to repeatedly reprimand his terrified subordinates for moving their shields from Octavian to protect themselves whenever a particularly loud rumble echoed around the valley. He repeated to them what other soldiers, more accustomed to that spectacle, had told him: it was customary in those parts, and nothing more had happened for years. This did not reassure them for they saw that the legionaries too seemed anxious: many of them wandered about in the shadows and rain instead of seeking shelter beneath a tree or a bush or beside the wagons. Even the Romans preferred to stay awake, choosing to spend a sleepless night which, in the event of a battle the next day, would mean them facing the enemy tired and at a disadvantage.

Ortwin hoped that no combat was planned. He was not certain that the gods would protect Caesar this time.

*

When Octavian saw the outline of Messina appear on the horizon, he was certain that everything would be all right. In spite of his subordinates fears, the detour he had taken around Etna had allowed him to avoid the enemy's manoeuvring to stop him and had threatened the flank of Pompey's lieutenant's army, forcing him to fall back and let him pass without hindrance. Messina would soon fall, giving him control of the Straits. The circle around Pompey was closing without a decisive battle. According to what his chiefs of staff had told him, Lepidus was already waiting for him in the city, and Agrippa, it seemed, had arrived and was waiting to discuss strategy now that the armies were reunited and the northern coast of the island was almost entirely under the control of the invading forces.

The triumvir was confident. He felt that in Agrippa he had his best resource in the field, and in Maecenas, someone who was covering his back in Rome. It was as if he were always in three places simultaneously, and his enemies could never surprise him. In spite of all the adversities he had faced, they were still there with him and for him – they were still a team, with more qualities between the three of them than any one human being could ever have had alone. Certainly more than Pompey, who until that moment had proved to be more lucky than talented, enjoying numerous gifts of fate which he had never followed up with any real personal initiative to give his opponents the coup de grâce. Well, now he would regret it.

For a long time, neither he nor anyone who was not one of the proscribed had been able to access the city that Octavian had been forced to observe for years from the other side of the Strait. Now, though, he saw close-up its famous sickle-shaped harbour, which had been an impregnable base for Pompey's pirates, where goods stolen from the commercial convoys plying the Tyrrhenian and Adriatic routes were piled up. He gazed down from the lowlands that overlooked it from inland and for a moment almost wanted to climb to the summit of the *Bimaris*, so nicknamed because from its peak one could scrutinise both of the seas that the Strait divided.

But now there was something else he had to do: he already knew that Lepidus would demand his part, and he sighed, remembering Antony's words. Antony had suggested keeping him happy, at least until he no longer needed him, and right now he needed him more than ever. He walked confidently into Lepidus's camp and went to the praetorium where the other triumvir and Agrippa were waiting for him. When he entered the pavilion, Lepidus was sitting down at his desk, while his friend came to meet him, gesticulating enthusiastically.

"Watch yourself," Agrippa whispered into his ear before Octavian reached the triumvir, "he's in a foul mood..."

Lepidus made no move to rise from the chair and waited for Octavian to approach him, returning his greeting coldly. The young man forced himself not to react and tried to assume his most affable expression. He knew how he wanted to continue the campaign, but it was advisable to let the other triumvir speak first regarding this.

Seeing that the other man clearly had no intention of rising, Agrippa picked up a chair for his friend and moved it over to Lepidus's table. Octavian sat down and instantly got to the point.

"I was anxious to meet you, dear Lepidus. I wanted to thank you for having kept Pompey busy this month and a half during which, due to the weather, I was forced to delay the invasion."

"I, too, had to endure the storms, and yet I managed to reach Sicily with almost all the legions," the triumvir answered irritably.

"Well, you lost two and a few cohorts, from what I've heard..." Octavian couldn't help pointing out. "I haven't even lost one, so far."

"But I didn't lose all the ships that you've lost," replied the other.

Octavian decided to bring the conversation back under his control. "Well, anyway... The second reason I was anxious to see you was that I wanted to know something: given your superior age and experience in war and the time you have spent on the island, what do you think it would be best to do now that we have Pompey in a condition of strategic inferiority?"

Lepidus seemed finally to relax, and Octavian restrained a smile, remembering how he had got round Cicero in the same way when he had needed him on his side, throwing him upon Antony's mercy as soon as he no longer needed him.

"Well..." the triumvir began, "I feel that we should take advantage of our numerical superiority to occupy the whole island with our troops, distributing garrisons across it. Without his stronghold, Pompey won't know where to go: he will be condemned to wander, and all his supporters will abandon him."

"But that would mean he would be free to build himself a new stronghold somewhere else, wouldn't it?" cut in Agrippa.

Lepidus looked at him with annoyance.

"He will not have the means to," he snapped. "Who will help him now that he has no kingdom to allow him to feed and pay his supporters? He has so far prospered because the outlaws knew that he would shelter them."

Octavian disagreed: Pompey could not remain free with his fleet – he must be forced to fight. But he had to say it tactfully.

"Lepidus, since our beloved Caesar died, Pompey has shown unexpected ability and we cannot simply hope that he will go away with his tail between his legs. I think you are right: we must continue to isolate him more and more, but by forcing him to fight, either on land or at sea."

That was precisely the strategy he had outlined shortly before with Agrippa: fleets in front of all the main bases and close enough to one another to be able to offer mutual assistance, and garrisons everywhere, with the legions ready to back them up. A long campaign which would require much patience but one that would inevitably bear fruit before the bad weather came, and Pompey would be unable to venture into the dangerous open sea to reach Greece or Africa or anywhere else to begin again.

He said it with all the tact of which he was capable. Lepidus stared at him for a long time, seemingly unable to find a suitable answer, but it was clear that there was something irking him. "That might be practicable," he finally admitted, "but not unless my troops feel that they are being commanded by me."

There it was – Lepidus was making his demands.

"What do you mean?" asked Octavian cautiously.

"I *mean* that I have so far acted as your subordinate, but only in order to allow you to recover from the various disasters which have befallen you," said Lepidus." But I have as many legions as you have, and I am a triumvir like you, so I do not see why I should take my orders from you and hold a lower position in the hierarchy. I want joint command."

Octavian was not particularly worried. Lepidus was too weak-willed and too indolent to hold any position for long, and he was too cowardly to even defend his own decisions. He might rage and storm, but he would soon give in when he realised that the effort of asserting his rights was too much hard work for him. Which, basically, was the difference between a great man and a man who only dreamed of being great. And that was precisely why he had relegated Lepidus to a marginal position in the triumvirate almost without him realising it and settling for only a nominal role. It was thanks to Lepidus that it had been possible to pay lip service to the law and maintain the form of the triumvirate without transforming it into a diarchy.

He nodded firmly. "That seems fair to me," he said finally, and was about to begin praising his colleague's talent when a soldier entered the tent to deliver a message. Lepidus looked at him with annoyance, noting that the messenger had chosen the youngest triumvir as the recipient, and became even more suspicious when Octavian's face broke out in a broad smile.

"What is it?" he asked in alarm.

"Apparently, we need look no further for Pompey. He has realised that he is trapped and has challenged us to a naval battle in the sea in front of Naulochus – three hundred ships against three hundred ships, with the winner taking everything…" said Octavian, who could barely believe what he had just read.

Agrippa too looked incredulous.

"That's not possible!" he exclaimed. "This is an unprecedented bit of luck!"

Lepidus tried to dampen their enthusiasm – if they were going to use the fleet exclusively, he would no longer be able to claim command of operations.

"I would say that the simple fact that it is he proposing it should be enough to deter you," he objected.

"And why? A decisive battle is exactly what we are looking for, is it not?"

"It means that he has everything to gain and nothing to lose," Lepidus insisted, "whereas for us it is the opposite: he is trapped and he knows it."

"But he is unconditionally offering us the opportunity to get rid of him once and for all and take his entire fleet away with us."

"Exactly! And you should ask yourself why! He is outnumbered and you want to face him on an equal footing, with a number of ships that *he* decides?"

"We will have something that he doesn't expect," said Agrippa with a smile. "He will be basing his strategy on what he has seen of the tactics we have used so far, and doesn't know that I've made some changes. Changes which will allow us to be victorious!"

"It is decided, Lepidus," said Octavian firmly. "We will accept this challenge, whether you agree or not."

It was with great relief that he saw that the other triumvir did not have the moral fortitude to oppose him: Lepidus bowed his head and glared at him with hostility.

But he said – and did – no more.

XXV

Veleda would have liked to have been aboard the same ship as Ortwin, but she could not deny that watching that magnificent spectacle without being directly involved might actually be an even more extraordinary experience. She stood next to Octavian, who was seated on his curule chair on the headland of Naulochus, at the highest point on the strip of land along which the legionaries of both sides who were not engaged in the naval battle had been deployed. Before her eyes was a stretch of sea crowded with six hundred vessels, three hundred arrayed in three rows for each side, which were in that very moment beginning to move forwards.

She saw Octavian tremble and clench the armrests of the chair, and could understand his tension. For all that she had never loved the Romans – and especially not him – she knew that the young man was playing for his life and was reliant solely on the skill of his best friend. She imagined what it would have been like for her if she'd been watching Ortwin fight a battle to reconquer her kingdom in Germany, and doubted she would have been able to stand the tension for long.

In addition to the exact number of ships to be used in the battle, everything had been agreed upon down to the smallest details. To avoid confusion, they had agreed to prohibit the use of fire and of any kind of incendiary bolt. In order not to confuse the ships engaged in combat, the turrets of the two fleet's vessels had been painted different colours: blue for those of Pompey, who was considered the son of the sea god, and red for those of Octavian, who had cultivated his ascent and his vendetta in blood. In absolute secrecy, the men had been given a password so that during boardings, the soldiers, armed with more or less the same weapons, would not confuse friend with foe.

Finally, it had been agreed that the land armies, stationed near to one another, would not engage with one another either during or after the battle. As soon as one of the two sides had abandoned the battlefield, the legionaries of that army would hand themselves over to the victor. And it was this possibility which made Octavian tremble, of that Veleda was certain: the triumvir had a powerful tendency not to comply with terms, and if Agrippa lost, he would probably have preferred to undertake a new land battle after the end of the naval one. In any case, she knew him well enough now to know that he would not let himself be delivered easily to the enemy, however things went.

Yes, she would have preferred to be aboard with Ortwin – there was the possibility now that they would die apart, and that was something she would never have wanted to happen. She had not even had time to say goodbye to him properly: her man had secretly asked Octavian to be able to take part in the naval battle, and the head of the sect of Mars Ultor had assigned him to the ship of Menodorus, whom he did not entirely trust, to keep an eye on him. Ortwin had told her nothing so as to prevent her from being involved in one of the most desperate undertakings he had ever been a part of. Sextus Pompey seemed genuinely invincible, or in any case favoured by fortune and the gods, and taking him on meant challenging a destiny which had so far always been against them. It was as though they were going up against sorcery rather than an ordinary adversary on the battlefield, and that made the battle the most dangerous in which they had ever participated.

The only real cause for comfort for Octavian and for her was the new secret weapon Agrippa had been working on over those last few weeks. If the triumvir had agreed to put his fate into the hands of his friend, it was because Agrippa had convinced him that he had come up with something capable of turning the odds in their favour. The harpax, the machine that the member of the Mars Ultor sect had devised, was the only thing that was not part of the agreements between the two opposing fleets, simply because Pompey was completely unaware of its existence and Octavian had made absolutely certain that he had not found out about it. It would be a surprise for the enemy fleet, and it was precisely upon that fact that Agrippa and Octavian were basing their chances of victory.

Veleda hoped that they were right as she watched the ships, deployed in good order, race towards one another across the sea, which grew white with the foam churned up by their keels. The entire scene was lit by the bright sun of the early September morning, and their slender silhouettes danced upon the ocean, climbing higher in the water as their speed increased and they neared each other, their turrets vibrating under the powerful thrust of the oarsmen, the masts and the yard arms swaying from the breakers caused by the simultaneous movement of six hundred ships, their prows cutting through the sea, their figureheads seemingly racing to outpace their neighbours.

It was an incredible, majestic, fantastic sight, thought Veleda, even though it was a sad prelude to death. All the soldiers standing around her and along the ridge watched in silence, holding their breath and sometimes putting their arms around each other as the two fleets advanced towards one another. And when the two sea monsters who extended their long tentacles along the sides of the ships were close enough to one another to engage, the sky was suddenly invaded by projectiles from the scorpios and bolt throwers in the turrets. A dense cloud of arrows and stones filled the air above the ships.

The firing continued from both sides until the ships' prows were almost touching, and then the crash of prows colliding, ships' sides smashing open, oars snapping, masts collapsing and men shouting rose through the wall of water that the impact of those six hundred ships had sent flying into the air.

*

Agrippa felt more thrilled than he ever had before on a battlefield. The huge responsibility that Octavian had entrusted to him, the tension for the imminent battle of which he was the protagonist and the fact that the lives of tens of thousands of men and the fate of his friend were in his hands were all things that he knew how to control. Someone had to do to this if they were going to make the Roman empire a proper place to live – a place without abuses and without an endemic state of civil war. He constantly reminded himself that he was working for the greater good, and that thought gave him the strength to go about his job and overcome the doubts that had gripped him more than ever before this decisive battle.

But what worried him as the two fleets collided was that it had been he who had convinced Octavian to agree to the battle on the basis of the device that he had invented. He would be the cause of his friend's triumph or ruin, and now that he was about to put the harpax into use, he was afraid that he might have overestimated its efficacy. If – in spite of all the testing he had carried out between his own ships in friendly waters and the changes he had made to render it more effective and robust – it proved not to give them the decisive advantage he had hoped, he would have to live with the guilt of having pushed Octavian to immediately accept this battle with Pompey instead of waiting for the right moment to attack him from a position of superiority.

Agrippa continued to assess when would be the best moment to bring his creation into play. He didn't want to do it too early, to avoid the enemy ships pulling out of the fight and escaping without there being a decisive battle. He wanted to wait until it would be hard for any of the ships to free themselves and so he observed carefully what was happening around him, trying to see beyond the individual vessels surrounding his own. For this reason, he had increased the height of the bow turret of his flagship, where he was now standing so as to be able to get as good a view of the battle in progress as possible.

To steel his nerve, he reminded himself that Milazzo had defeated Pompey a few weeks earlier, so Pompey was not undefeatable. He had stronger ships, able to withstand impacts with the enemy triremes and liburnas, and once the harpaxes were launched, the difference in tonnage would really make the difference. For the moment the smaller enemy ships darted around his own, trying to pull up alongside them and break the oars and rudders of the quadriremes while his flagship and the others attempted to ram them. And in the meantime, dozens of projectiles and rocks landed on the decks of the ships, forcing the crew and soldiers to seek shelter and making it difficult for the sailors to manoeuvre and for the archers and spear throwers to aim with precision.

Many ships, in fact, were moving aimlessly, and in the increasingly restricted space it was no longer easy to pick a target without risking hitting a friendly vessel. Only a few moments had passed since the battle had begun and already it was total chaos.

"Shall we launch, Admiral?" asked Agrippa's lieutenant.

"Not yet," he replied, raising his eyes to the nearest masts. There were still too many gaps through which the agile liburnas could escape. They had to wait. He directed the ship to the side of a trireme that had been blocked, aiming to ram it. The flagship's ram struck it close to the stern. The powerful swell of the water dampened the impact, even though the damage to the vessel was evident. The trireme disengaged with surprising ease from the bronze ram and soon, navigating almost blind, was once again out of the reach of the flagship.

The time had come to launch the harpax.

He looked around him once more. It was a free-for-all now, though many enemy ships were rowing their way behind his own to find room for manoeuvre. Yes, it was possible.

"Now," he said, and his assistant signalled to the catapult operators. The men quickly swung the metal-covered wooden rod into the housing for the projectile, arranging the various ropes that emerged from the rear end so they wouldn't hinder its flight and checking that the harpoon at the other end didn't make contact with the structure of the machine. Then the team's commander ordered them to prime the device, the cords went tense and the mechanism was suddenly released.

Followed by dozens of eyes, the harpax sailed in an arched trajectory through the air until it reached the enemy ship… and passed right over it.

A murmur of disappointment rose from the deck. Agrippa made a gesture of annoyance and banged the parapet with his fist. The enemy ship was too close. He ordered them to load again but told them to wait for his command to fire. In the meantime, the ship from Pompey's fleet had begun to move away, and when he estimated the distance was sufficient, he gave the order to fire again. The hook flew threw the air once more, landing this time in the middle of the enemy ship's deck. The men immediately began to pull at the ropes and the harpoon at the other end dragged along the deck, taking with it a sailor who had had the misfortune to be right in front of it. Smashing him into the parapet, the hook found purchase, crushing the flesh of the unfortunate man, and a yell of triumph rose from the deck of Agrippa's flagship. The commander could not help but rejoice too while the crew on the enemy ship stood almost paralysed: none of them moved.

"Pull in the ropes! Coxswain, change course!" cried Agrippa. "Archers, fire!"

Immediately the men deployed themselves along the ropes from the catapult to the parapet and pulled while the helmsmen and rowers slowly turned the ship to pull in the vessel that they had captured. Dozens of arrows suddenly filled the air between the two ships, hitting many of the men on the enemy deck. Only then did some of them awake from their stupor and, under their captain's orders, rush to try and detach the harpoon that had hooked them. But the few who managed to avoid the arrows stood with their swords frozen in midair when they realised that the thing was completely covered in metal.

Agrippa clenched his fists to give himself courage. If Pompey had known of his invention, he would undoubtedly have tied axe heads to spears to reach the ropes and cut them off, but there was nothing they could do with swords. The men leaned over the balustrade to try and cut the cords, but Agrippa had ensured that the metal shaft was more than two and a half yards long to prevent the ropes being cut from aboard the ship. And in the meantime the arrows continued to rain down. The two ships began to approach one another and the arrows were joined by spears and by stones thrown by hand. The enemy abandoned their attempts to free the grappling hook and began to try and row away, and for a few moments, the distance between the two ships remained constant, but then the superior weight of the quadrireme gained the upper hand and the trireme began to move closer.

When the two ships were flank to flank, Agrippa ordered the men to throw grappling hooks in preparation for boarding, and as soon as the two ships were parallel, the boarding ramps appeared too. While the legionaries were preparing to cross them, their commander looked around him: as he had predicted, his initiative had led other ships of his fleet to use their harpaxes too. There were ropes everywhere, running from one ship to another and constituting a kind of net suspended over the swirling sea, while the impact of the grappling hooks sent dozens of men falling into the sea, grasping desperately at the ropes their companions threw to them.

And the first boardings were already beginning, much earlier than would have been the case in normal marine combat without this new creation of his. The ships – all the ships – looked like pieces of a mosaic that were all being drawn to one another until they would be joined together in vast floating platforms.

*

These harpaxes are incredible, thought Ortwin as he clung to the parapet of his ship to prepare for boarding. Menodorus's flagship had just launched the miraculous harpoon and was winning the tug of war, drawing the captured ship inexorably towards it. Menodorus was behaving well, and so far it seemed that Octavian's confidence in him was well placed. What did not seem to be going so well, at least in the area in which they found themselves, was the progress of the battle. The blue ships of Pompey had managed to obtain territorial and tactical superiority over the red ships of Agrippa, setting various liburnas and triremes around the quadriremes of the squadron commanded by Menodorus. But the ship they had just hooked might be the key to winning the battle in their area: the enemy vessel was a quadrireme too, and therefore a flagship.

As soon as they were close enough, the men dropped the boarding ramp right next to the German, and when his grappling hook found purchase in the beams of the enemy's deck, Ortwin was the first to jump onto the gangway, glad for once not to not have to look around him to check that Veleda was managing. He threw himself onto the first opponent who tried to block his way, shoving him off with his shield and swinging a blow with his sword at the man beside him, who found the blade suddenly entering his eye. Now the way was clear he leapt onto the deck of the enemy vessel, almost losing his balance from the pressure of his fellow soldiers who raced behind him with the same momentum. It took him a few steps to regain his equilibrium, and he found himself with the tip of a sword pointed at his stomach. He managed to push it away with a sideways movement of his shield just in time, but his opponent reacted by swinging his own shield, which struck Ortwin's helmet, stunning him momentarily.

He staggered and only at the last moment did he see the glittering blade swinging toward his shoulder. But the rolling of the two ships repeatedly crashing into one another unbalanced his opponent, and his attack missed its mark. Ortwin took advantage of this and swung his sword horizontally at the man, into whose thigh it sank. The man collapsed to his knees, giving the German the opportunity to swing at him again, this time between neck and shoulder. Ortwin advanced towards the centre of the deck, his men behind him, and saw that they still had many opponents: this was a quadrireme like his own and could carry more legionaries than the smaller ships. He tried to form a tight line with five of his comrades and ordered a charge against an equal number of defenders. The two formations clashed almost like phalanxes in a furious exchange of blows and swings, shields and swords, headbutts and shoves, kicks and kneeings.

Ortwin found himself so close to his opponent that he managed to break the man's nose with the knuckles of his sword hand, and only when the man stumbled did he have enough space to bring his sword down on him, holding it like a dagger and piercing his exposed neck. Another opponent immediately appeared before him, and they crossed swords. The clang of their blades resounded over the shouts and sound of footsteps until the German managed to surprise him with his guard down and jabbed his sword at the groin of the man, who collapsed to the deck. Behind him, however, appeared a light infantryman with a spear pointed in Ortwin's direction.

The man immediately threw his weapon at the German, but Ortwin managed to raise his shield just in time to block it. The throw had been from close range, though, and the tip of the weapon went right through the shield, slamming into his armour and denting it, and slamming his shield into him in turn, causing him to stagger. He remained upright, though, and his opponent now had to defend himself with his sword. Ortwin cast his shield aside, with the spear still protruding from it, and launched himself at his opponent. After taking a couple of swings at the man, he managed to stab him in the abdomen, running him through and lifting him bodily from the ground on his blade before throwing him over the side of the ship into the sea.

He looked around. On the deck and all around the ship the battle raged. It had even become difficult to distinguish the legionaries of the two opposing armies, as they were not wearing identifying colours in the way the ships were. On the water, the situation could clearly go in favour of either of the two sides at any moment, and Ortwin hoped that was not the case elsewhere in the battle too, otherwise the challenge Octavian had accepted would be more of a gamble than ever. The dense network of ropes joining many of the ships together kept them relatively motionless, but at this point this was not an advantage for Caesar's men: their opponents had concentrated on their largest vessels and were in numerical superiority, probably with the intention of breaking through that precise part of Agrippa's deployment, and the harpaxes were preventing Agrippa's ships from manoeuvring. In the meantime, the enemy liburnas were doing their best to break through in order to back up their flagships and tighten the encirclement.

All Ortwin could hope to do in the meantime was to take possession of the ship he found himself aboard. That would be a great boost for their morale. He shouted the password – 'Atia', in honour of Octavian's mother – and ordered his men to gather closer around him, before leading them against their opponents, who were scattered about the deck, killing them before they had the chance to organise themselves to fight off the boarders. The intense fighting that followed gave him the chance to gain some space thanks to the pressure of his men's compact ranks, until much of the deck was under his control. Their enemies dropped one after another or tried to escape the battle by throwing themselves into the sea in full armour, relying on the proximity of other friendly ships to pull them aboard.

Finally, he realised that the ship had been conquered. From the turret, the trierarch was looking at him with a dazed expression on his face, giving only occasional orders to the coxswain. All that was left to do now was go over there and force him to surrender the helm. But at that moment, Ortwin felt a violent jolt that sent him and the other occupants of the deck crashing to the floor. He leapt to his feet and looked around him, only to see that Menodorus's flagship had cut the harpax ropes that kept the two vessels close.

The commander had seen a way out and was making a run for it, abandoning them on the enemy ship.

*

Popilius Laenas was excited about the harpax. With its grappling hooks, naval combat could become more like fighting on dry land, favouring his propensities and skills and making him feel as comfortable as he did in conventional battle. But there was also a chance that it might not work – and in any case, he had already had to deal with the swells and rolls of the sea which made him uneasy and prevented him from fighting at his best. With the harpax, however, the magical transformation from naval to land war happened quickly, meaning a soldier like him was still at the peak of his powers and with the exultation of the battle still intact.

Around him, he saw this his side was prevailing. Some liburnas had managed to break through the lines of oars on Octavian's quadriremes, but the wrecks of several enemy ships floated in the sea, their sides rammed and smashed, or harpooned and rendered harmless. That way, when the harpax brought his opponents closer, allowing him to cross the catwalk, he threw himself aggressively onto the enemy deck, almost jumping on top of the nearest enemy soldier. Rather than a battle it resembled a chaotic brawl, with the soldiers of the two opposing forces – impossible to distinguish from one another – rolling around on the deck.

Laenas swung his sword madly and it seemed to him that he had killed at least two people when he suddenly began to wonder if they had been friends or foes. In that vortex of arms, legs, armour, helmets, shields and swords – without the markings or clear formations which there were on a conventional battlefield – it was impossible to tell once you were in the melee. He found himself on his knees, pushed down by the pressure of the others, and a soldier fell to the floor right in front of him after losing his balance. Laenas immediately put his blade to the man's throat, but hesitated a second.

"Password?" he asked, pushing the blade against flesh.

The man looked at him in fear and hesitated. That was enough for Laenas: he pushed in the sword, skewering the man to the wood of the deck, then pulled out the blade, causing a spray of blood to spatter his crested helmet. When he got to his feet, he realised that many other soldiers were also covered in blood, which made it harder to recognise even those whose appearance was familiar to him. In any case, his goal was to capture the ship, and he had to reach the helm to damage it and put the coxswain out of action, but there were still too many obstacles between him and the bow. Worse still, some archers were continuing to shoot arrows from the stern turret, despite the chaotic crowd on the decks preventing them from identifying clear targets but still stopping him from moving forward.

He threw himself upon a soldier who looked to him like an enemy, and pushed him against the balustrade, holding his sword at his throat and hissing, "Tell me your password or I'll kill you right now!"

The man hesitated for an instant, and Laenas began to push his sword harder against his throat. "Neptune! Neptune!" he shouted finally. Laenas pushed him overboard and rushed over to two enemy soldiers who were fighting a pair of his comrades. "Neptune!" he shouted to reassure them, so they would allow him to stand at their side. His own men, who knew him, looked at him with bewildered faces, and their opponents, not immediately recognising the officer, hesitated. He took advantage of this to stab the one nearest to him and push the other onto the swords of his men.

"Now you know what to do!" he shouted to his subordinates. "Use their password to trick them! And now let's go and deal with the helmsman!"

He gathered another three men and together they marched towards the bow. Seeing them coming, the men in the turret began to fire at them, and additionally, there was a squad of five legionaries there to protect the pilot. Laenas led his men into the battle with a clear idea in mind. He immediately began a melee to confuse those watching, throwing himself upon his nearest adversary and kneeing him in the groin, making him double over before swinging his sword just beneath the rim of the man's helmet. The man's almost-severed head dangled from his chest as his corpse collapsed at Laenas's feet.

He continued fighting with the others, keeping an eye as he did on the archers in the turret and the helmsman, who in the meantime was trying to manoeuvre to keep the ship as far away as possible from the vessel that had harpooned it. He swung a vertical blow down on a soldier, slicing the arm with which the man held his shield off cleanly, and was once again sprayed with a powerful geyser of hot blood. Meanwhile, his legionaries were also picking off their opponents, and soon he found himself with four men at his back and no opposition. The archers hesitated, unable to work out who the survivors of the battle actually were.

It was time to take advantage of their confusion. "Neptune!" he cried out to the archers in the turret, who held their fire. Laenas raced forward, followed by his men, and threw himself on the helmsman. He ordered the soldiers to form a shield wall, and in the meantime slit the pilot's throat and grasped the rudder, hacking with his sword at the rowlock. In the meantime, he heard arrows thudding into the wall of shields behind him, and a sudden cry of pain made him realise that it was beginning to give. He continued to strike the rudder brace, going at it like a maniac, until finally it broke and the rudder fell into the sea.

Meanwhile, other soldiers had appeared behind him. He told the men to close the ranks of the tortoise and gave the order to advance, with the ship beginning to sway under the increasingly solid grip of the boarding ramps, grappling hooks and the harpax. The archers, forced to fire from an ever more unstable surface, were unable to aim their arrows with any accuracy, and before long the tribune was able to climb the stairs of the turret and kill them. From up there, he looked around: several of the blue ships were drifting aimlessly while others were already the prisoners of the red ones.

Things were going well.

*

Ortwin cursed himself for not having stayed on his ship to keep an eye on Menodorus. He had let himself get caught up in the frenzy of the fight and had gone over the other ship, but it would have been wiser to try and understand what was going through the admiral's head first. Now that he saw him running away, perhaps to join the enemy fleet because he thought they were going to win the battle, the capture of the vessel which he had boarded was of little importance other than to force Menodorus to return. He shouted to his men not to kill the enemy soldiers but to use them as a human shield as they advanced towards the prow. The line of hostages forced the archers in the turret to stop firing, allowing Ortwin to reach the helmsman.

He pointed his sword to the pilot's throat. "Manoeuvre us over to that ship," he hissed, pointing to Menodorus's quadrireme. The man hesitated, looking up at the archers who were now the only ones who could defend him. Ortwin nodded to his men, who now controlled the deck, to advance with the prisoners and disarm the archers, with whom there was also the trierarch. They raced off towards the stairs, fighting their way through a shower of arrows, but then the captain himself ordered his men to stop firing, and in a moment the turret was taken.

Ortwin repeated his request to the pilot, who this time obeyed. A soldier took his orders to the hold, where the rowers followed the movements of the rudder. The ship turned, its bow revolving toward the stern of Menodorus's vessel, and set off in pursuit. Fortunately, the sea was scattered with drifting ships, there was little space and the traitorous admiral could not head directly for the enemy lines but was forced to waste time attempting to avoid the obstacles in his path. This made it easy for the helmsman to recover ground, ignoring the cries for help and screams of pain from men floating in the waters full of debris, who at this point no one was any longer attempting to save.

A liburna ran across Menodorus's bow, forcing the freedman to slow down. He could quite easily have rammed his way right through it but now it was clear that he wanted to rejoin Pompey's side. His hesitation allowed Ortwin to get even closer, until the bow of his ship was nearly touching the stern of the flagship.

"Hurry! Throw your grappling hooks and lower the boarding bridge!" he shouted, then ordered one of the nearest soldiers to take his place guarding the helmsman. He approached the bridge, watching his men manoeuvre the grappling hooks until they were on the deck of Menodorus's ship. When they had succeeded, the ships moved closer still, at one point almost touching. It was time to board now, and the ramp crashed down violently onto the deck of the flagship. Ortwin summoned just ten men to come with him: there was no certainty that all the men on board Menodorus's ship agreed with what their commander was doing, and he couldn't risk losing the captured vessel.

In fact, when he climbed onto the deck, nobody tried to stop him. They knew him well, and that he was one of the closest lieutenants of the supreme leader. His presence on board might be enough to make it clear to anyone who was still undecided that Octavian and Agrippa still had their fleet under control. But what was happening around them was also fundamental in ensuring that all the men did as he said. Ortwin grabbed by the hem of his robe a centurion of the navy who was peering at him, undecided as to what orders to give his men, and asked, "Why did you do it?"

"We… Menodorus said that Caesar's fleet was losing and…" he babbled in embarrassment.

In front of the men on deck, Ortwin grabbed the man by the neck and threw him against the balustrade, forcing him to look out towards the sea.

The German knew that Menodorus was watching them from the turret, but right now he didn't have time to deal with the traitor. "Does it really look as though Caesar is losing?" he shouted, ordering him to observe the battle that was raging around them. "Tell me!"

There was, in fact, nothing that gave that impression. Yes, the fighting around them seemed fairly evenly balanced – in fact, compared to when Ortwin had boarded the other ship, the situation had improved in favour of the red boats. Paradoxically, Menodorus's attempt to escape had created space in which the rest of his fleet could move, and some ships had managed to find room to ram liburnas while others had harpaxed their adversaries, trapping them in the net of ropes. How it would all end probably depended on how the battle was proceeding in other areas, which it was impossible to tell from where they were.

"I… I don't know…" the disorientated centurion managed to stammer.

"Of course you don't know, you idiot," shouted Ortwin, slamming his face against the balustrade. "At the moment, nobody knows, and if we do lose it will be because of cowards like you who waver and choose the easiest solution. But fortunately, Agrippa and Caesar's officers are not like you," he concluded, lifting the man bodily and hurling him into the water.

Then he turned to the crowd, who looked at him fearfully. "Caesar is winning, I am certain of it. So what are you going to do?" he shouted. " Do you want to be remembered as the victors of this battle – or as the defeated, and branded as traitors to boot?"

The men were silent, but some of those who had boarded with him began to shout his and Octavian's praises. The soldiers began to mutter among themselves while Ortwin kept an eye on Menodorus, still hissing orders to the helmsman. Eventually, the men on deck shouted the names of Caesar and Agrippa as one and Ortwin commanded them to arrest the admiral and release the other ship, which at this point was theirs. Then he headed for the helmsman, put his sword to the man's throat and pointed to an enemy vessel, telling him, "Now turn. Point the prow towards that liburna. We'll ram it and do our bit to help Caesar win."

*

Mentally, Agrippa reviewed the conditions of the ships around him in his area of the battlefield, and then he ordered the flagship to sail along the deployment to observe what was going on farther away. He made a mental note of every wreck, every ship that had been captured, every ship with broken oars and rudders and every ship which had been put out of action, and what he saw satisfied him: more blue than red ships had been rendered harmless.

He called his men to attention.

"Soldiers! We are winning! Pompey's fleet has suffered numerous losses, and if we really want to put an end to this war then we must inflict the decisive blow now while he is outnumbered and in difficulty. Give the signal to attack to all of the ships within hailing distance! Turn the prow towards the Straits! We will force the enemy back into the narrow space between the two shores where we can trap them!"

His announcement was followed by a cry of joy that was so loud that it drowned out the noises of the battle. The horns blew and, one after the other, all the ships in the fleet able to do so turned their prows in the direction he had ordered. Agrippa had hoped from the beginning of the battle that he would be able to give that order: his plan for destroying the enemy fleet had been to prevail in the sea battle and then force them into a corner from which they could no longer run away. And now he had the chance to do it.

His ships danced across an ocean scattered with debris, bodies, and weapons just as they had done at the beginning of the battle. But this time they found no enemy bows awaiting them, but rather their exposed flanks or their retreating sterns. It was a chase, and the hunters were so much faster than their prey that many more Pompeian ships were soon overtaken and encircled and, their escape route blocked, forced to surrender. Most of them pulled down their turrets and cast them into the sea in order to be able to move faster, and in some cases they did so without allowing the soldiers inside them time to escape. The sea filled once again with wrecks, but Agrippa's powerful quadriremes ploughed through them all and continued to head inexorably toward their goals.

More rammings of the sides of other vessels, whose crews now cared only about escaping and put up no resistance, put them out of use, and the harpaxes captured new prey – and now their victims no longer even bothered trying to row away to escape contact. Agrippa continued to urge his quadriremes on to capture their opponents, as if they could hear him as he sailed from one side of the line to the other to check that the encirclement was uniform, and closing up any gaps where they threatened to appear.

When he entered the Straits and saw that, instead of using them as a route to freedom, the enemy ships were seeking safety among the beaches and rocks, he was sure that he had triumphed. In the distance, he counted about a score who would escape his encirclement and have time to reach Messina, but the others were falling into his trap. The first ships began to reach the coast, and some were even running aground. Their crews threw themselves onto the beaches or into the water and ran to the mainland. In the fury of pursuit, one of Agrippa's ships also ended up on the shore, where its crew jumped to the ground and began a manhunt, chasing the fugitives along the coast in a land battle that soon came to resemble the recapture of prisoners as Pompey's men gave up and surrendered.

When he saw that everything was under control, Agrippa continued parallel with the coast. His flagship and the others behind him were cutting off many of the vessels of Pompey's fleet which were further from the shoreline, and in the meantime they were flanked by Agrippa's ships, completing the encirclement. Meanwhile, there were more and more ships landing on the coast, some ending up against the rocks or grounded on the beach. In the end he gave the order to fire incendiary arrows: there were too many to capture them all, and so it was necessary to render them unusable. Soon a hail of fire rained down from the sky, falling on the ships along the coast and immediately sending up a curtain of flames, preventing any other ship from approaching the shoreline.

Those ships left in the middle had given up the fight now. One after another, they pulled in their oars while the legionaries on the bridges threw their equipment into the sea and the helmsmen abandoned the rudders. Agrippa tried to work out just how great his victory was so as to understand if it was actually decisive. He was eager to report to Octavian, certain that those watching from land would not be able to fully grasp how the battle was proceeding, and he wanted to reassure him as soon as possible: from where they were standing on the promontory, they would barely be able to distinguish the colours of the turrets, and now the air was thick with smoke from the fires it was even more difficult to understand clearly what was happening. But he was also in a hurry to find out wthat he should do with the enemy troops before Pompey, whose flagship he had not seen, decided to play some unpleasant trick on them.

When he was finally able to get a clear idea of the extent of his victory, he could barely believe his eyes: even if Pompey had managed to save himself, he no longer had a fleet.

He sent a liburna to Octavian. His friend must know immediately that they had won the most decisive, most incredible victory in the history of naval battles.

XXVI

Somebody had won. And to judge by the number of ships fleeing at speed with others in pursuit, it looked as though the victory had been an overwhelming one.

Octavian peered at them as he paced impatiently back and forth, attempting to distinguish the colours of the ships and trying to convince himself that his forces were the ones emerging victorious from the battle. But he couldn't tell with any certainty. He saw a wall of fire along the shores of the Strait near Messina and many ships drifting aimlessly in the sea, but he did not want to delude himself. The men around him reassured him that the victory was his, but he wanted to be certain. Further back stood Pompey's troops, and word had reached him that the tension was mounting. Where the flanks of the two armies almost touched, insults and provocations had flown, and in some cases there had been skirmishes which the officers had barely managed to break up and which were ready to explode again at any moment. In the absence of definite news of the battle at sea, there was a risk that battle would break out on land.

When he saw a liburna approaching, his heart began to thump wildly in his chest. That ship brought the information he was awaiting which would determine the course of his existence more than any of the other events he had so far experienced.

A man jumped down and ran over to give him a message. Octavian seized it from his hands with trepidation and read it: a few lines, in Agrippa's handwriting and with his seal, scribbled down in haste.

He felt his head begin to spin and he struggled to breathe, while all those around him waited anxiously for the response. He wanted to make the announcement right away, but he lacked the strength, and was forced to collapse into the chair from which he had arisen so long ago. The others remained in silence, not daring to ask him anything, and he realised that he must act like the victor that he was. He frowned with concentration, stood up, took a deep breath, puffed out his chest and attempted to speak in the proudest, most commanding voice he possessed.

"Friends! Soldiers! Citizens!" he declared "The pirates have been defeated! And forever! Of their three hundred ships, we have sunk twenty-eight, and have captured, destroyed, marooned or burned two hundred and fifty-five more. All the Pompey's most trusted admirals, like Demochares and Papias, are in our hands. And he has managed to escape with only seventeen ships. And we lost only three! *Three*, I tell you!"

He gloried in the ovation of the crowd as the wonderful news passed from row to row and he rejoiced in the first great victory which he had to share only with a man whom everyone recognised as his subordinate. No more honours for people like Antony or Lepidus, or for the Senate, or anyone else. Thanks to Agrippa, this victory was all his.

But now he must be worthy of his friend.

Promptly, he turned to the tribunes close to him. "Let's act quickly before Pompey gets it into his head to send orders to his troops here at our flank. They are ours now, according to the agreements: order them to yield. And you," he said, turning to a messenger, "go and tell Lepidus to march immediately on Messina and to take possession of it. We wouldn't want Pompey making it his stronghold: he has eight legions under Pliny's command inside, and they could become problematic if we do not hurry."

Then he turned to the man who had brought him the message. "Go straight back to the admiral and tell him to head towards the port of Messina," he said. "We'll blockade the city on land and from the sea, and then we'll see if that doesn't finally convince Pompey to surrender."

He turned to face the enemy troops. They looked disorientated by the orders issued by his tribunes. The officers did not know what to do but in any case refused to command their men to lay down their weapons. Evidently, they were waiting for confirmation from their own superiors. Confirmation which would not arrive because of the haste with which Pompey had fled. But his own men, exalted by the news of the awesome victory, taunted and provoked them, with the consequent risk of sparking off a pointless battle. Moreover, Lepidus's troops had already set out for Messina, so Octavian would have to face an army of the same size as his own.

He decided to put an end to the uncertainty and climbed quickly up onto a wagon that stood on the line between the two armies. Veleda hastened to follow him as did the rest of his bodyguard, who instantly formed a protective cordon around him. One by one, the soldiers who were nearest him gradually became aware of his identity and began to quieten down. Pompey's men too stared at him with curiosity, and soon he had their attention. When all were silent, he began to speak.

"Soldiers! The news that has reached you is true! Your ex-commander no longer has a fleet! And as you know, it was upon his fleet that he based his power: he showed it by choosing himself where the battle would take place and neglecting thus the value of his ground troops, whom he obviously did not trust enough. You do not know what to do now because you have not received orders: of course you haven't! He didn't send any because he was too busy running away like the coward that he is, with no concern for his men. Do you still want to sacrifice yourselves for such a commander? Sicily has now returned to Rome, and you too can return to Rome, be full Roman citizens, enjoy the same benefits as an honest soldier who is paid the state's salary, and not with occasional booty which you are forced to steal from your fellow citizens! The agreement provided that the defeated be pardoned and believe me, this is a great good fortune for you, because you can return to being honoured and respected soldiers without a scratch. Let's put an end to this long war that has created so much sorrow and suffering. Rejoice with me for what, now, is no longer just my victory, but *our* victory!"

A few moments of silence passed, and then his soldiers' cheers joined those of the men who had once been Pompey's army, and who then wasted no time in throwing their weapons to the ground.

*

Agrippa set up the blockade at the port of Messina, where only a few transport vessels were stationed, then, as the evening drew on, went along the coast to reach the camp where Lepidus had stationed his legions. Apparently, the city was the only place in Sicily where Pompey kept fighting forces. Indeed, to judge by the message received from Octavian, those in Naulochus had surrendered as agreed. Extraordinary. But there were eight legions inside the walls who would be willing to sell their lives dearly if their commander knew how to motivate them properly, and for this reason they had to make haste to set up a naval and land blockade and wait for Pompey to come and accept their surrender, forced out by starvation. What with the civilian population and forty thousand men in the garrison, it wouldn't be easy for Pompey to find the resources to feed everyone.

Agrippa landed by boat and went to the camp, followed by his bodyguard, which included Popilius Laenas, and the other squadrons that had landed with him. He marched like a victor, prouder than he had ever been before, and he wondered if this was how people like Furius Camillus, Scipio the African, Gaius Marius, Pompey the great and Julius Caesar himself felt after their first, great victories. He would never be as great as they, for he would always be in Octavian's shadow, but he would share their feelings of omnipotence after a victorious battle, and there was nothing that he enjoyed more. It had been Octavian who had absolute confidence in him and gave him the chance, and Agrippa was grateful that his friend had given him the opportunity to feel that emotion and hoped that he would be able to feel it again many more times in the future.

Suddenly, he noticed movement in front of the camp.

That was strange.

Darkness was falling, and he had expected everything to be quiet. Some men, in all probability coming from the city walls, were advancing with their hands raised towards Lepidus's fortifications. In fact, a long line of unarmed soldiers seemed to be intent on handing themselves over. The triumvir's legionaries went to meet them, took them into the camp and began fraternising with them. Then Agrippa noticed Lepidus moving in the opposite direction, toward the city walls. He sent one of his men to call him and the triumvir stopped to wait for him. As he approached, Agrippa noticed that he did nothing to hide his annoyance.

"*Ave*, Lepidus – what is going on?" he asked without preamble.

"*Ave* to you, admiral," Lepidus replied, assuming a triumphant and satisfied expression. "Things are going well, in some respects. Several deserters left the city after hearing of the naval defeat. They told us that Pompey attempted to set up a defence but found little support from among the officers and the troops so he immediately set sail for the East. It seems that he hopes to take refuge with Antony…"

"Antony? And why with him?"

"Bah! He hopes he will return the favour he did him by sheltering his mother in other times."

"And so the city is ours?"

"I am on my way now to talk to Pliny in order to accept his surrender – he has requested an interview with me between the fortifications and the city walls. And in fact, there he is," he replied, pointing to the commander and what remained of the eight legions stationed in the city.

"I say that you should not bargain with him until Octavian arrives. I am certain he will be here by dawn tomorrow. He is dealing with the enemy troops along the coast," said Agrippa, realising Lepidus's intentions. The triumvir wanted his own little victory.

"I don't see why. I am the one here, not Octavian."

"But he was the one who won the battle that forced Pompey to flee."

"Only the naval battle. I am winning the battle on land."

"I see no battle, only a surrender, the inevitable consequence of Octavian's victories."

"Victories he would not have without the support of my troops, who have been here on this island a month longer than his and who kept Pompey harried and busy. Please try to remember, admiral."

"Look, if they cannot run away that is partly because they have been blockaded by me along the coasts. We can at least agree that there has been collaboration between us..."

"Hmm, I'm not sure that I would agree. They started to surrender when Pompey left and before you arrived, so I will now officially accept Pliny's surrender."

Agrippa would have liked to stop him with all his strength. Messina should have surrendered to the true winner of the war, not to a subordinate – which was what Lepidus was, in reality. He had hoped that the garrison would hold out, giving Octavian time to arrive, but Pompey's escape had sent all his plans up in smoke, and now Lepidus, who had been marginalised for years, finally saw the opportunity to carve out his moment of glory. Of course, he was also hoping to incorporate Pompey's troops into his army, which made him even more dangerous. Agrippa would have insisted further, but when Lepidus rushed off to shake hands with Pliny – who was waiting for him ahead, a bitter, angry expression on his face – he knew there was nothing he could do.

Nothing except start a new civil war. But that would be Octavian's decision.

*

Popilius Laenas found himself in front of a mirror in a house in Messina that he was plundering, and saw that he was smeared with blood. It was not the blood that had sprayed upon him during the naval battle: he had cleaned himself up before reaching Lepidus's camp and he had also changed his uniform, disguising himself as a simple legionary once he was in town so as to remain incognito. No, it was the blood of the victims of his plundering and looting, and he realised that he had let himself get carried away again. He looked at the pair of old people lying slumped against the wall – the crippled woman holding the head of her husband in her lap – and ordered his men to leave her alone. Although actually, he said, he did not want any witnesses to connect him to the atrocities which had taken place that night. He stepped forward and slit her throat too, her blood splashing onto his boots.

He ordered the soldiers to search the house for everything they could find and not to hide anything from him then he went outside to take a look around. Exactly the same thing was happening in dozens of other buildings. And that was not all. He saw some soldiers chasing women and civilians down the street, throwing them to the ground and snatching their personal belongings from them, and killing them if they even dared react. He heard screams of pain and cries for help echoing everywhere and the crackle of flames rising from numerous buildings, adding to the glow in the sky which was only then beginning to push aside the darkness of the night.

Agrippa had sent him with a squad to check on what was happening in the city after Lepidus and Pliny had made their agreement. The admiral had been right when he had sensed that the triumvir wanted to add the legions of the garrison commander to his own and, to ingratiate himself with the soldiers who had been Pompeys – Lepidus had allowed them to plunder Messina side by side with his own men and so he now had twenty-two legions and plenty of cavalry on the island. A situation that made him as powerful as Caesar.

Once night had descended, the plundering had begun, and once in the city, Laenas had decided to take advantage of the situation to get his hands on some booty for himself. At the end of the day, if he and his small team could do nothing to stop the other soldiers from going over the top, there was no reason for him to just stand there watching while the others got rich. He had fought on the ships and had contributed to the victory and he thought it was absurd that the prize be given to soldiers who hadn't even got their hands dirty.

His men left the house with two full sacks and Laenas ordered them to make sure they were not noticed. In any case, Agrippa and their other fellow soldiers mustn't find out about it: the admiral had shown himself to be opposed to looting and had refused to allow his troops to take part. Laenas tried to hide from sight when he saw a team of legionaries belonging to Lepidus – or perhaps they belonged to Pliny, he had no way of knowing – walking down the centre of the road towards the Curia, and he envied them intensely: there they would find a huge amounts of booty without having done anything to deserve it. But he could not join them and so he decided to head for some elegant villas that had not yet been sacked. Until then, the necessity to keep a low profile had made him avoid the more elegant-looking buildings, but he was beginning to feel frustrated and before leaving the city he wanted at least a little satisfaction. He hoped that the raiders had left something for him.

He headed for the part of the town on the hill where the most luxurious homes were. The debris, corpses and fires in the street showed that the area had already been visited, however, and he regretted wasting the whole night with those unfortunates from whom he had taken at most some coins or jewellery. He walked confidently through the gate of a *domus* that seemed to have been spared from the general destruction. The doorkeeper hurriedly told him that the house had already been looted, but Laenas told the man to call his masters. Then he walked through the vestibule, reached the atrium, and barged into the tablinum, looking around him as he went. It was true that much of the furniture had been smashed: the floor was covered with debris and there seemed to be nothing of value in sight. But that didn't mean that there was nothing left. When the master of the house – a middle-aged man with a terrified expression – arrived, Laenas told him to call the rest of the family to the room. The man hesitated until Laenas put the blade of his sword to his throat and the man ordered the slaves to do as he had said. Soon, a woman who was certainly his wife and two little boys appeared.

Precisely what he needed.

"Now, tell me, senator," he said to the man, grabbing one of his children by the neck. "Where did you hide the gold?"

"What gold?" said the man, throwing his arms out wide in desperation. "Your fellow soldiers have taken all of it!"

"People like you hide their gold, so I'm sure that when the looting started in the low quarters you would have hidden yours pretty sharpish and just let the looters take whatever they found lying about."

The man was silent, looking in horror at the sword pointed at his son. Laenas grabbed the boy by the hair and lifted him bodily from the ground, preparing to swing his sword.

The mother burst into tears and stared at her husband with an imploring expression. "Wait!" said the man finally, falling to his knees. "In… In the garden, out the back, under the olive tree, there is a chest…"

Laenas threw the boy to his mother, who tearfully embraced him, but just as he was about to run to the garden, one of the soldiers he had set to guard the outer gate burst into the room.

"Tribune!" he shouted, earning himself an annoyed glare from Laenas, who hadn't wanted anyone to know his rank, "everyone is running towards the entrances of the city. Caesar has arrived, but Lepidus has closed all the gates and refuses to let him enter! It's civil war!"

Laenas made a gesture of annoyance. He couldn't be found inside the walls upon Octavian's arrival… But he couldn't leave the deserved reward of his efforts there either.

He decided to go to the garden before he left Messina. A few moments more wouldn't make any difference one way or another.

*

"Caesar, perhaps it would be better if you didn't get too close to the battlements..."

Ortwin and Veleda kept repeating the same thing in the hope that he would eventually listen to them, but Octavian was intent on personally challenging Lepidus, whose silhouette was visible on the fortifications on top of the embankment he had erected to prevent any access to Messina. He was certain that, as had always been the case before, this direct confrontation would expose the weaknesses and the indolence of the triumvir and persuade him to surrender once again. He, not Lepidus, was the victor – he was the supreme leader, and he would make sure everyone remembered it.

He was now close enough to the ditch to allow him to speak to Lepidus directly. Meanwhile, his shieldsmen had closed ranks around him, and the other soldiers who followed him were getting into formation along the fortifications, ready to attack him at any moment.

"So, Lepidus? Is *this* the way you thank me for having involved with you one of Rome's grand undertakings?" he shouted. "You have always complained about not having been at Philippi..."

"Without me, you would never have succeeded in this 'grand undertaking', just as you had never been able to do in the six years before I joined you. And now I have only started to take for myself that which I am due by right," the other replied.

"You came here as my ally, not to take over Sicily for yourself! So by what right are you doing it?" insisted Octavian.

While the two parlayed, the tension around them mounted and his soldiers occasionally shouted to Lepidus's men to persuade them open the doors.

"And by what right did you take for yourself those the territories we had agreed to divide among us when we formed the triumvirate? You and Antony left me only Africa... Well now I have Sicily too. But I will offer you an exchange: I will give it back to you if you give me back what you took from me at the time," said Lepidus. "A third of the empire."

By the gods, cursed Octavian under his breath. The possession of twenty-two legions was actually giving the idiot the confidence to stand up for himself in a way he never had in the past. The risk of a civil war – now, right when he thought he had eliminated every rival, at least in the West – was unfortunately becoming a reality.

"You ungrateful fool! What did *you* ever do to avenge Caesar? And yet we've allowed you to be the third most powerful man in the empire!" he insisted, in an attempt to remind the soldiers of both armies of Lepidus's failings. "You should thank me, and instead you stab me in the back. I had always thought that I needed to guard myself from Pompey, and now that I have defeated him I find that I have bred a snake in my bosom!"

"*You* are the one who ought to thank *me*," Lepidus said, "for never having hindered you. In fact, I actually supported you even when I disagreed with your policies. And I never attacked you when you were in trouble! I have always respected the treaties, even when they worked to my disadvantage!"

"Well you are not respecting them now! Do you really want to trigger a civil war just to further your silly ambitions? Don't you think the soldiers might have had enough?"

"You have done nothing except wreak civil war for your own ambitions, and you come to criticise *me* because, for once, I do the same? By what right?"

Octavian looked around him and stared around at the battlements. Nobody seemed to support Lepidus, while many were shouting Caesar's name. The third triumvir would struggle to find men to support his claims: the soldiers always sided with the strongest, not with who was right – provided Octavian's case had some merit.

"I defended the state from those who wished to overthrow it, and I have avenged the man to whom you owe everything," he proclaimed loudly. "And I did it in your place, because you have spent all these years standing by watching. If you are about to start a new civil war, it will be your responsibility alone. And as you have been careful to avoid gaining any experience in the field, you will be condemning to certain death the men who have the wrongheaded idea of following you – though I hope that there will be few enough of them. Even among your own men I am sure there are reasonable people who think you've gone mad. Do you actually think you have twenty-two legions to fight with? When the time comes, you will realise that you have much less than that!"

"My men are happy with the booty that I allowed them to take from Messina, and they will all be with me! Get out of Sicily: it is mine now. Go, I repeat, or I will attack you and wipe out your legions!" insisted Lepidus

"Your men might have their booty but they will not have the much larger prizes which are foreseen when the territories under my responsibility are pacified and the war ends. They will not have lands and funds, as it is right that those who have done honourable service should. I doubt that it is in their interest to exchange that for a handful of coins gathered while sacking the city!"

"We will see about that!" replied Lepidus. "It may be that in the end I too can give them their funds and land!"

Octavian realised that the other man felt too strong to compromise. He had to remove the ground from under his feet, and he knew that he could only do that in the way that Maecenas had taught him: he had to win round the soldiers before attacking him. It was upon them, he knew, that he must apply leverage. The legionaries knew that he would sooner or later have to face Antony and perhaps would be unwilling to undertake a war against Lepidus, who did not enjoy the esteem of the troops and until then had always been considered a fool.

Octavian left sentinels along the fortifications and returned to his own camp to prepare the propaganda offensive.

*

"Are you sure there are no risks, Caesar?" Ortwin asked Octavian as they approached the entrance to Lepidus's fortifications. They were surrounded by a robust contingent of cavalry, and the triumvir seemed certain they would let him in.

“After spending the night explaining to the soldiers what to expect if they join Lepidus’s revolt, I must harvest the fruits right away,” Octavian replied, sounding sure of himself. “And they must see me in person with their own eyes so as to make a comparison with that idiot!”

Ortwin knew what had happened. He himself had been part of the squads who had spent the night near Lepidus’s battlements firing arrows which bore messages for the troops. Some delegations had even come out to speak to them, led by their own officers. Caesar’s agents had received precise instructions – they were to be generous and indulgent, and not hesitate to promise awe-inspiring rewards to all those who refused to fight a new civil war. Ortwin also had the impression that money had already been circulated, sent by emissaries to the officers to persuade their troops. The messages, on the other hand, implied that anyone who supported the unjust claims of Lepidus would be deprived of the promised rewards at the end of the campaign: the principal reason most of the soldiers had embarked on that adventure in the first place.

Wars were won that way too, the German said to himself, shrugging his shoulders. But on the other hand, this was an unexpected epilogue, because Octavian had earned the real victory out there on the battlefield. When they were close to the guard at the entrance to the fortifications, Cesar's heir made no sign of stopping, continuing confidently forward as though taking it for granted that they would let him in, and Ortwin and Veleda had to increase their pace to keep their shields in front of him. The German stared into the eyes of the occupants of the garrison who, in fact, did not seem to have any intention of blocking their way.

Only one centurion advanced towards them and stood in front of Octavian, a hand's span from his face.

"Where are you going, Caesar?" he asked. "This is not your garrison."

The triumvir did not allow the man to intimidate him, however, and Ortwin appreciated the way he handled him. In the past he often struggled with his unwillingness to face difficult situations head on, but now it seemed that Agrippa's grand victory had finally given him the courage that he showed in intrigues and at his desk rather than in the field.

"What is it – have you not received your part, centurion?" replied Octavian scornfully. "You," he called one of the horsemen who followed him, "give me one of your pouches." The man handed him a small bag that jingled with coins and held it under the officer's nose. "And this is just a small advance. At the end of the war, you will have your plot of land," he said. "Do you really want to risk losing that?"

The other nodded, took the pouch and stood aside, letting the squadron of horsemen enter the camp. The men on the battlements were aware of his arrival, and began to climb down the ramps to meet him. They did not seem to have hostile intentions, but Ortwin remained on guard, peering around them for threats. A group of soldiers approached. "We are Pompey's men, Caesar," said one of them. "It is you who defeated us, not Lepidus!"

Octavian immediately took the opportunity to speak to the gathering crowd. "If Pompey was here now, instead of running away, he would confirm that he was defeated by me! And that this war is over! There is no longer any reason to fight. And now there are no more victors or defeated, but only soldiers of Rome, united by the common aim of collaborating to make our city ever greater and more worthy of the valour of those who fought for her!" he declared.

When he put his mind to it, he knew what he was about, Ortwin had to admit. It was no coincidence that Pompey's men interrupted him, calling him *imperator*.

"Forgive us, Caesar, forgive us!" they shouted.

"Do what is in your own best interest," he replied, "and you will need no forgiveness!"

The more impulsive immediately knocked down the nearest tents, took the insignia and the maniples of the centuria and deposited them at his feet, as the crowd became denser and the horsemen, at Ortwin's order, moved into closer formation around him. The German was beginning to wonder where Lepidus was and why he hadn't yet reacted. Evidently, he had lost control of his own camp and had perhaps even escaped.

But when he saw a centuria of fully armed soldiers running towards them, with the insignia of triumvir visible behind them he knew that Lepidus had only been preparing to react. He ordered his men to close the line. Although the men surrounding Octavian seemed to have taken his side, they were still in the enemy camp and ran the risk of losing everything they had won in the victory at Naulochus in a flash.

As he realised when he saw a spear flying in their direction.

Cries and shouts accompanied its trajectory, and when it landed, the weapon grazed the hoof of one of the horses, which responded by panicking and throwing his rider from his back. There was a gap in the protective cordon, and other spears soon began to arrive too, one slicing through the neck of one of the Germans. Ortwin shouted to Veleda to stay close to Octavian, who in the meantime refused to retreat and continued to shout to the crowd.

"Look, look at how the traitor welcomes those who come to bargain. This is how he receives your supreme commander!"

A spear struck Veleda's shield, right in front of the triumvir, and the woman was forced to bend almost in two to try and pull the weapon out, but other projectiles continued to arrive. Ortwin saw a spear flying straight towards Octavian. He pulled out his shield and threw it against the weapon an instant before it could hit the triumvir full in the chest, dampening its force and diverting its trajectory, but not enough to stop it from hitting its target. The tip struck Octavian into the abdomen, slamming him backwards and throwing him to the ground. With a start of terror, Ortwin looked over at Octavian's armour: it was dented at the point where the spear had struck, but didn't seem to be holed. He rushed over to him, helped him to get to his feet and then dragged him away, and together they ran back to the guard post while the cordon of horsemen resumed formation to cover the backs of the triumvir and his shieldsmen.

Assisted by the chaos that now reigned in the camp – many of Pompey's men who had surrendered and those who had been corrupted by money and propaganda looked on or actively hindered the passage of Lepidus's men – they managed to get through the front gate and through the guardhouse.

Octavian only stopped when he thought they had reached a safe distance, a few dozen steps away from the fortifications.

"Looks as though things have gone badly for you, eh Caesar?"

The voice was that of the centurion who had allowed them to enter. His tone was sarcastic, and he rubbed in his insult by twirling between his fingers the pouch full of coins which he had been given earlier.

Ortwin saw the expression of the young triumvir grow enraged, transfigured by hatred. In an instant, his humiliation at the precipitous escape from the camp forced aside his warm disposition towards the soldiers and brought out his cruel side, which the Germans knew only too well. Octavian turned to the decurion of the squadron accompanying him and shouted, "Kill him. Kill all the guards in the guardhouse. I don't want even one of them to be left alive."

The decurion did not need to be told twice. Followed by his men, he left at a gallop and attacked the garrison that, isolated outside the fortifications, could not count on the help of the comrades within. The horsemen launched themselves at the footsoldiers, overrunning them instantly thanks to their momentum and superior skills. After a short melee, all of Lepidus's soldiers finished up either trampled under the horses' hooves or impaled on their lances. When they returned, the decurion, with great sensitivity, handed to Octavian the helmet of the centurion who had insulted him, with inside it the pouch of coins. On the battlements, all were silent.

"You see, my dear Ortwin," said Octavian said with a new expression, which was suddenly more relaxed, as though he were satisfied with that blood, "Maecenas's propaganda is effective, but you also need a bit of intimidation. Here they must see not only who is the most skilled and who offers them the most, but also who is the strongest and the most vicious."

*

"He's coming, Caesar," announced the tribune in charge of the vanguard closest to Lepidus's fortifications.

Octavian finally allowed himself a frank smile, which he addressed to his principal lieutenants, Cornificius, Taurus, Messalla and Agrippa, who had gathered for the occasion. "I had promised you that he would come," was all he said, before sitting down in the curule chair he'd had set up on a small podium in the middle of his own camp. Ortwin and Veleda stood behind him, while two uninterrupted rows of soldiers formed to the sides of the small podium.

Octavian wanted it to be just as it had been between Caesar and Vercingetorix in Alesia, and Ortwin – who had fought in that battle – knew exactly how to recreate the scene. The triumvir wanted to link the two episodes and the two public humiliations suffered by the defeated in people's minds, and when it became clear that none were willing to continue supporting Lepidus's claims, he had prepared everything carefully.

During the night, he had subjected the fortifications of his colleague to constant pressure, putting the will of the defenders increasingly to the test, and as the hours passed, more and more of Lepidus's and Pompey's soldiers abandoned the city and flowed through the gates to Octavian's camp. Whole guard positions deserted together. And the more men abandoned Lepidus, the more the conviction of those determined to support him wavered. Overnight, there had been a genuine haemorrhage from one camp to another, which had not even been interrupted by the sunlight. An aquilifer who had left the camp with the standard of his legion had told him that Lepidus had tried to snatch it from his hands to stop him but he had replied that he would only release it when he was dead, and the triumvir had let him go in resignation.

At the first light of dawn, some of his horsemen had offered to bring Octavian his colleague's head, but he had refused. A living Lepidus was more useful to him than a dead one. And anyway, Antony might take it badly, accuse him of having gone too far and have a pretext for immediately declaring war on him. Cesar's heir had therefore limited himself to ordering Lepidus to hand himself over, certain that he would soon obey: he had always been a sheep and only the possession of a vast army had given him the courage to act like a lion. But without soldiers, he would soon revert to being the coward he had always been.

"You know, I thought he would have killed himself. It would have been better for him. That's what I would have done in his place after being abandoned by all and sundry," said Cornificius, when Lepidus crossed the threshold of the main gate and walked along the street which led to the platform.

"Who, Lepidus?" replied Octavian scornfully. "He's hardly the type. Antony might have, but not someone like Lepidus."

He couldn't help remembering that he had been about to do just that a month earlier. And if Ortwin had not stayed his hand, he would not been enjoying this moment of triumph now. He stared at the figure of Lepidus as it grew closer and closer. The man was almost running down the camp's *via pretoria*, without standards but dressed as a commander, with crested helmet and bronze armour, sword at his side in its scabbard. He seemed to be rushing so as to shorten that pitiful walk towards his humiliation. Meanwhile, a crowd of soldiers were gathering behind the two columns which lined the road, to watch the show.

When Lepidus was before him, Octavian rose from his chair. The humiliation was already implicit, and he did not want to give the impression of twisting the knife in the wound. Lepidus stopped at the foot of the podium, saying, "I salute you as the winner of this war, Caesar, and I give myself once more unto your will." Then he loosened his armour and laid it on the ground, took off his helmet and belt and put them on top of his armour and, finally, timidly climbed the two steps of the grandstand and knelt before Octavian.

Octavian hurriedly pulled him to his feet.

"That won't be necessary, Lepidus. I am not some Oriental monarch to whom you must prostrate yourself but a triumvir of Rome. Something which," and here he raised his voice so that those nearest might hear him, "… you are no longer. I am relieving you of all the authority which was invested in you for your betrayal of the cause you undertook to defend, and I take back from you Africa, which was assigned to you in the last triumviral division. You may return to Rome as a private citizen and continue to carry out your duties as *pontifex maximus*, the only position you will be allowed to hold until your death. I, as magistrate and supreme commander of Rome, take charge of the troops you commanded. I will bring back to the capital an army which is finally complete and united, consisting of forty-five legions, twenty-five thousand horsemen, forty thousand light infantry and six hundred warships. Without internal divisions, we are the strongest in the world. We are *invincible*!" he cried, basking in the cheers of his audience, which followed immediately.

Epilogue

The *quadriga* chariot crossed the finish line of the ninth circuit of Circus Maximus with a clear advantage on its nearest competitor while the remains of a wagon which had crashed into the central barrier hindered the passage of the third, forcing it to deviate from its course. The audience cheered the winner, on whom many had bet because he had been the favourite of Caesar. From the stands of the stadium rose jubilant shouts of the *auriga*'s name, which was quickly followed by that of Octavian, who was sitting in the front row with all his family and friends: one of the many rights that the Senate had granted him six months earlier after his victory over Sextus Pompey.

"I would say that we can go home now," he said to Maecenas. They were both sitting next to their wives, Livia and Terentia, and behind them were their bodyguards, Ortwin, Veleda and Popilius Laenas. Further back was the consul Lucius Cornificius, deep in conversation with Pinarius. "These games in honour of the death of Sextus Pompey have been a great success!" he added, adjusting the laurels that the Senate had authorised him to always wear on public occasions. The senators had also voted for him to be accorded a triumph, but he had limited himself to accepting only an ovation.

"And in honour of Mark Antony who killed him, always remember that," Maecenas reminded him. "We will have to work a bit more on the propaganda before we attack him, so as to weaken some of his support in Rome, where he still has many followers. For the moment, it would be wiser not to humiliate him too much after the heavy defeat he suffered in his Parthian campaign. Fortunately Lucius Pinarius is back with us and has provided us with many details about his conduct in Egypt that we can use to turn the senators against him…"

"We cannot attack him before we have consolidated our borders to the north. If we do not assume total control of Illyria and Pannonia, he might attack us there in the future," said Agrippa, who was sitting next to his wife Pomponia. He too, in all official occasions, wore on his head the naval crown, a new honour that Octavian had had created especially for him to celebrate his skill as an admiral.

"Then we can only hope," continued Maecenas, "that Antony doesn't discover our trick yet. Imagine what would happen now if he realised that Pompey had never actually had an interview with the Parthians to offer to become their new Quintus Labienus. And, before you ask me, yes, I had our agents do away with the Syrians we bribed to provide Antony with false evidence of their contacts."

"Antony has little enough to complain about!" said Octavian. "*We* are pretending not to know that he was about to accept Pompey's offer to become an admiral in a possible war against *me*! It was a good thing that Antony considered his alleged interview with the Parthians more dangerous than his offer was advantageous and executed him without looking into the matter too deeply. He has always been a shallow and impulsive man, fortunately..."

"Of course, now that he is the master of the East and depends upon Cleopatra for resources," said Agrippa, "he prefers not to risk further threats to his kingdom after the defeat in Parthia,"

"His *kingdom*? It's nothing more than a bunch of client states governed by a gang of debauchees," said Octavian. "You'll see, they will melt away like snow in the sun when we decide that it's time. There is no comparison with what we are creating here: a true empire, cohesive and functional, where all are striving in the same direction. When he dares take us on, he will discover that we are undefeatable. Now that his military power has been reduced and ours has increased, all we need to do is convince the people of his decline. And anyway, they will never forgive him for having sheltered the surviving murderers of Julius Caesar: Cassius Parmense,

Publius Decimus Turullius, Rubrius Ruga and Servius Sulpicius Galba. They were the only ones who had escaped our daggers, and he should have killed them too, as well as Pompey. It is a clear sign of his desire to harm me. The only pleasant surprise was that another of those murderers, Antistius Labeone, died in the battle of Naulochus."

He gestured to his court to move towards the exit, and as they watched him go, the people in the stands shouted his name anew, some even calling him 'god', which elicited a tremor of pride from the young man. His father had only been linked to the deities after his death, but the senators had voted to place his statue alongside the statues of the gods when he was just twenty-eight years old.

He left the stadium followed by his retinue of family and friends, who he watched carefully as he led them to his new home on the Palatine. It had been built at public expense by decree of the Senate after Octavian had ordered that the land, which had been struck by lightning, be consecrated to Apollo and donated to the citizens. In order to allow the crowd to witness his procession and thank him again for all he had done for Rome in those six months of peace after the victory at Naulochus, he took the longer route which passed through the forum.

He stopped in front of the column to which were attached the rostrums of the defeated ships and on top of which stood a golden statue of him clad in the robes he had worn the day he had returned to Rome as victor of the civil wars. At the base of the column, he read once again the inscription that the Senate had ordered placed there: "He restored peace, which had long been troubled by discord on land and on sea." Meanwhile, the citizens continued to shout his praises and thank him for having pardoned unpaid taxes, returned slaves to their masters, freed Italy of brigands, restored the food supplies, declined to confiscate assets from other proscriptions, restored the confiscated land to its rightful owners and personally purchased the plots of land with which to reward older veterans, the men who had fought for him since the war of Modena. Finally, he had showered the other soldiers with money, promising them new conquests of peoples outside the empire.

Accompanied by ever louder cries – "Caesar, Caesar, Caesar!" he walked back to the Palatine until he came to the foot of the hill and wished farewell to all those who would not be attending the meeting, including Agrippa's wife Pomponia, a worthy Roman matron of sound principles and customs, and the wife of Maecenas, Terentia, who seemed to already be making her husband suffer. He said goodbye to the consul Cornificius and the group of artists that the Etruscan always took along with him, and with whom he intended to create a body of literature to convince the Romans that they were guided by a man and a family with the divine right to govern. He said farewell to Horace, whose odes and satires he had begun to appreciate, and the other Epicurean poets Plotius Tucca, Aristius Fuscus, playwright and tragedician, and two more he had just met: a friend of Virgil, Lucius Varius Rufus, who had impressed Agrippa with a poem in honour of his victory at Naulochus, and the senators Cornelius Gallo and Valgius Rufus, talented writers who were willing to support his cause tooth and nail. He even gave a nod to Maecenas's slave, the young Gaius Melissus, who was learning – thanks to his master's teachings – to love culture, and proving to be a valued and educated poet.

Octavian paused for a few more moments with Publius Vergilius Maro, with whom he had met more than once in private, together with Maecenas, to conceive of a vast poem on the Homeric model. It would serve to draw a line of continuity between the events in Troy and those of the dawn of Rome, in which his own origins lay. According to the Etruscan, it would be the utmost expression of their policy of consecration of the family of *gens Julia*.

Finally, Caesar's heir dismissed the rest of the escort and the lictors, remaining alone with the members of the sect of Mars Ultor and his wife Livia. With his consort at his side, he climbed the hill, preceded by Ortwin, Veleda and Laenas and followed by Agrippa, Maecenas and Pinarius. He did not say anything to his wife: he wanted to surprise her, and he enjoyed her expression when they entered the Temple of Jupiter Capitolinus, where the Senate had given him the right to go whenever he wanted, without requiring permission. In the *sacellum*, everything was ready: the assistants had already stunned the sacrificial victim, which had been duly painted and decked with garlands.

Octavian covered his head with his toga and went behind the altar, leading Livia in front of it, while the others remained behind. His wife looked at him curiously, but said nothing: she was too intelligent to ruin the sacred atmosphere of the *sacellum* with questions that – she knew well – would soon all be answered. The master of Rome tore the guts from the sacrificial ram, raised them above his head and then passed them to the two slaves to put them on the burning stove a few steps away, and said, "Repeat after me, Livia Drusilla: I swear before Mars Ultor, on my dearest affections and on the children I have and will have in the future that I will do everything in my power to fulfil the aims of the sect of Mars Ultor."

"I swear before Mars Ultor, on my dearest affections and on the children I have and will have in the future that I will do everything in my power to fulfil the aims of the sect of Mars Ultor," echoed the woman, who seemed to be inhabiting her role fully.

"I swear to Mars Ultor that I will have no peace until I have punished all the still living murderers of Julius Caesar: Gaius Cassius Parmensis, Publius Decimus Turullius, Rubrius Ruga, Servius Sulpicius Galba, who have allegedly taken refuge with Mark Antony. That they come to the same end as those who Mars Ultor has already punished: Gaius Trebonius, Decimus Brutus Albinus, Lucius Pontius Aquila and Minucius Basilus, Gaius Cassius Longinus, Marcus Giunius Brutus, Gaius Servilius Casca Longo, Publius Servilius Casca Longus, Lucius Tillius Cimber, Quintus Labienus, Publius Sestilius Nason, Marcus Spurius, Quintus Ligarius, Antistius Labeo, Caecilius Bucolianus the younger and Caecilius Bucolianus the older, Sextus Pompey and Petronius."

Octavian intoned the names one by one, waiting for the new adept to repeat each one before pronouncing the next.

"I swear to Mars Ultor that I will do everything in my power and adopt all necessary weapons and resources, lawful or unlawful, to bring peace to Rome and transform it into a consolidated, prosperous empire, as Caesar intended."

"I swear to Mars Ultor that I will do everything in my power and adopt all necessary weapons and resources, lawful or unlawful, to bring peace to Rome and transform it into a consolidated, prosperous empire, as Caesar intended," repeated Livia with conviction.

"And finally I swear to Mars Ultor that I will never betray my friends, nor will I abandon this sect, to which I consider it a privilege to belong. May Mars Ultor turn his arrows upon me if I do not keep my oath."

"And finally I swear to Mars Ultor that I will never betray my friends, nor will I abandon this sect, to which I consider it a privilege to belong. May Mars Ultor turn his arrows upon me if I do not keep my oath." echoed his wife.

"And now you too are a daughter of Caesar!" exclaimed Octavian. Then he turned to the others who were present.

"Let us all share this dish to sanctify our covenant and consecrate ourselves to Mars Ultor!"

He gestured to the others to approach the altar and the slaves began to pass around the partially-cooked innards of the ram, which he himself distributed to the others, beginning with the new member.

Proudly, she returned his gaze.

We hope you enjoyed this book!

More addictive fiction from Aria:

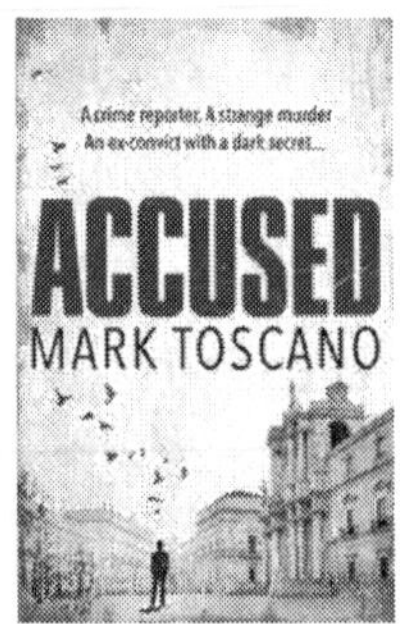

Find out more
http://headofzeus.com/books/isbn/9781784978853

Find out more
http://headofzeus.com/books/isbn/9781784978969

Find out more
http://headofzeus.com/books/isbn/9781784978907

Author's Afterword

I deviate from my intention to only write an afterword for the final chapter of this saga – which is the next – to say a few words about the main subject of this volume: the war against Sextus Pompey. Some of Octavian's military campaigns – from the war of Modena to that of Perugia, and from Philippi to Actium – have inexplicably obscured what, in my humble opinion, was his most difficult task. It took the future Augustus, in fact, years to defeat the son of Pompey the Great, and he suffered defeats and disasters that would have discouraged, or at least destabilised, anyone. And yet, thanks to Agrippa, he finally managed it with a deadly blend of determination, luck, political skill and unscrupulousness.

Of all the volumes of the saga of *The Invincibles*, and probably of all my novels in general, this one – which covers a period stretching from the end of 42 B.C. to the spring of the 35 B.C. – is the one where I was obliged to stay closest to my sources, which are so detailed that they imposed a series of hurdles. The war against Pompey is described analytically by Appian in the last part of the fifth book of civil wars. The Sicily campaign can genuinely be described as one of the greatest marine operations in history, a kind of *ante litteram* Normandy landing, and Appian's report provides us with all the details – battle after battle, march after march – forcing even the most imaginative novelist to stick closely to what has been described. All the episodes described herein are therefore real, as are, in part, the moods of the protagonists and many other details, such as the passwords aboard the ships or the colours of the turrets during the Battle of Naulochus, the march through arid territory or the night beside an erupting Etna, the frequent defections of Menodorus and the duels between him and Menecrates, and between Agrippa and Papias.

The unfortunate events which repeatedly involved Octavian's fleet occurred just the way you read them here and in the same sequence, as did the prolongation of the war that threatened to explode with Lepidus's about-turn. Appian describes characters, events, places, and circumstances with a detail rare in ancient sources, and which allowed me – or so, at least, I hope – to point the spotlight on a historical story that Augustus's future successes would overshadow, probably because it was the campaign in which he committed the most blunders and preferred to remember only the triumphant conclusion…

About Andrew Frediani

ANDREW FREDIANI is an Italian author and academic. He has published several non-fiction books as well as historical novels including the *Invincible* series and the *Dictator* trilogy. His works have been translated into five languages.

Find me on Facebook
https://www.facebook.com/andreafredianipaginauffi
ciale/about?tab=page_info

Visit my website
http://www.andreafrediani.it

About the Rome's Invincibles Series

Find out more
http://headofzeus.com/books/isbn/9781784978884

Find out more
http://headofzeus.com/books/isbn/9781784978938

Find out more
http://headofzeus.com/books/isbn/9781786692856

Visit Head of Zeus now
http://www.ariafiction.com

Become an Aria Addict

Aria is the new digital-first fiction imprint from Head of Zeus.

It's Aria's ambition to discover and publish tomorrow's superstars, targeting fiction addicts and readers keen to discover new and exciting authors.

Aria will publish a variety of genres under the commercial fiction umbrella such as women's fiction, crime, thrillers, historical fiction, saga and erotica.

So, whether you're a budding writer looking for a publisher or an avid reader looking for something to escape with – Aria will have something for you.

Get in touch: aria@headofzeus.com

Become an Aria Addict
http://www.ariafiction.com

Sign up to our newsletter
http://ariafiction.com/newsletter/subscribe

Find us on Twitter
https://twitter.com/Aria_Fiction

Find us on Facebook
http://www.facebook.com/ariafiction

Find us on BookGrail
http://www.bookgrail.com/store/aria/

Addictive Fiction

First published in Italy in 2017 by Newton Compton

First published in the UK in 2017 by Aria, an imprint of Head of Zeus Ltd

9 7 5 3 1 2 4 6 8

A CIP catalogue record for this book is available from the British Library.

ISBN (E) 9781786692856

Aria
c/o Head of Zeus
First Floor East
5–8 Hardwick Street
London EC1R 4RG

www.ariafiction.com

Made in the USA
Monee, IL
12 July 2020

36425824R00367